WOLF, WOLF

Eben Venter was raised on a sheep farm in Eastern Cape, South Africa and migrated to Australia in 1986. He has won numerous awards for his work, and currently holds an honorary appointment as professional associate in the Institute of English in Africa (ISEA) at Rhodes University.

By the same author in English

My Beautiful Death
Trencherman

Wolf, Wolf

a novel

wolf

Eben Venter

SCRIBE

Melbourne • London

Scribe Publications
18–20 Edward St, Brunswick, Victoria 3056, Australia
2 John St, Clerkenwell, London, WC1N 2ES, United Kingdom

First published in South Africa only in Afrikaans and in English by NB/Tafelberg 2013
First published in the Commonwealth (excluding South Africa) by Scribe 2015

Acknowledgements
Cavafy, C.P. *The Complete Poems of Cavafy*, translator: Dalven, Rae. New York/
London: Mariner, 1976
Doidge, Norman, MD. *The Brain That Changes Itself*, Melbourne: Scribe, 2008

Thanks
I would like to thank Riana Barnard, Francois Smith, Michiel Heyns, Lynda Gilfillan,
Madaleine du Plessis, Michiel Botha and Jo-Anne Friedlander for their dedication
and enthusiam.

Typeset in 10/14 pt Galliard by the publishers
Printed and bound in the UK by CPI Group (UK) Ltd, Croydon CR0 4YY

National Library of Australia
Cataloguing-in-Publication data

Venter, Eben, author.

Wolf, Wolf: a novel / Eben Venter; translated by Michiel Heyns.

9781925106404 (Australian edition)
9781922247865 (UK edition)
9781925113594 (e-book)

1. Gays–South Africa–Fiction. 2. Gay men–Fiction. 3. Fathers and sons–Fiction.
4. Cape Town (South Africa)–Fiction.

Other Authors/Contributors: Heyns, Michiel, translator.

839.3636

scribepublications.com.au
scribepublications.co.uk

At one o'clock on the dot, he walks into the room with a tray of food for his dying father. Privately, he uses the word *dying* in lower case – unlike the oncologist who rubs it in: I give your father another month or so. He's also taking along a request that he may be ashamed of. And yet he will – he *wants* to – ask his father for the cheque so that he can start his own business. Every word has been sifted and weighed; and lunch is tomato and lamb stew, his father's favourite.

He's surprised to find the old man propped up already, his back against two cushions – the willpower that must have taken. Without preamble, the voice issues from the decrepit body, forceful and peremptory, just as he remembers it. Pa wants to be moved from the bedroom to the study. Irrespective of Mattheüs's opinion concerning his condition.

'Now, this afternoon, Mattie.' He says: Now. This. Afternoon. 'No point in putting it off, my son. I'm here on borrowed time.' He inclines his head towards the spot where he imagines Mattheüs is standing with the tray of food, pinning him to the striped kelim, the eyes behind their closed lids holding him captive.

For weeks now, he's been mulling over the request, considering its consequences: in truth, it's a final favour to the dying man. His father would depart serene in the knowledge that his son is not a wastrel: Mattie will land on his feet again. He'd bought lamb and ripe tomatoes and baby carrots and left it all to simmer. He's thought of everything.

His saliva thickens in his mouth. The entirety of what he hasn't planned for flashes before him: double bed, mattress, bedside cabinet with pills and medication and special sweets for dry mouth, and the Sorbolene, all Pa's clothes and handkerchiefs and toiletries, slippers – the pictures on the walls can surely be left behind? – everything will have to be schlepped across. The bed remade, and pillows shaken down and puffed up and, finally: the frail body. And then the grumbling at the slightest mishandling. *Now*. It must all happen now. The cheque he wants to ask for, his carefully considered request, is fading into the background. He's beginning to tread water.

He's facing a man who's never been known for his tact, at least not in his own home. Who wants to be moved just as the week is drawing to a close, the day almost at an end. And his father knows perfectly well that Friday evening is his night on the town with Jack. Part of his plan was that they'd kick off with a double brandy, a shooter or two in between, then an ice-cold beer. (The cheque by now snug in his pocket.) At dusk he'd come to say his goodbye, his hand in his father's, with its thin, worn papery feel. Take my car, Pa would say, as always. And even though Mattheüs knew that he and Jack would get wasted, he'd take it all the same.

The study is on the south side of the house, while the en suite master bedroom is on the north; the mattress and base will have to be lugged all the way down the passage to the entrance hall and then left into the study, where they'll need to clear a space for the double bed and all. And then, what about ablutions and going to the toilet, has he even considered that? Up to three times a night while he's surfing the Net in the small hours, he hears Pa's toilet flushing.

'This afternoon, then, and it'll all be over and done with. I'm not asking for much, my son.' At the tail end of the instruction there's just a shred of a scruple.

It becomes, admittedly by mere degree, something between a request and an instruction. He places the tray with the tomato stew on his father's lap. It has been prepared according to his mother's recipe on page three of her dog-eared book. The only difference is the ground cumin that he adds.

He tucks the linen serviette into his father's pyjama top; he can smell the disease emanating from his body. Then he sits down on the wooden chair with its slatted sides and adjustable backrest and two fat cushions, the kind you come across in Afrikaner homes where old things are still cherished. The chair will go to his sister, which is okay; he's getting the house.

When he notices the frown about to form, he jumps up and adjusts the tray. The stew has sloshed around, leaving reddish-orange crescents on the rim of the plate. Pa's hands flutter about, his fingers groping for the tray, fossicking to find out what's what and where everything is.

Mattheüs sits down again. Beyond the French doors, which are always open to the fresh air except in a storm, are the wrought-iron security gates opening on to a small garden with a fountain, and flowers, white and pale-pink and yellow and so on, and two plovers on the patch of lawn that realise they're being watched and kick up a racket, a bird call with usually pleasant associations that now drills discordantly into Mattheüs's ear: his father's request throws him and reason goes overboard, so that it becomes a command pure and simple, raking up similar commands from his past with Pa, and smothering him under them.

In the meantime, Pa has sensed what inner nourishment is on offer today, and instead of taking up his knife and fork and eating like a good boy, his little paws clutch at the handles of the tray, his stretched skin translucent over the bone. Thin, thin. Weight loss, and a ring finger long since ringless. Clutch, release, clutch and release yet again.

Attuned as he is to his father's every move, he understands the drill: the request has morphed into an order, delivered with the brute force or, to put it more mildly, the authority of a man who in his prime had everyone at his beck and call, with his staff, twenty-five at one time if memory serves, all taking note of who was speaking. And in this selfsame house, proclamations and instructions prevailed 'because I love you', to ensure that the two offspring of his loins should stick to the straight and narrow, and there was a final set of rules specially for his wife, matriarch in her own right, but ultimately totally demoralised. Fuck.

'My son,' Pa once again directs his gaze at the spot where he imagines his son's head to be, where Mattheüs is still seated on the wooden chair that Sissy will definitely inherit, 'come over here to your father, please.'

The request that was growing into a command is tempered once again. This is Benjamin Duiker recalling that he is at the mercy of Mattie – he's the only one who calls him that – and of Samantha. Samantha, who arrives on Fridays just after one o'clock, which is to say any moment now, to toil in the footsteps of her mother, Auntie Mary, who on account of her arthritic claws has had to abdicate the task of keeping this house spic and span.

Pa wants him right beside him. Close enough to communicate, in the physical proximity of his son, the only true path open to him. While he's waiting for Mattheüs, his eyelids remain closed over the glaucous, blind eyeballs.

Now and again he slides the eyelids upwards, and the sight of what's become of his father's eyes, once deep-green and command-ing, makes Mattheüs just about shrivel up, even though he's wit-nessed it often enough.

Tempered. The command has been diluted to a relatively mild request. Nothing more. The request, surely one of the very last, of

4

an old man who wants to spend his remaining days in his study. But begging it's not, and never could be. Mattheüs would be highly embarrassed if he were ever to hear his father beg.

The books in the study – not that many really – are about trees, Pa's great love, and cars, his first love, and then there's the usual, familiar library: Langenhoven, the complete works, and Pakenham's book on the Boer War and Roberts's *Birds of Southern Africa* and Shell's *Succulents of the Karoo* and Goldblatt's *Some Afrikaners Photographed*, which his father regarded as a scandalous denigration of his people, and a concordance to the Bible in which you can look up the origin of a word like 'shibboleth'. Some of the top shelves have no books. Pa was never a great reader – never really had the time. So he put a White Horse Whisky horse up there, and a row of model cars, each of them a Mercedes. As a child, the car that made Mattheüs's heart beat fastest was the convertible, a red one with a suede top that you could unhook and push back to reveal the driver and his girlfriend and on the back seat another couple, and Pa's hand on his finger all the time to guide him, helping him push back the top carefully without breaking it. He was allowed to play with it for a while, and then the convertible was put back in its place, out of reach.

It's not just for the books that Pa wants to move there, it's for the atmosphere of the place. A cigar-smelling, masculine atmosphere, an inner sanctum, you're really somewhere when you're in there. The long velvet curtains are golden and his broad-backed desk chair is upholstered in gold brocade that scratches your bare thighs. In *High Society*, Pa once told him, Frank Sinatra and Bing Crosby sing that Cole Porter song in a study like this. A bit of a copycat. *High Society* – Pa chuckled.

He wants to bring something home to Mattheüs, something about himself. No secret, just a clarification. Just a glimpse. But he holds back. The son withdraws. He doesn't want to see inside, doesn't want to get too close to his father. Now, Mattheüs understands it, yet also doesn't.

There's a decorated Havana balsawood box with seven cigars inside it, seven for as long as he can remember, and between the two walls with their bookshelves, as in *High Society*, a fireplace, and to the left of that the liquor cabinet. His father's, built into the wall, which you can unlock, the lid forming a surface for pouring drinks. Mainly hard tack, ten-year-old KWV and even some older brandies, which he and Jack sometimes help themselves to liberally.

It's the atmosphere in the room, that's what he's hankering after. There, you can think like a man thinks. Elsewhere too, but there you can do so unhindered and without opposition. So: back there. Made deals in there while he was a businessman, it was his life. Moved huge sums of money around. Typed out carefully considered letters on the Olivetti. Urges and desires, especially when the velvet curtains were drawn. It all happened in there, Mattheüs knows it for a fact. A woman could be conjured up in your mind's eye, and every imaginable manoeuvre could be imagined there. One day, without knocking, he walked in through the half-open double doors and Pa and Uncle Diek Smuts, also a car salesman, were regaling each other with lecherous tidbits, their ties loosened, sleeves rolled up over hairy forearms (Pa's), jackets hanging from the coat rack with its curved hooks as you enter by the double doors, just to the left, and to the right the head of a springbok ram mounted on the cream-coloured wall.

Pa cut short what he was saying and looked at his son. He could have said anything to him then. His mouth was agape, words brimming. Contempt, anything scathing. But the words weren't spoken, he'll never know what it was. Only: he was not admitted to the circle. Come on, man, Bennie, he's big enough, Uncle Diek said then. Uncle Diek missed the point, though. It wasn't a question of being big enough. His father wanted to admit him, wanted him to experience his palpable charm, his passion and perseverance and principles, everything that made up his manly ego, but, as with an animal, instinct warned him off: you're dealing with a different kind of creature here. It was all on his tongue, in his glance: his son, his own, his flesh and blood. How, dear Lord, had this come about?

So Uncle Diek drained his glass and poured another drink at the cabinet. His male voice still lingers in the study. And Pa's – from then and all previous times, everything in there bears Pa's stamp. There's nothing feminine in the room, or about it. Even long ago, when his mother used to arrange roses in a vase, the petals, of whatever colour or smell, in no time developed a bruised, sallow, almost oily complexion. It's the room in the house that he most avoided when Pa was there, where he snooped most often when Pa was not there, where he went to hang out, brain-dead, curtains drawn, double doors closed, where in the pregnant twilight laden with scent he would listen to a wasp constructing its mud cocoon on top of a book marooned there, unread, forgotten. His, the study will be. He can't wait for this trophy. *The Battle of Blood River* picture, that can be chucked out. Just a touch here and there: he knows exactly how he'll rearrange things.

'You can take it away please, Mattie.'

'Pa, you only had a thin slice of toast this morning. How about a boiled egg? All the way from Sissy. A farm egg.'

'I can't even think of an egg. It makes me feel more sick.'

'It's the chemo, Pa.'

He removes the tray from his father's lap. Just the edge of the stew has been prodded at, and, shoving aside the stuff on the dressing table with the corner of the tray, he leaves it there and says: 'And Pa, how do you think you're going to manage at night when you have to get up?' Then he sits down, next to the hand on the white bedspread.

'You shouldn't take things so to heart, Mattie. You're so touchy. Pa can see this. I want you to be happy, my son.'

Then he knows that he's been right all along. He's been thinking on his father's behalf and he's come to *his* conclusion. To be asked in his final days for a cheque for a business venture, a takeaway serving cheap, nutritious food, can only give pleasure to the old man.

Both Pa's nostrils dilate as he inhales. He can hear the breathing, different to his, distressed. 'You get these modern commodes today. They're made of plastic and have almost no smell. They come with chemicals. I'd like to be in my study when I go. You know what I mean, don't you, my son? It was always Pa's hide-out when storms were gathering. My son.' His hand fumbles and lands on Mattheüs's wrist.

'Chemicals?'

But Pa doesn't reply. And the word bounces back with its merciless consonants, and he knows it was unnecessary to ask. If he really wants to, he can move his father.

So there they sit, the two of them. Mattheüs realises that he's definitely going to carry out Pa's request, Friday afternoon or not, and Samantha will have to skip the cleaning just this once.

Ever since the start of that Friday – the question had in fact wrestled him awake – he'd been obsessed with *his* request. (It almost scorches him.) Either he must grab the opportunity and have done with it, by far the neatest option: a request from his father, a counter-request from him. Then waiting for a reply with a stomach-churning sensation, almost like when E kicks in. Or he must wait until he's settled the old man; he can do this, he has a talent for creating cosiness. Whatever: the time is ripe. Go ahead and ask your little question right now, my boy.

By now Mattheüs can smell the congealing stew, the fat forming small white islands on the orangey meniscus of the gravy in the plate. Untouched. Pa was always mad for Ma's stew, but why not tell it like it is: his stew is every bit as good. Pa's hand on his wrist is just this side of human warmth, the skin so fragile that if you pulled it apart with two thumbs, you'd tear it.

So this is the moment. It's on the tip of his tongue: *Pa, I was just wondering if you could perhaps write me a cheque*. The sentence. Now. I can do it. The words pre-formed inside a layer of spit. It took him exactly ten minutes this morning to formulate the sentence just as it is right now. *Cheque*. The whole sentence pivots on that word. But he, he. He's always dithered in his father's presence.

He tries to synchronise his breathing with his father's. Pa's faltering, plucking at the available air in the bedroom. It's impossible. All that's required is Pa's signature on the fine line in the bottom right-hand corner. That's all there is to it. Yet he can't. He wills himself to exercise his will. Can't. He feels sweat trickling down from his armpits. Impossible.

Ever since returning from overseas, actually even before that on the plane, one little bottle of shiraz, one Windhoek Lager, then another, until the trollies vanished, he's worked it all out. Because to arrive in the country without some job in mind is beyond desperate. Therefore: a thousand times already. Thus. He'll go and fetch Pakenham's big coffee-table book on trees, the last one that Pa had paged through, saying at the time: 'It's all over now, Mattie. The pictures are blurry. Put it away for now, please. In its place. You know where, of course,' and place the book on his lap as a writing surface and fetch the cheque book from the bedside cabinet on the right and open it on the book and guide Pa's hand to the start of the line. The cheque by this time already made out by himself in block letters. Recipient: Mattheüs Duiker. The sum of so much and so much, only. And then the signature, that's what he's after. He suddenly jumps up and rushes to the French doors, flaps his arms at the plovers; he can't stomach their damn squabbling any longer.

'What's the matter now, Mattie?'

In the last ten days or so, the voice, always modulated and full of the cadences so characteristic of Pa, has started to wear thin in places. A word collapses, say for instance the 'r' in tomorrow, becoming blunter, depleted of expressive power. Oh, he could have died when he'd first noticed this. His father, oh, he'd wanted to hold him to his breast. In his sleep that night he'd wept, so that by dawn his pillowslip was stained with a track of salt.

The question on the tip of his tongue mingles with the anticipation of the finality that the signature will seal, so that he loses clarity and starts confusing the sequence of the two, and from behind, from behind the back of his chair, looms something misshapen with shoulders and arms attached to the shoulders, a massive thing: it's the incarnation of his vacillation in the presence of Benjamin Duiker. Now, previously, and all along. He's afraid he's not going to get his question asked. It's a fear that he despises: that it's so deeply rooted.

Wait. (It's already become futile.) The seventy-six-year-old hand is not going to rise from the bedspread and start moving, the signature is not going to happen. *The* signature: *BDuiker*, with the muscular, erect stem of the 'B' and the two perfect semicircles sprouting vigorously from it, the lower one slightly larger to stabilise and lend balance to its most important letter. The signature then flows from the lower, stronger semicircle to the upper loop of the 'D' so that it seems to grow from this semicircle, without your seeing how it's done, and from there swoops elegantly all the way to the bottom to execute 'uiker' in symmetrical letters, each with a perfect slant to the right.

On scraps of paper, or suddenly while reading, he sometimes grabs a pencil and tries, at a random whim, to forge the signature, say for instance on the blank edge of a page of the book he's reading: *BDuiker.* His attempt is pathetic. A dying swan or some such.

If he were to forget and put behind him everything, everything about his father, and he really does mean everything, all the reproaches and incomprehension and old, old grievances and misunderstandings and all that shit, all the unfinished business, and he knows there's still going to be a lot, and the hundred-and-one other feelings, his empathy too, his identification with a man like his father, then he would still cherish that signature. It's pure, that's what it is. It is masculinity, the essence of it, that engenders such a signature.

The temperature of Pa's hand has changed from lying against the skin of his own wrist. And he himself must be just about at fever pitch with anxiety over his lost chance. The simplest question conceivable, thirteen words in all. And spit it out he can't. By tonight he's going to be sick with self-reproach.

And by tomorrow the self-authored drama will play itself out again, from waking up to going to bed, with all its shades of bravado and might-have-beens. Every part of his business plan has been plotted in the finest detail, including his suppliers and recipes, the lot – he's just waiting for the money. The amount was not too conservatively estimated; he's taken into account unforeseen contingencies. Sundries, as they say. More ideal premises for his concept you couldn't hope to find. *To Let / Te Huur*, the corner store on Main and Albertyn Streets, Observatory, with a view of Groote Schuur Hospital, not that that really matters. Used to be a fish-and-chip shop, which does matter because it'll be easier to get a restaurant licence. The only question is how much longer the place will sit vacant, waiting for him.

Around one thirty, when Samantha walks in, he immediately announces that she needn't bother with vacuuming and dusting – the old man's orders.

She's not one to be surprised. 'If that's how Mister Duiker' – that's what she calls him – 'wants it.' She has her purple vinyl back-pack with her. He knows she'll be pumping iron at the UCT gym afterwards; she's a part-time student in Environmental Science.

They work fast and hard. From the wardrobe in the spare room, she wheels out a clothes rail that he's forgotten about and finds a place for it in the study. Shirts, overcoats and trousers are carried down in layers, then sorted out and hung up. Going-out shoes, church and casual, all in pairs under the clothes rail. The bedside cabinets, both of them. They take extra care with the medication, Samantha not needing to be told. They decide the double bed should be placed in front of the window where there's a bit of morning sun, and move the circle of armchairs to the right. All the time they're coming and going his father lies there small and frail, and by the fifth or sixth time Mattheüs comes in, his father's face increasingly deathlike – the comparison is inescapable – he feels bitterly sorry for him. This time, he's collecting his toiletries to take them to the guest toilet closest to the study.

'Pa?' he asks. The hand lifts from the bedspread and signals, nothing, no, nothing, and drops again. This is quite possibly his very last journey.

11

The wooden chair they leave for the time being. That's where they'll help him to, to wait there while they move the bed with all its parts. At three-thirty, Samantha comes in with a tray, tea and a milkshake for Mister Duiker. A sort of milkshake made with Sustagen Hospital Formula that has been prescribed for Pa to drink; strawberry made him feel sick, chocolate is out of the question, vanilla he can just about swallow. Mattheüs thanks Samantha for the tea. He doesn't expect much more from her than hello and goodbye, instructions she gets from her mother, payment directly into her bank account, or sometimes, at the end of a shift, a pasella via him via his father from a drawer in the bedside cabinet, from the purse with the golden clasp.

They tuck an arm under each wing and fold back the sheet and the bedspread – feeble human warmth wafts up from the bedding. With all the lifting and the propping up of his body, his pyjama fly flaps open, briefly exposing to view the grey hair and his flesh. Samantha's the one who takes charge and folds the flap back in place.

She is her mother's child. Auntie Mary was and probably still is very fond of his father, bless her soul back home in Jakkalsvlei Avenue, Athlone, close to St Monica's Maternity, where all her children were born, four of them in all. She cherished Pa as if he were one of her own, and passed on to Samantha a certain kind of solicitude with a bit of flair and banter (always); a tight triangle to which Mattheüs was never admitted. That's why he doesn't even look at her as she adjusts the fly of his father's pyjamas: it's something between her and Pa and Auntie Mary's legacy, and it's got bugger-all to do with him.

Pa is sitting on the chair. He supports his head with one hand.

'Mister Duiker okay there?' Samantha asks. 'We're taking across the mattress now and making it up nicely and then we're coming to fetch Mister Duiker. It'll all be over now-now.'

'Samantha, how's it going with your studies?' His head still supported on the cupped hand, he speaks into his hand.

'Mister Duiker, it's only going well. I'm passing all my subjects. Next year is my second-last and the year after that I'm finishing.'

Samantha stands arms akimbo in tight-fitting black lycra Adidas pants. She's looking at his father, and Mattheüs looks at her compassion for his father.

He's still brooding on the thing with the cheque and can't think it away. Viewed positively, the matter looks like this right now:

— Pa is capable of rationally considering his request for money. If he hadn't been capable, he wouldn't have asked to be moved.

— Pa loves him.

— Pa would like to see him get ahead, row his own boat. It's not as if Pa's given up on him. Any undertaking is better than twiddling your thumbs. (There's always the pressure.)

— Opening a takeaway with good, nutritious food at affordable prices is a noble undertaking. (He'll never get as rich as Pa, but he's living in a different era where you have to reach out and play your part, or you're a zero in the community.)

— Pa has money. No doubt about that.

Viewed negatively, the matter looks like this:

— The move, the mere thought of it, has weakened Pa so much that he should be left in peace to process it.

— It is underhand, to say the least, to pester a man for money when he's in a weakened state. (And that on account of his own failings. Is he convinced of his business plan or is it a belated convulsion of the dutiful son?)

— Pa gave him an advance to go overseas, an almighty one. (Now remember, Mattie, this is part of your inheritance one day.) When he was in a tight spot in Athens, he transferred some more money. To this day, Sissy doesn't know about it, though she has her suspicions.

Conclusion: He's not a ruthless person and doesn't want to be known as one. He should just let Pa be. (But it nags and niggles at him. He's got the money. Why not? And isn't he his father's primary carer?) No, he can't ask a man who's in such a condition. It's exploitation, forget it. On the other hand. No. Just put it out of your head. Everything in its own time. But it's such an ideal opportunity right now. No. No-fucking-no.

A mattress is an awkward thing to schlep and wrestle through a doorway, especially if one of its handles is half torn off. Besides, you can't drag the thing along by its handles alone – you have to give it extra support underneath where you can't reach, unless you have an abnormally long arm; in other words, you have to grab it somewhere in the middle on the two short sides, possibly tearing your fingernails.

'But it's queen size, why've you been going on about double?' Samantha's arms and neck are milky, like light-brown sea sand. She starts giggling with the exertion, which makes her even more attractive.

'Samantha, please stop it now, you're killing me,' and he gets the giggles himself in the passage with its old Cape clay tiles and two runners, so that the mattress slides down at an angle. He loses his balance and collapses, weak with laughter. Samantha relaxes her grip and places her hand over her mouth and then dangles it over the back of the mattress, and in the sliver of Cape sun from the skylight on her lips, glistening with spit, he feels the same sensation – as in this same house when she took over from her mother, but at its strongest right now just where he's lying looking up at her, at the insides of her gym-toned biceps – that her skin, her smooth beach-skin, is just a shade away from what for him is erotic and that he could get up and go over to her, to her kind, and annihilate that shade. He would be able to *have* her, is what he's saying.

'Mattheüs, come on, man. We must move. I'm not leaving here after five. It's my time, man.' From the white-and-mint-green house with the asbestos fence next to the United Reformed Church building, he often dropped Auntie Mary and Samantha off there, she has emerged with a self-discipline he can only dream of.

The bed is remade and even looks quite good in the light from the tall windows, as if it's been there all along and has appropriated a space for itself in the now overcrowded study.

Samantha apparently notices this as well: 'Mister Duiker will lie here nice and private. It's a nice little place for him, shame.'

They fetch him from where he's been sitting patiently listening, trying to figure out what's being done, everything, and walk him step by step to his destination until he starts protesting in a voice that Mattheüs knows, Samantha too: 'For God's sake, it's not as if I'm dead yet,' so that they glance at each other and shuffle quickly past the bedrooms, his and Sissy's, and the narrower door to the guest toilet that Pa will now have to try to reach at night in pitch darkness with arms flailing in front of him to find his way, come what may. It's his decision, let's see if he has it in him to apply his highly developed sense of direction in his own home.

The Murano glass vase, an aqua-green stork, its bill gaping to gobble up greenery, towers on its Imbuia pedestal to the left of the guest toilet and will have to be moved; you don't want the thing crashing down and cutting his feet. Slippers he'll always have to wear, Mattheüs must remember to tell him. Opportunistic infections must be avoided at this stage.

They make him lie on his left side, facing one of the big windows. He's said little enough throughout the whole palaver, a shock to his system. Samantha is still moving stuff around, making sure that everything is just so.

Mattheüs is squatting next to the bed by his father's face. Tentatively, lightly, he strokes the face all over with the flat of his left hand, starting with the clear brow, across the bridge of the nose and the tip and barely touching the jutting of the lower lip, his lips have retained their fullness surprisingly well. The pad of his thumb hovers on the lower lip so that it parts and closes, and the fleshy inside, almost moist, comes into contact with his bare palm.

'Pain?' Mattheüs asks.

Pa's head nods feebly.

Mattheüs gets up from his haunches and goes to the kitchen, where he takes a measuring glass from a sterile cabinet and pours Oramorph, a syrupy morphine solution, from one of three brown bottles on the bottom shelf of the Kelvinator and carries it back and thinks how wise it is of Pa to acknowledge his pain and to permit himself one of the most potent of painkillers. He himself can never resist the temptation to sniff at the bottle when he unscrews the top, and again when he replaces the cap and returns the bottle to its two companions. He's told Jack the stuff is in the house and they were both silent, not saying what they both thought they could get up to with it.

Pa licks the syrup from the crook of his arm. Then opens his eyelids, this time as if he really wants to survey his new, familiar environment. 'The wedding photos,' he says.

Clearly, so that it cannot be said afterwards that there was any doubt on this issue: 'Pa, we thought it wasn't necessary. It's not as if you can see the things any more.'

'It's not about seeing, Mattie. You of all people, who are so focused on the unseen. I want all of them here with me. And the one of me and your mother at the Mercedes plant in Stuttgart. I remember it as if it were yesterday. With her hundred-per-cent pure wool two-piece she was very stylish that day. And with a blue opal necklace that Hannes brought her all the way from Australia. Man, you two! You're trying to pull a fast one on me. It's not as if I actually have to see the stuff,' and he smiles mischievously, as if sneaking a bite of cake, and Mattheüs, who was on the point of getting irritated, melts a little.

He turns around with Samantha briskly at his heels, and fetches the photos from the wall above the bed – all of them, from small to large, the engagement, Ma with her first baby, Sissy, all. And to save time, he and Samantha pack towels between the glass so as to carry three or four at a time, and that's how they leave his parents' room, a devastated domain that won't easily, if ever, be inhabited again. They cart the photos in their frames and take down the painting of the baobab tree in the Lowveld and other pretty ones and some of the lesser ones, Pa's taste, and hang them in the study and stand them on the mantelpiece, wherever there's a spot, Samantha with an underarm whiff from all the pottering about.

'Pa, are you satisfied now?'

But the old man is asleep. On his left side, with the afternoon light through the tall windows fragmented by the long, pointy leaves of the frangipani beyond; light on his cheek, on the hillock of his hip, on his pyjama-sleeved arm lying exhausted on the bedspread. Thanks to the brown bottle, the old man will venture on distant journeys and arrive at fierce destinations. How his father used to warn him against substances and their consequences, things he really knew nothing about. Now he's off to zombieland himself. By tomorrow at breakfast, with a soft-boiled egg he won't eat, everything will be forgotten. Perhaps in an earlier fully aware era between father and son, if there ever was such a thing, he'd have noticed that. Whatever the case, he was too weak. He had thought the time was right, but then he wasn't ready.

@ *Clarence House*, Jack facebooks a quickie to Matt. *I = stink. Shower first?*

Matt: *Come as you are.*

Jack: *Okay, if you say so.*

So Jack doesn't change into fresh clothes. He likes fresh. Sounds exactly what it is. Okay, he keeps on his white shirt with the steel-blue stripe, blue tie with tiny pink dots, black pants, black nylon-and-cotton socks pulled up to just under his knees, and black pointy-toed shoes. Matt likes him like this, just as he's been teaching all day. Not that he lets Matt call the tune, but he knows when he has to please. Tonight he's got an issue, something he deliberately forgot to tell Matt. Let's face it, Matt is a weirdo. Not because he likes sweat. That too. It's just his whole mixed-up make-up. You don't even know where to start. Take him as he is, but just remember. He'd like to meet the guy who can unpick that number.

He shuts the door of his flat on the ground floor of Jonathan Clarence House, the floor of the grade tens and nines. The top floor is for the grade elevens and twelves, the boys' hostel where for the last three years he's been the youngest resident housemaster to date and loving every minute of it. The first time in his life, just about. He walks along a pathway between flower beds and reaches the spot where a tree root has pushed up the cement. Zilverbosch Boys' High is kept tidy, is very orderly and extremely PC. But he likes the root that refuses to conform.

Further down on the left is a lawn under the helluva big tree where only the grade twelves get to hang out. To the left is the sandstone main building with a wide staircase right to the double doors, locked at this hour. Above the doors is the school crest with an inscribed cement ribbon plaited through its narrow end: *Altius et Latius*. Embossed letters in pale blue on white. Come the April holidays, he'll clamber up there and repaint the peeling 's'. Funny, but that's a bit of untidiness that does bother him. He cares about the place. He says this without a grain of sarcasm.

During holidays, he's just here. Boys' voices absent from the grounds. He doesn't go home, to Worcester. No ways. He doesn't call on his mobile phone. His phone is private, reserved for good times. He's crazy about all the things he can do on his iPhone. When he phones home, he prefers to do the old-fashioned thing and calls from the phone booth with the graffiti scratches on the panes: *Why don't Zilverbosch boys play rugby? Cos they row*. 'Row' scratched out and written over with 'fuck'. Outside on the cricket oval hadedas are signalling. 'Not even for Christmas, Jack?' his mother asks. What kind of question is that? It instantly gets his back up. She's just asking that because she knows that's what mothers are supposed to ask. Maybe he's wrong. But all the same. He's not going home just to put his possible, only possible, wrongness to the test.

Blaze is the guard who sits in the hut at the gate of the grounds. Hey, Blaze. Good evening, Sir. Come dawn, the man will still be sitting there half asleep. One eye drooping, his radio on *Umhlobo Wenene FM 88–104*, and his mobile phone nestling in his hand. Next to him is his two-litre Coke, half finished. Jack walks right in the middle of the road, oak trees to the left and right on the pavements, their tops touching one another against the twilight sky.

He's walking, he's not driving. His beautiful silver Renault Mégane, every cent of which he paid for himself, he's pissed away.

18

To be honest, sniffed away, up his nose. Oh, well. He's still paying off that little trip of his. Buying a new pair of top-shelf shoes at Fabiani's, for instance, out of the question. No sweat. Sure was a blast while it lasted. Except for the end of it. Probably on the cards, anyway. He has a history behind him, ha-ha, with consequences. (And he's not talking about the money right now.) Matt knows most of the story. It's an issue between them. Jack can't even say how much it bothers him.

He lights a cigarette as he walks. On Fridays, the boys are rumbustious, to use an old-fashioned word. The metre of the stanza, he'll begin. And: If you'd only listen for a moment. With your minds and not your arses. They roar. Ag, forget it.

So he just tries to keep some kind of order. And now and then he takes the opportunity to talk about life issues, but not in a cheap or clichéd way. He can do this, he reckons he knows his boys. They respect Mister Jack van Ryswyk. They call him Mister Richie, he doesn't know why. When they talk about him in the corridors they don't diss him. They've got nothing to say about him behind his back. He'd even go so far as to say the boys love him. Notes are pushed under the door of his flat at Clarence. Innocent. Pure. Usually to do with their un-sorted-out sexuality. And who is there to talk to among the staff?

A watchdog behind one of the high walls bounds along to the tread of his shoes on the tarmac till he's gone past. Here, every house has its wall with electrified steel fencing at the top, and remote-controlled gates. The class of house with swimming pools and pedigreed dogs that Zilverbosch Boys' High pupils come from; definitely not him. As he walks, he eases down his pants and belt. Fashion. Matt thinks he doesn't know how to wear his pants. He stubs his cigarette out on a stormwater drain without slowing down: how's he going to break the news to Matt?

When he reaches Campground, the thoroughfare, he spots Matt on the other side on Carlucci's verandah before Matt sees him. Matt has tipped his chair back and is leaning against a wall with naively painted scenes of Venice. He picks up his half glass of beer and drains it in a swig. He's wearing a black V-necked T-shirt. On his wrist, his beer hand, is his broad dark-brown leather band.

Jack catches a vibe from Matt. Left, right, he checks for traffic, trots across the street. He recognises Matt's shallow breathing from here: he knows what kind of man is waiting for him tonight. Matt is in his hell-raising mood. He's just waiting for Jackie, as he calls him, so he can start. Maybe he already has, with Carlucci's waiters, quite a few of them ex-Zilverbosch boys, all of them handsome in their way and brimming with confidence.

He walks around the table and right up to Matt, who's been watching him, and shakes his hand, but Matt grabs him by the tie and pulls him in to himself, into his smell that he knows so well. Jack laughs.

And is still laughing when he walks into the restaurant to order two beers and two pizzas. What's he like with Matt? Whatever it is, he can't help it. He's on automatic pilot. And what kind of person is Matt, actually? Sexually, he knows what Matt wants from him. The man is insatiable. Even after they've drunk and danced through the night, he can carry on till dawn. Jack picks up the beers, takes a sip of his own and wipes his mouth on his sleeve. Returns to the old thought: he's too lightweight for Matt. He's on borrowed time.

Carlucci's is a standard little Italian joint. Their pasta and pizzas are tasty, but nothing out of the ordinary. At ordinary prices and served on a red-and-white checked tablecloth, not quite clean. An older man with grey sideburns is sitting with a much younger, dark-haired woman and a black boy wearing an upmarket CK T-shirt, probably an adopted child – that's the class of people who hang out here. A rainbow restaurant; and he's not being cynical now. Their pizza with roasted pumpkin and strips of lamb and feta and thyme is their best dish.

He leans in and notices how Matt, still in his tipped-back pose, spreads his hands in front of him and then runs them over his face like someone who's tired or has been thinking of something and has now done with it. Maybe he's misjudged Matt's crazy mood.

Matt signals to him *no*, he must shift in next to him rather than across from him. And immediately Matt puts his arm around his shoulder. Jack can feel the man's hands on his cotton shirt. He knows the feel of Matt's hands on his bare skin.

Matt tells him what happened today in their house. All of it, as you might read it in a story. What the morphine does to his father and all, and how he noticed Samantha's sexiness. (Jack laughs. Matt's obsession with the male body is above suspicion.) And how ugly and cluttered but in a way quite cosy the study seems now, and so forth.

It's a dream of a house. He'd never in his life been inside a place like this. Cape Dutch, number nine Poinsettia Road, est. 1890. He's visited there, though not all that often. He's eaten there at least once with Uncle Bennie and Matt, traditional bobotie with all the sambals in little dishes. The pain-in-the-Christian-arse Aunt Sannie from next door was also there that evening. Buggered up everything. Every conversation she sort of censors. Like, they were talking about the guinea fowl on the Zilverbosch playing fields. And how well they're adapting in cities, and then Matt mentioned his mother (Jack never knew her) and her recipe for guinea fowl that he still remembers. And then, would you believe it, Aunt Sannie barges in with quails this and quails that, a story from the Old Testament. The Israelites just caught them by hand, clearly impossible.

And that was still okay, but then they talked about the new digitally enhanced version of *Last Tango in Paris* showing at the Labia. Which Aunt Sannie hasn't seen and will most definitely not see, but from their talk she gathers what it's about. (Marlon Brando stuffing the slab of butter up Maria Schneider, and all that.) And then she started. Movies, food, manners, everything stuffed into a moral straitjacket so that you want to scream: please just fuck off back to your double-storey mansion from where, Matt says, she never stops spying on them with her binoculars on a tripod. Anyway, if it hadn't been for her, Jack thinks the conversation would have flowed more freely. As he'd like it to be with a prospective father-in-law, ha-ha. In his old age, Uncle Bennie is more receptive to and curious about almost everything. Okay, so he has his little list of thou-shalt-nots, but he's a Reformed Church man and doesn't force the stuff down your throat like Aunt Sannie who belongs to a charismatic thing.

Carlucci's verandah is packed. The rainbow customers eat and drink and chatter, and schoolkids with mobile-phone glow reflected onto their boyish faces don't miss a single word of the table talk as they thumb away on their mobile phones.

Again and again, Matt comes back to the cheque issue. The unsigned cheque. 'Two more beers and two tequila shooters,' when the waiter brings the pizzas. It's a Malawian guy, Fulumirani. He sends just about every cent of his earnings home to his family. Tall and blue-pitch-black and built like someone who's grown up doing manual labour and got his toning that way rather than by hanging around in gyms. Fulumirani always laughs about the meaning of Fulumirani: long trip. He wants to become a journalist.

'Matt, I'll skip the shooter. I can't tonight. I have to – Something's turned up.'

'When I ask him again – okay I haven't yet, what am I saying – when I ask Pa, I'll go all the way and ask him for a hundred thousand more. Okay, now I can see how it works. That's why I had to wait. Why it wasn't possible to ask him today. I can see it all clearly now.'

Two shooter glasses arrive at their table, green-and-gold Springboks. Jack and Matt both look to the left. With compliments to Mister Richie from an ex-pupil.

'Off to California on a swimming scholarship. Lucky devil. No, but he deserves it all the way,' Jack says about the ex-pupil. 'Are you here by car?' he asks Matt. He's referring to Uncle Bennie's. Mercedes E-Class, white, but it never looks plain white to him. It's a kind of ivory or meerschaum. And then the camel-brown seats inside.

'Or maybe I must just do it on my own.' Matt pushes away the pizza; he's eaten only three wedges. He looks back to get the waiter's attention for more drinks and then rests his head on his hands clasped together behind it, making a triangle of his arms. 'Maybe I should try to do it all on my own steam. But how?' He addresses the table from the bowl of his arms. Jack knows the hair on his arms well.

'Aren't you going to finish your pizza?' He leans across and takes Matt's pizza and slides it in front of himself. Personally, if he'd been Uncle Bennie's son and come back from years of travelling around overseas, he wouldn't be asking for money. Not that Matt doesn't deserve it. Totally. I mean, look what he's doing for his father now. That's sacrifice, that, first-class sacrifice. His sister won't be driving all the way to the Cape just to mope by the bedside of a dying old man, day after godforsaken day. But if you add it all up, say for the few years or so that he's known Matt. What he's talking about is access to bucks. That's what Matt's got, which other people can only dream about. Access, that's what counts. No, to be honest, if he'd been in Matt's shoes he wouldn't have had the guts to ask his father for yet another cheque, half-dead or not. His father. Fuck it, when he thinks of his own father. Mechanic for a while, and then chucked it all. Where's he now? Gone without a trace, pal. The cunt ditched his own family. His mother, him. Jack his son? No ways. East London or somewhere. Who cares.

'Maybe I should shut the fuck up. You'll do what you want to anyway,' Jack says, taking another wedge from the pizza that now, at room temperature, is even tastier. Another round of drinks arrives. Jack pushes his shooter across to Matt.

'What are you on about, Jack? Why should you shut up, about what? You've said almost nothing all night. What's the matter now?'

'Matt, listen, please don't be pissed off with me. I forgot. You also forget sometimes. It's a question of totally, as in *totally*, impossible.'

'What?'

'When I'm finished here I have to go. Can't go out with you tonight. Please, Matt.' (Matt's way of turning to him and looking at him from under his eyebrows.) 'You've also got your responsibilities. I have to get up very early tomorrow morning. Me and Jamie, the English teacher. He can't drive. He hasn't got a licence. A total retard. We have to take nine boys to Misverstand

Dam. And the boat. It's out at Moorreesburg. Totally impossible. Can't wriggle out of it. I have to drive. You've met Jamie. Red hair. Straight and shy. Matt?'

'If there's one person on earth who knows how to put a fucking crowbar of a spoke in my wheel, it's you, Jack. I don't understand. After this whole day with all its shit, and you don't want to go out with me.'

'I want to, I always want to. But not tonight. Give me a break, Matt. It's my job.'

Matt grabs the Malawian waiter round the waist as he passes, orders another drink, and leans across to him: 'Will you have a last beer with your lover or is that too much to ask?'

Way over the limit, he slides in behind the wheel, and despite Jack's (responsible) jibes he drops him at Clarence, and, as expected or not expected, Jack won't let him come in even though he's told him he's desperate for a blow job, and so he kissed him passionately and Jack it was who gave in, yielded in spite of himself and got out, tore himself out, driven by a sense of responsibility you only develop when you know there's nobody to wipe your arse if you fuck up, because you've *got* nobody.

At that moment, in the almost ominous half-light of the Zilver-bosch grounds, wild figs dripping with early dew and rows of clivias in single file with their bottle-green leaves, he experiences a sensation of unravelling; he's all fired up, and so, in a spirit of good will, one might say, he releases his Jackie to go where he must.

Then he drives out of the gates and the guard with the nice teeth waves at him. He pulls up some distance down the road, just outside the Zilverbosch grounds, to look for the bottle of water that's rolled in under the seat and tunes his iPod to Proton, a Chicago radio station that streams electronic music, plugs it in and lets the powerful speakers pump it out all round him and sits like that for a long time, smokes one, two cigarettes and downs the whole bottle of water, gets out and angle-pisses against one of the high security walls, slowly, as a man who was hoping for something else pisses. An ADT security guard comes cycling past, 'evening brother,' he says to the guard to keep up the lingo and the ADT guard with the crackling two-way set nods uncertainly and pedals on. He shakes off and spits to one side and reckons he's sober enough to drive to town. With drum and bass permeating his body on the N2, he thinks of nothing at all, and keeps his head empty and open like that without even trying.

The club is pumping already. Heat pours from the entrance so that you get that familiar club fug as you approach. He walks in, flanked left and right by two bull-necked bouncers, one black and one white, both dealing with stroppy clients, both dressed in black with bouncer batons, black leather, in the right hand.

He orders a Black Label from one of the bare-chested bar-boys with attitude, and moves over to one side to light a cigarette, and soon, say on the third puff, Daniel sidles up to him. Daniel pronounced in the French way, a man who always cosies up to him because he judges him on his jeans and classy Adidas shoes as someone with money. Warm breath in his ear, Daniel advertises his wares. He trusts him, but also not. Each man for himself – he follows Daniel down and on the stairs to the lowest level where the cubicles of toilets number one, two, three, and four come into sight, and the darkness turns blue-black. As he steps down onto the floor strewn with unidentifiable objects, for a split second he sees this gateway to hell through the eyes of Benjamin Duiker, the total destruction of everything decent, then rejects the vision and enters cubicle number four with Daniel, the only available toilet, not that you'd expect to find toilet paper or a toilet seat for your arse or anything similar there. From his pocket, a small Ziploc with the goods. R100 tonight. He uses the word '*partager*', a French-sounding word that seems to mean 'partake'. Daniel now offers rather to *partager* his body, tasty, smooth and muscled, in exchange

25

for the money for the shit. He supplies, Mattheüs pays, Daniel keeps the shit.

'Wait a minute, wait a minute.' As turned on as he was a moment ago, he's now more in the mood for the shit in the Ziploc that Daniel has stuffed back into his jeans pocket. He is given what he wants. He trusts the man.

And so he drifts off, and he hadn't even wanted to – or had he? Back among the clubbers on the first level, he no longer contemplates them with quite the same heartfelt compassion as before. They now seem hard and narcissistic, even the women. He hadn't wanted to, you see. Drowsily, he squeezes past the crowd to the counter and orders two seriously sugary cans with a high concentration of caffeine, and pays laboriously; it takes an hour, or so it feels. He sways off, and downs the cans one after the other. Daniel walks past once again, winks (he trusts him), looking for new clients. He hadn't wanted to. All he'd wanted was to mingle with the people and to love everybody.

When he gets outside, dawn is breaking. A feeble little drizzle edges seawards from the mountain and moistens his skin. He must, must get to the fish-and-chip shop in Observatory – the premises he wants to rent and bind to his name to contractually. He walks fast, but not so as to appear afraid, across to the BP garage. Three people slouch up to him and ask for money and food and shit; he avoids their eyes. He joins the back of the queue snaking through the shelves of sweets and biltong and magazines to the cash register, and buys a bottle of water allegedly from the springs of Franschhoek, and cigarettes. To round it off, he selects from a perspex cabinet a chocolate doughnut, its lower crescent dipped in pink icing sugar, forges his way out, and walks to his father's car. Tonight's car guard is Etienne, in a pink-and-white striped Lacoste. He pays him R15 for the white car that's standing there without a scratch or a dent.

He glides onto a stretch of freeway, and beyond the city centre he slips off to Main and cruises calmly through Woodstock and Salt River, with all the grey security doors lowered over shop windows and locked at pavement level with industrial padlocks, a never-ending wall of exclusion in the early-morning hours. In Observatory he parks right across from his shop on the corner of Main and Albertyn, still with the *To Let / Te Huur* sign on its window. He mutters a little prayer of gratitude that the place is still there. This week he must take the bull by the horns – cheque, contract with the owner of the building, licence to trade as a restaurant. Another week, then it's all settled. Then he can start his new life. The old man will be pleased, no doubt about it: something of his entrepreneurship in his son after all. Always knew his Mattie had it in him. He laughs at his sudden clench of fear at the plan, and gets into the car; Pa would call it having little faith. If the shop was fated to be taken, the sign would definitely have been painted over with 'Let'. He aims and takes a photo of it with his phone. It's his proof that it's fated to become his. He stuffs the rest of the doughnut, sweet solace, into his mouth.

When he presses the remote at their gate – there's also an intercom where you can punch in the code – his electronic music is turned down out of consideration for the old man, who is by now lying wide awake (pondering his life). Just then, Aunt Sannie from next door walks out onto Poinsettia Road, freshly bathed and all dolled up. She's carrying food wrapped in clingwrap, and has Janneman on a leash. She places the food on the lid of the green dustbin in front of her gate. It's leftovers of her famous Madeira cake that has started to mould; he can see the green from here. She's leaving it out for the bergies. Then she prepares for her morning constitutional to buy *Die Burger* or some milk, looks up, pretends she's only just noticed him, waves exuberantly, and just about yanks little Janneman's head from his obese body. Behind his shades, Mattheüs nods just enough to register a greeting, presses the button of the passenger window to cut her off, and drives inside.

The strange thing is that in the entrance hall he now has to reckon with a presence just to the right, in the study. In fact, one of the double doors is ajar, not as he'd left it the previous afternoon, which means that the old man went to the toilet during the night.

He pops his head round the door. 'Morning, Pa.'

'Mattie, come here.' The voice extremely feeble so early in the morning.

'Pa, do you need anything? So, how did it go in the night?'

'Do you know, I now have to sit when I want to make water? Have I told you this?'

'Pa.' He's feeling the chill, his system sluggish with drink and Daniel's cocaine and the all-night action. Back at home it's okay to be defenceless, like he is right now; he's just not equipped to listen to his father.

'You know, Mattie, this illness drains the last little bit of manliness out of you. It's a terrible thing to endure. If I didn't have my faith, I wouldn't have made it. My rock and my salvation. There's nothing or nobody else to cling to. Pa wants you to remember that one day.'

'If Pa is okay with everything now, I'll get going.'

'You must just leave some toilet paper in there for me. I couldn't feel if there was any left. Apart from that, I don't need anything, my son. I thought perhaps you could come and sit here for a while.'

He looks at the person in the bed. Pa is lying on his back with his face turned to the window. The curtains are half-drawn, as he left them late yesterday afternoon. The water carafe on the bedside table isn't empty yet; there's no need to go all the way in, up to the bed. There's enough light, it's nice and friendly there. The problem isn't the light, though – something Pa can still sense. It's the smell. The study, with its pleasant blend of smells, is a thing of the past. He's sorry about that, sorry for Pa who'll never again smell things like he used to. When Jassie had to be put down, also from cancer, his father said, 'No, I'll never get another dog. Jas was my last. Did you see how he shied away from me? I know, my son. It's the cancer. The after-smell of the chemo. Jas stopped knowing me as his owner long ago. Poor animal.'

His father turns his face to the study doors, to him.

'Can't now, Pa. I'm dead on my feet. I need to sleep.'

'But did you enjoy it, at least? It's already morning, you know.'

'It was all right. Just a club. Nothing special. If Pa doesn't need anything, I'll be off. I'll make breakfast a bit later. After you've listened to your usual stuff.'

'You need the rest, Mattie. Go and lie down for a while. I wanted to tell you something I remembered. My mind is sometimes so clear in the morning.'

'I smell bad. Smoke and stuff. Pa doesn't like it.'

'I like the smell of beer on you. It's nice. I just wanted to tell you something. But it can wait.'

'G'night, Pa. Sleep well or whatever,' he whispers to soften the impact. He has to get away from there. Not to be cruel, but he simply can't right now. He turns away from the smell, caustic, the skin of a body cooling down permanently, just giving off a metallic dampness; appalling to have such a chemical smell on a human being, you can't imagine it. He tiptoes to his room, turns the key, and as the metal tongue slides into its groove, a tremor runs through him. A warning that he has to get to the toilet. He knows it and knows he can avoid it, it comes and goes and is really only a physical sign that he's about to enter the frontiers of his own world. He's had it – head on the pillow and he'll be gone. But he doesn't allow himself that. He pushes himself, his nerve endings exposed; man, you must try to understand it. It's a bit like shingles. The agony of your desires, the blessed, unconsummated desire that urges him on beyond all rational thought. He's operating only at the level of his last remaining senses.

The curtains remain drawn, and in the bluish glow of his laptop, always switched on, he goes across to it, swipes the touchpad of his seventeen-inch screen, clicks on the bar at the top, and opens Bookmarks, chooses a porn site, shudders afresh with the pressure in his arse, raw randiness, and, while waiting for the site to load, peels off his stinking clothes. Wearing only underpants, he grabs the computer and places it to the right of him on the bed, folding the blanket so that the screen faces him at the optimal angle for sharpness. His bed is unmade; Samantha never comes in here, it's his choice. He snuggles into the blankets and makes himself comfortable on his right side and explores the website while one of the videos starts up. Most are pirate copies distributed over a network of sites. All are hosted on Tumblr, and each photo or video on a site is linked to another site, apparently hundreds of them. If breach of copyright causes a video to be wiped on one of the sites, you can download it on a whole lot of others. He opens up eight videos, checking if the actors are his type, and if not he closes them one by one until he eventually finds one that's to his taste – brown Brazilians in a palm forest – the cigarette still unlit between his lips.

He skims through the formula of every video: courtship (sic), undressing, touching and feeling, groping and gripping, oral fuck and the final full fuck of penetration. Over and over, the images flicker on his retina, switching on that part of his brain that helps him to manufacture a private erotic experience and take himself in hand and bring himself to the point of satisfaction – but not all the way – and to click over to the next video with its variation on the formula and then over to another that opens full-bore on the penetration scene and makes his hand, the palm sticky and smeared with the mucus of spit and pre-cum, fall open, and makes him keel over onto the right-hand corner of his computer, and his eyes flicker, not in time with the action of the penetrator, but slower, heavier, so that he falls asleep in that haven of his bedroom, his clothes crumpled on the floor next to other clothes from other days, and odd shoes in and out of the wardrobe, his towel from his last shower over the wardrobe door, and recipe books open and turned over on their faces, other, older, possessions from his childhood, all the smells familiar and not unpleasant, Jack likes them, few other people ever have any contact with them, above his bed a photo of himself and his mother under the willow on Pa's family farm in Laingsburg, socks worn and unworn on the floor and the carpet, on the desk a Coke, and a square box of soil with the experimental sprouts all half-dead or etiolating from the continuous darkness, three containers of deodorant (the one he likes best has a smoky, nutmeg aroma, almost like a wholesome man-breath, if such a thing exists), DVDs, several books from the time (age seven) that he started reading up to now, a small framed black-and-white photo of Kafka as a young man with middle parting and collar and tie that he'd bought on a bridge in Prague, lots of other objects directly or indirectly connected to his development and self-development. Okay, so Jack's been in here many times. But essentially the room is for his own use, his castle.

He opens his eyes. There's a man on the screen whose symmetrical chest hair follows the twin undulations of his pectoral muscles to his sternum, the man is sitting handling himself on a blood-red sofa covered in some easy-wipe material, the man has milky droplets on the snail trail from his navel to the fringe of his fuck-fur and remains like that freeze-framed on the red sofa, legs spread wide.

The tip of Mattheüs's index finger starts moving automatically, tickles the touchpad to the next website, all of them in Bookmarks. There are up to seventeen different sites, apart from the extensive Tumblr network, which he regards as the ultimate porn site and which, strangely, he keeps secret as if other people mightn't stumble upon it. He finds two actors who take his fancy and arranges the pillows behind his back and leans back and picks up the crumpled underpants, lifts himself and puts them on again and takes hold of himself in the green-and-white elasticised cotton material and follows the whole on-screen ritual again until his head is light, his body chilled with sweat, the fluid he still manages to produce thin and watery, and yet he floats on, on, the images no longer on the screen but fused onto his retina, impressed upon his brain, which after one-and-a-half-years of obsessive porn-watching needs a daily fix, otherwise you'd find him hanging about hungry, jittery with a day's worth of quick-fix jobs, his mood feverish, though he did make an exception for his father's tomato stew and simmered and supervised it for a whole day, the preparation efficient and just this side of rushed – you can't have that with food – at last, like now, to reach his source of nourishment in his darkened room. There's nothing more to be said.

At one stage he lowers the volume, thought he'd heard a shuffling at the door or his father ringing the bell. Nothing. He switches from the video he was watching and surfs to a new one, twenty-eight minutes long, as the window in the bottom right-hand corner tells him. He moves the cursor until he finds his kind of action at the thirteen-minute mark and carries on manhandling himself, striped underpants half on, half off, until he falls asleep again, wakes up again facing a frozen image and slides his index finger along the pad at once, hunt and peck, now completely independent of his conscious self so that the longer he carries on, the less he knows whether the images are spooling in front of him or inside him. After each doze he wakes up without any memory of dreams, at most a single, persistent image of the porn star François Sagat bending over and tying his shoelaces on a beach – he's on sea sand, a perfect butt if ever there was one – which he wakes up to, and eventually after the fifth or sixth or seventh time he wakes up without any image in his head, without remembering anything of the twenty or thirty films he's run through, no action that stands out, not a single actor he can recall. He'll be able to sleep now, purified at last of the urge, until it returns like a monstrous thirst after an orgy of eating salt: that's how he understands it without wanting to mess with it or relieve himself of it, without ever telling everything to Jack, or to anyone.

Benjamin Duiker turns his head on the pillow and lightly touches the hands of the clock. (When his sight started to go, he peeled off the convex face of the alarm clock with his penknife.) It's half past eight.

The first chore is to sit up and put on his slippers. Groping for the left slipper, he touches the floor by accident and rubs his two fingers together. Mattie will have to have some vacuuming done here.

The second chore is to make his way across the room to the door. Last night he bumped himself against the corner of the desk;

the other two must have moved it from its original position, which he has a good idea of. He'll take that bruise to the grave with him. There's quite enough time before the start of the service. A Pastor Mikey Bruins of the Apostolic Church, Parow South, is taking the service. They've got such a soppy way of saying 'Jesus'.

He's got himself as far as the door. He's light on his feet, he must tell Mattie that. There are so many things he still wants to tell him. See, he always had such a heavy tread. His staff always knew when he was coming. He liked leather soles for working shoes. He wore German shoes, the Marc brand, and he preferred a rich brown colour. His heavy tread meant that he had to have them resoled often, on the market square in front of the city hall, there at Solly's. When Solly held out his properly resoled shoes in a paper bag and he opened it to inspect the handiwork, which was never actually necessary, he could smell the food Solly and his family had eaten at home. His sense of smell was always pretty sharp. If he had to smell now, it'd just be an old withered leaf.

From the top of his head to the tip of his toes he's lighter. He's lost how much fat and bone mass? 'Mister Duiker,' Solly used to say, his worker's hands touching his own as he passed the paper bag, 'I'm told Mister Duiker's cars are selling like hot cakes.' And then old Solly would roar out his laugh, to this day he'd be able to pick it out from other men's voices and traffic noise. If only he could get out once more to mingle with the creatures on the Lord's earth. What kind of unthinkable place is it that he's headed for? There is no true revelation in that regard. Dominee Roelf agrees. About that, you're left in the dark for the time being. What he wants to tell Mattie, now, is how unusually well he's feeling this morning. The nausea has gone down a bit. Not gone altogether, but it's bearable. He's learnt to live with it. And that's why he's such a featherweight, it's the oddest thing on earth.

He stands still there, with his old body that can't even dent the inner soles of his slippers (can you believe it, Mattie?), and tries to listen down the passage to his son's room. He suspects that part of his hearing has come back since he's had to rely on just four senses.

Mattie is still awake. He was convinced he'd gone to sleep. He hears a rustling and voices. He must remember to tell Mattie about his visions after taking the morphine. It's enough to really scare him.

Mattie. Step by step he walks on. It's wide and easy and open here in the entrance hall. He goes into the toilet and touch-feels until he's seated. He can't get the child out of his mind as he sits, waiting for it to come. His urine stinks, he thinks. A miserable little piddle, too, and it seeps out, all burning. How he remembers the day on the dam wall on their farm when he and Hannes wanted to see who could piss furthest. He was sixteen, grown up, he had a bull of a prick already and his stream arched thick and high. Out of sheer jealousy his brother knocked him over, and as he fell his piss sprayed a sort of drizzle.

When he's finished in the toilet and has checked that he's done everything there that needs doing, he gets up to listen again down the passage for Mattie. He's unsettled, his child, he can hear it even from Mattie's breathing when he bends over him in his sickbed. Mattie never sits with him for long. What he manages to get of Mattie's time, he more or less has to steal. 'I'm coming in a minute, Pa.' But he doesn't come. He asks him to peel his apple, anything, just to keep him by his bedside a little longer. It's no use. His heart bleeds for his son. He'd hoped that the overseas trip he financed at considerable cost would motivate him. But Mattie returned with a renewed restlessness. He pities him with all his heart. He doubts Mattie's faith in the Almighty. It hurts him very much. If only Providence would make him end this thing with Jack. It's a passing phase, oh, he's never doubted that. Even though Sannie from next door says differently. Mattie has his head screwed on right. Not quite *his* head for business, but still, quick on the uptake. Look, let him put it like this, this Jack chap is not a bad boy. But for Mattie, no good can come down that path. What on earth are these influences that have now sucked in his son too? If only Mattie could see it in that light. He prays every day for a change of heart – except when he has to swallow his dose, there's no time for prayers then. If only he'd find someone to share his life and set up home and settle down. Mattie's such a good-looking boy. Now that he's lost his sight he wants to say it to him: Mattie, come here so that I can touch your face.

He passes his desk and sees-remembers his things there, the fountain pen in the blue glass globe with inlaid bubble eyes that always make him think of a frog. Daimler-Benz engraved on it. It was a gift from the time he was chosen as one of the ten best dealers in South Africa, when his whole trip to Germany was paid for. His wife's ticket he paid for himself. Heavens, those Germans knew how to treat them. They were waited on hand and foot. *Schweinebraten*. The taste of it nauseates him, as he now remembers it.

At the back of the desk on the right is his old Philips tape recorder. A reel-to-reel, as they used to say. He'll use that. All his secretaries over the years, Leandra Kruger, Jeanette – another Kruger, had such a hard time with her weight – and then the last and prettiest of the bunch, Jaydee Minnaar. He often dictated his letters on the Philips and then they had to type them out with no mistakes on the Duiker's letterhead. But Jaydee Minnaar made many a slip, from the very first sentence. The soft flesh of her palm suddenly on his forearm: Mister Duiker, I'll fix those little things for you in a jiffy. He overlooks her slips – how else?

He shuffle-walks to the radio on his bedside table, switches it off and returns to his desk, where he starts pottering about. He takes the odd break, he knows it's the only way, to save scraps of energy, otherwise he'll be flat on his back in no time. The arum lilies outside the study windows – he must make a note to tell Mattie they'll be needing water. It hasn't rained for a while. He manages to set the Philips up in the middle of the desk, right in front of his hands. Bought in 1962, if memory serves. Quite a decent machine with its dark-brown lid (which he locates by touch and lifts off) and its tan undercarriage with ivory-coloured knobs and silver finish. His index finger explores and finds the three oblong knobs right on the left: play, record, and pause. He sits down, the effort obvious from his breathing, and feels first the left-hand reel, then the one on the right. The tape is indeed neatly wound on the right-hand reel.

His meticulousness. There's not a single possession in this house that he didn't look after and maintain. As he tried to do with his people also. And yet.

He can get going now. He leans forward slightly to the spot where the built-in microphone should be and feels his balls in their old sack slipping down over the edge of the chair and wiggling in the crotch of his pyjama pants. There's even a brief spasm of pleasure. All set now.

First he rests a bit, shifts in his chair, leaning his head against the broad backrest. Jaydee Minnaar. Listen, there wasn't a single part of her silk-stockinged legs that he didn't ogle on the sly. Of course, she cottoned on. Mister Duiker this and that, all lips and nails. And then she pretends to cover up her low-cut neck a bit. Now, there was a girl who proved to him that pretty needn't be dumb. Diek and he, the two of them, they could fire each other up just talking about her.

He presses the central button to record, 'One, two, three,' then presses pause. He locates the rewind button in the centre of the machine and presses it down to rewind and test. His voice doesn't sound as worn-out as he expected. Just thin. He'll make a point of speaking more from the pit of his stomach. Funny taste that was in Mattie's tomato stew. He picked it up immediately. He can't stand it when Mattie doesn't tell him things. If only he would talk, the child. If only he would open up his heart a bit.

He presses record again and starts talking:

My dear son,

Pa has so much that he wants to share with you. It's a bit of an effort, this living together, your father knows. He doesn't deny it. It's hard for you and me to talk to each other. I suppose that's just the way the Good Father created us. Look, me and my father, your Oupa Ben, as I remember all too well, we only talked to each other about important things. You may well regard them as unimportant.

Mattie, please excuse me if I stop talking every so often, my child. I'm drawing on my feelings here, and I'm not going to press pause every time

I need a break. This is not about sounding good. I'm just trying to say it as it comes from my heart, Matt. More than that, your father can't manage.

No, as I say, your Oupa Ben and I, we mostly talked about how to keep the sheep alive in the most economical way, how to make money on a farm, and which of the farmers in the district were farming badly, going under. And we talked about cars. Your oupa was also fond of cars, of all machines, actually. One thing you have to understand, Bennie, a woman is another kind of thing. They don't think as we do. That's the kind of thing we discussed.

Anything you might say was a bit more private, we never touched on that, your oupa and me. And round about sixteen he said to me one day: you'll have to start shaving, Bennie. You're a man now. I don't want you to leave the house looking untidy. Go and look in that white cabinet in the bathroom and take my old razor for yourself. And he also told me to wash properly down there when I'd done my thing. And none of that unnecessary fiddling. Pa doesn't want that. See to it that you save your seed. You know, don't you? All that kind of stuff. Yes, Mattie, we know each other, man.

Mattie, what I want to tell you is about the time when Hannes and I saw a sedan for the first time. Up to then my father had only had the Model T Ford with the side flaps. A real dust magnet.

Then the day arrived, a morning as beautiful as any you can get there on the farm. Ag, I remember it as if it was yesterday. It was summer, and the miraculous rains that year made the thorn trees flower in one mass of yellow. They made these huge pompoms, too beautiful.

Suddenly we heard something coming, a car's engine with a different kind of sound. And different it was. Uncle Jaap in his Buick. A 1946 Roadmaster, a shiny brown one, as I remember it. Very posh. It had a wide vertical grille in front and a small silver mascot on its nose. Too showy for words. Let me tell you now, Mattie, it was the most beautiful thing on earth for me, that car. Nothing could touch it. See, stretching from its front wheels to the back, the most beautiful fender, streamlined and everything, all the way to the back wheel. The Americans knew what they were doing. Picture it, almost like a long wave breaking. With a bit less chrome, because of the war. You know, everything was in short supply.

Man, Hannes and I, when Uncle Jaap came driving past and pulled up in a cloud of dust, Hannes and I fell on our knees there and then and smelled the tracks of that car. In the sand. Rubber and dust and the exhaust that had left behind a whiff of gas. I can still smell it in my mind. Hell, man, Mattie. A sedan it was, one of the swankiest cars you could get around here in those days.

Uncle Jaap got out, white gloves and all, smiling broadly. He'd shaved himself a pencil-line moustache like in Hollywood. Errol Flynn and the boys. Ever so slightly hard-arsed. How shall I put it? A real man. With that car, Uncle Jaap was for me everything a man should be.

If only you could understand that about your father, I thought, Mattie. That's why I'm talking to you now. Your father wants you to understand him, even if only a little bit.

Mattie, I've finished now, my son. Pa is tired of talking. But I hope you can hear everything clearly, as I meant it, and that you're not bored with all the inbetween stuff. Please excuse your father's silences, my son.

Your father.

With his computer next to him now in sleep mode, Mattheüs wakes up. It's dark in his room, twelve noon and thirty-two degrees outside. The back of his head has made a dent in the pillow, the slip and stuffing are drenched in sweat. He disentangles himself from the sheet that has wound itself around his waist and crept in under his body, everything sopping wet. He sits up, grabs the computer that's slipping down, and puts it on the floor. From the (recurring) dream full of delays, full of places that can never be arrived at, the anxiety about that obstruction and resultant overheating of his body, his thoughts sludge lava-like to one of the last fucked-up heart-to-hearts with his father, as he calls those conversations.

Pa wasn't quite blind yet by then. It was December exactly

four years ago, just before Christmas and shortly before he left for overseas, a red-letter day because it would have been his mother's birthday and Pa extra-full of shit, you have to know him to know how full. And why? Was it because of the commemoration of his mother's birthday or because he'd been waiting all bloody day for the man to come and fix the remote-controlled gate, him up and down on the lawn with his cell, or was he fretting all over again about his son who was going nowhere with his life, or was it just the illness? But the NHL or non-Hodgkins lymphoma was under control, the oncologist positive about the new treatment available. Pa had this dogged expression on his face whenever he talked about his illness. Almost an arrogance in the face of death; he'd convinced himself that he was not ready to go yet. Or was it just the hot, dry Cape day, or what? How can you get into his head?

If there's one thing that drives him insane, it's when Pa invites him to the study and seats himself in his great golden throne and he, Mattheüs, sits on this side on that pathetic office chair, switching position from knees clenched and legs spread wide. It was stuffy in the study even though the windows were open, or at least that's the way it felt.

'Shouldn't we switch on the fan?'

'You'll be the death of me before I'm dead, you and your sister.' He reached over his desk and pulled the in-basket closer to him and started riffling through a lot of stapled-together stuff, looked like accounts or something.

He passed one across to Mattheüs. 'Have a look there if you don't believe me. Every month the electricity just goes up and up. How's it possible? Is it that computer stuff of yours?'

Never mind Eskom's stuff-up and never mind their directors with their fat-cat salaries, no use mentioning those. Facing him is the man now claiming back the account to slip it into its place. His face is reddish today. But it's not a healthy shade of red. The forehead bigger and broader in relation to the lower part of his face, his cheeks more hollow since the treatment.

Funny thing that happened to Pa after he sold Duiker's Motors and retired. (Although he never could or would truly retire.) His mother, fucking hell, he drove her mad those last few years together. It got so that she couldn't buy anything for herself. Then he started going to the supermarket with her. Beeline for the 'specials' shelf. He made her so nervous, the poor woman. Mattheüs can remember her hands one day, making scrambled eggs for him, trembling witnesses to her inner life, her extreme effort to keep a grip on herself. By that time she was frazzled. And that morning, it was all about the price of a dozen farm eggs (free range). She refused point blank to eat factory eggs or chickens. She believed that the mash or the stuff they fed them gave her a rash. Under her arms, at the back of her knees and in the crook of her elbow. Strong rooibos tea helped. Sorbolene. But the inflamed redness, the exposed nerve, kept coming back. Each time with renewed vigour, fury, almost.

Pa got a bee in his bonnet about money. A condition that got worse by the day. Fuelled by a fear that he'd sink back into poverty, like his father during the Depression and the drought of '33. Who knows, really? It wore Ma out completely, *he* did, and to this day it's the principle determining every cent that's spent in the house. Single-layer toilet paper, tinned jam. You just end up using more. Or throwing it away.

What's odd about the money thing is that it's not applied consistently. (Thank heavens.) About his overseas trip, Pa said: Fine, you can have this much. Pa gives it to you with an open hand. The car he can have whenever he wants. Sissy's children are given huge cheques on their birthdays. Ridiculous, they're just kids. But as for his mother in her final years, she was no longer allowed to buy the classy shoes she was accustomed to. She certainly had taste, paid R2 000 to R5 000 for a pair of shoes. 'But my dear wife, have you gone off your head?' Then he'd get really furious. 'You'll have to wait until I'm dead before you buy those shoes. That's blood money you're spending. Good Lord, how many years have I worked my fingers to the bone for you?'

'Pa?' In the study where he's been summoned, his father looks at him and then looks away again. He takes his penknife from his pocket and trims the nail of his pinkie and then looks at him again.

'It's not easy for me, this thing. You know I respect you. Your opinions. Even if you see things so differently from me. Not that I can see why, either. It's not as if your mother and I made a mess of our lives. Our way of life.' He stopped there and put the penknife in his pocket and sat with his hands folded in his lap, in his light-khaki pants. He was wearing a pale-blue button-down shirt and was clean shaven as always. It was a Saturday, even on weekends he never let himself go. (Men are such vain creatures, he said often and with mischievous relish.)

He knew in advance what his father wanted to talk to him about, and resistance to the man grew in him like a huge turd. He refused to sit out the conversation, not again. 'Yes?'

'Yes, Mattie, yes. That's what I want to say to you. You're a Duiker, my son. A man. You're my only hope of continuing the family line. When your old father is dead and buried, he just wants to know that something of him survives on this earth. It's only human, Mattie. That's how people throughout the ages have thought and lived. Please don't tell me that you're the only one who's right.'

Mattheüs wanted to puke. He got up and adjusted the fan to blow straight onto the fucking office chair where he was sitting.

'Look, Mattie, Pa doesn't want to upset you. You know I want nothing but the best for you. Only the very best, my son.'

Pa shifted in that broad chair of his so that his left shoulder pointed at Mattheüs. The old man was trying to tone down the confrontation, you couldn't accuse him of not trying in his own way. He had after all mellowed in his old age. A breeze blew in the scent of frangipani, just a whiff; it was too hot outside to release the full aroma of the pale-yellow blossoms. He would endure a few more sentences and then get up. He wasn't going to let Pa mess with him. It happened too often in the past, too many heart-to-hearts that settled in his unconscious and lurked there, slumbering for years, and suddenly on the beach at Clifton Four where he'd fallen asleep on his stomach in the sun, it would sneak in like some thief of a nightmare and scald his skin as he lay there, overwhelmed by a surge of emotion.

Pa, in the meantime, was carrying on about all the old stuff in his usual way, ag, he knew it all. He managed to shut himself off completely, neither hearing nor seeing, he sat there, and Pa thought he was listening and taking it in and even dared to hope that today he'd make some headway. His father had become smaller of stature, that's for sure. And looking at him like this, if he himself could curl up, foetal and vulnerable, and then think of Pa, a man deeply capable of compassion, of love, the man in his beautiful suits returning from work, transactions involving thousands and thousands concluded, success on his lips, when he thinks of him as he was and how he'd made and shaped himself to be the man he wanted to be, and when he thinks of him as he thinks of *him*, his son Mattheüs, and as he wants him to be, then he really does empathise with him. He could curl up and forlornly howl on his father's behalf. Yet he could also react in this way to his father.

'Pa, wait a moment. It's terribly hot in here. Aren't you hot?' He unbuttons his shirt and goes to the liquor cabinet and pours himself a stiff brandy. 'Do you want anything to drink?'

This time of day, broad daylight. Pa doesn't even deign to answer, but nor does he dare comment on the liberty his son claims in pouring himself a drink. Given the circumstances, Pa is holding out for the best possible outcome.

'Mattie, if there's one thing I want to impress upon you. Just one thing your father asks you nicely.'

Here it comes. He gulps at the brandy that is much too good to be swigged like that, it burns all the way down to his stomach.

His father knows that his son is now knocking back his ten-year-old KWV like water, and shifts so that he is facing him head-on again. He's picked up his letter opener and tick-ticks the silver blade on the desk. Anger is the only way he can say what he has to.

'You know this house is open to your friends. It's always been like that. Your sister had lots of parties here. Open house right until the day she got married and left. That's how it is. Pa is more than happy to know that you want to entertain your friends, boys or girls, here at home. And now, now it's Jack, your big friend. Look, Mattie, let me put it like this, I've got nothing at all against Jack. He's got a respectable job. It's not child's play nowadays to be a teacher, that's common knowledge. Jack is welcome here any time. He knows it and so do you.' The blade of the paper knife lies pointing towards the crystal tumbler of brandy, or at least what's left of the drink, in Mattheüs's hand.

'But there's one thing you must understand, and Pa has no choice but to say it now. I've always been honest with you, Mattie. I don't want you and Jack to come into this house and sleep together or whatever kind of unmentionable things you get up to. That's your business. But not in my house. I won't allow it. It flies in the face of my principles. I firmly believe that humans weren't made to live that way. In my house, no. And absolutely not while I'm still alive.' The violence in his voice subsides. He looks away from his son. The brutality of what has been said here and has been laid bare by the saying, its implication for him and Mattie, is almost too much for him as well.

He softens. There's a weariness in his face. 'Once I'm dead you can do as you like. Then you stand alone before your God.' He looks at Mattheüs in the hope, perhaps, that a grain of something will come of it, understanding or assent, however half-hearted, as long as there's something to cling to.

In the study, Mattheüs gets up from the chair he's been sitting on and that he hates anyway (after the *Battle of Blood River* picture, it's the first thing he'll chuck out) and, as he gets up, he grabs his glass to drain the remaining liquor in one go and stalks out with his hand on his back, as if he's just fallen or wants to ward off a shot or something – what with having his back to the enemy and his head spinning from the sudden shot of alcohol – but he keeps walking straight ahead, out of there, blindly. He has the capacity to commit some atrocity, he's already far gone, if he were only goaded enough.

So that's what one of the fucked-up heart-to-hearts with his father looks like.

He sits on his bed with his elbows on his knees in the overheated nocturnal darkness of his room, and the additional heat generated by the memory, and before that the dream, builds up in the bowl of his body. He plucks a hair darker than the rest from his thigh.

Then there was also the thing about the elusive cheque book in his dream. Scoured his father's room even as far as the bathroom cupboards, and the frustration fierce and just as real as in the world outside the dream, the fear that he won't find the cheque and that his father's going to die and then how long, a year, before the estate is sorted out. Then at last, it felt like hours, he found the thing, hidden under the socks in his father's drawer. Flipped it open immediately, only to find that a cheque to the amount of R500 had already been made out to him, signed *BDuiker*. Ridiculous. Can't be. What's he supposed to do with R500? He swings around where he's standing at his father's wardrobe with the open sock drawer, and when he looks around him he is suddenly in the study, inside already, and his father leaning against the doorway still in suit and tie and all, like a movie star, Cary Grant or one of those old-time actors, and his father holds out a hand, palm open, to receive something, and he comes closer with the cheque book, expecting that he's going to change the amount, it's a slip, that's all, and when he's almost reached his father so that he can even smell him in his dream, his father's hand flips over and he lifts his index finger and then the erect index finger starts oscillating like the needle on a speedometer, to the left, to the right.

Mattheüs gets up and then collapses onto his bed again, collects all his memories and the dream and all, and tries to drive it out into the outer darkness, as the Bible says. He lights a cigarette, crouches into his sweat and picks up the computer from the floor, wakes it up and surfs to a site with hard mechanical NYC-style porn and drips oil on himself and beats off so hard that the veins bulge on his temple, and when he comes he flings himself backwards to catch the sperm on his stomach: it burns his skin and he lies like that till his breathing stabilises and he calms down.

He's seventh in line in the row of chairs against the wall with their maroon seats that you just know aren't clean. Capital Bank is a bank for lame ducks and losers. The grey paint selected for the walls can't be smudged by children who've come here with their mothers; most of them are single parents come to beg for a micro-loan.

He found parking easily, opposite the Observatory Library, a sturdy building that he refuses ever to enter again because he's persuaded himself that they stock only easy-reading pulp. Once when he asked for help from the librarian – one with far too much lacquer and gel on her hair, a woman who'd be more at home in a shoe store – she looked at him dumbly and started searching for Doris Lessing on the computer. 'How did you say that name was spelt, sir?' No idea who the writer was, even though she'd just received the Nobel Prize for literature.

Mattheüs has chosen this branch of Capital because it's just a few blocks from the premises he's eyeing that still says *To Let / Te Huur* on its window, which is getting filthier by the day, so that all you can make out inside are shadowy forms. But he knows the serviceable stainless steel counter is still there. The walls outside, especially on the street side, are also (fortunately) scrawled with graffiti, which he himself has contributed to so as to downgrade the place even more and force down the rent.

Next to him in the queue is a mother with three children, all snazzily dressed and speaking English, a kind of Cape Flats primary-school English that you can hear is not their mother tongue, because she with her loser handbag from Ackermans and the pungent spray-on scent speaks crappy English herself, and what's more she's going to speak it to Mr Isaac Smit in cubicle number one; what's the bet he's also Afrikaans.

Clients occupy cubicles three, four, five, and six. This is the bank with the lowest service charges in Africa and the greatest willingness to take risks and to recruit men and women other banks wouldn't look at twice, all under the benign gaze of the president (centre), the minister of finance (right) and the governor of the reserve bank (left) in gilt frames against the dull-grey wall behind the cubicles. The three persons in the portraits, leaders all, do absolutely nothing for him. They only contribute to the growing ridiculousness of his mission. Listen, Mattheüs, let Pa make this clear to you from the word go, this is a Mickey Mouse bank you're sitting in today. No, my son, if you need capital for a business venture you make an appointment with the manager of one of our big banks. Then you're on the right track from the outset. Here you won't achieve anything, my son.

The queue moves on. The man at the head of it in his pin-striped suit gets up and goes to cubicle number two, Mrs Leslie Sikhosana. His long fingers clutch the briefcase that he's holding against his jacket, he is tall and thin himself.

'Do you think he's from Ethiopia?' he asks the woman next to him, an unusual openness to strangers attributable to his nervousness or the futility of the whole damn thing; he doesn't have a single asset to offer as surety for the enormous loan he wants to apply for.

The woman looks at the man he's looking at. 'I really can't say,' she says and turns the page, one of the Capital Bank brochures she's picked up, in glossy white, pink and grey. He's disappointed; most Capetonians are always ready for a chat. Main thing is to remain positive. In spite of. Fuck, he won't do and never has done as well as Benjamin Duiker. He just wonders whether Capital grants loans as big as the one he wants.

'Spaza shop,' she says out of the blue, apparently having once again inspected the tall man with the fingers. 'They all start businesses and rip off the Africans who can't buy at Checkers. I feel sorry for them.' Then, in Afrikaans, to the child, who's starting to irritate the baby next to her, 'No, Jodie, leave the baby.'

She starts paging again and he starts what he's never stopped doing. The cheque is a goner. Pa is too frail right now. He just can't be so callous. He must have been blind not to have seen, the day they first arranged his father in his sickbed in the study, how Samantha folded the sheet one last time, straight as a ruler, under his father's withered, pyjama-covered arms, just as she was taught by her mother, neatly, and how she hung around there as if she guessed that he wanted her out of the way, which was of course the truth.

'Let's leave him to rest a bit now. It was a lot of stress for him. You may not think so, but it was,' Samantha pronounced. Just one more time he wanted to try to make his request, his eye on the bedside cabinet they'd carried in, on the drawer where the cheque book lay. And Samantha stops him with her glare: don't you dare bother the old man with your dirty business.

The queue in Capital Bank moves on again, so that now he's sitting at number two, and he wipes the clamminess of his hands all along the seams of his pants, an appropriate pair for the occasion. A hip-hopper, younger than him, with 'cool' written all over the torn bum of his jeans, gets up and saunters extra-cool to cubicle number one; DJ equipment or a record company is what he probably wants. He'll get nowhere in that outfit of his. The mistake he makes is to keep on his sunglasses. That's disrespect towards the bank clerk. He's had it before he's even started.

Cubicle number five is manned by an auntie, *Mrs Tanja Botha*. If only he could get her, he prays under his breath, and when he opens his eyes, he finds little Jodie from next door watching him. He laughs. 'Who do you want to talk to?' he asks the woman next to him, who is showing not a trace of nerves.

'Ag, I get what I get. It's my life policy. They're not stuck-up, you know. They give you what you ask as long as you pay back the instalment on time, you have to be on time and so on.' She looks at him. 'You're not worried, mister, are you?' And takes a packet of Sparkles from her handbag. The children all get one, and he does too.

'I wish I could get Mrs Tanja Botha in cubicle number five,

if you know what I mean.' He has a yellow Sparkle, which he swopped with little Jodie, who wanted his red one; children always want the red one.

'OK, I make a deal. If I get Mrs Botha now, you can go first before me. You whites help each other. I respect that, you know.'

And that's the way it turned out. Cubicle number five is vacated and Mrs Tanja Botha pushes her pale-mauve reading glasses back up the bridge of her nose and peers at the next client, Sandilee, that's her name. And Sandilee nods at him, friendly, and he gets up with the sweat literally running all down his sides under his respectable Ben Sherman checked shirt. There is hope. He takes the Sparkle from his mouth, and without getting his fingers sticky he drops it into one of those tubular trash cans, and sits down on the maroon chair in front of Mrs Tanja Botha. He pulls the chair in so that he can lean his arms on the edge of the desktop, ready.

She introduces herself and he introduces himself to her, all in Afrikaans to make sure she knows he's one of her lot, a bit sidelined nowadays what with affirmative action and all, a young white man, she *has* to lend a helping hand, never mind Capital's regulations. He tries to regulate his breathing, and by the time she asks, 'And how can I assist you today, Mister Duiker?' he's calmer, with his father's mantra like a distant buoy in stormy seas: The one thing you must never ever do is throw in the towel.

'Well, yes, that's a large amount, Mister Duiker.'

'You can call me Mattheüs, Mrs Botha.'

'We'll have to look very carefully at your business plan. You know the recession is still biting. People tend to eat in, you know. Takeaway. Well, we all know the big names, the Wimpys, the KFCs, they're not suffering any damage. We're talking market share and sustained publicity. Their customers know they can eat cheaply there. But if we're talking restaurants and that kind of more special-ised place, they're the first to feel the pinch.'

'Mrs Botha, you must please just understand that I'm not aiming for a restaurant. I'm not even thinking of it. My premises are just down the road. *To Let / Te Huur*.' And from his back pocket he produces the folded A4 – limp, sat-upon – and opens it out, the writing politely angled towards Mrs Tanja Botha. Upbringing. If she can't see it.

There's a hand-drawn map with the premises circled in red: Duiker's Takeaway. Good Food for Good People. He starts explaining everything to her from A–Z, even a recipe or two, including his suppliers of good cheap meat and dried beans. Atlas Trading Company for his spices, does she know the shop? A second-hand cold-storage room he'd come across in Goodwood at so much and so much, there's an industrial gas stove he has his eye on, takeaway containers in recyclable materials, a bit more expensive, but he's going to try it anyway.

'How about your microwave? There's no way you can get by without one of those in a modern kitchen. I baked the most delicious apple cake in my microwave the other day. Twelve minutes, can you believe it?'

'Did you sprinkle cinnamon on it?' he asks, certain that naming the spice signals a breakthrough. Now he wants to know (enthusiastically) whether she realises that most takeaway food is of a low, extremely low, quality; and to make things worse, it's usually unhealthy. Cholesterol, heart disease, all those complications. He wanted to add *fattening*, but bit his lip as he'd taken up position across from Mrs Botha and had a view of her spare tyres, four on each side, which is to say eight in all, compressed into summery lilac, though it's cotton at least, thank heavens for that. Mrs Botha has to realise that it's a service he wants to render to people of middle or low income. A thoroughly ethical undertaking. He can show her the premises when she has the time. He looks at his hands on his side of Mrs Botha's desk. Let his father lie there in his deteriorating, at times befuddled, ever-judgemental, troubled, whatthefuck-to-call-it condition. His loan will be approved and sealed this very day.

'Mr Duiker. Mattheüs. I can see you've got your head screwed on right. My next question to you is about surety. Your assets. If your restaurant flops, and believe me this can happen to the best enterprises, just like that. Capital must at all times be assured that it will be able to recover the loan. That's how it works with us. What do you have to offer as security, young man?'

'There's the Mercedes E-class. Pa paid just over half a million for the car.' Is he totally out of his mind? He removes his hands from his side of the desk where they've left two damp marks. The car is going to be his, but this hasn't happened yet by a long shot. That's the point. It's not his car. Pa could linger for months or even a year, it doesn't matter what the oncologist says. As long as they make sure his father eats. He must eat. If you don't eat, you die.

Mrs Botha is looking at him attentively. Her left hand is resting just above the open V of her lilac dress.

'That car is worth a fortune, Mrs Botha.' Stark raving mad.

'I don't quite understand, Mattheüs. You say your father paid half a million for the car. For your use? Whose car is it?'

'Mrs Botha, that car can cover my debt any day. Triple. Over and over. There really is no problem here.'

'The bank would first have to appraise the asset. Cars depreciate very quickly. We need to know the condition of the car. Every six months you would have to bring the car in for an assessment. And if it's found that it can't be sold at, well whatever, then that's it. How much do you want to borrow?'

It's not as if he hasn't said. He says it again.

'Mm. That's a tricky one. Cars, to be honest, are not our ideal security.'

'Mrs Botha, you're welcome to come and do an inspection. Perfect. There's not a scratch on the car.'

'Well, I'm not the one who'll inspect the car. Tell me, what year's model are we talking about? I'd also need the purchase contract. We have to verify the ownership of the asset. Without that we can't accept the asset as security. It's problematic. How about property?'

'The house doesn't belong to me, Mrs Botha. Not yet.' He's pushed his hands in under his thighs and taken them out again. He's got a raging headache. 'Mrs Botha, I'm going to have to excuse myself for the time being. I'm not feeling too well. I need to rethink things again. Back to the drawing board, as they say.' He puts out his hand as a last brave gesture.

Mrs Botha lifts herself a fraction from her chair and places her fleshy hand in his. 'There's a water cooler right next to reception. Feel free to help yourself. And come and see me again. You can make an appointment now, while you're here, with our secretary, Millicent du Preez. And Matthéüs,' she gestures with the hand that's just rested in his, 'things run their natural course. I quite like your concept. Though I'd recommend more beef in your recipes. And remember, of course, your chicken must be halal, otherwise you lose the Muslim community. Now go home and think about what other assets you have. There must be something you can offer. You're the type who'll go far one day, I can tell by just looking at you. Here,' and she flaps open her mobile phone. 'Isn't she lovely? Just turned eighteen.' She leans across and gently nudges his arm with the phone, showing a girl with a small pinched face and a bushy mop of blonde hair.

He feels like vomiting. Rushes to the water fountain, empties three of the plastic tumblers. He doesn't even consider making another appointment. The woman of a while ago is putting her case in cubicle number one and, judging by her relaxed pose and her giggling, is succeeding. He puts on his sunglasses, he'd selected the Diesels today, and goes and stands just outside the entrance to Capital Bank.

He's beaten. His father would have a word for this: you allowed yourself to be humiliated today, my son. He can't believe how dumb, how fucking idiotic he was to think that he'd get such a big loan with nothing to show. And then he pulled the Mercedes out of the hat. He'll end up on the street one day. How's he ever going to maintain that huge big house of theirs after his father's death without a good, a very good, income? Of course, he could sell. He can't believe that he went and mentioned the Mercedes.

He has a second interview this afternoon at 4:20, with Lucinda. Symes@capetown.gov.za, on the second floor of Media City. Found everything out at the Civic Centre, in that gigantic foyer where these days you can buy samosas from a rag-and-tin kiosk on the staircase. Not that he minds. It's a matter of finalising a permit to trade as a restaurant or a takeaway. Lucinda Symes is the person. Got the telephone number, everything. He remembers now that a poster was stuck up in front of the civic centre. There was a strike threat. In order to ensure the safety of staff and the security of the Civic Centre and all government buildings, admission is currently restricted. Visitors will be admitted provided they can furnish proof of an appointment and produce their green ID document for inspection.

Back at the car, he switches on the ignition and turns the air conditioning full on so that he hears the engine hiccup as it revs, and punches in Miss Lucinda Symes's number, a landline; he'll keep it short. While it's ringing, his hand lies on the queasy pit of his stomach.

'Is that Miss Symes? Miss Symes, this is Mattheüs Duiker. I can't make it, I haven't got my ID with me,' he says out of the blue.

'The gentleman with the takeaways and the stews and stuff. Mister Duiker, that's just the mess left over from the strike. Never mind. That's over and done with, that stuff. You can just give my name and come up in the lift, second floor. They were supposed to remove that poster a long time ago.'

'Miss Symes, I really can't make it today. I've been to the doctor and so on, I'll have to come some other day.'

'Well, that's all right then, Mister Duiker. So we'll see each other some other day. Have a good afternoon.'

He sits in the car for a long time – it's hard on the engine to idle with the air conditioning full on – then again finds Miss Lucinda Symes under contacts and presses call and lets it ring twice. Then his courage finally fails him. Another day, maybe. He presses stop. He knows she won't phone him back. He pulls away and drives off. He has a last vision of himself dishing up his delicious lamb-and-butterbean stew from a twelve-litre stainless steel casserole and sees how chuffed the customer across the counter on Main, Observatory, is with the massive helping, but what strikes him now is that the vanishing takeaway concept matters less and less to him. A pipe dream, nothing more.

But still he digs in, clings to his dream, pictures himself in his pressed black Italian apron and his white T-shirt that he'll freshen up just before opening time, half past eleven, with the logo of a tiny man holding a larger-than-body-size spoon in front of him with a cheeky wisp of steam curling up from it. Everything becomes vaguer and even dirtier, that's what surprises him most, the filthiness that spreads over every aspect of his takeaway – even the pile of recipes, collected and carefully copied, starts looking like a heap of shit to him.

'Sannie, is that you?' Benjamin Duiker hears someone entering the gate, walking along the paving in heels, climbing the three broad semicircular steps up to the generous slate-paved stoep and opening the front door. Sannie from next door, of course, has the gate code, much to Mattie's disgust.

'Sannie?' It can't be anyone but her. He senses her presence. A big woman, not unattractive, just a bit coarsely put together, something she can't help. A year older than him, but doesn't look it. Self-satisfied, rather too much so. He often thinks: if something should happen to Mattie, and with Sissy far away on the farm in Laingsburg, Sannie will be his only recourse.

'Good heavens, Bennie, I *thought* I heard your voice coming from this end of the house.' She flutters in in a haze that he recognises and kisses him on the lips; drops of sweat migrate from her upper lip to his. 'My word, Bennie, and now they've put you in here. And not even a bathroom for you. Where do you relieve yourself?'

'It was my choice, Sannie. I want to spend my last days here.'

'Don't you talk like that, Bennie my boy, it's not as if you're on your way to heaven just yet. I pray for you every night, you know. Funny, I thought I heard a commotion over here. Must have been when they were moving you. Mattheüs and Samantha, must have been those two. Did they at least help?'

'Everything, Sannie.'

'I brought you some milk tart. It's leftovers from the sale. We collected five thousand for Coronation Park. You know, Bennie, the poor-white Afrikaners near Krugersdorp. They have to make do with tents and caravans. No, we have a lot to be thankful for. I'm flying up next week for an appointment with Fanie Putter, their self-appointed mayor. Shall I go and make some tea for the milk tart?'

'Later, thanks, Sannie. Just leave it in the fridge.'

'Oh, I know who'll get his hands on it.' She comes up to him. Sannie thinks now that he's lost his sight it's her duty to talk to him with her body. Her breath scorches his neck. 'You must eat, my friend. Otherwise your body can't heal itself. Listen to me, I know what I'm talking about, Bennie.'

'But aren't there jobs for those poor people? There must surely be something they can do. You have to be able to make your own way in life, Sannie. I've always believed that.'

'There's nothing, Bennie. They're at the mercy of other people's charity. If we from down here don't help them, they'll all go under. Our pastor Roy Rabinowitz is going along with me for the Big Baptism. They first have to confess and confirm their testimony with the baptism, Bennie. Then they're one of us. That's how it works. They don't just get stuff. They must first become members of the Silver Cloud Christian Fellowship. Only then do I write out the cheque. By now they know this. We've been saving souls out there like never before. You cannot live by bread alone. Those people are starving, I tell you. Starving.'

Benjamin just lies there. Fiddles with the strip of sheet folded over on top of his pyjamas. Silver Cloud. He says nothing.

'Can I read you something, Bennie? I've brought along some of our pastor's sermons. Just say the word. I'm happy to sit here with you for a while. I suppose you don't have much company. I don't see lots of people driving in here.'

'My thoughts are just about enough for me, Sannie. A whole larder of memories. I remember every little thing as if it happened yesterday. Have I told you about the dwarfs I saw the other day? Imagine, three of them sitting over there on the windowsill. All in a row.'

'Bennie?'

'I'm telling you, Sannie. I don't believe in such things, but a man can't lie either.'

'What do they say?'

'They don't really talk. The three of them just sit there holding onto the windowsill so that they don't fall off. It's been a few times now that I've seen them there.'

'It doesn't sound altogether right to me. One has to be on one's guard, Ben. Has anybody else seen them? Mattheüs?'

'I've been wanting to tell Mattie.'

'Bennie, shall I ask our pastor to come and have a word with you? Do you feel the need?'

'No thank you, Sannie.' He turns his head away from where she's sitting. She thinks he's a child. He lies there, saying not a word; she sits and fiddles. Mouth shut, but not for long.

'Bennie, I'm on your cell. Call me anytime, please. I have to take Janneman to the vet. He's got a terrible rash under his tummy again. I don't know what it is.'

'Probably fleas, Sannie.' He hears the big body getting up. Kleintjie, her husband, must have had his hands full with the woman. Only detective novels for her. And then every Saturday evening his palaver with the braai, the same each time, with lettuce and onion rings and tomato slices and Aromat. Eventually they didn't want to go any more.

Sannie kisses him on the cheek and squeezes his hand. 'Bennie, I was wondering if you didn't perhaps want to make a contribution to Coronation Park. Every bit helps. Their need is great there.'

'How many of them are there?'

'Bennie, I … Pastor estimates around three hundred and fifty now. Most of them in caravans. Anything will help. And as I say, it's souls for the Lord.'

'Well, pass me my cheque book, then. In the drawer here.' He gestures limply.

'For how much shall I say, Bennie?'

'How much do your benefactors usually give?'

'Well, the last was from the AR Foundation. They gave generously, fifty thousand.'

'Well, then, you can make it ten.'

'Ten thousand?'

'Yes, Sannie.'

'Heavens, Bennie. The Lord will bless you abundantly.' She bends over, the cheque book in her hand jutting unnecessarily into his breastbone, and kisses him again and plops down on her chair.

'Remember to fill in the counterfoil.'

'Done. Here you are, Bennie.' Then she points his finger at the place he should sign. And he wonders whose pen it is, because he knows the feel of his own.

@ Clarence House, Jack facebooks Matt. *Nothing can go wrong. Please check the time. Miss you!* ☺

It's just after five-thirty in the morning and on the chilly side. He considers taking a photo of himself to send to Matt, but decides against it. The boys are busy arriving, some of them straight out of bed and having dressed without washing. Rowers who don't stay in the hostel are dropped off by their fathers. Moenien Albertse is dropped by his mother in a pitch-black BMW with tinted windows. When she opens the window to say goodbye, he sees her fancy headscarf. They're Muslims. Moenien rows at number five on the stroke side. For a grade ten boy, he has one of the most perfect torsos Jack has ever come across. The white boys refer to boys like Moenien as 'gam'. Not great. There's nothing he can do about it. Not everything at Zilverbosch can be bright and beautiful.

It's going to be just him, Jamie, and the boys. It's the new red-headed English teacher's first time out with the boys. Jamie is excited because he's afraid of something going wrong. There are the eight rowers and the coxswain. No problem.

Jack drives the minibus with the trailer and boat and all the oars. He's wearing a white, long-sleeved T-shirt with jeans, the T-shirt not tucked in. He's thinking of Matt, that's why he notices the T-shirt. What do you say so early in the morning? He's got nothing in his head. Steering wheel in his hands, Jamie next to him trying to stay awake out of politeness and making small talk.

Behind them are the boys, with their iPods and bottles of Coke and water. Some of them have put on Axe deodorant. There's the rubber smell of their designer runners, some of them have pulled their hoodies over to sleep – he knows their register of smells.

They know him. He comes out of his shell at braais and so on. But when he has spoken, he's spoken. That's only fair. Taking out a handful of boys is no big deal. Just enjoy it. He doesn't think ahead of this or maybe that happening. That's the difference between him and Matt. Matt can see ahead a whole day or night, like a movie; and if things don't turn out as he expects, he's surprised or disappointed. Matt sees him like this (okay, not all the time): shirt tucked into pants, hairless strip around his ankles from wearing socks every day. The over-conscientious teacher-type who prissed up after one disastrous sex trip.

In the rear-view mirror, he sees some of the boys fooling around on Mxit. Some are taking mobile phone photos of one another, with all the obligatory finger signs. And then everyone has to look at the photo. They're cool with Moenien. There're no problems.

Mikey comes and puts a hand on his shoulder. They're on the N7 now. Mikey is the pack leader. He's blond, ungainly from growing too fast, and informed and clever at storing observations and information without ever officially sitting down to study.

Mikey knows the Wimpy won't be open at this early hour, but asks all the same if they can stop there. Jack gets his sense of humour, but without showing too openly how he enjoys it. The distance between him and the boys is just there. It's not as if he plans it in advance. His instinct tells him that it's the only way, otherwise they take advantage of you. The boys know he's gay. It won't be a problem at Misverstand Dam. It's not a problem at Clarence or anywhere else. Ever.

At eight o'clock, they pull up at Misverstand. A brilliant day. The boys are frisky, Mikey not quite daring enough to be reined in. He sees to it that they put up the two-man tents right away, because when they come back from rowing they won't want to do it. He knows them. He's seen to it that he got a site with a river view, as usual.

Hennie Strydom, the trainer, arrives under his own steam. This evening when the braai begins, he'll travel back to his just-married wife. Hennie and he, what can he say. The man probably thinks he's going to hit on him. Even if he'd been his type, heavy artillery, ha-ha, he wouldn't have dared. He's got far too much respect for himself and for Zilverbosch.

The shell is held in position, and the boys in blue-and-white vests take their places, and so does the cox on this clean, clear day, with the sun on their shoulders.

'Ready to row,' shouts the cox, whose main job is to steer the boat on a straight course. Jack knows most of the commands by now. Rowing is such a proper kind of thing to do. These outings have a soothing effect on him. As if everything falls into place for a change.

He and Jamie sit on the shore under a blue-and-white tent with the Zilverbosch logo. As a rule he doesn't smoke in front of the boys, so he lights up now. He inspects Jamie. Freckles are sprinkled across his nose and slightly pubescent cheeks. His eyebrows are ginger, his irises light-green. He has an open, innocent gaze, as if he's not altogether present. You don't easily get anything out of him. He's too reticent, and definitely straight. From a rich home.

There's his car and all. Jack laughs. He's got a nose for guys with money. It helps.

He gazes over the calm blue surface of the dam. On the other side are contoured hills where wheat farmers sow their seed. By now the wheat would have been long since harvested. With any luck, you'll see some blue cranes strutting and pecking on the lands. Their tails and trailing wingtips. He looks at the cloudless sky, he hears other human voices further along on the water's edge. No complaints.

'Square on the ready,' the cox shouts, and Jack doesn't see their boat again. They are somewhere on the twelve-kilometre route. When they get back, there will be sandwiches and cold meat: plenty of carbohydrates, plenty of protein. He and Jamie will have to prepare it, but there's more than enough time. Everything's running smoothly. He can't think of anywhere he'd rather be than here.

As dusk approaches, he prepares a fire in the special brick braai area. The two bundles of thornwood he'd bought at Swarries, the bar here at Misverstand, are ready and waiting. Jamie does everything he tells him to. Bumbling and butterfingered. Jack reckons the guy has grown up with other people doing everything for him.

'Have one.' No, he doesn't want a drink.

'Have one,' Jack says again. And then he takes one of the eight beers he'd brought along.

The boys huddle together to one side. Now and again one drifts over to them, Mikey or Herman or Rory or one of the other grade elevens. Talk about nothing in particular, and joke with him. The new English teacher might not as well have been there. If nobody has come by for a while, Jack looks across the hump formed by the lawn to check on the boys on the other side. He likes keeping an eye on Moenien.

When the chops have been arranged head-and-tail, tail-and-head on the grid, and the first meat fumes are billowing up, he remembers a time long ago when he was small enough to run around naked in places like this. They were camping. There were gum trees; he can't remember where. He's banished most of this stuff from his life. And yet, tonight. Later in that place, when the wind came up over the water, there was also a dam or maybe a river; his mother had called him and dressed him. He remembers how he liked her mother-hands on his damp skin, and how nice the braai smoke was all around him. And his mother asked him: Can you smell the pine trees, the pine resin? It's such a small thing to remember, nothing out of the ordinary. And no nasties with it.

Jamie is next to him with a stick to put out flare-ups. In effect, he's alone with the boys. The guy's a dud.

Liquor? It'd be naive to deny it. Vodka mixers, that kind of thing, bottles hidden in the boys' tog bags. Mikey? Yes, he'd say so. He'd rather warn and inform the boys – searching their bags is out. It's not expected of him, and he'd regard it as an invasion of their privacy.

After the meal, he and Jamie are sitting in front of their tent. He's on his fourth, Jamie halfway through his second beer. The boys' tents are haphazardly pitched to the left of them: the boys are all bunched together beyond the tents, away from the authorities. Boys' voices that have broken and become men's voices mingle with those of boys who have the high-pitched laugh of birds.

It's still early in the year, the so-called slave period of the grade tens is still in force. To be a slave to a senior boy means having to report to his bedroom for no reason at all on a Sunday morning, you owe him all sorts of favours. During your slave period you subject yourself voluntarily to initiation.

Jack knows most of the rituals from previous years. He tells Jamie about it all. It consists mainly of silly games and stays within certain limits. It's actually quite innocent and the boys find it hilarious, the seniors as well as the slaves. Jamie fiddles nervously with his chin, but then.

Jack has got up a few times to check on the boys from a distance, just to let them know that he knows what they're up to. Jamie goes along the first time, stays behind after that. The light from one of the lamps is shining on the backs of the seniors, all of them in the dark-blue Zilverbosch tracksuits. In the centre of the circle are the slaves, the three grade tens, including Moenien, all in vests.

Jack stands watching, beer in hand, the boys' laughter comes and goes, dies down when a senior claims something from a slave, then roars loudly when the slave obeys. He can hear the younger boys in the centre of the circle laughing too. He is satisfied. Walking back the last time, he stops again and listens, but without turning around and looking. And then, with the mingled taste of beer and braai chops lingering in his mouth and the damp dam air of the summer evening on his bare arms, he again experiences something of that sense of well-being from his early childhood. It's transient, though, and he leaves it like that. He has no wish to recall any further or to force himself to remember things from later years.

On his back on the blow-up mattress, he lies in the tent. Pure bliss. Next to him on the other mattress, Jamie has turned his back to him, uncommunicative, in a too-big, white T-shirt.

Jack likes his job. He likes explaining a poem and seeing the revelation dawn on their faces. Okay, only a few. He likes the energy of the boys. How it flares up and dies down and goes crazy and dies down again. From one of the other campsites he hears the sawing of an accordion and raucous singing. The boys he no longer hears.

He waits for sleep. He doesn't need to. He could lie like that all night, hands on his underpants. The boys sleep in pairs in the tents. They're safe, that's all he needs to worry about. If he sleeps, his dreams will be sweet like those of a well-fed dog. He tries to listen to Jamie. Young, doesn't snore yet. Heavily PC, this one. Won't touch a cigarette. The new teacher's motto will be 'due diligence', Jack decides. The requisite sense of duty, à la Jamie. His own approach relies heavily on the senses: listen and you will hear, look and you will see.

The side of the tent gets wetter and colder deep into the night. Crunch-crunch, some creature nibbles the grass outside. A hare or something. He picks his nose and flicks it away and puts his hand back on his underpants and lies there wrapped in his own body. He thinks of nothing.

In the course of the night, he is woken up by someone outside their tent. He crawls out of his sleeping bag, unclips the tent flaps and stands there on his knees, shining his torch. It's Mikey. He raises the torch to shine in his eyes. His blond hair is off-white and unwashed.

'Something's happened, sir.'

Jack gets to his feet and shines the torch up and down the boy. He's wearing his tracksuit pants and a pitch-black vest. He is serious. The torch plays slowly over his face, from left to right. Jack knows him; he wants to know everything. Mikey's mind is usually in overdrive trying to think of something witty to say. None of that now. Won't cry easily. At this moment, Jack sees him as an incarnation of the words of Cavafy: 'his hair uncombed, uplifted, his limbs tanned lightly' – but that's irrelevant.

Then Mikey whispers that he's pissed on one of the grade tens. Immediately, Jack realises that this could cause trouble. All the details, please. Firstly: who was it? Mikey says it was Moenien Albertse. Moenien had been standing in the middle, surrounded by the senior boys. He could have left the circle if he'd wanted, but he didn't. Then he, Mikey, took his dick out of his pants and started pissing on Moenien, because he had a piss on board.

'Did you mean it like this? Did you plan it in advance?'

'I suppose so, sir.' He'd taken aim and started pissing on Moenien from where his gym pants started, no higher, no piss got onto his T-shirt, he's sure of that, and then all the way down onto his legs and knees and onto his feet. He'd saved up a helluva piss, that's the thing.

'Was Moenien barefoot?'

'Yes, sir.'

'So on his feet too?'

'Yes, sir.'

'On his chest?'

'No, sir, you can ask anyone. Ask Moenien, all of them. Just from his gym shorts down. No higher.'

'On his hands?'

'No, sir. Maybe. No, I don't think so. He took his hands away. Out of the way.'

'How long did it take?'

'I can't say exactly, sir. A piss is a piss.'

'So what did Moenien do then? When you'd finished.'

'Moenien laughed, sir.'

'Do you realise the consequences of what you've done? You could be expelled?'

'Yes, sir. Not exactly, sir.'

Jack shines the torch straight in his face. He can't see any remorse. Mikey's expression is clean and shameless. For Jack, that's the deciding factor. There's no ulterior motive here. It's permitted because it's possible. That's what he reads into the blond boy's face.

'Okay then, Mikey. I'm going to have to think about it. We can talk again tomorrow. In the meantime go to bed.'

'Sir?' Then Mikey wants him to hug him first before going back to his tent. The boys do that. In that brief moment of physical closeness, the boy is at once vulnerable and unconsciously erotic. (To him.) Easy to exploit the younger one then, but Jack is a rock in that respect. Simultaneously hot-blooded and cool. One foot wrong and it's bye-bye Zilverbosch. He's often discussed it with Matt. The scarce commodity of integrity. What he knows is that a weakling is not the man for Matt. He's inherited that attitude from the old man.

After breakfast the next morning, two slices of white bread with sausage and tomato sauce in between, they have a heart-to-heart, Mikey and Moenien and the two of them, he and his young colleague. Right there in front of the teachers' tent. Jack knows what he wants to say. He sees the mist rising from the dam, leaving a damp film on everyone's arms. He looks at the crows flying up from the ploughed fields on the other side of the dam and then settling in patches on the brown soil. He looks at Jamie. His unshaven chin is ginger, the stubble varies from golden-red to whitish-pink as he moves his head in the morning sun, his shoulders hunched up in a green tracksuit top. Jack suspects it's not the damp. The man is uncomfortable about the conversation with

Mikey and Moenien. He doesn't know what to do next. He's afraid he'll put a foot wrong.

Moenien seems relaxed, and in the course of the conversation it's clear that he's been unaffected by the pissing. It was nothing. He's even proud of it, because as a rower and a bullshitter, Mikey inspires respect among the juniors. While they're talking, Moenien is squatting on his haunches. He loses his balance, and Mikey takes him by the shoulders to right him.

The race thing, thank heaven, isn't dragged into it. (Jack had been afraid of that.) Among themselves, he and Jamie and the two boys decide that not a word will be uttered about the whole affair. Neither to the parents nor to the principal, Mr Richard Richardson. Nobody's been harmed, nobody need suffer any further on account of a rash deed. Mikey shakes Moenien's hand and apologises. Moenien says it's cool.

When the two walk off, Jamie wants to go and pack his stuff inside the tent. Jack calls him back. He looks at his colleague. 'You're sure about this, are you, Jamie? It's the right thing to do? It was a joint decision?'

Jamie nods.

'You're absolutely sure, Jamie?'

He nods again. Jack puts out his hand. Deal. The redhead glances at him briefly. As in, almost not. He doesn't open his mouth again. Then Jack sees a puniness in the man that puts him off. And knows for sure what he's suspected all along – he and the teacher are never going to hit it off. He's seen something in him that's too close to the bone, something about himself he doesn't like any more. He's long since outgrown it, that's for sure.

Pa wants one of his pale-blue shirts to wear to the oncology clinic. And his tweed jacket.

'Pa will be too hot, it's not cold outside.' He helps him with his shoelaces, on his knees while tying them for his father. Perhaps it is better here in the study after all. Pa hasn't been morose since moving here. It's the clinic visits that make him anxious, in fact even before he got sick, that he'll fall or wound himself, or that somebody will hurt him by handling him roughly.

'And Pa's cheque book lying out here in the open?' He picks it up from the bedside cabinet to put it back where it belongs.

'Oh that, yes. No, just a little help I gave to Sannie and them.'

'Yes?' He flips to the last counterfoil. He hates this kind of thing before he's even finished reading. He hates Aunt Sannie for strolling in here as if the place belonged to her.

'Pa, I know this is your business and I suppose I've got no say in it; who the hell is the Silver Cloud Christian Fellowship?' He hates it that Aunt Sannie's been in here handling his father's cheque book.

'Oh, that. You've looked. But no, I don't mind if you take an interest in my affairs, Mattie. I'll never hold that against you. Not in my condition.'

'Who is the Silver Cloud, Pa?'

'You see, it's this charity organisation of Sannie's. It all goes to the poor whites up in Krugersdorp. Apparently there are more than three hundred of them. I can't remember offhand the name of the caravan park, but that's where they live. All of them in caravans. Apparently those people are having a really bad time.'

'Silver Cloud?'

'You'll have to ask Sannie about that, Mattie. She's the treasurer and so on. She administers the charity. But we have to get going now, son. I want to get it over and done with.'

He takes his father firmly by the arm, tries to anticipate his needs and helps him along when they get to the Panorama Clinic, which looks like the Cape Grace Hotel, but is actually a hospital; just look at the kinds of flowers and the size of the arrangements in the entrance hall and you'll know more or less what your bill will be. Pa is on the Motor & Allied Worker's Insurance, he's paid in literally thousands since selling his first Chevy. (It was only later that Benjamin Duiker, once he'd become a truly outstanding salesman, acquired the Mercedes-Benz agency. In his father's words: that's not for every Tom, Dick, and Harry.)

Through the lobby, he leads the man – good morning, Mr Duiker – and they trundle along on this day, Wednesday of every month, he with the old man with the sunken cheeks, his father who still looks human – fuck it, you must see him post-chemo if you're thinking walking skeleton. And all the time, during the drive here along the N1 and throughout his mutterings, if he so much as brakes a bit too hard or the back of his father's head tilts back a millimetre in pulling off at the Parow off-ramp – other people, normal passengers entrusting themselves to the driver, wouldn't even notice the hiccup, whatever – throughout the drive here and now in the lift as big as a medium-sized storeroom (dreadful in there, a real terror trap), up to the oncology unit, his mood is darkening, which makes it impossible for him to behave equably, like he was when he got up after jerking off, without even watching porn; he did, after all, greet the day or at least the morning with a measure of self-control, and the success contributed to an invincibly positive attitude and even deep compassion towards the man he's going to help today to do one of the most terrible things you can do.

Now that resolve has been scuppered, he's the hell in, and all because of two words: Silver Cloud. A preponderance of curlicues in the capital S and C, the handwriting of an imbecile or a dyslexic moron, on the last counterfoil that does his head in: what the hell is going on here?

The transparent liquid, almost like liquid KY, suspended from a frame on wheels, everyone knows the contraption, and a tap at the top of the pipe leading to the needle, drips over a period of five hours drop by drop into his poor father's body to finally destroy such little function as his organs are still capable of.

Just ask him, Mattheüs, when he's holding the oblong Belleek dish, decorated with grass-green clover leaves, under Pa's chin. Ask him what he sees emerging from the innards of this human being. What the colour is of this vomiting forth, and he'll tell you now: this man is going to die, and it's not because of the overabundance of so-called CD20 cells that convert the normal lymph cells to cancerous lymphoma cells. Why his father chose that delicate little dish – his mother used it for petit fours and not even always, well, he assumed that, as with all other things, his father wanted nothing but the best. If he must puke, let it be in Belleek.

Fuck. Brown gunge, an unholy brown, a colour you associate with the devil himself, not that he believes in that trumped-up creature. This sludgy slime that Pa tries to void his body of and that the body itself rejects, for heaven's sake – even if Professor Jannie de Lange, the oncologist, can't see it – is an alarming colour, if ever there was one. It's the consequence of the MabThera manufactured in a laboratory as anti-CD20 treatment. But while the self-destructive mechanism is switched on, intentions undeniably good, the healthy organs are also attacked and destroyed.

Mattheüs takes his father's wrist, the one without the needle, and bends down and presses his lips against the cool, scared skin and stays like that with bowed head, handkerchief out of his pocket so that the other patients undergoing chemo, family and loved ones, in that waiting room stinking of sickness and suffering, shouldn't see that there are tears. Such physical closeness between father and son is uncommon. He's never kissed his father like that.

Later he fetches a *You* from a pile of magazines and flips it open on a photo of the Beckhams, the most impeccably dressed family on earth, and hangs his head low; tears won't stop, he's crying about more than just this.

Only by recalling the lurking name of Silver Cloud Christian Fellowship can he temper his sadness. He'll forbid the bloodsucker to enter their yard. As soon as he's home he'll phone the technician to come and change the gate code, so that those who have no business to enter can be locked out for ever.

Ten thousand. Just like that. He smells a huge rat. And he, primary caregiver, can't bring himself to ask Pa to help him with a cheque. Or, *or*, he can talk to Aunt Sannie himself. It's just that the woman has a way with him. She fetches him when she's spotted him on the screen at her own gate: oh, that's Bennie's Mattheüs, plonks him down on her cream-coloured puffed-out sofa in her sunroom with its uninterrupted view of their house (those binoculars are hidden somewhere), and then the tea arrives with those golden-brown koeksisters, no bigger than a smallish thumb, the syrup tempered with a dash of lemon juice. The woman has something of his mother or Granny Fransien (on his father's side), or the universal mother, and with her broad, hospitable lap she draws him in, all the way.

On the N1 back to the city Pa sits hunched up, clammy with all the injected MabThera combined with chemo and finally paracetamol or antihistamine to prevent allergic reactions.

To think about the treatment as Mattheüs does is impossible for his father. Professor Jannie de Lange can't put a foot wrong in his blinded eyes. It's a matter of grasping at the last straw. And outside the Panorama Clinic, on the raised parking reserved for doctors and specialists, you can see them lined up: the latest models on the market, the fruit of long and reasoned conversations with men and women on the verge of dying: the operation and the treatment can prolong your life, Mister Duiker, so many of our patients have benefited immeasurably from it, extended their lives, now they can look forward to cake and cool drinks under a willow tree with their grandchildren, ag, it gives us such pleasure (modest little chuckle).

Just once, as they slip onto the Muizenberg exit, does he admit to having doubts about Aunt Sannie coming to beg for her old projects.

'Does Pa believe in them?'

Pa doesn't reply. Mattheüs thinks it's deliberate. He tugs at the seat belt, which is hurting him, he says.

'Ag, rather put on some nice music for us, Mattie.' Now he knows it's deliberate.

Back home, he gets him into bed as soon as possible. His glass of milk with vanilla Sustagen on his bedside cabinet.

'Take that stuff away, please. I can't even look at it.' This makes Mattheüs wonder if it's the beginning of the end.

Pa doesn't want to lie down yet. He remains sitting with his legs dangling from the bed. Mattie must first help him with something. He's embarrassed to ask, he says.

'Oh good heavens, Pa. I do everything for you in this house.'

'Yes, but at least there's Samantha too.'

'She's only coming on Wednesday, Pa.'

'You're a good son, Mattie. You're good to me.'

He looks at his father as he says it. He is glad that he's said it. He is very, very glad, he can't say how glad.

'What must I do for Pa?'

It's the left toenail that's growing inwards. His father wants him to cut a notch right in the centre of the nail so it can grow out of the flesh.

'My feet aren't dirty. At least, I don't think they are.' He tries to laugh. Sunlight falls on the bald head with the last baby fluff on the temples.

'It's nothing, Pa. I'll fetch the nail clippers.' But it is something, after all, and they both realise it. It's an intimacy forced on them by necessity, which wouldn't have happened by choice under normal circumstances.

He kneels and takes the foot in his hand and places it between his knees. His father's blindness makes the physical exchange between the two of them, two men, even more intense. What makes it easier is that he no longer experiences the foot as flesh. It's a transparent, white, porcelain object, cold from disuse. It's no longer a limb for walking; its function is lost, he thinks, as he manoeuvres the clippers to cut the nail at an angle. A broad flat toenail testifying to good foot genes, now chalk-white and barely distinguishable from the skin on the arch of the foot, with a pink rim on the right where the nail is vindictively penetrating the flesh.

'Wouldn't scissors be better?' Pa is scared he'll hurt him, he can hear it.

'I'll go fetch some.' He gently lets go of the foot. On the way to his father's old bathroom where the sharp-pointed scissors are kept, he lifts his hands to his nose. Neither sock nor sweat nor foot he smells, he wishes he could. It's just the alien, rusty-tin after-smell of the chemo that's remained on his hands.

The little operation is performed successfully. Mattheüs is relieved. 'Does Pa want to know how I did it?' Not really. Pa draws his legs up and wriggles them in under the sheet and bedspread. 'It's a very neat little V I made there for Pa. Nobody could have done a better job.'

'They say your nails and hair carry on growing even when you're in the grave.'

Mattheüs has no answer to this. He takes his father's hand, that's all. Then Pa places his right hand over his. He clears a space on the bed and sits waiting for Pa to release him. He doesn't know how long it is that he's been sitting there with his hand in his father's. His thoughts are in such turmoil that he eventually starts feeling ill at ease, starts muttering: let go, let go, let go of the hand that tingles and throbs and wants to be released from between Pa's two grey, lukewarm hands. On top of it all, he's tussling with a suspicion about his porn-goggling: that his insides, steeped in all the lascivious images, are sweating onto, infecting, someone as exposed as his father; and Jack to a lesser extent – though he's not really vulnerable.

'Pa,' he says out of the blue, 'I need hundreds of thousands to start my business, Pa. More, even.'

He withdraws his hand from his father's without really knowing that he's doing it and gets to his feet and walks away from the harsh sunlight into the interior of the study and catches sight of himself there in daytime dusk in the mirror above the mantelpiece, an unusual mirror for a study, one with *Castrol Oil* diagonally emblazoned across it in red paint, both mirror and letters stained in antique style, a relic from Pa's days as a petrol station owner in Observatory. On this side as well as that side of *Castrol*, Mattheüs sees himself as he is right now, confronted with his own cold, manic glare. And he seems to himself a predator, one that will tear the food from the beaks of its own children, his gaze hard and his eyes round and distended like those whatchamacallit birds in the Kruger Park, and he feels sick, because *that* he is not. And his request to his father was not how he meant it. He leaves the room.

In the small hours, he half wakes up and gropes for his computer on the floor next to his bed and surfs to Done-in-Darkness where he begins browsing and then clicks on Watch, chooses a video and sets it going, making the cursor jiggle along impatiently to the relentlessly hard penetration scene that he gazes at with the dull stare of a third- or fourth-generation porn junkie, force-fed on a diet of hardcore, long since relieved of the need to think, his flesh immobile and heavy on the bare mattress (the sheets have shifted), with the hand now coming into play and working himself up, only to let the computer slide down onto the floor immediately afterwards, and then sinking into the sleep of a primitive being.

By daybreak his body is mobile again and he picks up the computer and positions it on his abs, and the index finger seeks and finds. There's no sign of a single thought or recollection or even the slightest attempt at self-stimulation. Only the lethargic weight of his own body that drags him down, down, following its own impulse, his forearm lifting clumsily with the hand forming a funnel, and the rhythm again, but slower by a beat or two, until the fluids flow from him.

He sleeps. His father's bell rings from the study. It's now just after six in the morning. It's a copper bell that used to stand on the dresser in the dining room. When there were people for dinner and the first course was ready – the dining-room table seats twelve – his mother grasped the bell with thumb and index finger on the flat handle with its image of the Union Buildings and rang it enthusiastically, swinging her arm to and fro, ran like a schoolgirl from the dining room into the entrance hall and left into the sitting room where the guests were standing or sitting with their drinks, and there she swung the little bell in a big, wide curve and laughed, her voice pitched high with a merry top note, almost like the trill of some songbird or other. Then his father swung round, infuriated, and uttered something that is terrible to utter about your wife in front of guests.

The bell has intruded upon his dream and he remembers thinking while dreaming: Can't come now, Pa. You should be aware of the time. I'm still sleeping, I'm only human. And his father said: Well, then, that's all right, Mattie. And he remembers how terribly grateful he was to his father in his dream. Almost tender. You need it, my son, he hears him say. And how happy he was for a long time afterwards that his father had given him the break, because usually he demanded immediate attention. So the bell subsided into silence and he remembers how nice and contented he felt about it. For a long time afterwards.

For a third time his sleep is interrupted. By now it is about eight o'clock, and the Cape morning in February of that year is pumping heat already, and the side of Table Mountain where UCT and Rhodes Memorial are built is splendidly and clearly visible from their front stoep; you could count the pines with their umbrella crowns all around the memorial. The computer is still open on a new video, twenty-three minutes into the film where he must have paused it, so that now he need only tap it lightly to set it going again. This time he allows himself to slip into the scene. The two are amateurs and have selected their bathroom floor as the perfect location to set up the camera, probably on a surface next to the hand basin so that the lens peers down at their bodies; one is still wearing his green underpants, and the light is a yellow, murky affair. It's the kind of amateur porn that Mattheüs prefers and bookmarks. He slides into it, even longs to be going at it with the two on the tiles, tiles that he imagines would get slippery under the back from the sweat and stuff so that you'd have to anchor yourself to something on both sides. The pace of the action is lazy and deliciously lethargic because of the high temperature outside. Mattheüs takes longer this time, his energy drained, hours it takes, right until the morning of the next day, or so it feels. (In the meantime he's got hungry, and thought of two fried eggs and crisply fried rashers of bacon and sweet fried tomatoes – in fact the only thought that has occurred to him in the course of that threesome session.)

Now there is only the last bit of conserved energy to release, his body grateful that the end is in sight. From his head and right through his body to the backs of his knees and down to the insides of his soles he is aware of pressure, the back arches, the thighs stretched to breaking point, and as the pressure builds, a continuous buzzing starts up in his inner ear, voices he hears, indecipherable and even reassuring, his mouth totally dry, and then at last the meagre, transparent fluid. He comes into his left hand and lets it dam up there. Only he, his body, knows it. Nobody else has ever seen it or ever will. Jack, nobody.

He sleeps in until twelve. He showers under lukewarm and then cold water and even tries to recall one of the porn stars he watched, but can't. Even though their build and technique differed, there in the cubicle where he is slowly stabilising under a shower of water, they become mere clones of each other. Each a generic copy of the original. Who is it? And what is the ideal fuck in any case?

He shaves. He'll drive out to the beach today and get some sun. He's pale under the gills, inside too, and he wants to go and burn it out. In the mirror he sees that the hot water has left a pink rash on his shoulders. What he does know for sure is that he can't reach a point of satisfaction with porn. If he were to think he could, it would be a lie. He doesn't intend cutting down, either.

Back in his room he half-opens the curtains, dresses, and selects a pair of sunglasses from the string suspended on his wall like the mouth of a smiley. Seven pairs of sunglasses in all, only the Diesel pair genuine. The others all cheap imitations that look and feel just as good.

The bell. He can hear it's not the first ring, that. The tongue strikes the copper lining, pure geriatric impatience. Must be hungry or something. He goes out without putting on deodorant.

My dear son,

I can feel the heat of the day behind me on my back. I'm chained fast, that's for sure. It's His will, I'm not complaining.

This morning my heart is full. I feel the need to talk to you. Also to Sissy. I miss my daughter. Imagine, I spent all night thinking of that town in China that Sannie read to me about, which only makes tweezers. Can you believe it. Now we can buy the stuff here for a pittance. How the world has changed. Your mother was very attached to her tweezers.

My heart is full. I was very angry that I had to ring and ring my bell the other day and you took no notice. Mattie, that's not the way to treat your father. Look, I was really very angry. Much, much angrier than I let on to you. I restrained myself. It's no use, my son. I was angry, but I'm not going to upset myself any further.

You see, that is what I'd like to share with you. In days gone by I would flare up for nothing and then immediately afterwards suffer terrible remorse. You all know me like that. My staff knew me like that. Now I saw my anger coming. Is that how your generation does it? You're always talking about being in touch with your feelings. You can see now that your father has learnt a new lesson in his old age.

But I don't want it to happen again, Mattie. Understand me well. Look, I considered having a nurse for a few days a week. But won't you say when I'm dead: Heavens, Pa certainly wasted our money. No, I reckon, as long as you're still here. Look, I'm not such a nuisance yet. Or so I believe, at any rate. I do after all have Sannie next door as well. You must feel free to talk, Mattie. You talk to me so seldom.

My son, you may think I'm stupid, but Pa isn't, you know. I can sense when you come in here with my medicine. Or with the tray, doesn't

74

matter which one. I know you probably want it all to be over now. Over and out, as the saying goes. You want to move in here and do as you wish. Not much respect for your late father will remain.

I just wish we could talk to each other. Men are such odd creatures. My father, Grandpa Ben, said so himself. A man is a strange thing. Look, it's not as if my father and I talked much about life, as I've said before. He wanted to make sure of my religion, that I believed and was living my life righteously, and that I would experience eternal life. That was his only concern from when I was a child to his very last days. He always wanted to know: Benjamin, do you believe in the one, true God?

Years ago, when I was just a whippersnapper, I was playing in the irrigation furrow on our farm. I was making my own miniature farm with its own lands and furrows, and for sheep we children always used the little cypress cones. So I was struggling to make my own dam with its wall and everything. Ag, I suppose I was three or four years old. All day I played there in the shade of the tall poplars. Then my father walked past, he always wore his hat on the farm, and he had his pipe and tobacco in his pocket. That's how he went around. He saw me struggling. He took the spade standing there and cut big fat sods and threw a strong, wide wall for me. So then I had my own dam on my farm. Do you know what that meant to a child like me, Mattie?

So that was how Grandpa Ben and I communicated. I bear him no grudge for it. My father was an outstanding example to me, throughout my life. I suppose that that's how it is between men. Now I don't know about you, Mattie. You don't talk.

I'm tired right now. I'm pressing Stop.

Your father.

@ Grade Twelve class, Jack facebooks and posts it on his Wall. *Has anybody got anything to say about van Wyk Louw's* Die Beiteltjie *that hasn't been said before? (Make no mistake: I like the poem.)*

75

Steve (an ex-pupil of Jack's, not gay): *Imagery too simplistic. Overrated.*

Jack sees an e-mail arriving in his inbox. He opens it while carrying on chatting. It's from the principal's secretary. *Mr Richardson requires a meeting with you at the end of this period if it suits. Thank you, Layla.* With a smiley. Red flag, that's what he sees.

When he sits down in Mister Richard Richardson's office and looks up at the photo of the state president – oh, shit. Nothing, he's done nothing wrong. Or has he? His premonition kicks in again, as in automatically: why has he not seen it like this before?

The combination of him and Mikey and Moenien Albertse at the Misverstand Dam was wonky. From the start. He, Jack, with his libertarian discipline and Mikey the blond bully and Moenien who is stuck with the white boys' nickname for him, no matter what. That word. Moenien stood out. Or did he? Was he the third ingredient in some kind of concoction? And not forgetting the holy innocent Jamie.

He shifts on his chair, a standard office chair with green upholstery and a round back. A wide-awake chair. He must have changed position a hundred times by now. Knees open or right leg dogleg and butch with right ankle on left knee or right leg tightly folded around left leg, more feminine and fairly common among men. Uptight is the word that Matt sometimes uses about him. Matt doesn't *get* him, so to speak. One day he's going to surprise him. He's going to tackle him. Hurt him. Blow all his preconceptions about him sky-high.

He quickly picks up the framed portrait on Mister Richardson's desk. It shows him and his wife in a half-and-half traditional Transkei outfit, even though she's actually from Wiltshire. Terribly PC, the whole lot. And in front of them the three daughters. All three of them nice and sallow like daddy. And right in front the Labrador that you can immediately see is fed far too much.

Five years at Zilverbosch, two years as housemaster. Have there ever been any problems? A definite no. Mister Richardson, come on. He must realise what he's got in him. Gay is no problem here.

Once he thought that for a change of scene he'd apply for a post at Gimnasium. First question they asked him was whether he was married. Fucked-up way of asking whether he's gay. Hello? This is the twenty-first century! Check your Constitution, people.

Jack saw the failed application as confirmation of his status quo. That afternoon, he bought the double CD/DVD of Tiësto, the Amsterdam DJ with his dirty sexy mixes. He was, he *is* happy.

'Jack, my apologies, man.' Mister Richardson takes his seat behind the desk, under the president's photo. He's wearing a navy-blue suit and white shirt with old-fashioned collar and navy-blue tie with the Zilverbosch crest. Nothing odd about him. 'Coffee?' He buzzes the intercom and orders two from Layla. 'Look, I'll get straight to the point.'

Misverstand Dam. No ways that an Englishman is ever going to pronounce that name correctly. In any case, that's irrelevant. So shit got spilt. He's itching to know who. Wouldn't be Mikey. Must be either Moenien or Jamie, the hypocritical arsehole. How pathetically cautious people can be. When Mikey came to tell the pissing story at their tent, Jamie was doubtful at first, then he was just plain shit-scared. How clearly he now sees what he didn't want to see before.

Gifted teacher. Popular with the boys. Loyal to the ideals and principles of Zilverbosch, says Mister Richardson. Get to the point, please. Cigarette, or he'll die. One in his hand, at least, as a crutch.

So it was Moenien's mother. She smelt urine on his shoes (brand-new Nikes) when he got home. Moenien had apparently stuffed the tracksuit pants into the washing machine very quickly, but his mother fished them out and saw the stinking stains. In this very office she'd come and vented, she couldn't stand it any longer, no matter how many times Moenien told her: Mommy, it doesn't matter, it was just boys' games. No bloody way, that's not how she saw it. Those white shits pissed on my son's gym pants. Brand-new Adidas and not cheap either. Does Mister Richardson think it's fair? And does he think for a moment that she's going to shut up about it in the new South Africa?

He had to proceed with great care, says Mister Richardson. The woman was seething. He hoped she wouldn't play the race card as well; racial harmony was a feature of Zilverbosch. Jack looks at Mister Richardson's lips talking and talking and getting moist with all the explaining, he can see their fleshy insides. He carries on and says he made how many excuses to the woman. He is sure, he eventually said to her, that Jack acted in good faith.

Moenien's mother persisted in being upset and insulted. She wants Mikey to be expelled. It's a very serious matter. He soothed and coaxed for all he was worth, says Mister Richardson. But it's turned into a huge embarrassment.

A gentleman, Mister Richardson, no doubt about that. Putting out fires, that's all he was trying to do.

'And what about Mikey now? That boy doesn't deserve to be expelled on the basis of a single mistake,' says Jack. Who doesn't like Mikey Greeff? That shit-stirring glint across his eyes, morning, noon, and night. He does his best to confine the discussion to Mikey and Moenien.

Between the two of them, says Mister Richardson, he doesn't want to lose Mikey for Zilverbosch. He's an outstanding rower and an excellent swimmer. To get to the point. Jack freezes. He's been waiting for this all along. Where does he fit into the picture?

Another cup of coffee? His cup has formed a blue scum, in the circumstances untouched. Mister Richardson carries on. This and that. It's a sensitive matter, extremely sensitive, for him as principal, et cetera. Which has to be sorted out, of course. What? For the first time in the course of the meeting Mister Richardson says not a word. He looks up at the air conditioning unit on the wall behind Jack. Plump drops plop in slow motion onto the strip of wooden flooring just inside the door.

'Is it a little too cool in here? Or is it my imagination?'

Is he out of his bloody mind? Jack is sweating as if he's shagging. And for the first time since he's kicked the habit, he wants coke or speed. Craves it, actually.

Jack, your discretion, says the principal. And where may I ask was the teacher in charge? Moenien's mother demanded to know. Crux of the matter. Okay, so that's how matters stand. Here we have it at last. Couldn't he have spat it out right at the start? That's how over-politeness can really screw up a man who's trying to be straight and honest.

And then the bummer: Clarence House. The tremendous responsibility with so many boys under one roof. His role there as housemaster. Well, the way things stand at the moment. Jack's capacity for discretion, that as well, is being questioned. (His sweat begins to stink, acrid – Matt would like him now.) It pains him to involve Jamie as well, but he was there when it happened. A witness.

'Yes? What did Jamie have to say?'

Mister Richardson looks at him and shakes his head. 'Right, let's leave him out of the picture. It's unnecessary to drag him into this. He's a new arrival.' It seems that Mister Richardson has already gone too far even in mentioning Jamie's name. The man is covering up for Jamie, that's what's happening. Whatever Jamie has said about Misverstand, and how he handled the matter, was probably undoubtedly definitely not what he and Jack had agreed upon that morning in front of the tent. Jamie was the fourth toxic ingredient of the Misverstand excursion.

But Mister Richardson, they, the governing body, won't come to a decision. Decent-to-his-eyeballs Mister Richardson is leaving it up to Jack. He, Jack, must now calmly go off and reflect on the matter. Mister Richardson says he respects his integrity. His decision, whichever way it goes, will likewise be respected.

'I believe your decision will be in the interest of our school.'

Dickhead. Why don't you just tell me to my face? He's just written off Mister Richardson as well. Decency? Please, spare me that. The man is spineless.

Money. The root of his panic. What he earns now is gobbled up by debts. (Plural.) Hundreds, thousands of rands run up in his wild life. Hey, Jack my man, how about that thousand you still owe me? – texts just about daily from his creditor, Okechi, the Nigerian. Sometimes late at night, so that he gets the fright of his life. His car long since pawned. Has he mentioned that? He's calculated that after another two years as housemaster at Clarence, where he doesn't pay a cent in rent and even receives a stipend, he'll be in the clear.

He fiddles with his mobile phone. Matt. Wants to text him right away. Get drunk tonight to celebrate his downfall. He's buggered.

And of course, of course, says Mister Richardson, pleased as punch with the bit of good news, in his position as the Afrikaans teacher he is above suspicion. Permanent and highly appreciated. (In a predominantly English school like Zilverbosch he's managed to draw full Afrikaans classes, twenty-four grade elevens, nineteen grade twelves – that takes some doing.)

'By when must I decide? I mean, by when do I have to? I mean, by when must I inform you of my decision?' Rotten, that's how he feels. He can't wait to get the hell out of that over-cooled office.

'I thought I'd give you a week or so. What do you say, Jack? The ball's in your court now.'

One strike and you're out. Incredible. 'I. Well. It's tricky for me. To be honest, Mr Richardson, I have a lot of debt.'

'We all have debt, Jack. That's life, nowadays.'

Mister Richardson is turning his back on him. This is a principal he hasn't known until now. Watch it, Jack. Don't chuck out the baby with the bathwater. You're on your own, pal.

'I'll see. Well. It's difficult.' Jack regains a little strength. 'My reputation at Zilverbosch is spotless. If there's one person who knows this, it's you, Mister Richardson.'

'Of course, Jack. And for that I respect you. That's why I'm asking you to take the decision yourself.'

'Fuck,' he says behind half-closed lips.

'I beg your pardon?'

'No, nothing. It's nothing.'

'Well, then, that's that, Jack. I trust that we can rely on you. Till next week, then.' Manly handshake. Wedding ring set with a tiny diamond.

He walks out of the main building and sits down outside under the wild fig in the grade twelve garden.

@ Demise, he facebooks his bosom friend, Charnie.

Charnie: *What?*

Jack: *It's started.*

Charnie: *What are you talking about, J?*

Jack: *They want to chuck me out of Clarence.*

Charnie: *Ag, don't be silly. They can't.*

Jack: *I'm finish & klaar x.*

'Hello, hello, hello. Bennie, it's me. Sannie.' She flutters in just as he's rubbing Sorbolene onto his hands. Comes over and kisses him. He knows it must be boiling outside from the heat she radiates.

'Wait, pass that here, Bennie.' She takes the jar of Sorbolene and starts massaging his fingers one by one with a gob of the stuff, a skill acquired in her days as a paramedic. She has plump, round fingers and she's working very gently.

He sinks back until he's lying flat, ouch, and without withdrawing his hand from hers. 'Heavens, Sannie.' He almost feels as if she's doing something that only a woman can do with a man. He's secretly pleased that there's still a bit of man in him. He realises that the chemo and the pain treatment have smothered most of the passion left in him.

'Other hand.'

He gives it.

Then he must have drifted off, because when he wakes up, Sannie is no longer next to him on the bed.

'Sannie?'

'Over here, Bennie my boy.' Oh, she's sat down on the chair next to him with a bowl of something.

'Bennie, I've made you the most delicious blancmange. With just a touch of granadilla. It won't make you feel sick. Come, sit up so I can help you.'

He feels the shape of the bowl. Square, they don't have pudding bowls like that. Pudding spoon stuck bolt upright in the middle of the dessert, enough to make him laugh. Soft, he presses it. It's all spongy. He eats slowly while Sannie talks non-stop. Search him, he's got no idea about what. He was always a slow eater and an excellent shitter. But now, good grief, he doesn't even want to talk about it. He hands her the bowl when he's done. He's eaten about three quarters, he'd say.

A breeze pushes in through the open windows. It's balmy and lovely and caresses the back of his neck. He can't tell when last he felt so good.

'Professor Jannie de Lange. Hell, there's a man who knows his stuff. He'll still get me out of this pesky thing. It's not over with me yet.'

'Your oncologist, Bennie?'

'I believe it was ordained from above that I should end up with a man like that.'

'Our lives are constantly in His hands, Bennie. Let His will be done, we must abide by it. It's our Christian duty, Bennie. I'm going to take you out to Kirstenbosch one day. You tell me when you're ready. You're looking so pale today. I knew you'd enjoy the pudding. I know you men.'

'Sannie, won't you bring me my cheque book over there, and also my pen. I want you to write for me.'

Sannie gets up and puffs and pants to the bedside cabinet. 'Bennie, we haven't yet handed over your donation to Coronation Park. It takes time with those people. In the meantime, it's safe and sound in the Silver Cloud Christian Fellowship Trust. Nobody can touch it. We're preparing for the Big Baptism. Ministering to the people. You must know, Bennie, some of those people are hardened. It's the drink, if you're asking me. We're having small silver-cloud coins made. Everyone who confesses and is baptised gets a silver cloud. That's how we'll know whether this one or that one has been saved. Then the cheque will be handed over.'

'Oh.'

'Who should I make it out to, Bennie? Say the word and I'll write.'

'Mattheüs Duiker. For the amount of five hundred thousand rands only.' He crosses his arms over his chest. Pleased. Show him the man who can take a sum like that from his back pocket without flinching.

'Heavens, Bennie, but you really are one of the most open-handed people I've ever come across. I only hope your son appreciates it. He's just been overseas for heaven knows how long. This is an almighty pile of money, this. Not to be sneezed at. I only hope.'

'Mattheüs's head is screwed on right, Sannie. He's got a very shrewd business concept.'

'Then that's fine, Bennie, I just thought. I just want, how shall I say. You're number one for me, Bennie. Your welfare, that's what I think of before anything else. I'm not going to allow anybody on this earth to take advantage of you. You can take my word for it. Not that I'm – Mattheüs, I mean, he's your son.'

'Where must I sign, Sannie?' She places the pen between two fingers of his right hand, then guides it to the dotted line.

Sannie can't help marvelling at how evenly the man can still write. Not like an old man at all. She wonders as she so often has in the past, she'd never actually say it, but she does wonder whether Anna appreciated and cherished this remarkable husband of hers in the way he deserved.

'Put it back in the drawer, Sannie. Thank you. I'm going to doze for a while, I think. I'm almost without pain today. It really is wonderful, medical science today. Come and kiss me goodbye.'

'Tell me, Bennie.' He can hear she's standing at the foot of the bed. 'Does that other one still come around?'

'Who? Jack?'

'Between you and me, Bennie, I don't have a good feeling about that man. He may be a teacher and all.'

'Goodbye for now, Sannie.'

He pulls up the bedspread. The bed supports him as gently as you'd carry a child, he sinks slowly, contented and without a single distraction. It's the mattress, inner-spring quality. He's never believed in buying cheap stuff, no matter what Annatjie accused him of in later years. Take a look now inside his wardrobe, there's a Rex Trueform there that he bought in '61 at Stuttafords. One hundred per cent new wool. You could step out in it now to meet the queen.

Somewhere near the door of the study, Sannie is taking her leave with a final grumble: 'You must see to it that your beliefs are adhered to, Bennie. This is your house and nobody else's. I can only hope that that son of yours respects your principles, because the Lord only knows I can't see that he has many of his own.'

He pages through his recipes as if it's an old photo album, precious recipes collected and copied and annotated. Got this one last year from his ex-South African friends in Antwerp: black mussels with their beards plucked and properly rinsed and then steamed in white wine and a chiffonade of celery, carrots, and leeks with a dab of cream; okay, that may be a bit rich for his takeaway. He closes the file and hides it in the bottom drawer underneath other papers and resists the temptation to refresh himself with porn, he resists it three times, and lies down on his bed trying slit-eyed to be just a human being, an ordinary human being with happiness and a future, that's all.

When he wakes up, he masturbates to an old favourite that he's bookmarked, dries himself with a cum-encrusted towel and goes to the kitchen to make some food.

He decides on a frittata in the big pan, a wedge for Pa, a wedge tomorrow for Samantha, and the rest for him. The secret of a frittata is very finely grated Parmesan beaten into the batter, and when you're sure the first layer is cooked through, always on a low flame with the lid on, you grate more Parmesan on top and put it in the oven at 130°C, you just have to keep an eye on it.

Didn't add tuna this time so that Pa can at least try the thing. Very ripe tomato. He reckons the old man needs something acidic. Ag, who'd know? And who ever thought he'd last this long – there goes the bell as if on cue. He leaves the whisking for the time being, you have to whisk in lots of air otherwise your frittata will be too dense.

'Pa?'

He's pushed a cassette into his antique radio-cassette player, it's *boeremusiek*. 'Mattie, come and listen to this. Hendrik Susan and his band. Man, I know it's not your kind of music, but give the man a chance. He was master of the concertina years ago. Just listen this once, Mattie. Listen: the Moepel Waltz. Just this once. For Pa.'

He leans his elbow on the mantelpiece and looks at the man sitting straight up in his bed, both arms lifted, doing dance steps.

He tries to get into the music, really he does. Of course he's heard it before in the house, but now he tries to listen as if it's the first time. He even tries to think what kind of porn you'd screen to the concertina music. He tries everything. He looks at the man making small movements with his upper body and arms, as if he were dancing with his partner of long ago in some town hall. The pyjama sleeves have slid down over the pale arms and light catches his blue-white nails, and the only emotion he can summon up is an admittedly rather stale pity for the man.

'I'll have to get going now, Pa,' he says softly. 'I'm busy making us something.'

He thinks his father hasn't heard him, but he presses the stop button on the radio-cassette player, drops his arms and fixes Mattheüs with a blind stare as only he knows how.

'Do you know what puzzles me, Mattie. It's what you do with yourself the whole blessed day. In that closed room with the door always shut, hours and hours every day. Do you think it's normal for a strong young man like you? Pa can't help wondering, you can't blame me. Not that I want to tell you what to do.'

In the kitchen, he immediately fetches a beer from the fridge and goes out onto the paving outside. This is where he's thought about reviving his mother's herb garden, so that he can harvest seeds and pick fresh stuff to use in his takeaway. Ag, the hell with it all. All of it, please. One tattered basil plant has remained, its sweet leaves chewed ragged by bugs. He violently uproots the plant and flings it over the back wall to the neighbours. Let him admit it once and for all: he can't wait for his father to peg off.

The year before last, while he was staying with his friends in Antwerp for a while and they got him a painting job via a friend of a friend, her whole flat was full of glass, glass tables and glass shelves with glass knick-knacks, she was a lesbian, not that that had anything to do with the glass obsession, whatever, he had to be so careful with the paint splashes that he only got home in the evening after dark – it was more or less always dark there – more exhausted than you should be after a day's painting, and that's probably why he reacted so strongly to the parcel from his father. Carefully wrapped, a parcel containing magazines, *In aller Welt*, the Mercedes Benz trade magazine, and with it the killer of a self-help book, *How to Be the Best Car Salesman in Town*. That was his father's way of inviting him yet again – he'd often done so either directly or indirectly – to become a partner in Duiker's Motors. Duiker and Son. It was so damn tragic that he could only react to it with anger. Raging anger, he got angrier and angrier at that pile of propaganda, as he thought of it years later, and he was unable to forget it. The mighty established business with a reputation all over Cape Town: You could be a millionaire, Mattie, listen to your father. And he, the only heir, a total loser.

He tries to banish the memory from his system – now, previously, the old, old callus – he smokes two cigarettes and goes indoors, whisks the batter so that it splatters the work surface with yellow goo, lights the flame, puts the lid on and fetches another beer. The tragedy is this: the aversion that he's retained for the antagonist, for the harm that man has done him, increasingly becomes a projection existing in his own head and nowhere else. He's unable to associate it with the pale man in his sickbed; it has long since ceased to have any bearing on him.

The intercom at the gate rings. 'Mattheüs?'

It's Jack. Jack has a habit of turning up suddenly, without an SMS, a neutral tone of voice on the microphone like an announcement at a station, knowing very well that there's another person in the house.

Mattheüs presses the button, checks his frittata which is cooking slowly from below, quite safely, and meets Jack just as he enters, his expression complex and also remote, especially, as if to protect himself; he's come to know him like that. He pulls Jack over to him and pushes his hands between his jacket and shirt along his sides and strips him of his jacket; he can smell Jack on the lining of the jacket, on the dark blue under each arm of the blue shirt. 'Jack?'

He carries the jacket as they walk before sitting down in a sheltered corner of the stoep, safe from prying eyes next door, from *her* upper storey she has a one-eighty-degree view of the Duiker garden. While walking, he fishes Jack's cigarettes and lighter from his inside pocket and lights up for both of them, Jack's hand on his, cupped around the flame.

'What's the matter, Jack? Just say something.'

The story emerges in fits and starts on the wrought-iron bench with its red-and-white striped cushions, a *Garden and Home* scene it could be. 'Fucked' is the word Jack uses once, twice, three times, and Mattheüs develops a sense of vertigo, as if it's not Jack but rather he who's losing his balance.

A sensation that intensifies when Jack says: 'The carpet's been pulled from under my feet. How unfair is that, Matt? Hey?' On and on he tells the story with emotion and in detail, and gradually Mattheüs starts to see in this carpet of Jack's a red thread that he's weaving into it, at first surreptitiously so that he doesn't see or notice it at all, but then a more vivid red and more noticeable: does Matt have any idea how much money he still owes?

He should never have come back, should rather have tried to

make it overseas, rather fail there if he has to fail at all. Jack is in the shit, he with his business somewhere far in the distance once he's long since run out of energy; that's how things now stand. He's limping along and Jack's following him with his red thread that he now sees so clearly that the rest of the carpet fades from sight till eventually it's all red thread. 'Matt, I'm moving in with you. That's the only solution. You must help me. I mean. We're in a relationship. Hey? I've got nothing. I've got a few weeks left and then I have to be out of there. I'm coming to stay here, Matt,' and he bangs the red-and-white cushion with his hand.

Mattheüs gets up holding his head and walks up and down the long stoep, right as far as the yellowwood door at the end leading to the study where Pa will surely have been buzzed awake by the intercom or made out Jack's voice or is simply lying there wondering who it is with his sense of right and wrong, his law, fuck knows, towering like a horse's hard-on. And he all the time with his head in his hands: how can he? He can't possibly let Jack come and stay here. It's non-negotiable with a bullhead like Benjamin Duiker who probably in that filthy backyard of a mind of his tries to imagine what it looks like when two men fuck, and how at the end of that broad highway they arrive at the great open portal of hell and that, that most deeply sinful of things, he will never ever allow under his roof, may God have mercy on him.

He rushes indoors and grabs the pan of frittata from the flame, takes off the lid and puts it into the oven that he's preheated, and fetches two beers from the fridge. On the stoep, it's now Jack's turn to sit with his elbows on his knees, cupping his head in his hands, waiting for an answer, for mercy. For the absurdity of this situation (there are four bedrooms in this house, only one of which is currently occupied) to vanish like the morning mist.

'Are you praying, Jack?' Mattheüs gives a wry laugh. 'Here, another beer.'

Jack accepts gratefully.

He must have dozed off, for he becomes aware of a shuffling at his bedroom door that wasn't there before. It'll be Pa.

Since the old man's moved into the study, the toilet visits have been going well. The commode's been put on hold for the time being, for which he and Samantha, not forgetting Pa, are all grateful, none of them too keen on that whiff. Although he must admit that Pa's toilet, when he's been to clean it with Jik and a scrubbing brush, has never emitted anything but the most discreet of odours. Not exactly perfume, but far from revolting. It's one step away from the chemo, that's what it is.

'Pa?' Actually, he doesn't want to be heard. Old man must learn to stand on his own two feet, it was after all his choice to move.

He lies dead still and listens and swallows when the spit collects. (He's just zapped through three short porn videos, at most six minutes of heightened attention.) Nothing. He waits for a sound that will make him get up, though he'd prefer at all costs to prolong his siesta, the immediate, post-randy, total immersion on a hot afternoon, his favourite of all sleeps.

He must have dropped off again. He's startled by the sound he's been waiting for as he lies there. Things are toppling off the bookshelf, the first on the right as you walk towards his bedroom, which means that Pa has lost his way; it's miles past the guest toilet. He has no business in this part of the house. He waits for a few minutes more and sighs and slips into his trousers, stumbles into the left leg and hops to the door, which he opens in the meantime with his free hand, and peers out into the daylight gloom of the passage, his eyes heavy with sleep. 'Pa?' Nobody.

Three coffee-table books have fallen down, he steps over them. The guest toilet door is closed and he hears flesh rubbing against cloth, an old man's sound from a mouth. 'Pa, can I come in?'

'Ag, Mattie, my boy, I thought you were never coming.' The

voice is that of a man sick and tired of struggling.

'Pa, what's the matter, then?'

His father is sitting on the toilet with his hands crossed over himself when he hears Mattheüs enter. The head remains bowed, the shoulders puny and afraid, so that Mattheüs, as so often at his father's sickbed, blanches at the man he sees in front of him. The daylight through the ribbed glass above the toilet reflects some of the pink of the bowl and the seat – his mother's idea of décor – onto the side of his father's thigh, if you can still call it that, onto his hands and his bald, drooping head and contributes to the dehumanisation of this man, so that Mattheüs yanks down the roller blind (also pink) behind his father, leaving only the subdued lamplight on either side of the washbasin.

'You know, I don't even know if I can tell this to another person,' he says, attempting something brave, something like a wasted smile, some remnant from the arsenal of this once fearless man. 'But I suppose I can tell you, Mattie, you are blood of my blood after all. Man, I've been sitting here for I don't know how long. Just water, that's all. Just a little dribble. You'll never know what it feels like, Mattie.' He lifts his head and keeps his hands crossed over the sparse pubic hair. 'Mattie, I can no longer produce what I have to every day.' He's on the point of crying, this man. He lifts a hand and grabs at air. 'It's a terrible thing, this, to have to endure.'

Mattheüs squats in front of his father. 'Pa, I think the time has come for us to find a nurse for Pa. It's the side effects of the Oramorph. Didn't Professor de Lange warn that this would happen? There are ways. Enemas and things. We must find out. Why is Pa only telling me now? How long has this been going on?'

'Mattie, no. I don't want a strange person fussing around me. And I don't want to squander your, your and Sissy's, money. Listen carefully now. Go to our old bathroom and look in the cupboard there, the left-hand one, I think. Where your mother used to keep her things. There's a flat box in there with plastic gloves. Go and fetch them for me and let me put one on and try to get this stuff out of myself. How long, you ask? From when I started having the chemo, that's how long.' The voice rises. A hand now on each pyjama knee.

'Pa, I. It's not the best, I mean it's hardly the recommended way to get your shit, if you'll forgive the word, out of yourself. Not if you're a sick man. There are better ways. There are pills to loosen your bowels. Pa is very weak in any case. I don't think you'll even be able to.'

'Man, you mustn't underestimate your old father. Go fetch them for me, please. You say pills? My system can't cope with even one more pill. Now go. I'll wait here. Bring me the things and then go and make your father some tea. Without milk.'

Later, in the study, he's sitting with his father having tea. He has his tea with ginger biscuits from Aunt Sannie. They don't talk about the business with the blocked shit. And Pa doesn't say whether his plan worked. Easy to talk about baby shit or dog shit on the lawn, that's part of everyday life. About your own, and then with your son of all people, that's more difficult. Pa keeps the honour of his personal life intact, and Mattheüs would never be the first to mention it.

He eats six ginger biscuits, and on his seventh he notices that the drawer of the bedside cabinet is open just wide enough for a mouse to get in. He leans across, suspicious, and yanks open the drawer and notices at once that the cheque book is lying at an angle and not lengthwise next to Pa's fountain pen as he always puts it away, and as he knows Pa – neat in his person and his possessions – would do it.

Pa with the mug of tea. 'What's the matter, Mattie? You mustn't upset yourself, man.'

'Has Pa been looking for something? Someone's been busy with the drawer.'

'There's something for you, son. Open the cheque book and have a look. Pa's been thinking about you a lot.' He slurps the lukewarm tea to corroborate it all.

Mattheüs flips to the last, recently written cheque. In a fraction of a second his eye scans every jot and flourish. His hands tremble as he holds it, the sanctified-by-his-father cheque book, and he's glad that Pa can't see him. He blushes, he's overcome. His legs feel light, his arms take flight; in the wink of an eye the takeaway on the corner of Main and Albertyn becomes a reality. Duiker's, the logo in a warm orange-red on the window, he sees it all as if the shop has existed for years, he even smells his food, lamb chops and lemon and thyme with small white cannellini beans, his first stew in a stainless steel casserole. He sees a line of people all along the pavement digging into their purses for the right change and licking their lips and looking up to see if the queue is getting any shorter; he sees Duiker's Takeaways in Plumstead and Muizenberg, eventually even in Khayelitsha and Langa, fucking Stellenbosch, everywhere, he sees it more clearly than he can ever imagine his own life or his personal history or any aspect of himself. He's leaving behind his pathetic limbo existence; he'll get real. He'll trim his wick at night, and all cravings suppressed once and for all, he'll fall asleep exhausted like ordinary people, his hands still smelling of turmeric, no matter how much he's washed them. For the first time in his life he'll enter the realm of the hard-working. He'll be happy, Pa already is.

He takes the mug of tea from his father's hands and hugs him and holds him for longer than he can remember ever doing. He is, as they say, dumbstruck. He is far too embarrassed to mention that it is more than he had hoped for. He is overwhelmed by the gift, by the generosity of it. (How did things go so totally wrong with the allocation of his mother's monthly allowance at the end of her life?)

'You see,' his father says against his shoulder. 'You think I've forgotten you. You think I don't know you, Mattheüs. But I know who you are, even if you don't believe this.'

'Ag, Pa.'

'I wish you every success, my child. This is your big chance. What are you going to call your place?'

'Duiker's, Pa. Just Duiker's.' And looks over his father's shoulder at the curtains that are too tightly drawn for this time of day. Cry, he won't.

'Heavens, Mattie. And you're only telling me now. Give me my tea so that I can finish it.'

Mattheüs flops down with the cheque book still open in front of him and then he realises what it is that bothered him: who wrote the cheque? He examines the handwriting on the cheque, pages back to the counterfoil, and almost chokes. The low-down brown-noser.

'Pa, you didn't really get Sannie to write the cheque, did you?'

'But how else would I have surprised you?'

'Aunt Sannie, of all people. There's Samantha. Dominee Roelf. I'd prefer it if Pa kept money matters between us.'

'Sannie wrote, and that's that. You know, you mustn't under-estimate her part in caring for me. You're not here all the time, and now with this thing of you setting up a business. What am I supposed to do with myself all day and every day, Mattheüs? You tell me. I can't lie here the whole blessed day counting sheep.'

'I was just saying, Pa.' And how she'll shoot off her hypocritical prissy mouth about him being thirty-two already and never having had a proper job: what kind of a man is that?

'I see a fine future for you, Mattie.'

'Thank you, Pa.' He's already texting Jack. He wants to get blind drunk tonight with Jack and persuade him to do the thing men do best with each other, for the first time, the man's going to have to get over that little violation against him. Outrageously, mindlessly dead drunk for the very last time, and after that it's all work and no play.

'There's enough there for a bakkie as well. You're going to need a bakkie with that type of business. Or how did you think you were going to cart all that stuff around?'

'I noticed that, Pa.'

Pa laughs, his hand cupped around the mug of tea. Light flush on the cheeks. So it must have gone well with all that scratching around in the backside. To flush out everything inside you after months of hoarding: may the gods be thanked.

Mrs Lucinda Symes, second floor, Media Building, Roggebaai. Had garlic last night, he can smell it under the musk-flavoured Beechie. Oh, she's ever so pleased to see his face again. She knew it was a winner, that idea of his. Told her husband, she did: somebody should do it here in the Cape. Junk food is taking over and everyone's getting fatter and fatter and diabetes everywhere. Go and talk to Health if you want to hear about all the misery.

Licence to trade as a restaurant issued by the City of Cape Town/IsiXeko saseKapa/Stad Kaapstad. Stamped and filed in the mighty system of the Municipality of Greater Cape Town, with only someone like Lucinda Symes and a password having access to it and being able to change it, say for instance by transferring it to a new owner or somebody, or if you have rat dung in your storeroom, to suspend your licence, or if you sell salmonella chicken and poison twenty customers, take it away from you, Mattheüs Duiker, ID number so and so.

It went quickly. Every afternoon Jack turns up, shirt tucked into his trousers, and without the smile that melts Mattheüs's heart so. He's carrying a six-pack of Windhoeks. The two of them stand on the sidewalk – not too close to the street or a taxi will slice off your backside – unscrew a beer and watch the progress. And Jack, without looking at him squarely, keeps up the frown of so-where-do-you-think-I'm-going-to-stay that he's using to try to force him into a thing that cannot be, not before his father passes away. And Jack knows that.

The signwriter arrives; it takes him two days. He arrives every day with two little kids clinging to his legs. Things have gone crazy at home with his wife, and his mother isn't all there most of the time either to be able to cope with the two; you can see he dotes on the pair of them.

The logo with the little man and a spoon that's bigger than his body, the spiral of steam curling up from the spoon, he draws it just as it is on the sheet of paper. Talented. The children play with a doll and his mobile phone, and there are two bottles of chocolate milk for them, all on a tarpaulin he's brought along. Next thing, he puts the apostrophe after the 's' of Duiker's Takeaway.

'That means there's more than one Duiker. It's just me, Kosie. This is my business. It should be between the "r" and the "s".'

'I thought it's Mr and Mrs Duiker together in the business.' And when he sees Mattheüs says nothing, Kosie says, 'It's like that with signwriting, Mr Duiker. You look at the letter in front of you and forget it's a word.'

He laughs loudly and changes it at no extra cost, his mistake.

Cash. Everyone wants to be paid in hard cash. Including the guy who installs the walk-in cold room.

'My problem is that I want to claim back from SARS, that's how it works.'

'OK, sir, I'll let you have an invoice, no problem. I bring it tomorrow in an envelope and everything, addressed to Mr Duiker.'

'That's when I'll pay you.'

'Hey, Mister Duiker, you can't do that. Services delivered, services paid for.' And it's true, the cold room's up and running and set to the correct temperature.

He walks out to where Jack is chain-smoking and asks what he should do. People walk by and stand to watch Duiker's taking shape. And he hopes it's starting to look like a place where they'd want to buy food on their way home, to get the wife out of the kitchen for the evening. Jack says he's trusted the cold-room man this far and should trust him all the way. He's got his number, too.

So then he pays him seventy-five per cent of the costs just to make absolutely sure that everything's in order with the cooler motor and everything, and the man – Sam de Beer is his name – pulls off in a huff in his dilapidated bakkie. Learnt it from his father, Mattheüs explains. Nobody's going to do him in.

'You're going to have to relax, Matt. That's all I'm saying. You're

the one who says food tastes like shit if it's prepared under stress.'
Jack is moody as hell.

When it starts to get dark, they sit with the last two beers on some crates inside where, Mattheüs thinks, it smells of paint and steel shavings spat out by an angle grinder, of a promising new business.

'I'm thinking I'll move in here. I'll sleep back there in the storeroom on a blow-up mattress.'

'Jack, you're crazy. How long do you still have in the hostel?'

'A week and a half. Maybe you think I'm joking, but I've got no money, as in zilch, for a flat.'

'Jack, man.'

Mattheüs suddenly gets up and walks outside into the air, blown clean by the wind for a change, there are still quite a few people around at this time of night, which makes him wonder how late he'll keep the takeaway open. For now, though, he wants to get away from Jack, much as he loves him, just to stand back once again and to look at his new baby.

It's not that he's not thinking of Jack's dilemma. He's just fully preoccupied with his business, that's all. And when he looks at that little orange-man logo with his big steaming spoon he's almost scared to be proud (what if it all capsizes again). And yet this time he's displaying something, at least something of his father's entrepreneurship.

The next day, supplies start arriving from wholesalers, one twenty-litre tin of sunflower oil and cans of tomato purée and fine sea salt, and so on. At the Atlas Trading Company in the Bo-Kaap, he selects his dried beans himself, as well as rice and whole spices. He carries the stuff from his bakkie into the storeroom, the bags of rice and lentils and split peas and cannellini beans are placed on a wooden pallet to protect them from the damp. Precautions against everything. He thinks of everything because the whole time it feels – he can't shake off the feeling and maybe that's what it really is – as if this is his last chance.

A stocky little bugger comes up to him and asks if he can help, and Mattheüs has to stop and think, doesn't want to put a foot wrong (the last-chance anxiety). He checks the guy up and down, this man who speaks bad English with a French accent, Emile from the Congo, he says his name is, as hand-on-hip he cockily waits to see if his offer is accepted; then his finger points at the logo. Oh okay, the little man on the logo with the big spoon looks like him, get it? Oh well, okay then.

He watches closely how and where Emile puts the stuff as he also checks out his appearance. He has perfectly rounded biceps, though on a miniature scale, and broad hands, one stuck into a black leather glove with three-quarter fingers and holes for the knuckles. No, he doesn't want to be paid, only when the bakkie's empty. He can give him some food once he's opened his shop. So then Mattheüs fetches him one of Jack's beers from the cool-drink fridge. But he flaps his hands, protesting with laughing white teeth. So, is he a Muslim? No, not that either, and accepts the Coke that Mattheüs holds out instead and takes elaborate leave and expresses gratitude and waves, thank you, thank you, as he walks off, a weird sort of a person and just a little too good to be true, with the knuckles of the right hand peering through the four holes in his glove.

During Jack's last week at Clarence House he starts posting messages late at night on his Facebook Wall. Little ball-biters while he's watching porn, and when the message arrives he can't stop himself from looking each time. Jack with three open suitcases, half-packed, and a box full of books. He took the photo with his mobile phone so that you can just see his bare legs and his Jockeys and the luggage. Caption: *Jack and his earthly possessions prepare for departure.*

At first, he thinks Jack may be losing the plot. Then, as this carries on night after night, he reckons it's Jack's way of dealing with the eviction. A journal of the last days at Clarence House. Jack in front of the main entrance of Zilverbosch (*Altius et Latius*) captioned: *Shortly after Jack van Ryswyk formally resigned as house-master of Clarence House in the office of Mr Richard Richardson.* Jack is looking straight at the camera and comes across as emotionless, scary, so autistic.

It becomes almost impossible to watch, say, a twenty-three-minute video uninterrupted, without receiving two or three Facebook messages from Jack. Once, he actually comes while Jack is on-screen in front of him, the video minimalised. It's Jack in front of his shower curtain with its plunging dolphins, water drops on his bare shoulders, and the caption: *Just finished showering on my seventh-last night in Clarence. Two notes from boys pushed under my door. Too personal for Facebook, will share later. Gist of the messages: Sir, we need you. Go slow don't go – stuff like that. How do you think I feel?*

What to say? While's he's daubing the last spots inside Duiker's with the deep-orange paintbrush – he's chosen this food colour for the wall behind him, it attracts hungry people – or while he's sharpening the two Füri knives on the fine whetstone bought from a Chinese wholesaler, or while he sits with his pen brainstorming daily menus, Jack haunts the back of his mind with his logic of the twin-gabled house in Rondebosch with its two bathrooms and four bedrooms of which three are currently vacant. What crooked logic in a city of three million people with a mixed first- and third-world economy, and what kind of out-dated decree is it that forbids him such a house? And while he's picking pebbles as big as insect eyes and just as grey as the lentils, from the lentil heap, he thinks of how impossible it is for someone like Jack, who never grew up rich or privileged, to understand a decree founded on his father's religious convictions, and besides, there's Jack's deliberate refusal to want to understand it, his reproach, and where it could take their relationship, possibly on to the rocks: you don't want to help me, Matt. What kind of a person are you?

Then, on the Tuesday before the Friday he wants to open Duiker's Takeaway, he hears his father talking on the phone, which still surprises him, after the blindness, how he remembers numbers, Dominee Roelf's, Aunt Sannie's of course, Professor Jannie de Lange's, it's a long list. Mainly it contradicts any assumptions that the old man is on his last legs, he could stay on in that study until next year, as high and mighty as ever and almost cheerful on the trajectory of his sickbed: now sitting up straight, with flushed cheeks, chatting to Aunt Sannie about the old days, then dozing off or coming to after a dose of Oramorph, and the flood of images he was then subjected to. The hallucinations are so totally alien to his experience that he can't help wanting to share them. Dwarfish creatures in a row on his windowsill, with dangling legs in knee breeches, discussing him in a confusion of tongues, it would seem, and always maliciously, or so it sounds to him. Mattheüs is fascinated and encourages his father to tell all, only too pleased that for once he's been shocked out of his bourgeois complacency. Aunt Sannie, hands cupped under her chin, is convinced it's all evil, and when Pa sometimes becomes too agitated as a result of these fantastical visitations, he hears the woman muttering a prayer over his father.

The person at the other end of the line turns out to be Professor de Lange, who tells him: No problem, Bennie, it's entirely up to you. It depends on how you feel. Remember to take the brown bottles along in case the pain suddenly overcomes you. Perfectly fit for a three-hour trip on the N1 to Laingsburg and then a further forty minutes or so on a dirt road that could be bumpy, to the family farm: Luiperdskop. He feels the need to see Sissy and the little girls. And old Hannes, his brother.

'No, Pa. No. You know I want to open on Friday.' (He's talking to a wall.) 'Friday has always been my target date and you know it. Friday is ideal. There are lots of people in the streets and they've been paid and want to treat themselves. It's the psychology. I've thought of everything.'

With a sick man in the car, things can go wrong; he sees it all in a fraction of a second with his special gift, call it what you will.

He sees Pa screaming with pain when they drive through the Du Toitskloof Tunnel and the man still refusing to turn back. There's a thermos flask of tea and sandwiches, sweet and with Marmite, and the subtle hints that he's braking too hard or: are you sure it's safe to overtake, Pa miraculously aware of where exactly they are on their journey, as if navigating with a third eye.

Samantha is busy with a duster and vacuum cleaner in the study when Pa announces the weekend outing to Laingsburg. Mattheüs signals that she should leave, it's private. Dusts here and dusts there, she doesn't leave, silver DKNY logo across her chest.

Pa clutches the sheet in his hand, the fingers contract and let go and do this again. He shifts a little and prepares to get up from his supine position to slowly sit up, his irritation clear from the glow on his face.

'I thought Pa was the one who wanted me to start the business. I don't understand this change of heart. We can go, don't moan. I'll take you. Just let me get going first with the takeaway. Everything's ready, my lentils are soaking in the cold room. Everything's ready to go. But I will take you, Pa.'

He struggles into a sitting position in the bed. With his head at an angle, he slowly wipes his red forehead from right to left. The dusting behind them has abated. Bees outside hover over the frangipani blossoms. A deathly hush descends. And just before his father gets going – he recognises the signs – Mattheüs permits himself one last thought in this study that is now infected with the strange smell that the sickness has brought into it. Everything; he's going to change everything.

'Mattheüs, you have twenty years or more ahead of you to make a success of that business. My months – no, it must be weeks by now – I can count on my two hands. It's not as if your father doesn't understand you. Once a business has got its teeth into you and you start making money – it's a wonderful feeling. Pa wishes you every success, Mattie, every blessing. All that I ask of you is three days, three, that's all. It'll be my last time at Luiperdskop, for all we know. I need to be with the little girls just one more time.'

'And if something happens to Pa there?' (Should they ask Samantha to go along?) 'There isn't even mobile phone reception there. There's nothing. How do we get hold of a doctor? You've weakened a lot, Pa, I can hear it on your visits to the bathroom. All the way to Laingsburg and back.'

'Ag, bugger you, Mattheüs. Laying down the law to me. You'll take me to Sissy and the little girls if it's the last thing you do for me. You can open that business of yours at the beginning of next week. How many years were you away overseas, it's not as if there's such a tearing rush right now. I won't make it to Luiperdskop again. And old Hannes, he won't come here. Terrified of the city. He probably won't even attend my funeral.'

Mattheüs listens with his head tilted to one side like a bantam, a stuffed bird on the mantelpiece that you can move around at will, put away, even; he's of no account in this house, and Jack wants to move in, *here*. All he knows is that he knows for sure, like before, as always, that he must switch off from what he hears, otherwise he'll say or do something (that's the only wisdom he's acquired with age) that he'll regret almost immediately, just like Benjamin Duiker.

'Shall I go and make Mr Duiker some tea?' Samantha coos behind his back.

Mattheüs goes to the liquor cabinet to pour himself a drink. Why can he no longer tolerate the pact between Pa and Samantha? He knocks back one drink and pours a second. And what does it really matter to him?

'We may as well leave tomorrow morning, early, I thought. Remember to check the tyre pressure for me, Mattie. You know it's written on the inside of the door.'

'Yes, Pa.' With his finger, he wipes a spilt drop of brandy from the wooden surface and then licks it off.

Never say die, as spoken and performed by Benjamin Duiker and emulated willy-nilly by Mattheüs Duiker. Luckily, the welder is coming this afternoon to install the security door, he starts strategising. He's had a special steel door made with an ornate 'D' at head height, and on either side of it two laurel branches with leaves, all of it in steel, very attractive and much more expensive than your usual steel door. In *his* damn condition all the way to the farm. Okay. He gulps. He's powerless. Okay.

A few years ago and exactly one day before he was due to leave for overseas, his father invited him to Duiker's Motors for a guided tour: just for you, Mattie, so that you can see for yourself what happens there, Pa doesn't think you really know what he does. (Pa is as excited as a little boy.) They started in the workshop with the impressive hi-tech machines connected to cars to diagnose the engine, just as you would a patient. He was introduced to John and the old man, Oubaas Smittie, and to Syd Dlamini and Dave and Benji, Vepi and James, all the grease monkeys who in their red-and-grey overalls with the red Mercedes star on the chest didn't really look like grease monkeys at all; and they all looked at him either curiously or amiably (Oubaas Smittie) or sneeringly, son of the boss, well, well – spanners in their back pockets – what kind of boss would *he* make. Then on to *Spare Parts / Onderdele*, all along the steel shelves, every spare, big or small, each with its own serial number, filed in pigeonholes. He had no idea where all these things fitted into a motor car; some of the parts he found beautiful, min-iature sculptures, and there, too, he was introduced to the spares specialist, Novak the Serbian, with a square head and crew cut, a real porn look, who assured him that Duiker's Motors stocked only authentic spares – go and check in Goodwood if you want generic cheap stuff – and then he was introduced to Providence, the spares assistant with a sucker in his cheek who nod-nodded at everything; these people, he must say, were very friendly, probably on account of their work with the public, where you have to maintain a pleas-ant facade or you're out. After that to the showroom with its green polished floor; ag man, you could eat off that floor, that's the way he likes it, says Pa. His empire. His life. And who will take over from him? A lifetime of calculated advance planning and shrewd transactions. There is only one, the first-born, the son, his, and he *is* proud of him, he's the one who'll be able to take it further. *Must*.

By this time, Mattheüs was feeling like he did as a child when, at

Goodwood showgrounds, they entered the ghost tunnel on a mini-train with flapping apparitions every now and then, right there in the dark on the rails, which never scared him, not even once; only right at the end, suddenly, the hand of a ghost, bigger than any human hand, limp and clammy suddenly around your neck just when you thought or hoped it was over, the ghastliness of that hand belonging to an unknown creature existing somewhere outside his life, and it was that same ghastliness that he experienced that afternoon in Duiker's, more and more so as the afternoon wore on. It was as if it wasn't even his father any more who was carrying on like that, but rather an apparition of almighty proportions immortalised as The Arch-Antagonist, present only in his head.

In a corner visible from Buitenkant Street, a gigantic arrangement of proteas and strelitzias and greenery, always fresh, and then he was introduced one by one to the Mercedes models on the floor as if they were characters, and that was where his resistance, which had been mounting all afternoon in the brightly lit, air-conditioned, slightly rubber- and pine-airfreshener-smelling rooms, melted away. There his father displayed his love of cars, his knowledge of every detail, his admiration for the sophistication of German technology, his love so true and strong that for a moment it relieved the ghastliness, almost completely he would say, so that he was no longer aware of it. You'd have to have a heart of steel not to succumb to such enthusiasm, and he'd have liked to bid the afternoon farewell in that haze of exhilaration to go and down a double Klippies and Coke in the bar lounge not too far from there, but then Pa played his trump card.

He took him into the nerve centre of Duiker's, took him right inside his office, surrounded by the luxury that came with such a long and exceptionally successful career in the motor game, as his father put it. One of the two secretaries fluttered in, and Pa was at that stage so involved in his story that he introduced her to Mattheüs only in passing. 'On a plate, Mattie. You can become a millionaire here, man. We can do up the office next door for you just as you'd like it; Pa won't begrudge you a cent. It's all yours, and then, then, you'll be able to do as you please. Have you thought of that? For a man who earns money, nothing can come in his way. The world is at your feet.' And then everything, everything came back. 'And what about my overseas ticket?' Pa gave a kind of snort-chuckle, like a very rich man looking at a poor man counting the coins in his hand for the single cigarette he wants to buy. 'Your overseas ticket, forget it, it's money down the drain all in a good cause.' Mattheüs walked his index finger up and down the blood-red suede upholstery of his easy chair, saying nothing because he had nothing to say. His heart was raw, his insides gutted because of the man in front of him in his elegant suit, every seam straight and every button in place. Nothing to say to him. And he would never go there again, that he knew. He'd go overseas, and when he came back his father would be retired. That was the last visit, Pa's very last stand. He was limp and lame. 'Mattie, but can't you see the potential?' And it was as if the whole office, an extension of the man Benjamin Duiker, was proclaiming his father's taste, was talking to him. He felt completely lame. Thick-tongued. And sad, very. 'Forty, fifty years I've spent building up this business. Not for me. For you. You are my only son.' He couldn't stand it any longer. He had to get away from the domain where his father grew larger than life and powerful enough to persuade him to do something he could not or would not do. He pulled his handkerchief from his jeans pocket and blew his nose and walked out – he could still manage to do that. He could flee his father's physical presence, but he couldn't switch himself off from his wish, this final attempt. He was completely overwhelmed.

And that's when he opened the door of one of those brand-new Mercedes models and got in, turned the key once to switch on the radio, Cher was singing 'Believe', perfect timing, as if it were meant just for him, because he was totally shattered, and he sat slumped like that, his head on the steering wheel, for the duration of the song.

'Mattie, so who did you decide to use as your butcher, you never told me?' asks his father, sitting up in his sickbed in the study.

'I used Uncle Hentie. Pa knows him. Not so? He does halal,

everything. But not kosher. I'll always do lentils or something for Jewish customers or for Hindus and anyone who doesn't touch meat. I've thought of everything.'

'Yes, I can see you have. Ah, here's the tea now.'

Mattheüs recovers from the shot of brandy. In his father's presence issues a string of instructions to Samantha about the journey, that's the only way to get her to do things for him.

He pours a last shot, leaves the study and cancels the Friday meat and vegetable order for Duiker's Takeaway, postponing it to Wednesday; he's so calm he actually feels cold, and he phones Jack to tell him about the complication. And he says to him, excited, 'Do you know what, Jack, I'll pay your bond for a flat. I've just thought of it. I've got money now, haven't I? Why didn't I think of it earlier? See if you can get hold of a flat this weekend.'

No response from Jack at the other end of the line.

'Jack?'

'I'll have to think about it first. You make deals with me, I know you. If you give, there's always something you want in return. You say that's how your father is, but you're just the same, Matt.'

'Fuck you, Jack.' He cuts the connection.

An hour passes while he packs his weekend case and can't get Jack out of his mind. Samantha packs for Pa: 'But of course, Mattheüs,' she says when she sees how he's ordering her around. She knows exactly what he's up to, and doesn't sulk. Simply gets on with the job. Helluva mature, that he must grant her.

Then he's off in his second-hand bakkie to Zilverbosch, with a cigarette that he lights and then immediately chucks out, and he pulls up in front of Clarence without parking in the proper place and marches into the hostel with its characteristic boys' hostel smell and arrives at flat number 2, Mister Jack van Ryswyk, and takes the packet of cigarettes from his pocket and clutches it so as to have something in his fidgety hands, doesn't think about what he wants to say, just the raw emotion (for Jack, at his sexiest then), so that he hammers on the wooden door without thinking.

'Jack,' he shouts. Where is the bastard?

A door opens further down the passage. Pitch-black curly hair and pitch-black eyes peering out: 'Mister van Ryswyk's gone out, sir.'

'When did he leave?' It's none of this guy's business. And yet.

'Can't say, sir. Maybe half an hour ago. Can I take a message for Mister van Ryswyk?'

'No, thanks.' And he turns back to the light falling through the entrance onto the wooden floorboards of the passage with its linoleum runner. The curly-top, probably a grade tenner, will have noticed that he's there for a reason. This generation is damn intuitive.

In his bakkie, he lights up at last and phones Jack on his mobile phone that's switched off and stays switched off, every quarter of an hour Mattheüs phones him, phones him till he's crying with rage when he drives into their garden (he's been to Carlucci's, asked the guard at the gate of Zilverbosch, everything) and keeps phoning, but now at intervals of half an hour, an hour, and eventually two hours, during which time he makes spaghetti bolognese garnished with chopped celery for him and Pa.

On the hour that night until about two o'clock or so, there's stuff on his News Feed from Jack, nearly every time with a photo. The redhead, the English teacher Jamie, is in three of the four photos.

Must clear things up with Jamie, Jack writes. *He avoids me in the corridors. Thinks I'm a fool. To Sea Point for a beer or two. I think you'll understand, Matt*. With a photo attached of him and Jamie at La Perla, outside on the terrace. *His* place, that. He introduced Jack to it.

On his rumpled sheets, with the blue glow of his laptop screen on his face, Mattheüs gets more and more worked up with every Facebook photo. The one that Jack sends now was taken at dusk next to the Sea Point swimming pool, precisely when there's an apricot glow on the Atlantic Ocean and the calm water of the pool. Jamie stands in the light, Jack's arm draped around his shoulder, against the railing of the promenade that curves past the Sea Point pool with its symmetrical paving, palm trees behind the two heads

106

and late-night gulls, thousands of them swooping and swerving just to drive him mad; and that's what Jack manages to do, a jackal through and through, and if he thinks, if he just thinks of everything he's invested in that man.

Every one of those places he showed to Jack, Jack cooped up in that hostel flat until he, Mattheüs, met him and restored him to life. Jack, who polishes his shoes at eight every evening, real small-town loser, a glass of box wine from his mini-fridge, empty except for the chocolate Jack can't live without, alone, just him, nobody else with him or in his life, okay, the hostel has two floors of boys, but that doesn't count, just Jack on his ownsome watching that miserable show, *Muvhango*. And he keeps clinging to the scar of that night during his 'wild time', to the fatal thing that befell him against his will and without his knowing anything about it. (Is that possible, Mattheüs wondered, but without saying it.) Whatever the facts, Jack's shy about that night, he had to fill in the details for himself. He understands what a painful thing it must be to process, and funnily enough, Jack doesn't really want to process it though he's long since healed, Jack is strong. He persists in clinging to it and punishing Mattheüs with it: you're not going to have your way with me. That's Jack.

The last photo to be posted is of the redhead on his own, still leaning against the swimming-pool railing, a profile pic, the evening's orange glow illuminating the freckles on his cheek and the bridge of his nose, and no matter how pissed off or by this time sad Mattheüs is, he must admit it's a sexy photo, which he immediately drags and drops into his wank bank. After that, nothing more from Jack – must be tired – and Mattheüs, also buggered and by now worried about getting up in the morning and driving all the way to Laingsburg with a half-dead person, for one last time obeys the peculiar wiring of his brain that needs a fix of porn before he's done and tries to go to sleep.

They set out before dawn, Pa frozen to the marrow as Mattheüs helps him with his hundred-per-cent wool duffel coat with its bone toggles, pure vintage and desirable, and leads him to the car where he's already started the engine and put on the powerful heater. When they've negotiated the set of half-moon steps and reached the paving leading to the garage, Pa presses on his arm to bring them to a halt.

'I know this time of day, there's dew on the lawn. Am I right? And the exhaust fumes of the car, I can still smell them. I don't know if there are still roses. Are there? Perhaps one or two late ones. I suppose they're already forming their rose hips.'

'Yes, Pa.' And he takes him to the car where he has to help him out of his coat again before getting in, Pa can't tolerate stuffy heat.

Mattheüs has, as he predicted, had a bad night, and when he did manage to snatch some sleep, he found himself in a landscape seething with images.

Now he tries to keep a cool head, he tries to be nice to Pa so that nothing can go wrong. He wants the whole weekend to be like that, so that he can return to the Cape in a positive frame of mind and start his business. When Pa has been settled, he fetches the basket with two Granny Smiths, whole-wheat sandwiches (Marmite only), a thermos flask of black tea, his right arm circling the plastic container with two bottles of Oramorph – two means playing it safe – and then all that remains is the thing with Jack, which he can't tidy up as nicely as with his father, who's almost like a baby, he now realises; it's like travelling with a baby. The dawn is breaking as the gate slides open and they pull away. In the rear-view mirror, an apparition in a mauve dressing gown comes striding up. Aunt Sannie. Does she always get up so early or does she have some kind of intention?

'Bennie, Mattheüs. Wait, I've got something for you.' Who can be so chirpy so early in the morning. She's brought a Tupperware container with a face cloth freshened with orange peel, and a few strong plastic bags. 'For the nausea, Mattheüs, I thought you wouldn't think of it.' He takes it from her and touches her hand, warm like a mother's.

She peers at Pa. (She hasn't brushed her teeth yet.) 'And what's with you, Bennie, sitting there like a frozen chicken?' And makes the old man laugh.

'Sannie, make sure our house isn't burgled. We're off to the farm. Probably my last time.'

'Ag, don't be silly, Bennie. You've still got plenty of strength. Mattheüs, look after your father well, my boy. It's a privilege, remember that.' (For fuck's sake.) 'And bring me back some of that excellent Laingsburg biltong.'

Mattheüs takes his foot off the brake and slowly begins to move forward with Aunt Sannie skipping along in mauve slippers next to the window, which he's also slowly rolling up. 'Bye, you two, bye-bye, Bennie,' she gushes in the wake of the snow-white washed and polished Mercedes, the sanctimonious old witch.

As the car gets going, he battles the temptation to make a quick call at Clarence to see Jack. From his expression in the half-open door, he'll be able to see if the bastard is there on his own or not, and if he didn't spend last night on his own in his flat, he'll be hounded by the thought all the way to Laingsburg, something to chew on obsessively. Jealousy in its various shades of green, he can say in all honesty, has never been something he's indulged in; it's his vulnerability right now with his ailing father and the putting off of his business that makes him want to be sure about Jack, and the conviction (another thing he wants reassurance about), please, that Jack won't hold it against him that he can't move into number nine Poinsettia Road right now. He glances at the man sitting next to him, hands folded on his lap, his dead eyes straight ahead of him. At the T-junction before the common he turns left onto the M5, which means that he's decided not to check up on Jack; he'll remain exactly as he is, suspended in a state of speculation.

After a while on the N1: 'Are we getting to the garage with the Woolworths shop, Mattie? Because I want you to stop there. I want you to buy sweets for the three little girls and something nice for Sissy, whatever you think.'

'How does Pa know we're there?'

His father laughs mischievously. 'If you've grown up on a farm, you have a built-in sense of direction from early on. Just that one time in Stuttgart, no, really, I said to your mother, the sun will come up on that side of our hotel tomorrow. I was completely wrong then.' Ever since leaving Cape Town he's become more and more perky.

Then, while picking packets of sweets, it strikes him that Jack, looking at it rationally, hasn't even acted terribly out of character. Jack is keeping to his logic and getting back at him for not wanting him to move in. Essentially, what Jack hasn't known for a long time or has never known, in fact, is that the son must respect the father and stand by him to his very last day, though it's not as if that's what he always wants to do; it's more of a given, ingrained in his very nature. The realisation gives him a measure of composure.

And Mattheüs (okay, add three packets of Mini Liquorice All-sorts) resolves to do everything he can to make things pleasant for his father, because he won't be going to the farm again. This is the last time. He loves him, that much he can say. It's a particular kind of love. With Jack it's more complex. At least there's now a half-baked sort of certainty that Jack won't dump him. It's a game Jack enjoys. Can you imagine what kind of low he reached with that whole Zilverbosch business?

Then shit hits just this side of Worcester. And the realisation that this weekend can't possibly run smoothly; no matter how hard he tries, fate is out to get him in multiple manifestations and from every possible angle.

Flat tyre. Left or right rear. A tiny red eye winks on the dash-board. As his body temperature rises, affecting the hair on his forearms and thighs, and he becomes aware of his overheated face, his non-driving hand shoots through the steering wheel to cover the red light, which makes him laugh, anxious, and even more anxious about Pa's hands grabbing at both sides of the sheepskin seat covers.

'Mattie?'

'Flat tyre, Pa. I know.'

'Then you didn't have the tyre pressure checked?' Impatience, the merciless Benjamin Duiker version.

'It's not that, Pa. I did, but it's not that.'

'These are brand-new tyres.' His impatience now unbridled.

'It must have been a nail or something, Pa. How would I know? I thought these cars didn't get flat tyres.'

'That's a stupid thing to say. All cars get flat tyres.'

He allows the speed to drop from 110 to 90 to 60 to 40 km/h and keeps well to the left inside the yellow line. Trucks and cars and minibuses rock the car as they roar past. As is to be expected of a car of this class, it keeps its balance amazingly well. Involuntarily, Mattheüs calls up a hard-core porn image as an escape from a situation bordering on the unbearable: this is no place to stop. Too dangerous. There are desperately poor people in this country, opportunists lurking in the Port Jacksons next to the road or the vineyards fuck-knows-where, and there's the Mercedes marooned and inside it only a decrepit old man and it's exactly what it looks like: money, wallets, mobile phones, watches, petty cash in the cubbyhole – whe's de gun, you whitey cunt? – Pa's Florsheims, sunglasses, all the larnie stuff, at least he left his laptop at home.

And him busting his gut; he can't even guess how long it's going to take to change the tyre. First, all the luggage has to be unpacked and then you peel back the grey carpet from the bottom of the boot where the spare wheel lies in its cavity together with the tools in a pitch-black bag with two white gloves – Germans think of everything – the process apparently user-friendly, but the Merc, my man, that's another story.

The small green dot, small, notably small, of the BP Ultra City in the distance: does he see it or is it only because he so badly wants to see it?

'You have to pull over now, Mattheüs. This very moment, or you're going to drive that tyre to shreds and then you're on the bloody rim. You can cause us a lot of damage here. A tyre like that costs a fortune, we could still have this one retreaded. Pull off, Mattheüs!'

'Okay, Pa. Just keep calm, please.'

He keeps trundling along at 40 km/h in defiance of his father's command and gobbles up the highway, so straight and careful his course inside that yellow line that he persuades himself that his father isn't even going to notice that they're still moving. That's all he keeps telling himself, and he becomes extremely positive about the ever-larger green lights of BP Ultra City, convinced that they're going to reach them. The wheel spanner, you see. Scrabbling between the hairs on the skin of his forearms there are tiny creatures like crabs, as in STD, he means: the wheel spanner is not with the spare wheel where it should be, neatly in its proper place.

He was, to put it mildly, pissed out of his mind; three o'clock, half past three that Sunday morning with a perfumed pickup hot on his heels, not what you'd call super-svelte, but that time of night, beggars, you know what they say. The two of them were making their way through the clubbers to the sauna for a last bit of sensual pleasure, the brain long since fucked, when he gets an SMS from Abrie Spannenberg, sturdy, strapping, a nicer guy you wouldn't find; with his glowing, freckled face you could eat him on the spot. His wheel spanner is missing. Could Matt maybe help him out? He and his pickup boy go outside and take a deep breath and cross Strand Street and walk to his car where Etienne, by now high as a kite, is standing guard over the Mercedes. Abrie arrives and hugs him with his usual warmth. The spanner is taken out from under the spare wheel; Abrie does it himself. 'Listen, Matt,' Abrie knows late-night horniness when he sees it, 'why don't the two of you move on along? I'm coming into town on Wednesday, I'll deliver the spanner into your hands.' Oh fine, that's absolutely no problem, he trusts Abrie one hundred per cent, coming from such a stinking-rich, exclusively Mercedes-driving, apple-farming family in Grabouw. And he and his pickup walk up the road and turn right and right again and dive into the steamy pit of the bathhouse, where he shakes off pudgy-bum, randy as hell, in a cloud of steam and exchanges him for more muscle and less flab. The spanner has yet to put in an appearance, he realises, disappointed in Abrie, while they traipse along at 40 km/h as if in stationary slow motion, if such a thing exists. (Does Pa notice?)

'Mattheüs, you're going to get me very, very angry now. That tyre is on its last thread by now. You're messing me around now.' And he hits the floor with the soles of both shoes to signal: stop, stop.

'How can you possibly think we could stop here? It'll take me five minutes or more to unpack all the stuff just to get at the spare wheel. Then ten minutes or more to jack up the car. Then fitting the wheel, and so on. By that time we're surrounded. It's not going to take them longer than five minutes to notice there's a rich man's car parked next to the road. Has Pa thought of that? On a silver platter. We are prey, Pa, did you think of that before beginning to shout at me!'

Pa is silent. He scratches at the sheepskin and moves his hands to his knees in dark-brown flannels and pat-pats and then his hands fall open on either side of his legs, imploring in helpless rage.

'You always have an answer. You get me down, Mattheüs. You'll wipe me out long before I'm dead.'

'Listen, Pa. What we've got here is a flat tyre and a chronically ill elderly man and a guy on his own who has to change a tyre with superhuman speed and all this with South Africa. That's it. I don't know what kind of stuff you're on about now.'

He guesses five, at most seven, kilometres to Ultra City, and he has to figure out how not to tell Pa the damn wheel spanner is lying in the boot of a gay apple farmer's car – promises, promises – and his only hope is that there'll be other Mercedes cars at Ultra City. Mercedes owners are known for their helpfulness to fellow Mercedes owners; in the old days, he remembers, two Mercedes passing each other would flash their headlights to affirm their exclusive camaraderie.

Pa utters not another word. He looks even smaller as he sits there, and from under the closed lids two tears trickle down his cheeks in the saddest way imaginable.

Ag, Pa, give him one chance, just one, and everything will be all right. But he keeps silent, overwhelmed by the situation; he should never have given in on the issue of this journey.

Three kilometres, can't be much further, his indicator flashing already. The plan looks like this: he'll find a safe parking spot with an open space next to it to change the tyre and be on the lookout for another Mercedes so he can go and ask whether he can borrow their wheel spanner and then quickly pour Pa some black tea before he starts. Maybe there'll even be someone to lend a hand.

As he turns off, he feels the last layer of rubber peeling away from the now unrepairable tyre so that they're crawling along on the rim of the wheel, which for the first time really scares him. The spare wheel of a Mercedes, he knows, is slightly smaller; it's a temporary affair. If the rim of the flat tyre has also been irreparably damaged, they're way past shit street and his father, he can guarantee this, just this side of a stroke.

'Mattheüs, you're going to have to help me to the toilet now.' The fury has given way to an exceptionally icy chilliness.

'No, that's fine, Pa. I'll just. I'll see if I can find another Mercedes guy to help me, then we'll be done in no time.' He switches the engine off. His whole body is trembling. They're safe.

'Another guy? Listen, Mattheüs, I can see very well what's going on here. You're too bloody useless to change that tyre yourself. God Almighty. Help. Me. Here.' He's got the door open and is trying to get out.

'Listen,' while they're moving along, step by step, to the rest-rooms, 'I know old Gawie van Straaten, the manager here at Worcester Mercedes. Old pal of mine, also been in the motor game for many years. Find his number so I can talk to him. Let him come and help us, for God's sake. We can't carry on mucking about like this. What does that rim look like? Anything left of it? Honestly,

Mattheüs, I might as well tell you, today you've really disappointed me.'

He dials directory enquiries, relieved not to have to listen to any more of the old man's whingeing. All he sees before him is a Mercedes workshop with those perforated panels from which tools are suspended; he sees a wheel spanner, ten or even twelve of them.

'Oh, Mr van Straaten? No, he left the Worcester branch a long time ago. He's gone to Umhlanga, they offered him a manager's position. His wife, you know, is from Natal. They're terribly happy there.'

He asks, hoarse but firm – he'd ordered a coffee at the Wimpy and knocked it back boiling hot while waiting for his shitting father – can they please, urgently, his father is sick to death, send a wheel spanner to Ultra City, Mercedes E-class, he'll pay every cent, please please, who's he talking to now? Wendy. Wendy, please, he's begging here. His father is dreadfully ill. He'll need some morphine any moment now.

Short silence; he thinks he's going to dissolve. 'Okay just for you, Matthew. I'll see who I can find, we're clean-out of them here. Give me your number again? Okay, got it. Now, how come you people travel without spanners?'

He sees his father stumbling out, led by one of the BP men in uniform. He gulps down the last of his coffee and runs across; he'll probably write himself off today on top of it all. He takes over and thanks Sebego and announces that Worcester Mercedes is sending someone to help – Gawie van Straaten was transferred to Umhlanga years ago.

'Mattie, I couldn't get anything out this time either. I need a dose of that medicine. I've got a stitch here in my lower belly. It feels as if it's a blade working its way into my guts.'

@ Carlucci's, Jack facebooks. *Anybody out there?*

He has a last beer from one of the slender Peroni glasses (36-24-36) that comes with this particular brand of beer and walks in the direction of Matt's house, about half an hour's walk or so. He walks tall and smartly, not like somebody who's been drinking. He thinks of nothing in particular. Several beers in quick succession have left him light-headed, even a bit happy after the previous few out-of-sorts weeks. He chooses the right turn each time to get there by the shortest route. Seven cars pass him from behind, and four on the other side of the street. As he gets closer, he meets two ADT guards on bicycles. Both look in his direction. What? Okay, that's their job. He nods. Red trumpet shapes in the dark-green hedges, quite pretty, and the blue-flowered shrubs, he doesn't know their names.

Then he is in front of the Duikers' gate. The forbidden gate. The gate is made up of three steel panels pompously spanning the double-laned driveway. At head height there's a border of fleurs-de-lis, but welded in such a way that the steel tip of each flower looks more like a spear that'll rip your arse apart if you try to clamber over. Jack peers between two of the steel spears, an opening as wide as a hand span. From the garden, two concealed lights shine onto the two gables at the front of the house. On the stoep, there are two coach lamps on either side of the broad front door with its upper and lower halves. Over the garages, a floodlight. Lining the driveway, three ground-level lights on either side, and to the right in a bed of shrubs and stuff there's also a bright floodlight illuminating the lawn. To get in, if you can, and to get yourself from the gate to the stoep without being noticed, and to hope that the front door is unlocked, and then pass through the entrance hall and down the passage on the left all the way to Matt's bedroom, is a superhuman task. Jack looks up and down the street and then presses the intercom button. He holds his ear against the box and listens to the static crackle that the open circuit transmits to him. It's an empty house. Nobody inside. He releases the button and pushes his hands inside his pockets, just standing there.

An ADT guard cycles up. 'Can I help you, sir?'

My friend lives here, he says. Just checking. No, no need to worry. They do the checking. That's their job, day and night. The guard looks at him from under his cap. Jack offers him a cigarette, which he accepts gratefully. He hangs around a while longer on his bicycle, the cigarette tucked into the top pocket of his bottle-green uniform, for later. He's not altogether reassured. And yet there isn't quite enough either to make him suspicious.

'Good night, sir.'

Jack loiters there for a good five minutes or longer. And does his reconnaissance. He looks slowly from the driveway to the far right of the garden where a narrow river-pebble path runs around the house. On the south side of the house there's another gable, exactly like the two in front, and underneath the gable are the windows of the study Uncle Bennie has moved into. He's been in the study three times, each time in Uncle Bennie's absence. On each occasion, Matt poured them drinks from the liquor cabinet. He would lift the bottle with a flourish, elbow in the air, as if the place belonged to him. And they'd sit there, chatty and cosy. Matt, this must be what rich people feel like, he'd said. Matt said he's never in his life felt like a rich person. Then, with legs spread wide on either side of Matt, he sat on his lap in the big armchair and playfully cuffed him in the ribs. Matt liked that, Matt likes all physical contact.

Just call me Uncle Bennie, the old man has told him several times. Still, he has kept the necessary distance between him and the man. He's not so dumb as to be fooled by Uncle Bennie's thinly veiled homophobia. He feels most at home in Matt's bedroom. It's completely different from the rest of the house, where everything's in its place, everything hand-picked to complement the Cape Dutch exterior and interior architecture. Behind Matt's closed door, definitely closed, one, dim light is burning. The curtains are also drawn. Honestly, when he thinks of it. No, he couldn't even say what colour the walls are painted in Matt's room. And always with a frisson of sex hanging about the place. And on Matt's computer, as if he didn't know it, as if he hasn't known it for a long time, hundreds of porn videos bookmarked. That's how things stand now. Not for ever, hopefully. Whatever. When you find yourself in Matt's room, you're in a Matt-created space with rules à la Matt.

The Duiker home is on a corner, so there are no neighbours on the right-hand side. To the left is the double-storey belonging to the Sannie woman. If he stands in front of the far left panel of the gate, he's out of sight of that house. (The light in one of the upstairs rooms has just gone on. It's exactly 7.15 in the evening.) If he stands in front of the central panel, he can see most of her house. From in front of the right-hand panel the whole house is visible. So he assumes that his human head amidst the steel spears must also be visible from her top storey. He observes all these things, stores them away, and doesn't give them another thought.

@ the Duiker home, he facebooks his friend Charnie.

Charnie: *Thought Matt's gone to the farm? With the old guy.*

Jack: *Have a master plan.*

Charnie: *What?*

Jack: *Can't tell. Plan = a bomb.*

Charnie: *Bomb?*

Jack: *Bomb of a plan.*

Charnie: *As long as you don't fuck up, please Jack.*

Jack: *OK, cool.*

Charnie: *X*

He positions himself in front of the central panel of the gate and turns his back on the house and takes a photo of himself. He dawdles along. Twice he stops, the first time still within sight of the house, and sends the photo he's just taken to Matt. The last time, he stops opposite a house where a watchdog is barking hysterically. Yes, yes, he talks to the animal. Then he reaches the furthest corner of Poinsettia Road, where you can catch a last glimpse of the steel-green gate.

In the late afternoon, when the surrounding Karoo changes from a dry, steel grey to pale yellow, they approach Laingsburg. Pa's neck lifts from the support, emerges from the coma into which he's been plunged, straining to the surface almost like a duck that's dived down and is now coming up again, his neck indeed like that of a duck that's lost some feathers on account of age or in a narrow escape from a jackal attack – a lonely neck, Mattheüs thinks, and wishes that he could wrap it in one of his woollen scarves, if only it had been a bit colder. He feels the need to protect Pa from the gaze of Sissy and to a lesser extent that of Uncle Hannes. How the three little girls are going to see their grandfather, he couldn't give a damn about; they're children, and children accept everything. And about whatshisname, Marko, his brother-in-law, as long as he sees to it that his, Matt's, glass is full, he's at peace with a man who can hardly bring himself to discuss anything with him other than the weather.

And that while everybody knows, he and Jack for sure, that Uncle Hannes is also gay and has been all those years in those flapping white trousers of his with the pressed turn-ups and ironed shirts, unbuttoned just enough to accommodate the paisley cravat on a Saturday evening at a braai with beer and brandy on a goddamned Karoo farm. The last time Uncle Hannes came to Cape Town, it feels like so long ago, he and Jack took him to the new Labia Theatre to see that gay cowboy movie *Brokeback Mountain*, and the man just about swooned. For the rest of the weekend, he tried to analyse the movie with them, not that there was much to analyse, rather a question of giving voice to his need, and then when Pa or Sissy came into the room unexpectedly he clammed up.

'This is where those terrible floods were,' Pa says as they enter the town at 40 km/h, there's always a speed cop with a camera hiding under a thorn tree to the left.

And then there was the old man clinging to a log who got washed away into the dam and saw his old wife clinging to a log on the other side of the dam, and he called out: is that you, Marie? Mattheüs finishes his father's story, because if he has to hear it one

119

more time he'll go mad.

His father's head bobs as they cross a speed bump. Mattheüs looks at him, shudders when he sees how he flinches at his son's tone of voice, a blow with the fist, and at the point he wanted to make, to drive home, by rattling off the story himself without allowing the old man the opportunity to enjoy the nostalgia of retelling the story himself.

'Sorry, Pa, I didn't mean it like that,' but he knows he's saying it too softly for his father to hear, his father in any case switched off again, withdrawn into his morphine world.

On the other side of Laingsburg, past the koppie where peeling whitewashed stones urge, *Dra Wol / Wear Wool*, he turns off to the right onto a tolerable dirt road as far as the railway line, where he stops, checks for the Shosholoza Meyl, the name of the passenger train that he's never managed to figure out properly, then further on along a dirt road that has by now turned into a two-track that takes you thirty-five kilometres or so to Luiperdskop. The snail's pace on the dirt road seems to revive his father, weak as this he's seldom seen him before. This is either going to be the end of him, this visit, or he doesn't know what.

He phoned Sissy last night and warned against shock: 'You haven't seen him for a long time, Sis, he's deteriorated enormously in the meantime. You'll have to prepare yourself.'

At the other end of the line on that telephone contraption – a chair with a padded square cushion edged with gold braid and next to it the raised table with the phone, all-in-one – she was silent. Then said: 'Thank you, Matt.' And he could hear it was heartfelt, which made him feel more positive about the visit.

With the headlights now on the double-track ('Mattie, have you switched on?'), blond grassy fringes on both sides of the road, the two of them drive on. Mattheüs has half opened his window, hoping to breathe in the veld, and is worrying that he's made a mistake in not bringing his laptop. Behind the farmhouse you can climb the mountain, and then there's a plateau with a flattish black rock, which last time he'd marked with a pile of rocks – if the baboons haven't chucked it over yet – where you can just get a signal. The fact remains – and it's enticing right there in the dusk with the veld wafting in at the window – he's got an archive of porn pics on his computer, an impressive collection built up over the years, which could see him through a weekend with no signal if things got too heavy.

Pa says he needs one of those dry-throat suckers which Mattheüs, without taking his eyes off the road, fishes out of the cubbyhole, tearing off the cellophane with his teeth and placing it in his father's extended hand.

'He didn't give me enough for the farm. Daylight robbery.'

'Ag, Pa, you're not really going to start on that again.'

His father is on about Oupa's will, where Luiperdskop was left equally to him and Uncle Hannes. But then it turned out that, at about this time, Sissy married Marko, a rich young guy from the Nelspruit area, who wanted to clear out of the north ('the Western Cape is the only place where a white man can still survive'), and so he bought the farm after a terrible fight with Pa and Uncle Hannes, especially Pa with his sharp head for business, and so in the deed of sale there was a clause granting Hannes the lifetime right to stay on the farm – and stay he has ever since, in the rondavel in the yard with all his dogs, but Pa still has twinges of dissatisfaction at the agreed purchase price.

His father sucks at his sucker and nods. He understands, he'll obey his son. Digging up old bones, that's not why he got Mattheüs to drive him all this way. He asks for his window to be opened just a bit, pushes his nose out into the dusk, filled as it is with arid aromas, shakes his head. His sharp sense of smell has abandoned him. As the best smeller in their family, he used to be able to tell when the potatoes started sprouting in the darkness of the store room, he could smell their mother's monthlies, which he didn't mention, at least not to her.

The double-track takes them through a drift overgrown with thorn trees, and across a cattle grid that makes his father vibrate in his seat. A little pepped up after all at the prospect of being on the farm, he leans forward, he knows exactly where he is.

Mattheüs checks his mobile phone: the signal is still two bars strong. This is probably the last spot on the road where there's a signal. Two messages from Jack. The first is banal. Jack is getting dressed to go out. And then: Something unexpected has happened with him and Jamie. Nothing to worry about. It's what Jack doesn't say that Mattheüs finds disturbing. With yet another photo of him and the redhead teacher that evening in Sea Point, one not sent to him before. He carefully inspects Jack and Jamie as he tries to interpret the photo. Jack's smile is artificial, saccharine, to say the least. He knows what he might think of the two of them together like that, but he doesn't want to go there. It'll frustrate the hell out of him here on the farm. With his thumb, he wipes the image from the screen and switches off.

'It's dry here, isn't it, Mattie? That's how it seems. I know this farm like the back of my hand.'

'Looks like it, Pa.'

'Sissy said they last had a spot of rain in January. Nothing much to talk about, though.'

The farmyard comes into view in front of Mattheüs, the single-storey farmhouse with its red corrugated-iron roof and light-brown fifties-style face-brick walls, nestled between tall poplars and American ash trees. He perceives it not in the present, but rather as a visual memory one keeps remembering, years later, a landscape painting from your grandparents' home, until the activity in the yard between the house and the outbuildings draws his attention. There are floodlights and people and Marko's four-wheel drive with its hunting lights on and then another bakkie with its doors open, two farm horses saddled up and dogs everywhere, two ridgebacks and dogs belonging to the farm workers, four men still in today's blue overalls. He notices another farmer as they drive up, both he and Marko have guns over their shoulders, and both walk up to the Mercedes.

First to reach them is Sissy with her corn-blonde hair tightly pulled back in a ponytail, and her wide smile with the even white teeth; he's forgotten how attractive she is. Her three daughters also there in the background, giggly and curious, but hesitant as farm children often are. (Oupa is seriously ill, see to it that you behave yourselves, or something of the kind to school them in advance for the visit.)

Sissy opens Pa's door, takes him carefully (he can see she's not forgotten his report on Pa's condition) by the shoulders, kisses him on the forehead, as they tend not to do in their family, it's usually on the lips. 'Pappie, ag heavens, my dear Pappie.' (Since when has she called him that?)

Sissy is wearing pale-yellow tights with matching shirt, loose and feminine with a pattern of pale-yellow flowers and a perfume that wafts in the dry air. Marko comes to shake hands, affable, genuinely so, asks how the trip was, and so on, then helps Pa out of the car, in passing handing his gun to the other farmer, who is introduced as Frans; for the rest, the whole farmyard with all the other people and dogs has settled into a lull at the sight of the figure, helpless between Marko and Sissy, she who apparently can't stop saying: 'Pappie, we missed you so.'

A jackal hunt is being planned, which accounts for the activity in the yard. Five lambs killed last night, seven the night before. No, things can't carry on like that. Pa brings it all to a halt, raises his hand; it's now even quieter. They are standing on the rough lawn that in the stark white floodlights appears more yellow than green and is clearly only just being kept alive. He wants to know, he says, he just wants to know if they don't tie bells to the lambs' necks. And has Marko made sure that there aren't gaps in his fences. To which Sissy replies, 'Ag, Pappie. My dearest, dear Pappie.' Marko laughs in a way that can only be described as good-natured, which makes Mattheüs think that he can't be altogether an arsehole, and in turn gives him hope that the weekend may after all go quite smoothly.

Apart from that, a drowsiness overcame him on the dirt road, especially the last bit to the farmyard, more or less from the railway track, with the smell of herbs and dust given off by the half-dead scrub and the almost-not-sweetness of the granaatbos here and there that is opportunistically sprouting yellow blooms.

It's a to-and-fro chatting, with dogs that break loose and jump up, the three children who huddle behind their mother, waiting to be told what to say and how to behave with their oupa. Shy, they've only ever seen blindness in sheep.

'Come closer, so that Oupa can touch you.'

They press forward until their children's heads are under the old man's hands, extended waist-high, suspended there.

'This is Anna,' (she was named for her grandmother), 'this is Leona, say hello nicely to your oupa, Leona,' when she wants to squirm away, 'and this is Leeutjie,' the youngest.

From the direction of the rondavel, positioned at some distance to the north of the farmhouse under a copse of bluegums on bare soil, Uncle Hannes comes walking with his clutch of dogs – a mix-and-match little fox terrier mongrel, a sheepdog with gentle eyes, and two smaller dogs of mixed parentage. Pipe in hand. 'Goodness gracious, Bennie, there's nothing left of you,' he smiles, literally pushes Sissy and her children aside and hugs his brother, hands him back to them so as to hug Mattheüs in turn, 'Such nice sturdy shoulders, my goodness, man.'

The people all cluster together on the stoep with its six yellow bulbs in six old-fashioned bakelite shades evenly spaced on the ceiling, and wicker chairs and a bright-red geranium in a barrel, an outstanding specimen and Sissy's pride. Here, Marko and his friend Frans take their leave after receiving a basket containing two thermos flasks of coffee and four two-litre bottles of Coke from the kitchen. The jackal hunt will keep them out until daybreak.

'What does his oncologist say, how much time does he give him?' Sissy asks later, at table.

'They no longer tell you that sort of thing, Sissy.'

It's only the two of them here. Uncle Hannes had one glass of merlot and then excused himself; he prefers eating his food in the rondavel. For Pa, she's made fresh weak black tea – he'd only eat one of the left-over Marmite sandwiches – and put him in bed, so exhausted that one couldn't tell whether he was even just a little pleased to be there.

Mattheüs doesn't sit down, even though the food is on the table – this is regarded as impolite.

'Come and sit down now, Matt.'

From where he's standing on the other side of the open-plan room, looking back at Sissy as she dishes up, glancing every now and then at the clock above the sideboard, he indicates that he's coming. She's jittery, with the dogs and Marko out till who knows when. He parts the curtains in front of the big sitting-room window and looks at the yellow lawn lit up outside, with its encircling bed of agapanthus which Sissy is still trying to keep going, a fine example of how people around here battle against barrenness. He closes the curtains. The food has been dished up, she's looked at the clock again. Towards the back, down the passageway, the antics, shrill and silly, of the three children in their bedroom are heard once or twice, and then no more.

Next to the wall clock hangs a calendar with a photo of the local Laingsburg rugby team. Mattheüs inspects the players and notices the flank, third row, second from the right, hair straight as flax, sallow-skinned, broad shoulders filling out the rugby jersey, one more peek, and turns around to sit down. Sissy gazes at him: impossible that she could have followed his train of thought, the thoughts that now unspool, while he sits down and unfurls the serviette from Ouma's trousseau (he doesn't mind that she got it, it belongs here), as Sissy holds her hand out to his to say grace: unspool in the total silence of the room, the silence outside in the farmyard where nothing is stirring, with only his sister's voice rising and falling to intone the prayer with the necessary respect, with the last word, amen, a mere whisper, only her lips, wide and full like Pa's, breathing on it, and then she lets go of his hand, his thoughts opening like a sluice in the wake of the prayer, the futility of his takeaway concept, leaving him astonished at the sudden and overwhelmingly negative idea that he will *not* succeed in opening Duiker's Takeaway next Wednesday, and even if he does, it's doomed to failure.

He, Mattheüs, day after day in a takeaway, with customers chronically insistent on friendliness, on a little extra, no matter that he started at six that morning, and he, he of all people thinks he'll be able to handle it. He gets up.

'Sissy, give me a minute, please. I'm going outside for a moment for a cigarette.'

'What's the matter, Matt? You can smoke in here, man. For you, I'll make an exception.'

Should he take her into his confidence or not? Poultry, jackals, carting children to school on a dirt road, outfits at the new Worcester Mall, the Swartberg behind them like a bulwark against the coast, in front of them as far as the eye can see, the Great Karoo: the sum total of her world that hardly at any point overlaps with his. She probably shares Pa's image of him as the wastrel of the family, although she's never said it, it's even possible that the assumption is a fabrication: he's overwhelmed by a wave of self-doubt.

'I wanted to start my takeaway on Wednesday, my idea of good food at affordable prices for ordinary people – low-income, poor people, you know. And now, ag, I don't know. I don't know if I can. Or if I should.'

'I've heard about the business.' She stuffs a chunk of lamb into her mouth and says nothing more. He shouldn't have told her about it. Stupid exposed prick he's made of himself, that's all.

The fireplace in the lounge area of the room has been stacked, even though it's still only February. Pages of the Sunday paper have been scrunched up into pieces the size of a tennis ball and put on the grid, with kindling criss-crossed on top. He bends down and blows his cigarette smoke up the chimney as he hears Sissy chewing. He glances at her over his shoulder. She eats, wipes her mouth with the serviette, fills her fork again, looks up at the clock, carries on eating, apparently unperturbed.

And then there's Jack, whose loyalty he doubts right now more than ever before. And what about his own loyalty, his loyalty to Jack? Has he ever told the man that he loves him? And then there's Pa in the guest room, his pyjama-covered arms crossed over his chest on top of the sheet as he usually does even when it's cold – his uneven breathing barely audible – lost somewhere in his morphine valleys, the dreadful alienation it must make him feel, ag, Pa. And there's the ever more constricting matrix of his own porn obsession, the action and effects of which become clearer by the day, the deformation of his brain that causes or activates the hunger, the images that feed the new circuitry, and in gorging the obsession is intensified, with his sex ever more bent and battered to conform to a closed circuit where only he and the screen in front of him exist. He shudders, puts out his cigarette on the stone floor of the fireplace, tries to turn his back on his last thought, tries, really tries, and again takes his place at the dinner table.

'Your food's going to be ice-cold now. Matt, my question just now. How long?'

'What does it really matter, Sissy? We all die when we have to. They don't know. He could live for years, still.' (He doesn't really think so.) 'Professor Jannie de Lange didn't say,' he lies.

'Ag, come on. Don't lie to me. They know very well how long their patients have to live. They deal with cases like this every day, they know exactly.'

He looks at all the food on the table. There's roast lamb on an antique oval serving dish that also belonged to Ouma. Then there's roasted pumpkin with cinnamon, sugar and butter, as well as frozen green peas from the Laingsburg Spar, a pyrex dish with Tastic rice, and a pretty floral jug, also Ouma's, with fresh mint leaves in boiled water, everything sober, honest.

'I like your food, Sissy. I've missed it. Pity Pa can't enjoy it. He always did love his food so much. He ate with such enjoyment.'

'A fortnight, a month, six months?' The children's voices unexpectedly rise again. 'I …' Sissy looks towards the passage. When the noise dies down, as she expects it to at this hour of the evening, she glances once again at the hands of the clock, and then back at him.

Slowly, he spins the serving dish with the leg of lamb and finds the small chip that he knows, the one that Oupa carefully filed down so that all it left was an even dent on the lip of the dish.

He rubs it. 'He doesn't really eat any more. So you can think for yourself. I still manage to get him to take some of that Sustagen powder – he can only handle the vanilla – but apart from that, not much. You must watch him this weekend, Sissy. It gets to you, you know, twenty-four seven. And the daily deterioration. That's the worst to see. And don't think he's an easy person. As you know. I've nagged him to get a nurse, but he says he doesn't want to squander your and my inheritance. When he can no longer go to the toilet on his own, maybe then, he says. He's almost there, I think. But he's okay, I mean, it's not that I'm complaining. He's not that bad. The morphine helps a lot. It completely knocks him out.'

She's shifted backwards so that the low-hanging light illuminates her from the neck downwards. In her hand, a glass of merlot: 'Do you hold it against me?'

'What?'

'Ag, you know what I'm talking about, Matt.'

He lays his knife and fork side by side, as they were taught to do, wipes his mouth, folds the serviette, and places it to the left of his plate where it had originally been set. 'Should we take the food to the kitchen before I smoke here?'

She flaps a hand dismissively. 'Do you realise you've adopted many of Pa's mannerisms?' He tries to gauge her tone: compassion or plain vindictiveness? He thinks he knows, even though there's hardly any light on her face. She's also got something of Pa. The direct, tactless way of talking – attacks, in effect. Her broad, open forehead and the broad smile, when it appears, are pure Pa.

'I'm his primary carer, there's no doubt about that. As I say, it's not always easy, but I'm not complaining. I'm okay.' He half-fills his glass, as they do in the city, not all the way to the top, like here.

'I think only one person at a time can care for somebody. That's the way it is in most of the families I know around here. One child knows exactly how, and takes over the care. I've got no problem with that. Nor do you, apparently. This business of yours. Wouldn't a restaurant selling liquor make more money?'

He becomes wary of her. 'That's exactly what I don't want to do. I want to do something for the poor people of Cape Town. A small contribution, maybe. Nothing more.'

'And who'll look after Pa then?'

'You!'

'Ag, don't be ridiculous, Matt. You know as well as I do that it's totally impossible for me. I've got three children and a husband to take care of. We're up against a drought of close to seven years. Do you think it's easy to keep this farm going? Pappie, won't you quickly write me out a cheque, we've run out of feed for the sheep.' (So she knows about the cheque as well.)

'Don't start your nonsense, Sissy.' He picks up the second bottle that's been standing open at the far end of the table and fills both their glasses.

'I warned Marko, I knew you were coming here with an agenda. I can't get away from here. I can't go and look after Pa, it's out of the question.'

'I'm joking, Sissy. You needn't take everything so damn seriously. It was Pa who wanted to come here. I think we owe it to him: let him enjoy it. It's his last time, he won't come again. D'you know, what I'm sorriest about is that he can't smell the Karoo veld any more.'

'But who's going to look after him when you're working all day? How many days a week is this takeaway thing of yours open?'

Little shit. Sometimes he's tempted to tell Pa to change his will so as not to leave her a cent.

'There's Aunt Sannie next door and there's Samantha, I think she'd take on more hours if you offered, and on Sundays I won't be open, I don't know yet. We'll figure it out somehow. We always have. And Pa doesn't need someone with him all day, every day. As long as he can phone. Thank heavens he can still manage that.'

'I hear what you're saying, but I know you're holding back. You resent me, I can see it in that look of yours. D'you know what, Matt, even if I could, I wouldn't look after Pa. I'd force him to get a nurse or I'd pay for one myself. He's too much for me. I don't want to mess around with our relationship at this stage, I want it to remain just as it is between me and Pa. How are Samantha and them?'

'Okay. They're okay.'

Then Sissy starts telling him things. He hears and also doesn't hear; even though some of it is new, he knows the kind of stuff she talks about. The wine has made him slightly drunk and subdued, and he'd rather be in the company of his computer. He digs out his mobile phone and waves it over the table as if it were a fan. 'Do you still have no reception here in the bundu? Why doesn't Marko put up an antenna on the mountain? There are ways of doing these things, you know.'

'Do you think for a moment money grows on trees out here in the veld? Do you know what, Matt. Oh, let it be. We'll leave it right there. In any case, you think I don't know anything. You think I'm stupid. Do you think I don't know about you?'

Without waiting for his reply (she's convinced her deductions are correct), she switches on the television and for a long time they sit there watching junk. Sissy has settled herself on the four-seater couch, her legs stretched out, every now and then she wiggles her toes against his thigh: she's not in a huff.

'What's keeping the men at this time of the night?' she asks again.

On the opposite wall of the sitting room, she's hung a copper frieze of a pride of lions. It's not his taste. And yet. The total seclusion here at Luiperdskop, the silence both outside and inside, in spite of the TV racket, soothes him, brings him to rest in a wholesome place. He wakes when Sissy suddenly gets up. The men are back earlier than she'd expected. That's either good news or bad. She's on her feet looking at him.

'One last thing, Matt. If I may. I always feel I have to tiptoe around you. And what for? What the hell for? But okay, that's another thing that I won't go into right now. Just this one thing: please don't let Pa's will be tampered with. He's told me what he's left to everyone and I know what's in it. That's all I ask of you. Nicely, please.'

Fucking hell. He refills his glass, right to the top like they do here, and lights another cigarette from the butt. Sissy gets up with her arms folded across herself and unlocks the front door and goes outside. 'Hey, you people,' her voice echoes across the yard. 'Hulloo-hulloo-hulloo, yes, there we are, Devil, don't jump up, hello, my doggie. Did you give the jackal a hard time, my dog? Oh, here's Socks too, ag, Socks, look at that blood on your nose.'

The men come in, full of themselves – not with conceit, just full of the experience they share with each other as well as the other four and the horses and dogs, all of them waiting there down-wind in the veld with a cigarette and a swig from the hip flask, speech reduced to a single word, to breathing, waiting for creatures that are a hundred times more cunning than they are at night in the open veld. Now they're back with the experience – only two jackals that they'd managed to finish off in the veld, one a knackered old thing – and left old Grootpiet behind in the veld with his dogs, which is the only way of nailing the creatures.

It's the exclusivity of the experience that he'd never be able to share in, Mattheüs thinks as he watches Marko pouring drinks for Frans and himself without asking him, Matt, whether he might not also like one. Khaki shirts and camouflage pants, Marko in Jeep boots, Frans in running shoes, that and the smell of gun oil, of dust and veld and a bit of blood, conspicuously macho: he doesn't cut it, he's not one of them. Hunting is normal, the checking of the magazine before slipping the gun into the hatstand is routine, Frans who now in full view of the company digs wax from his left ear and inspects it in the light; that's how men here go about it, men who make a living from cattle in the veld, who marry and make children, the day's work done, you crawl into bed next to your wife and if your luck is in, you get to admire her, not her, but her sex with all its parts, get to make love to her there, the miracle of it and the loveliness of it, the normality of that smell of hers with all the additional nuances that he can hardly describe from first-hand experience (the other one he knows a little better), and that here on the farm is presented as the norm without a second thought, so much so that it's difficult not to succumb to it and start doubting your own normality.

Marko drops into his chair. 'Fuck, I'm knackered,' Sissy on his lap with his arm around her waist, his hand holding the glass on her thigh in yellow tights.

He'd fallen into an unusually deep sleep after a failed attempt at vividly calling up the flank in the rugby photo, second row, third from the right, for the kind of stimulation that made him realise the value of internet porn. He was still thinking of this when he'd apparently drifted off again on the single bed with its second-rate mattress and yellow floral sheets, then woken early. Now he's up and about in the balmy February morning, up the mountain among the spekboom where he hop-skip-and-jumps to the flat rock where his pile of marker stones has been tossed about, as he'd expected.

Two messages come through on his iPhone, each with a photo. Another one of Jack and Jamie, which is to say emotional blackmail, and the second is a mysterious one of Jack in front of their gate at number nine Poinsettia Road. Both messages are cryptic, the gate one says: *Look who came calling*. It's impossible to get clarity on Jack's motives. Behind and above him he hears baboons beginning to go about their business. From here, there's nothing he can do with the messages, he's not even going to reply to them. He's not going to get jealous, that would be out of character for him, and he won't get upset or whatever. He switches off his mobile phone, starts running downhill as fast as he can without losing his step; if he sprains an ankle, he can't open on Wednesday.

All the way down to Uncle Hannes's rondavel with the barking dogs, he runs, and smells the coffee. Uncle Hannes says he's been waiting for him. Uncle Hannes is wearing sunglasses even though he's indoors; he's dressed in his usual uniform of flapping turn-ups, pale-pink shirt and cravat, his bald head lightly oiled: 'You can still be handsome if you try, Uncle Hannes,' to which his uncle smiles, putting his cup of coffee with two aniseed rusks in the saucer in front of him. The dogs have the freedom of the house and lie down wherever they like, on the chairs or on the lynx-pelt bedspread on his bed, a rickety old thing. Just not on his lap when he's dressed like this – Uncle Hannes chucks off a small one that tries its luck.

Even though it's not real coffee, it's good. His current reading matter with its guinea fowl feather bookmark lies on the coffee table – F. Scott Fitzgerald's *The Great Gatsby*. Uncle Hannes notices him taking it all in and winks. He says he's been thinking about Mattheüs's visit; there's more than enough time here in the Karoo to reflect, and has decided to share something with him this time that he's always kept to himself. He doesn't look at Mattheüs while he talks, then he gets up, opens the drawer of the dresser and takes out a framed photo. He says he trusts Mattheüs because, after all, he knows about him and Jack, how things are between them. Mattheüs must please remember that he regards this as completely private, it must remain between the two of them, please, his father, dear old Bennie, ag, to think that he's also on his way out now, but there you are then, it goes without saying that it's a matter that Bennie cannot and never ever could or would deal with. He taps his middle finger on the glass in the frame, then brings the picture across, the four dogs tracking him with their eyes.

'So that's my Paul.' He pronounces it 'Pole'.

A black-and-white street photo of a man from the nineteen-fifties, legs crossed and cigarette in hand, coffee cup on a round table in front of him, forming part of a row of tables and wicker chairs on a sidewalk, with a plate-glass window behind them both, clearly recognisable as a bistro in Paris or some other French city.

Uncle Hannes has meanwhile turned round – two dogs jumping to the floor as they misinterpret the movement as going for a walk – the dresser is opened and he takes out a bottle of brandy, adding a stiff slug to his coffee. Mattheüs nods and is given one too. Clearly a weighty matter this, for Uncle Hannes.

A Free Stater is how he describes the man; he'd left for overseas one day and never came back to South Africa, not to his people and nor to their Free State farm, never once. Can you imagine? So then Paul said he should come and join him, there's a life awaiting them over there. He painted a very, very rosy picture of it all, but then, sadly, there was no money. He couldn't very well beg from his father; that was out of the question. And by the time money did become available, when Luiperdskop was left to him and Bennie after his father's death, and later when Marko came along and bought the farm from them, 'Ag, good heavens, Mattie, by that time I'd long since lost touch with Paul.'

He fetches a blue envelope stored in a plastic bag; this then was Paul's last letter, 1964, after that he never again replied to his, Hannes's, letters. He suspects he'd said something he shouldn't have. Uncle Hannes ends the story there, sits down, letter in hand, avoiding Mattheüs's eyes.

They remain sitting like that, surrounded by Uncle Hannes's possessions: the horns mounted on the curved wall, knick-knacks consisting mainly of found objects from the veld or from the mountain, long blue-grey crane feathers pushed between two books and pointing upwards to the cone-shaped thatched roof, a handful of old marbles in a bottle, a dried tortoise shell, reddish stones with fern fossils – that kind of thing. On the green waxed stoep by the door – there is only a single entrance to the rondavel – sparrows peck away and scurry about. A wedge of morning sun slants in upon the two of them, warming the dusk inside.

Well, Paul probably gave up on him, you can't hold it against him that he didn't want to keep the hope alive. Paul realised that he'd never make it to the other side. He was a curly-head, as Mattheüs can see, it was fashionable in those days to keep your hair quite short. But as he remembers Paul when he was still in South Africa, he also had a curl at the back of his neck, 'A scandalous little kiss-curl,' Uncle Hannes laughs wryly, that's what he remembers about him.

Mattheüs gets up and holds Uncle Hannes's head close to his

body. Uncle Hannes responds to the gesture by hugging him too, though clumsily, the dogs' eyes once again on the two of them, then he pushes him away, gets up from the chair rather heavily, and taking a cloth he walks over to the kudu horns above the dresser to whisk away a cobweb that he's spotted. He says he appreciates Mattheüs's sympathy, however that's not what he was seeking in telling the story. He's long past self-pity, long past it.

'Life on the farm teaches you to put up with a lot, Mattie. Otherwise you go under.'

Another slug of brandy for each of them in their coffee – mostly brandy by now, the coffee having been drunk. 'Ag, Mattie, what more is there to say?' Throughout the years on Luiperdskop, first in the main house and later here in the rondavel where, as he can see, he's made himself reasonably comfortable. Throughout the years he's seen droughts come and go, changes in the breed of sheep, merinos replaced by the hardier dorpers, his mother buried first, then his father. Bennie's success with the beautiful German cars he observed from a distance, and he, what about him, was he left behind? No, he wasn't, he persuaded himself. He visited his friends, both men and women, in town, the librarian in Beaufort West, a few of the farming families, ag, all in all no more than a handful. He regained hope, yes, hope, and then lost it again as the interminable years passed, ag, Mattie. And what is he actually trying to say with all of this? What can he say? 'Mattie, to be absolutely honest, I don't know.'

There was something else. There is. He supposes he can, ag, he doesn't know how to. There was a sentence in his last letter, Mattie must understand, there was a sentence that he'd written and which he later realised – of course when it was too late – must have been the death knell.

'I find it dreadfully difficult to say it, nobody has ever heard it, I suppose it's the kind of stuff that you'd sit and spout to a psychologist. The sentence, then, ag, Mattie, you see I can hardly get it out, anyway, I went and wrote: *I want to hold you close to me day and night, my Paul*.

He believes that this was the end between them. After that, Paul's letters from Paris dried up. That letter was overburdened with neediness, 'Do you understand, Mattie?' That sentence had put the wind up Paul. The man will come over to Paris and smother him. He's used to nothing out there in the dust and sticks, he yearns for you-know-what, and that's still okay, but a man who's too starved is of no use to anybody. Everything, it was all in that sentence, Paul couldn't read past it.

Now, whenever he goes for a walk with the dogs, he likes going to the wetlands, 'you know, don't you, where this is on the farm, at the back, to the north-east, there's strong spring water there,' that discordant sentence keeps echoing in his head. At night, when he's lying in bed reading, drifting in and out of the story as sleep overwhelms him and he eventually lets go and his mind clears again and he picks up the book that's lying on his stomach and he carries on reading, as a rule he's then at ease and contented, until the time comes to close the book and turn over and try to sleep and then, then that sentence returns with a vengeance, you might say, to haunt him. Year in, and year out. He's tried all possible techniques, some of them picked up from self-help books, for instance, you pretend that the sentence is a material thing and you go through the motions of wrapping it in a parcel, sealing it, and sending it away. He's prayed, too, everything, but that sentence keeps echoing in his ears. With a single stroke he destroyed the most precious thing in his life, once and for all. There's nothing to be done about it. It's irreversible.

At this point, Uncle Hannes is so upset that in getting to his feet he bumps the coffee table, and the cups and ashtray and things all tremble a bit and a few books fall to the floor. He clutches his forehead and moves to the far side of the rondavel, to a room divider with three silk panels painted with pale Chinese boatmen, and there he sinks to his knees, his head hanging in shame, the dogs all around him, wagging their tails. 'I was unwise. No, too eager. Too greedy. My Paul got cold feet, and who can blame him? Everything wiped out in one sentence. Lord, have mercy on me.'

A little girl peeps around the door of the rondavel: 'Mamma wants to know if the uncles want bacon and eggs for breakfast?' Mattheüs nods and gestures to her to leave. She seems to understand and ambles off home.

He is touched by the confession. He tells Uncle Hannes that he is too hard on himself, 'please, Uncle Hannes, after all these years, still so much self-flagellation,' and knows, as he's saying it, that these are idle words that will make no difference. This is the life story of a hermit on a farm in the Great Karoo, caught in his own cycle of reflection and regret, a torment that becomes more and more of a burden as time goes by.

Uncle Hannes at last gets up from among the licking dogs, fetches the photo of Paul in the wooden frame and puts it back in its place. Then he walks to the hand basin right at the back, next to the shower cubicle that's closed off with a plastic curtain, and washes his face.

He offers Mattheüs more coffee and pours a third dash of brandy without waiting for a reply. He says he's heard of Mattheüs's business in the city and he wants to wish him every success. This time he fetches something from the wardrobe, rummages among the shoeboxes at the bottom and produces a box, a purple shoebox with Florsheim printed in faded gilt. He sits down, opens the shoebox, and produces an object inside a leather pouch. 'Dassie hide.' He holds it out for Mattheüs to take. 'It's yours now.'

'But what is it, Uncle Hannes?' He's suddenly suspicious.

'Open it. I'm giving it to you today. You'll need it.' Mattheüs opens the soft hide and finds what he expected, a pistol that he leaves inside the pouch on his lap, a blue-black colour, just a shade off black, in fact.

'I can't accept it, Uncle Hannes. Thank you very much, but it's not me. If someone started shooting at me or whatever, I don't know. I suppose it'd be a case of my time has come.'

Uncle Hannes suddenly becomes quite animated. He says Mattheüs is being a bit too, how shall he say? The men who have their roots on this farm have never been shy. So, where's he going to work? Where is his business? Main Road, Observatory. Well, now, that's one of those gangster streets, isn't it? He's there all alone on the premises and it soon gets late, with his whole day's takings on him, 'It's a cash business, not so?' No, Mattie must keep his wits about him, give it a bit of thought.

Matthéüs holds out the dassie-hide bag with the gun; Uncle Hannes starts fiddling with the thing, showing how it works. Here, he points at the barrel: Beretta. It's the Cougar 8000 series, the Italians used to manufacture it, now it's made by Turks. You can't get any better. Easy to conceal, he's taken it to Cape Town how many times, walked up and down Adderley Street with the thing in his trouser pocket, through the Gardens, everywhere, ready to take on anyone looking for trouble. And nice and light, too, it's like walking about with two rather than one in your pants, he jokes.

Matthéüs is surprised and pleased at Uncle Hannes's sudden high spirits after his sad story. But on the matter of weapons, a gun, he and Uncle Hannes part ways.

It's got a double-stack magazine, Uncle Hannes continues, like a real weapons instructor, it's a nine-millimetre, he says. It takes fifteen rounds, here's the safety catch, on the slide, easy to handle. Here, take it, feel how it sits in your hand. It's got a lovely grip. A pity I lost the holster. But the dassie hide's also fine, actually even better.' When Matthéüs still doesn't hold out his hand, Uncle Hannes takes his right hand in his own and places the gun in it.

'So there, you see,' says Uncle Hannes when he notices that Matthéüs is beginning to show an interest, and positions the butt of the gun so that it fits into his palm, or at any rate feels as if it fits, he's not used to weapons at all.

Uncle Hannes sits down with one of the smaller dogs on his lap, now permitted in celebration of the transfer of the Beretta, and no doubt also as consolation for his eternally lost Paul.

Should he, Matthéüs wonders, must he accept it? Or is he completely crazy now? He immediately conjures up a couple of scenarios like the one sketched by Uncle Hannes, even though he's never in his life walked down Main Road, Observatory. Late afternoon on that street, behind his counter with the left-over food and especially the day's takings, a weapon might be useful even though he'd never want to use it. On the other hand, if you do have one on you, you can always threaten; he can reconcile himself with that, he can imagine himself in a situation like that. Beretta, he reads on the barrel. Quite neatly made. Actually, damn good-looking.

The rest of that day, he and Uncle Hannes practise target shooting with the Beretta, faded Coke and Fanta cans in a row on a ridge far away from people and animals; he couldn't say why or from where, maybe it's something in his genes, but after a while he's an ace shot and nails the cans one by one. When Marko comes to have a look, he hits five out of the seven cans, while Marko hits four. Cut or with a foreskin, hard or flaccid between the legs, an older guy all beard and bush on sand-coloured sheets in a sleazy motel, images from his photo archive flash across his mind when he stiffens his arm, takes aim and pulls the trigger.

And yet. The steaming piles of dung from this morning's milk cows, for instance, are also there, and Sissy with the dish of crisply fried bacon, and Marko, ag, he's got no evil intent, and the soil where they're standing, the dryness of the air that he breathes, and the tiny grey veld birds – after a while these things come to constitute the chief content of his consciousness.

All the time, too, he needs to know how Pa is getting along. Wants to go to the kraal, and makes Sissy and the children take him there. He wants to go to the dip tank where his father drove the cattle at the start of winter to prevent tick paralysis. All over the farm there are particular places he wants to go to, and mostly he has to be driven there. Mattheüs never goes along, just needs to know where his father is each time. And has he had his Sustagen yet, and so on.

'You're not his keeper, after all,' she says. But he is, and she knows it. She listens to him even though she doesn't like doing so.

'It's high time Pa took a nap,' says Mattheüs when they return from a trip in Marko's 4×4 bakkie to the cement dam in the kraal closest to the farmyard. That's where Pa used to collect weaver-bird eggs as a child, he wanted to go and have one last (he says this himself) look.

At dusk, he suppresses the impulse to climb up to the flat stone to check his messages. And then remembers Uncle Hannes's hand gesture, how at the end of the shooting session he handed him the Beretta, pushed it at him, as it were. There, take this thing away from me. The looking away and then, looking up again, the sudden alarm, there, in his urgent glance: don't you get it? Take this thing away from me.

He fetches a beer from Marko's bar and walks into the veld on his own, due west; his arm held out in front of him is orange-brown in the light of the setting sun. He sits down under a thorn tree, emptied of almost all thoughts of Jack and of his business that must open on Wednesday, or not. It takes honesty to admit that it's happened to him on this barren farm, among people with ways that are not like his (Sissy uses Aromat), far away from the city that he regards as his heimat, his true homeland.

When he returns to the farmyard and walks into the sitting room, Pa is in the recliner with a rug over his knees and earphones plugged into his ears. He's listening to *Liewe Heksie*, Sissy explains. He's had a wonderful time today. Look, his cheeks have even got colour.

He bends over his father and takes his hand. Pa knows immediately from his touch who it is: 'Oh, it's you, Mattie,' and the earphones are pulled out. Pa draws him closer to say into his ear: 'I've done everything I wanted to do. I'm ready. We can get going quite early tomorrow. They really don't know how to handle me here, Mattie. I'm ready to go home.'

Sissy (she's making rusks to be taken to Cape Town) immediately demands to know: What is he saying, what is it this time that Pa doesn't want to share with her? She tends to be distrustful.

He's just saying that he's ready to go home. 'Oh,' she says.

For the first time ever, in his role as his father's primary caregiver, he feels superior to his sister. Maybe that's not the right word: equipped, better than she is with her husband and three children and chickens and orphaned lambs and whatnot that she has to see to; the fragile body of their father, that she cannot deal with.

When she kisses him goodnight in the passage with the triptych of wedding photos on the wall, she again asks him to please see to it that the will is not meddled with (her phrase). Mattheüs does not answer her. It's clear that the intimacy between him and Pa unnerves her.

My dear son,

Pa doesn't know whether this could perhaps be one of his last recordings. It's getting too much for me, the talk-talk-talk. If the Lord wants me to go, I resign myself to His will. But I want to believe that it's not my time yet. I can feel here on the desk the flowers that you put into a vase for me. What kind are they? Oops, Pa can't find the pause on the old Philips. I suppose they must be daisies. Ag, my child, what would I do without you?

I'm going to get right to the point here. Not that I really know why now, of all times. That's how thoughts and all kinds of things enter my mind. Pa has always wanted to tell you about the doors of the Mercedes. Pa thinks you may not realise exactly what has gone into those doors. The technology and the refinement. All I really want is for you to appreciate those doors as I appreciate them. Look, all those years before I got the Mercedes agency, it was always General Motors cars, as a matter of course. Chevs and Pontiacs, and so on. Also quite good cars, mind you. And then, later, all the Japanese cars came along. But it was only with the Mercedes that I discovered how a door should really shut.

Ag, I remember it very well, the model, a pitch-black 220S, you know the one with the fins on either side of the boot, it was one of the most beautiful Mercedes cars they ever made. A cousin of mine, Karl-Hendrik, you know, the eldest son of my Uncle Jan, came driving up one afternoon to our house in Observatory in his swanky car. Get in, he said to me, and he drove us to Sea Point. Once we were there, he told me to get out and to get back in again and then to shut the door. Ag, by that time I was in love with the car already, the red leather seats and the creamy-marble steering wheel and the beautiful walnut of the dashboard, there was no comparison with the Americans. So I got out as Karl told me to, we always called him Kallie. An attractive man, looked after himself too. Women? Listen, there wasn't a woman on this earth that he couldn't sweet-talk.

So anyway, I got back into the car and closed the door behind me. No, he said, get out again. You closed the door too hard. It's not necessary with a Mercedes. You bring the door to within a few inches of yourself and then you just pull it ever so lightly towards you, that's all that's required. So I did as Kallie instructed me, and then I knew exactly what he meant.

It's a kind of lubricated click into its lock. Man, the Germans knew just how. It's not those tinny doors of the General Motors cars. Here you're dealing with a totally different class of craftsmanship. Do you know, as I'm sitting here, I can hear exactly the gentle click as the Mercedes door neatly shuts.

Ag, I know you and Sissy and your mother sometimes looked at me askance when I asked you please not to slam the doors like that. And sometimes there was more to those looks of yours, especially your mother's, than just a look. It's not as if I didn't notice it. I'm also just human, you know, Mattie.

You can say today, yes Pa, it was only a door, after all. Your cars came first, then your family. And perhaps that's how it was. Pa just wanted to teach you appreciation of the outstanding technology of the Mercedes car. In the end it may have been a way of understanding something about your father. After all, it was those cars that earned us a living, that sent you to university and overseas, everything we have.

You'll say you understand me, Mattie. And I suppose that's also true. You're right. You're an intelligent person with a soft heart. Ag, I find this such a sad business. I'll have to say more about it next time.

I simply wanted to tell you about my appreciation for the door of the Mercedes, so that you can understand. And old Kallie, the show-off. You know, Mattie, if I really have to be straight with you today, I was sometimes jealous of my cousin. His way with women, man, that takes some doing. Now I don't know how it works with you people, but it's not easy, Mattie, to be with only one woman all your life. That's a thing that becomes a real burden for a man when he starts pushing middle age.

Now I'm tired and I'm going to finish off for now. You're a good son to me, Mattie. That's what Pa wants you to know, my child. Pa is by no means perfect either.

Pa.

It's the day before the opening of Duiker's Takeaway. While his lamb-and-tomato stew is simmering, and the pot of lentil dahl (with boiled butternut for a bit of sweetness under the chilli) is cooling on a special rack, he slips away to have his hair cut at Chauvel's. 'Jeez, Matt, why are you so tense?' he's asked when Vaughn washes his hair, massages his scalp and also gives him a bit of a shoulder rub.

He wishes he could say he's not scared. He's scared his business concept won't come off, he's scared he doesn't have the stamina for all that standing and cooking, on your feet all day long, and he's scared all his father's generously donated money will go down the drain – and what will Sissy say then? – and he's scared his father will finally give up on him. Just this once, he thinks. If not for his own sake, at least for the sake of the old man so that he can go to his grave contented. And the one thing he's always been confident of, the flavour of his food, he's even scared about that. While Vaughn is rubbing product into his hair and starts styling it, standing back and checking and working his head again with nimble fingers, he texts Jack (chilly ever since he and his father returned to the city on Monday) please to drop in at Duiker's to test his food.

Mirror behind his head. He has to be off, no more time for this shit; and as he leaves: 'You must remember to come and support me, you lot!'

'But you're the one we're after,' shouts Vaughn, pulling his lower lip down with a long finger.

Into his bakkie, changing radio stations and changing to another again, and still Jack hasn't texted him back. It's four o'clock; he stopped teaching long ago.

'Jack?'

'The person you have called is not available.'

He races to Zilverbosch, and concentrates on shifting his attention from his disappointment about Jack (which could trip him up) to the savoy cabbage pickle with chilli, fresh ginger, and sesame oil, rather like the Korean kim-chi, which he wants to get done before this evening. Red-faced, he knocks at Jack's door, walks in without waiting for a response.

Jack is standing in the middle of his flat like a person who has just moved into a bare space and now has to decide what to do next. It is bare indeed, everything has been taken from the walls. Jack's stuff is all lined up: one large suitcase, one medium-sized suitcase, and a small one lying open on his bed for the last few things, one box with books, and another box with all his pictures and smaller stuff. But that's not the point, and he sees it written all over Jack's face. In the rush and bother of driving to the farm and the opening of his takeaway, he's forgotten to remember that it's Jack's last day; he has to clear out of Clarence by tomorrow. Mattheüs doesn't know what to say. Jack didn't let him know either whether he should give him a loan for a bond on a flat. Jack is killing him with his criticism.

'Ag, Jackie, man.'

And he hugs Jack from behind and kisses his neck with a body that smells of food. Where will he stay? Jack shakes his head against his lips.

'With Charnie?'

He refuses to say. Jack frees himself from his embrace and says he's okay, he's worked it all out.

Does he want to come along to the takeaway? Mattheüs is embarrassed to ask him to come and taste his food, but he does need someone for that, he's feeling sick to the pit of his stomach and in Jack's presence – inexplicably – even more scared that his business will fail.

Jack says he has to pack a few more things, arrange some stuff, until what time will Matt still be there, he'll come by later. Mattheüs leaves the place with the echo of Jack's very specific tone of voice in his ears, brusque, low, threatening rather than accusing, and the whole way, in thickening traffic, focuses only on the ingredients of his cabbage pickle.

So then fate chooses the little guy as his food taster. The metal roller shutter over the counter is raised and Mattheüs is chop-chopping when he spots him among the pedestrians: Emile, the Congolese. He has a huge dog with him, a Rottweiler cross, only bigger and more brutish, tugging at his chain, Emile's hand still covered in the leather glove with the half-fingers and the holes for the knuckles. Emile calls to him excitedly, ties the monster dog to the lamppost and comes to lean on the counter with folded arms, his head only just visible.

Is he going to use cassava leaves in his food, he could let him have some? No, he says, he really is open to all suggestions, but for now he's only going to prepare the food he knows. The short-arse won't leave. Behind his shoulder, on the pavement, the dog is huffing and puffing, slobber drooling from his gums. There's a slight prickliness between them, and Mattheüs inevitably reacts with caution. He wishes he would leave now. No, no food for sale yet. Tomorrow.

At one stage, he has to fetch something from his bakkie parked behind his premises in the four-bay parking area. But he first has to lower the roller shutter, and gestures to the folded arms to get off the counter. Wait, wait, Emile signals, one hand without, and one hand wearing a leather glove: he'll keep an eye on the place while he's gone. There's his dog. Diamond is his name, nobody will come in here.

At this, Mattheüs feels a terrible anxiety, followed by a sudden urge – involuntary, as sudden urges tend to be. 'Watch out,' he shouts, and drops the heavy shutter, the short arms pulled back from the counter just in time. From behind the closed shutter – it's one of those with a steel bar along the bottom that you screw into the wall on either side with a key – there's a howl of indignation. Mattheüs remains standing where he is in the glow of the neon – he'd selected the warmer, daylight type – and tells himself the hell with him, he did the right thing. He has a drink of water from the bottle next to his chopping block, goes out by the door, double-locks it, closes the steel door too, and pretends not to know that Emile is standing right there with the dog that is by now tugging hard at its chain.

'It's my business,' says Mattheüs as he walks off.

In the meantime, Emile has lit a cigarette, holding it between thumb and index finger in his cupped gloved hand: '*Je te comprends.*'

Mattheüs, in turn, understands exactly what he means. Emile implies that he understands everything, more than the takeaway he sees in front of him, whereas in fact there is nothing more to understand. And that's what Mattheüs instinctively doesn't like.

Back with the grater, a piece of kitchen equipment that you grip comfortably with the left hand while grating lemon or naartjie peel against calibrated grooves, everything must be unlocked again and the roller shutter raised. The small guy's still there, squatting next to the rump of his dog, eyes fixed on him, unblinking.

Mattheüs opens his iPhone for a last check, a photo posted on his Wall, no comments. Jack snapping himself in his empty bathroom, middle finger raised in front of him in the traditional up-yours sign. Crude. Okay, if that's his attitude. He's certainly not going to come and taste. So let him spend his last night alone in the hostel. But in spite of his efforts to persuade himself, he can't shake off the chill. All right then, life goes on, and he decides, against his better judgement, to call Emile closer.

Again he comes up to the counter to lean on it with folded arms, the face now open and friendly – the power of persistence – and one after the other, Mattheüs dishes up tablespoons of the tomato-and-lamb stew, the lentil dahl, the chicken curry with coconut milk and fresh coriander, and the cabbage pickle that still needs to soak a little. For each dish a fresh spoon, to prevent saliva on the licked spoon, heaven forbid, from fermenting the food; it's standard hygiene for a commercial kitchen. And maybe it was destined to be this way, he laughs with sheer relief, everything's okay and everything's going to be okay, with none other than the midget Emile, the ordinary street eater, as his first taster.

Emile grabs the plate with all four spoons in it, wanting to squat on the pavement and eat it all. But Mattheüs says no, he has to rinse his mouth between each taste, here's some water, so that he's tasting each dish on its own merits, understand? He nods and takes the plate again, raises the spoon with the lamb stew, his black shirt lifts, and Mattheüs sees his ribs, the taut skin darker than that on his arms and face. He bolts the portion and rinses so that he can try the second one, the chicken and coconut dish. That one's gone too, then the last two. Greedy, like someone who hasn't eaten properly for a long time, everything tastes *délicieux*, *délicieux*, *délicieux* to him, he says. (Is he totally out of his mind, having his food tested by a famished hobo?)

Then he dishes some of the chicken-and-coconut curry into a container because he does after all have pity on the human being (the ribs), and manages to wring it out of him that this was the tastiest one – the creaminess of the coconut milk, of course. He must go now, Mattheüs tells him, he has to finish and lock up.

Emile is already taking the last mouthful of the food that he's just given him, sticks his tongue into the container, chucks container and plastic spoon aside, the dog straining on its chain towards it all. Dustbin, says Mattheüs, but not before Emile has cadged a cigarette from him too, and encourages him again to leave, which he's actually going to do now, the dog chomping at the plastic container, its head reaching almost to Emile's chest. Three, four times he looks around and grins toothily at Mattheüs, and he really does hope that it's nothing more than ordinary friendliness.

Another one from Jack: @ Clarence House. *Early to bed tonight. Got two DVDs from the boys to watch. They won't let me go. Good luck for tomorrow. Will come check it out.* ☺

147

Pa is already settled when he gets home and peeks in. There are slips of paper with messages from Samantha and Aunt Sannie; the latter wasn't supposed to come today already. Pa's week is divided up among him (Mondays, Tuesdays, and Sundays), Samantha (Wednesday and Thursday afternoons) and, against his will, Aunt Sannie (Fridays). Dominee Roelf has agreed to take Pa to oncology for his radiation tomorrow. The dominee is an old family friend, not all that young himself, but still amazingly open-minded for his generation, not a bad preacher, a man he trusts with his father. There's also a bowl of soft Hertzog cookies, 'for your father', from Aunt Sannie, and Samantha has made a list of the week's food that she's prepared for Pa: vegetable soup; tender chicken pie, the filling only, Pa doesn't like the crust any longer. Every dish marked, on the second shelf of the fridge. And: Will you please cut his nails?

He reads Jack on Facebook while he's drying his hair: *Meryl Streep is seriously the best*, and while he's getting dressed he's got his computer on his favourite porn site already and quickly checks through the day's additions, and there and then decides on a video, his deferred reward, and walks barefoot to minister to his father's needs.

'You're so warm, Mattie,' Pa says when he helps him sit up to drink his glass of Sustagen. He holds the back of his father's head, the scalp moves gently under his hand as he takes small sips. His father knows he's looking at him.

'I can see a future for you, Mattie.'

In the dim light of the desk lamp, his father looks beautiful. The sunken cheeks, the just-visible stubble on the chin – odd how the beard is apparently also inhibited by the chemo – the soft, sparse hair like that of a newborn, the movement of the eyeballs behind the lids as if still trying to make out something in the dusk, even if only the heat radiated by his son's body. And it's his father who makes him feel what it feels like the night before opening his own business: a sensation he can compare only with the jumpy but throbbing-thrilling anticipation before you-know-what.

He says he knows Mattie doesn't actually have any kitchen

hands yet, and that's good, in the beginning one has to put one's own shoulder to the wheel. (He's glad his father can't see how tired he is; and he's only just started.)

Hard work's never killed anyone, says his father. One of his golden rules was always to greet all his staff in the morning as he walked in. One by one. He always made sure to look them in the eye and in that way he could tell whether they were still happy or not. The words are uttered in measured tones and remain hanging between him and his father; what might once have been a handy hint now becomes something intimate between the two of them.

'I rely on you, Mattie,' he hands him the empty glass, 'help me to the toilet, then you can carry on with your own stuff. You must have plenty to think about. Remember to be careful with your money, son. Pa knows how it is. But feel free to speak if you're really in a tight spot.'

The steel gate with the fancy 'D' for Duiker's Takeaway – that monster of an account still has to be paid. The welder cheated him, that's for sure.

Inside his room, he involuntarily prepares himself even though he's knackered; a pile of cushions against the headboard, computer to the right next to his side, his breath just beginning to race. Either he'll sleep very well tonight – he's warm, the sustained physical labour still heating his skin – or he'll toss and turn, reviewing the day's events. He gazes over the flickering images at his room, his nest: the photo of Kafka; a CNA poster of Michael Jackson that he's always wanted to take down; a photo of a wild fig tree with a bonobo monkey, on its own for once and yet clearly on the prowl – it's the ape species that humps incessantly (not for procreation, purely for pleasure); the string on the blue-green wall with his sunglasses; a small framed photo of his mother that he knows without quite being able to make it out, she's on Blouberg Beach on a clear day, and she's running at an angle with her arms stretched wide like somebody pretending to fly, set free, in the moment. If only he could hide in this den of filth for ever and ever, his hand always at work. He drifts off with his hand gone to sleep by his side, the computer also dormant, the security of the room overwhelming.

From far away and detached from his craving brain, the sound of the intercom comes buzzing down the passage, into his room and all the way right up to him, animating his slumbering body. The first thing he does is reach down to the towel on the floor and wipe both his hands. He shuts the computer. Listens. Whoever it is has stopped ringing for the moment. There it is again. Pa will wake up if he isn't awake already. He picks up his pants from the floor and puts them on, and again the buzzer sounds. Chances are slim that it's one of the ADT guards. They phone you on your cell or on the landline, as instructed by the client.

He presses the button to activate the screen of the CCTV system: two sharp-pointed ears. A dog – except that a dog doesn't reach that high. He keeps pressing the button and peers at the blue-grey night scene of the pavement and section of road covered by the cameras at the gate. The dog's head, larger than normal and wolf-like, stares straight at him. There's something about the hairiness of the dog hairs and the oddly impassive gaze of the dark pin-hole eyes that doesn't look quite right. And where's the rest of the dog-creature's body? He knows who it is before the deliberately hoarse voice comes over the intercom.

'Matt,' says the dog-mouth, 'it's me. Please open up.'

'Jack, are you crazy? What are you doing here this time of night? What have you got on your head? Wait, I'm coming. Stay right there.'

Barefoot, he runs past the half-open study door with the desk lamp burning (all night – Mattheüs's decree), no rustling or snorting coming from there, which means absolutely nothing, and out onto the paving, silver-tracked by nocturnal snails, the lawn ghostly white with dew that's just starting to smell of the fresher autumn dew.

He slides the gate open to the breadth of a man, and there Jack is, dressed up in his pitch-black, bulging-in-the-fly jeans, cowboy style shirt with rivets for buttons, and the pièce de résistance, the dog's-head mask fitted to his shoulders where it fans out hairily like a luxurious fur collar, slopes up to a neck with tufts of silver hair, followed by the head with its extra-long gleaming snout, a bit moist with dew, even, and inside it the eyeholes that Jack peers through, his real human eyes glittering as he lifts and lowers his snout and turns it this way and that for Mattheüs, to make him laugh, to win him over, and then come the pricked ears, attentive and muscled with fine ear veins and hairs for better hearing, wolf's ears, no less; and last of all, cheeky and right between the ears at the top of the forehead, a stiff tuft that shivers lightly in a breeze that has just come up, or possibly as a result of Jack's inner state, his pent-up anxiety about this moment, the true nature of which Mattheüs only realises when he notices what's to the right of the gate: Jack's pitiable pile of luggage moved close to the wall to escape the gaze of the two CCTV cameras – the big suitcase, the medium-sized suitcase, the small one and the two boxes tied with rope, each with a cleverly made rope handle, and finally a Checkers bag containing bits and pieces. (It's both pathetic and admirable that Jack's earthly possessions are reduced to three suitcases, two boxes and a plastic bag.)

'Jack, have you gone completely crazy?'

Jack goes down on all fours and trots on the spot. The cocked head looks at him with vibrating whiskers, and deep inside is the glint of real eyes. He announces that he's moving in as a dog, his name is Wolfie. Uncle Bennie won't mind, of course. Doesn't he have a soft spot for dogs?

'Get up, for God's sake, Jack, you fucker. You're out of your mind. Take that thing off.'

'I don't want Aunt Sannie to see me. Just until I'm inside.'

Mattheüs looks at the double-storey house next door; he's paralysed with wanting to laugh and wanting to cry and heightened excitement at the thought that this is the dawning of a new era. At last the commandment forbidding him and Jack to bed down together under the paternal roof has been defied, a thought that he simultaneously shies away from as it approaches, comes closer, making him fumble for the cigarettes that he knows are in his bed-room. Jack fishes out his own packet.

Mattheüs again peeks at Aunt Sannie's double-storey through one of the gaps between the gate's fleur-de-lis tips. Night in all the windows on the upper level, downstairs only the security lights illuminating her garden.

Jack gets to his feet, slowly lifts the dog mask from his head until it drops behind his back, hanging from its elastic, the dog muzzle pointing heavenward, and gives Mattheüs a wet, spontaneous kiss.

'I love you, man. Do you really think I'm going to move in with Charnie in Pinelands or into some depressing flat when I can sleep in your bed, Matt? In your house, with all those empty bedrooms just standing there.' Jack carries on talking, but his whole body is shivering. If Mattheüs wants to, he can phone a taxi and send him packing.

Mattheüs looks at the wolf's muzzle that is now perched on top of Jack's head, the mouth open, immobile, with fangs made of hard plastic or something that looks horribly real, and then strokes Jack's back, all the way up to under the mask until he finds Jack's shaven head, that irresistible eroticism of a smooth male head that makes him take his tongue from Jack's mouth, but before he can say anything, Jack says: 'Well, is Wolfie being invited in?'

Way down in the street, Mattheüs sees an ADT guard approaching on a bicycle. 'Stand inside the gate so he doesn't see the mask behind your back.'

'Everything okay here, Mister Matthew?'

He knows him, it's Christopher. The guard shines his powerful torch over the luggage, over him and Jack, and again over Jack so that the rivet buttons glint on his black shirt, and stops on Mattheüs's face.

Mattheüs signals to him to cool it, this is his friend, he's coming to overnight here, just got off the plane.

'He has lots of luggage, I see.'

The man has a sixth sense for the unusualness of the situation, for the tension of the unfinished conversation between the two men. He must divert his attention: 'How is your sister, Chris? I've been thinking about her.' Christopher's sister, a lesbian, was recently raped in Khayelitsha by three young men: to try and 'fix' her same-sex orientation, the *Argus* reported. Both the incident and the fact that Christopher knows Mattheüs is gay have established a strong bond between them.

'She is suffering all the time, the criminals are out on the loose.' His sister bumps into her rapists every now and again, and then they taunt her.

'He's flying out again tomorrow,' Mattheüs says when he notices that Christopher is still looking askance at Jack, who's standing his ground in the gap at the gate.

'Cigarette? Jack, give Chris one of yours.' Then he says goodbye, they also say goodbye, and Mattheüs sends his regards to his sister. Christopher cycles down the street with his crackling two-way radio, the torch flashing this way and that as he passes the homes of ADT clients.

'Come in, then,' says Mattheüs.

They haul in the luggage, the gate slides shut and locks. They must get the stuff to his room without making any noise. Mattheüs has by this time plotted the whole scenario: his room will now be inhabited by a second person, his loved one. His father is blind, but by no means an imbecile, and will know within days what's going on. Samantha will spot the traces of another presence in the house: Jack almost always pisses past the toilet; Aunt Sannie with her don't-miss-a-thing binoculars, oh hell, what does he care? Must he really, at the age of thirty-two, and a few hours before opening his own business, try to pretend to an ADT guard that Jack isn't coming to stay? Is that what his father expects of him? That he should abandon Jack, not lend him a hand in his hour of need? That's surely not what Pa's own dominee proclaims from the pulpit.

And Jack. He's stark staring mad, the man. To arrive here like this. And he himself is mad about his insistence tonight. It's so not-Jack. Mad about that, for sure. Jack with that bald head of his above the wolf mask on his back, now walking purposefully, with a suitcase in each hand, up the three fan-shaped steps, into his new home.

'Mattie, what's going on, son?' from the study.

He knew his father was still far too attuned to anything out of the ordinary in their house. Until he loses that sharpness, he won't surrender his spirit.

Tempered till now by the excitement of the situation, his anxiety about Jack's arrival as a guest returns, a disturbing kind of thing that grabs hold of him, grapples with him. Something like a sin, though he doesn't easily think of any of his deeds or thoughts in terms of sin.

Mattheüs chooses a kelim where he deposits the last suitcase and box that he's carried in, and walks to the study. As he enters the sick air, his anxiety over the impostor intensifies, his loved one notwithstanding, and above all there's the realisation that the new era could very well become an age of anxiety, and that the honourable status that he's maintained up to now is starting to show cracks, even though he may not agree with its underlying ethos. It *is* a kind of sin, this. Not against his progeny, because he doesn't have anything like that, but against his ancestry.

And he remembers the dawning of another growing anxiety during his high-school years, and how immeasurably upset he was about what was still to come and would still come. One evening at table it happened, a summer evening in Cape Town it was, and still full daylight outside, with a roast leg of lamb and roast potatoes for supper, a special leg sent from Luiperdskop to the city, and Pa getting up, his jacket draped across his armrest, and with the sharpened knife starting to carve the leg against the grain – he'd never manage to slice it like his father did, not so thin – and then exploding: 'Good heavens, do you think I can't see that the leg is totally overdone?' And a slice of meat on the carving knife is pushed in front of his mother's nose, which she turns towards the dresser decorated with her copper pot of hydrangeas. 'Dry. Can't you see, all the life roasted out of it.' He hurls the knife down with a clatter, wipes the fat from his hands on the serviette, chucks that down too, takes his jacket from the armrest and clears out.

And for the first time he hears his mother swear. 'Piece of shit!' If only she'd shouted it after Pa, who by then had started his car to drive to town, but she mumbled it into her chest, where it collected and became toxic. Then he, Mattheüs, realised that everything was falling apart, that it had fallen apart a long time ago; what he'd just witnessed had only been the aftershock, and it wasn't even about the leg of lamb. He was then in his second-last year at high school and understood what was happening in their home, had in fact always understood, but was only then able to verbalise it.

Addressed to the sickbed (his gaze on the steep hillock made by the old man's feet at the foot of the bed): 'It's me, Pa. I thought I heard something at the gate.'

'Who was it?'

'Scavenging dogs or something, Pa. I think somebody further up in the street let their dogs out on their own to go and do their business.'

'So late?'

'Yes, Pa.'

Jack is in, the smart-arse, and he's not going to get him out in a hurry. To be honest, he doesn't want to, not after his tremendous effort (he radiated tension, his stare urgent, not once did he look away from him); buggered if he's going to do that to him.

He's tired. Tomorrow at five-thirty, no, five o'clock to make sure, he must get himself up. He must go to bed now.

He kisses his father on the forehead, leaves the room, this time closing the double doors.

They quietly carry the luggage into Mattheüs's room, lock the door, strip off their clothes and crawl into bed. Jack cuddles up against Mattheüs's back, behind his buttocks and in the crook of his legs, and Mattheüs immediately drops off to sleep.

He wakes just before dawn as he usually does, gets up from Jack's encircling arms, goes to the bathroom and listens in the direction of the study whether everything is okay with his father. He crawls back into bed and drops off almost immediately, only to wake suddenly at daybreak, minutes before his mobile phone alarm is due to go off, to a vision, Old Testament-like and therefore dramatic, a hand writing on his sea-green wall above the string of sunglasses, the commandment, fourth or fifth it must be: honour thy father and mother as long as you live – the one that Dominee Roelf read out Sunday after Sunday when he unwillingly accompanied his father to the Reformed Church, Gardens, and which would be read out again the following Sunday, and had been read out by Dominee Klaas too, before Dominee Roelf, his mother then in the last years of her life, hatted and gloved in the pew, all of them listening to the commandment echoing all the way back to his baptismal dominee and even further into the past, Sunday after Sunday, to keep the memory of it alive in the minds of the sinfulness-inclined congregation, a commandment enjoining his people, his tribe, and himself, in a very particular way, not to stray from the ways of the fathers or you'll be burnt to a cinder. As a reflex to the writing hand, a rebuke if ever there was one, his hand gropes around on the floor for his computer, which he wants to flap open to seek consolation on his favourite porn site, but with Jack next to him it's way too unprivate.

A month, two at most, then Pa won't be there any more. Couldn't Jack have hung on for just a while? He closes his eyes. Behind him, Jack is bed-warm and now, just before dawn, hard. He squeezes shut his eyes that are wanting to open.

'It's Sissy, Pappie.'

'Oh, it's you, my child. Are you phoning from the farm?'

'Now where else would I be phoning from, Pa?'

'No, it's just that. It feels as if you never phone me.'

'Ag, don't be ridiculous, Pa. I phone every Wednesday and every Sunday. Pa knows that very well. Why do you do this to me? But tell me, is Pappie settled in again at home?'

'I'm alone here. Mattie, you know, has started with his business. Dominee Roelf is coming to fetch me soon for the chemo.'

'I really hope Matt doesn't neglect Pa with him being out and about all day and every day with that business of his. Couldn't he have waited? No, so now at the very end he has to go and do exactly what will take him away from home. No, really. Ag, I don't know, Pappie. I'm just saying.'

'It's his prerogative, Sissy.'

'Prerogative.' She pauses a while on the word. 'I mean, couldn't he have waited a bit, Pappie?'

'Couldn't he have waited for what? For me to die?'

'No, I mean. Ag, I don't know. Pa knows what I mean. Listen, one of Pa's socks got left behind. Shall I post it? Pappie must say if there's anything I can help with. I can always drive down. Cape Town isn't that far, after all. I mean, if there really is something.'

'Sissy?'

'Yes, Pa?'

'It's a terrible suffering you have to endure when you're old.'

'I know, Pappie.'

'Do you know, when I lift my old arm against the light, it's all flabby skin. And I always had good solid arm muscles. Do you remember Pa's arms, Sis?'

'Ag, heavens, Pa. My dear, dear Pappie.'

'Well, my child, I suppose I must get myself ready. Mattie has put out my clothes.'

'Pappie sounds a bit off-colour to me this morning. What is it? Is something wrong?'

'How would *you* know what Pa is going through?'

'Ag, Pa. I hope it goes well with the chemo and all. Tell Matt to phone me.'

'Goodbye, my child. Give my best wishes there.'

'Same, Pa. And remember I love Pappie very much.'

'Me too, my child.'

@ staff room, Zilverbosch, Jack Facebooks. (Does he post it Public or Close Friends only? He decides on Public.) *Get this: a Grade Elevener asked me, the teacher with the least discretion on the planet, for counselling. Is Mister Jack van Ryswyk on the official counselling committee? You must be joking. Tell me: how does this tally with my so-called lack of discretion?*

Mister Richard Richardson is a total prick. (He wishes he could facebook that too.) Whenever he happens to come across him near his office, Mister Richardson's greeting is abnormally friendly.

There wasn't time to eat at Matt's this morning, so he takes out the Tupperware with his lunch. He balances it on his knees. The container isn't greasy underneath, he's checked. He opens it. A cold chop. It's a loin chop with a narrow strip of fat that's now congealed yellowish-white. The belly of the chop is grey and also hard. It's one of the nicest things you can eat, a cold chop the next day. Matt taught him that.

This morning he opened the fridge in Matt's kitchen to take out the milk. Take the chop, Matt said when he saw him eyeing the side plate with the cold chop. Now it's the chop itself that's got him all frazzled.

Look, if you were to ask him what kind of person he is, Jack would always say his senses come first. He hears and sees how a situation looks, he licks and spits, he acts on his senses. But now, this chop. It's as if he can't even bring himself to taste it. The chop represents the house that he's entered. By force. It may in future become his chop, but at the moment. Let's face it, in all his life he's never taken a chop from his own or his mother's fridge, as the chance of there being a chop in one of those fridges was zero. Sauerkraut, don't even ask why his mother developed a taste for that. That's all he can remember from their fridge in Worcester. The stinking bottle of old cabbage; hours after his mother had opened the thing and helped herself, the smell still hung in the air in that kitchen.

In the staff room there are two circles of fifties-style armchairs that have been covered a few times, nothing luxurious but also not shabby, in the style of Zilverbosch. Along one wall is a counter with a hand basin and an urn with coffee- and tea-making things. There is decaffeinated coffee and herbal tea for the abstemious. Along the opposite wall there are pigeonholes containing all kinds of crap, and to the left of that a notice board with black-and-white xeroxed covers of the counselling books available to boys and counsellors. There are titles such as *Dare to Succeed* and *Raise Your Game* and *The Quest for Masculinity* and *The Secret of Happy Children*.

The boy will soon come in, probably confused about his sexuality. Jack doesn't have to plan what to say to him. He talks to the boys like an ordinary person. That's what they want. No shitting about. They see right through you.

He points and takes a photo of the chop inside the transparent pale-green container on his khaki chinos. He doesn't share it, unusually for him. He's mainly trying to figure out what's going on here.

He's forced himself upon the Duikers' Cape Dutch house, I suppose you'd say residence – that's how he's started thinking about last night's entry. And with all those counselling books in front of him and him now having to give advice, he doesn't know what to make of his own scheme. Matt was so nice to him this morning, so friendly and loving and warm and sincere. Take the chop, Jack. This, after he'd forced Matt to open the gate so that he could invade number nine Poinsettia Road.

With his index finger he up-ends the chop so that it lies leg-in-the-air. Payback. He's going to have to give the man what he wants. And that's connected to the thing he can hardly bear to think of. Do you understand? If he even begins to remember the incident, he wants to puke. It's a whole lot of veiled images; if he could, he'd delete them one by one.

That morning, he'd woken up on his stomach. With his hands

159

folded under him. Never sleeps like that. That was the first thing that hit his drug-fucked mind. That, and then all the other things, the sour air in the room with a picture of one of those palm-fringed beaches ridiculously high on the wall. And the slimy blood and coagulated blood on him and also on the polyester sheet around him. And the pain all the way, up and up, right through his very being. And the shameful taste of it. And the knowledge, immediately, that his life from then on would be marked by it. That's more or less all he wants to say. And all that he could tell Matt. And finally: when he hobbled out of there like a crippled fucking penguin to the taxi that had to take him to emergency, he had the presence of mind to look. He wanted to know where he was. Where it had happened to him. Cabana Hotel, Rooms available from R199, corner of Loop and Marine Streets. And the man who helped him out, a tall Nigerian in jeans and a pink Lacoste polo shirt, who didn't look back. Just walked back into his hotel and pulled the security door shut behind his butt.

More? No, he can't.

He turns the chop on its side again, looks up to check that nobody's coming in, and smells the goodness of the meat. Then he presses the lid closed all along the square of the container. He could get all worked up about the thing that he's taken that doesn't belong to him. And the only way he can think of it in his stupid way, is to pay Matt back. And that's the shit of it. He's zipped up tight, he is, and he accepts it like that. That's his status quo as a sexual being. He slips the Tupperware container back into his pocket for later.

After another minute or so, the boy comes in. He's come straight from cricket practice, a second-team player. Jack shows Joey where to sit and puts him at ease by telling him a few things about his own life, and asks some questions too to loosen him up even more. They talk for more than an hour. No, Joey, put that out of your mind, he says when the boy seems to connect his sexual confusion with his relationship with his father, which was far from close.

Afterwards, in a spirit of deliberate indiscretion, he asks Joey if he can take a photo of the two of them. Joey says cool, and stands next to him with his white cricket shirt and his cream pullover with the two Zilverbosch-blue stripes bordering the V-neck. (Usually it's the other way round, boys ask if they can take a photo of Mister Richie on their cameras.)

When Joey leaves, he boils some water for coffee and facebooks the photo of the chop to Matt, without any caption. What is there to say?

He takes a piece of shortbread from the cookie cupboard, sits down and facebooks Matt: *Give me a week. If it doesn't work out, yours truly moves out. Promise.*

Bad coffee. The biscuit crumbles creamily in his mouth. Jamie comes scurrying into the staff room with Philippa, the history teacher, gets a fright when he sees him there, greets him half-heartedly, and deliberately chooses the other circle of chairs to sit down. The man doesn't know how to behave.

When Dominee Roelf brings him back from oncology, Samantha is there to help him out of the car. She's God's blessing, that girl.

'Look how they've mistreated poor Mister Bennie again.' He lifts his head up to her, tears running down his cheeks. Salty water, that's all, which he can no longer hold back. He hears it all – thank you and phone any time – somewhere above his head between Samantha and the dominee. Dominee Roelf, he may as well say it, is one of the old sort of Christians, very rare these days.

His back supported by Samantha's arm, they walk together into the house. She has a tissue handy, which she uses to dry his cheeks. Tears they definitely are not. Once more, twice at most, he'll have chemo, and after that, nothing. Professor de Lange said as much. Truth to tell, he'd expected it.

The oddest thing has happened to him. 'Samantha?'

'Yes, Mister Bennie?'

He can't say what it is. It's too odd for words. But he knows. He knows. After today's session he experienced the sensation, the first time ever, of no longer being conscious of his own weight. Look, he was always stable at just over 90 kg, always kept his weight in check by jogging and going to the sea for a vigorous swim. Now he's, ag, he can't say it out loud. He thinks of himself as a dragonfly on a lily pad. Should he share this with a young person?

'Samantha.'

'Yes, Mister Bennie?'

'I think take me to the toilet first, my girl.'

'Okay, Mister Bennie.'

'There's nobody inside the house, is there, Samantha?'

'How does Mister Bennie mean now?'

'Never mind,' he says. 'Just leave it.'

Then she carefully directs Mister Bennie so that he can hold on to the toilet seat. He loosens his pyjama pants and lowers himself. 'Nobody's going to fool me,' he mumbles.

He'll have toast with Marmite, he says after being helped into bed a while later. When Samantha brings it, he doesn't touch it. And when at last he does hold out a hand for it, the bread is rock hard. He feels the need to say a very specific thing to Mattie and he lies there thinking how best to say it. Mattie's going to need advice now that he's started his own business. He lies there, wondering how to get up and put on his slippers and get as far as the desk to make a recording.

He wakes up to the sound of Sannie's voice coming in by the front door and walking up to him. The afternoon has already passed, he can sense it, and his body has still not taken on its weight. It's as if there's nothing lying in his bed. Samantha must have just about finished inside. She'll come and say goodbye and then take a bus to her little house in Athlone. He says little house, but it's a decent place. Spic and span. He's been there several times. Old Mary. Shame, he really should leave her something in his will. He must get the attorney to come by.

'Good Lord, Bennie. What have they done to you now? No, really, I'll have to go and talk to Professor de Lange.'

'What's that, Sannie?' He's too tired for Sannie's nonsense. He'll have to call Samantha and tell her to show her out.

'Finished, Bennie. Finished, finished, finished.' She sails up to him, Sannie is always draped in a lot of cloth, he wouldn't quite know what it is today. Her hand explores the bedspread so that she won't sit on him, at least. Then up she gets onto the bed, with her hand on his arm.

He says nothing more and hopes his eyes don't start watering again; Sannie will find it impossible not to take it as a blubbering. And he really doesn't feel up to that. Why is Samantha not coming?

Sannie gets going on the thing she came for. She switches on a soppy voice like some of the dominees who don't know how to be serious in their sermons without being sentimental. Decrepit as he is, she mustn't think he doesn't notice. Her hand is boiling hot, folded around his arm. Won't keep him long, she says. She's just quickly bringing the good news that Silver Cloud has duly handed over its donation to the Coronation Park people – she's talking about the caravan people. Oh, and if only he could see the joy. All of them, apart from two stroppy gents, dedicated their lives to our Precious Lord, as Silver Cloud demands. 'As you know, Bennie, it's not a matter of handouts.'

He says nothing. Samantha will have to give him some of the Oramorph. His body has become a mere instrument for registering pain. Strange, the path the Lord wants you to walk on the final stretch.

She comes in. 'Samantha?' He lifts his hand, not the one under Sannie's protection, and makes a gesture that he knows Samantha will understand. The girl is more attuned to his moods and things than old Mary was in those days.

'Mrs Sannie, Mr Bennie is very tired. He should really rather be resting now.' She comes and takes the woman by the arm.

'My goodness, let go of me! I know my boundaries.'

'Sannie,' he murmurs.

She kisses him on the lips, a cloying rose fragrance that brings him no joy, and then pitter-patters out. Reaching the door, a parting shot: 'You mustn't let them treat me this way, Bennie. I'm one of *your* people, you know. Remember that.'

Shortly afterwards, Samantha brings his morphine and carefully helps him to sit up, with almost the same solicitude as Mattie, it's just that with Mattie there's something more in his touch, must be that he's his own son. Then Samantha also says goodbye. He pays her by debit order directly into her savings account, there's no problem on that score.

Once only and not again, he tries to get up, just halfway, and tries to plan the route ahead, each foot in a slipper, then the six paces to his chair, shuffle in, and then press Play on the Philips. He sees himself doing it, clear as daylight, almost more real than real life. But when he gets to the talking, speaking the right words where he knows the built-in microphone must be, he gets stuck. From that point on he can't think ahead. Mattie. He can't think how he wants to say this very specific thing to his son. There's nothing but nonsense in his head. At first just a tiny bit, like a feeble stream. Then an eruption of all kinds of monstrosities and things that look as if they still need to be shaped, things that he's never seen in all his life, and that he can't distinguish from one another. Things that are nothing on earth to do with his words to Mattie. This makes him unhappy. There's no direction any more in the overwhelming flood that he's experiencing inside his head. He is inside it, irredeemably, a Benjamin Duiker he can make neither head nor tail of.

'Is that you, Sis?'

'Now who else would it be, Pappie?'

'I'm so glad you're phoning, my child.'

'Pappie, I can't talk, I must rush to fetch the kids in town.

Ballet and stuff. I just wanted to ask, does Pappie know that Uncle Hannes gave Matt his Beretta? Do you know about this business?'

'Mattie mentioned something like that, yes.'

'Oh, well, then that's all right. I just wanted to make sure. No, I suppose there's no problem then. Marko and I were wondering, because Uncle Hannes has never had that weapon relicensed. I don't want Matt to pick up trouble with that thing. That's all, really. I must run. Love you lots, Pappie.'

'Yes, my child.'

In the first three weeks or so, when he arrives at his business in the morning, parks behind the premises across the way from the laundry, walks round the corner with his rucksack – Uncle Hannes's Beretta still untouched in its dassie-hide pouch – unlocks Duiker's Takeaway and lights the gas flames one by one, he experiences an increased sensual awareness, a high. All he can compare it with was before Jack's time, when he used to take a weekly trip out to Kalk Bay, in the afternoons it was, and called up from the street to his fuck buddy – who came out onto the balcony, wearing only a vest – and then walked up the stairs and entered the bedroom where the bed had been prepared with all the paraphernalia, such as condoms and lubricant and a few toys and cigarettes, all that stuff strewn over the bed, ready for use in the purple and red bubble light of a single lava lamp, and then it comes on, like a fit, a throbbing sensation in every fibre of your body.

But something else gets added to the mix, something he's never experienced before. It's as if he's entered another sphere, one of survival, where he's acting beyond the limits of his body's abilities. The constant standing on his feet, the carrying to and fro of heavy saucepans, keeping track of the number of orders (any over-ordering of fresh vegetables or meat, and he's had it), keeping track of recipes, of seasoning and tasting (he reaches a stage where he takes a spoonful of sauce and tastes it, and then tastes it again and again, without knowing any longer whether the flavour's okay), keeping his humour and patience with customers, his enthusiasm (fuck) in describing the food when he sees someone hesitating, the pain in his arse then, the faint trembling of his hand around a glass of Coke when, at about three or four o'clock in the afternoon, he has a chance to sit down.

And then getting up again for the chunk of beef that still has to be cubed and marinated in his curry mix (nicely spiked with extract of tamarind), the job itself energises him, and there at the counter another customer already: a mother with her two children in white school shirts: good afternoon, Madam, and he's switched on, in gear, and remains like that, just like that, right through the afternoon as he sells someone a container of lentil dahl, or some chicken curry to the next customer, every one of his muscles and senses primed.

Between customers, and with his preparation for the next day under control or at least planned according to a sequence, Mattheüs looks out over the counter and over Main all the way to the Groote Schuur Hospital tower and even further up to Table Mountain with its wind-blown pines, and the sight makes him think of his mother, he doesn't know why – if she could only see him now. His mother sitting next to him with his clasped hands, feeding him the words of the children's prayer in a voice that he's learnt to recognise as her night voice. On his boy's knees, he is then with his mother and gentle Jesus – at the deepest level it's a matter of that all-embracing security. And maybe that's what made him think of his mother. If Pa goes tomorrow or next week, and Jack also decides to push off, and all other safety nets disappear, then he'll know at least that he's made it, competent and capable, here at Duiker's Takeaway with his Italian apron. He'll keep standing on the perforated spongy plastic carpets among his pots that are like pals, his cold-room meter on a safe five degrees C, here he'll hold the fort, his eye on the passers-by on the pavement: is this my kind of customer or not? That's how powerfully he experienced his new business in those first three weeks.

When he and Jack arrive home, Jack lying flat on his seat in case of prying eyes over the fence, he first goes to the study and takes Pa's hand in his. Pa is calm, there are no problems. Mattheüs keeps his mobile phone in his pocket all day, ready for any emergency calls. He notes a contentment in his father that in the early phases of his illness was variable in nature and has now become complete. Either he's accepted that his death is very close, or, so Mattheüs would like to believe, he's terribly grateful that his son has at last found his feet and he no longer needs to worry about him.

He tells his father about the wheat farmer from the Caledon area who came to buy food from him, Francois was his name. In town for shopping. A bit skimpy on the meat, but tasty, he said about the lamb stew. So he fished out an extra chunk of meat from the pot and put it on top of Francois's helping, keep the customer satisfied.

If he added more meat, he'd have to push up the price, he tells his father. Pa's eyes mist over with a smile, tears trail from the corners of his eyes. 'My son,' say his lips voicelessly. Mattheüs carefully folds back his father's lips (at the end of each day he cleans his mouth with sterile soap), and inserts one of the dry-mouth suckers. In his last conversation with Professor de Lange – and may he just once more say how little he appreciates the man's pietistic way of treating his father – he said they could try chemo one more time, but he thinks the possible benefits of such treatment are minimal at this stage.

'The organs have all had it, not so, Professor? It's the chemo that's going to kill him, not the lymphoma?' Professor de Lange, horribly thin-lipped, gratefully took out his mobile phone that was ringing in his pocket and took the call, and Mattheüs walked out of his dirty-pink-and-grey consulting room without a goodbye from either of them.

When, that day, Francois the wheat farmer had finished his stew, wiped his mouth and left – he provides serviettes made from grey recycled paper, only one per person, please – he immediately got going on his kitchen routine, and with a special spoon he scooped lentils from the drum to be soaked for the next day. He skims from the top, he's chosen the lentil drum to hide his Beretta. He keeps it in the dassie-hide pouch, he doesn't really want a lentil to creep up the barrel, you never know with these things.

Like an oiled machine just made for this work, is how he thinks of himself after only a week. (Though the piles of invoices pushed under the steel door do shake him up; quick calculation on his calculator, is he in the red yet?) Outside of his routine, or in it, and even while he's serving customers, there is always the furtive burning in his head, manifesting itself either as a blinking in his eye or as a twitching in his crotch, the craving for an hour or even less if necessary, as he'd got used to before Duiker's, to delve into his porn archive and give himself what his brain is asking for.

But opening his computer and searching for his porn sites isn't the same any more. It's between the two of them, him and his computer, and with Jack around there's one too many. Jack in the evenings there in his bedroom, fooling around on Facebook in his underpants – strange how his desire then closes in on him. How he repeatedly returns to Jack in his bedroom and on his bed. Maybe the time has come to rein in his pleasuring, even to shake it off, he whispers to himself. But does he want to? That's the question.

Sometimes Emile comes sauntering along to Duiker's, some days he doesn't see him at all. He suspects he chooses his days and times carefully, and then again he thinks no, he's labelling the guy. Emile is an impoverished Congolese refugee intent on survival, he's only human, he's doing what anyone in his situation would do. Also, none of the cheek of his previous visits, only happy smiles. And when he comes, he always ties his dog up two posts further along the pavement, as Mattheüs requested: 'You're going to scare off my customers with that monster.' From his pants pocket he produces a pair of two-rand coins, never anything more than that, which he uses to buy food. Mattheüs dishes up half a container, that's the most he can give. Emile squats right there and devours the food in an instant, and Mattheüs, who can't help watching from the corner of his eye, gives him the job of emptying the rubbish bags into the bins behind the shop in exchange for another helping. But Mattheüs doesn't allow him inside – Emile so eager – rather carries the bags to the other side of the steel door to be taken away from there.

One day, when Emile comes back after dumping rubbish again, he's eating something with his hands, out of a cut-off Coke bottle. Mattheüs notices that it's the last of the fermented lentil dahl that he'd had to throw out. He tells Emile it'll make him sick, but he eats everything he's got right there, he doesn't mind. Why does Mattheüs's cheapest food cost eight rand, while here at the back you can do a load of laundry for seven rand, he wants to know. Mattheüs explains how a business works. If your expenditure exceeds your income, you're buggered. Does he understand that? And dishes him up another half-container of food for the job he's done. Well, it seems Mattheüs has forgotten he'd told him he used to own a restaurant in Boma, he and his brother. On the beach on the west coast of the DRC. He knows everything about business.

'I also have to make a living,' Mattheüs tells him. What does he think it costs to establish a takeaway?

He's just saying, says Emile. Just saying. He doesn't want to make Matthew angry. He has a wife with *trois enfants* at home. Then he politely says goodbye, and once again gives a wave over his shoulder as he walks off.

The incident leaves Mattheüs troubled. And it's not about Emile, who he's really not scared of. (He tells himself.) Rather about the disintegration of his brief sense of security, the one that made him recall his mother.

His last chance. Duiker's will either make or break him – this, while he's counting the day's meagre takings, the shutter already lowered, of course. What's happened to Jack? Two short-arses who by the look of them could be related to Emile – though their presence might also upset him – have just disapprovingly (tongues clucking) examined his menu and prices, and stalked off to the

169

chicken place further down the road with its rancid oil that you can smell miles away.

@ bus stop, Jack messages him. And minutes later on Facebook so that his 640 or however many friends can also comment on it (if they still give a damn): *Is it wrong to still feel kicked in the jack because Mister Richardson forced me out of the hostel?*

Finally, Mattheüs digs the Beretta out of the drum, shaking a few lentils from the folds of the pouch, slips it into his pocket and goes to the back, where Jack has now arrived and is waiting. Mattheüs with four containers of food for him to taste. Everything is told and retold and swapped; Jack says he smells of curry and oil.

Jack lies flat when they drive in at the gate. Mattheüs is convinced that Samantha knows of his presence in the house, Aunt Sannie without a doubt, and his father probably has a hazy awareness of Jack on debauched sheets over there in his son's room.

Mattheüs admits the situation with him in the house unnerves him. He can't help it. It's not a question of not wanting Jack with him. It's just. He can't handle that as well. What does he mean by 'as well', Jack immediately wants to know from his supine position in the bakkie, his shaven head glistening in the floodlights of the driveway (next door, Aunt Sannie's lights are also already on). Mattheüs shows him the fever blister on his lip, throbbing, he's stressed to the limit, he says.

He immediately goes to sit with his father, who still seems contented, his expression clear and open. In fact, he didn't phone once today. After a while he lets go of his father's hand, only to pick it up again in his own when he realises that that's what he needs right then. The old man has become like his child, he'll miss him. He'll miss the caring. Funny, hey?

The hand with liver spots and ever-vanishing capillaries, the skin loose and fragile over the bones of the hand – there is no longer anything about the body of this dying man that has the power to upset him. The cheeks that become even more sunken when he sucks at the Sustagen with the straw (how skull-like it seemed to him at first), the gaze of his unseeing eyes, even the shock of the few remaining pubic hairs, hard grey wires that have lost their way, he has seen it all in his father.

'But have you made at least something, Mattie? Sometimes it takes a year to start showing a profit. Tell Pa if he should lend you a hand again. Mattie?'

He was far away in their old house in Observatory with Pa's lush or rather glistening bush right at eye level, both of them, father and son, drying themselves in the steamy grey atmosphere of the bathroom. Those days, there was only one bathroom for them all in that old house.

'Yes, Pa.'

'Yes what? Must I help you with your overheads? You must speak up, son. Don't wait until you're in trouble. You know if a man doesn't pay his bills he soon gets a bad reputation among suppliers. And very soon, too.' It's tired his father out, all the words. He won't say much more than that tonight.

'No, Pa. Thank you, Pa, I'm still all right, thanks. I've worked everything out well, Pa will see. It's going to work.' He's never considered that his own father – now he comes to think about it – was a sexy brute in his prime. Is he allowed to think that way about his own father? (Jack would open the question for debate on Facebook.) Can you help what comes into your head sometimes? Can you say: okay, this thought or that image I'm not going to conjure up when you know very well the thought or image is already fully formed and right there, an adder in your bosom.

'Some chicken soup for Pa, I see Samantha's made some. Nice and thin. Pa won't struggle with lumps.' Then Mattheüs answers softly in reply to what he's just been wondering about. 'Maybe yes.'

With an effort, Pa turns his head to him. 'What. My. Son?'

'No, I'm thinking, maybe Pa can help me a bit after all. There are some bills that are only coming in now. The coffee machine I have to pay off every month, but I forgot about the deposit.' (He's sold only four coffees. Maybe he should hang out a banner or something.)

'There you are,' his father whispers, 'I thought so. Go on, write out another hundred and fifty thousand and let me sign. Then I'll have done with you for the time being, Mattie. Then you can continue on your own for now. A man has to, you know.'

Pa signs almost totally illegibly. Mattheüs can only hope the bank will accept it like that, and he puts his father's hand back by his side and goes to the kitchen where Jack is up to no good. Not really, it's actually very funny, the funniest thing he's seen in three weeks.

Jack has left on only the overhead light above the stove; the rest of the kitchen is dark, the blinds up so that Aunt Sannie has a good view from her sunroom on the first floor across the way, which is exactly what she's enjoying at the moment. There she stands in her mauve dressing gown with no shame; why ever should she be ashamed, spying on them? And Jack on all fours with only the wolf's head showing over the counter, the wolf's ears just above the windowsill, turned towards Aunt Sannie. The pointed ears – each tipped with a tuft, almost like a lynx – wiggle. He doesn't know how Jack does this: they taunt and tease the vigilant old matriarch holding a mug of coffee or whatever it is in her hand, probably laced with something; they don't trust her piety one bit, and her judgemental disposition is doubtlessly being kick-started right then, like a lawnmower being yanked to life by its cord, she who is firmly founded on a rock, a righteous one, exactly like dear Bennie with his wastrel of a son, and she shall neither falter nor fall, not now or ever in all eternity. Aunt Sannie lifts her mug in salute, takes a sip, over and out.

'What the fuck, Jack,' Mattheüs fetches a beer from the fridge.

The game is over, Aunt Sannie has seen her fill and switched off the light (in a while she'll switch it on again), and they take their food to the bedroom to eat it in privacy.

Mattheüs hardly glances at the show that Jack has started watching, episode four of *True Blood*, the vampire story from the American south. His smouldering desire has returned (it's never really gone), his need to go to his archive now or rather, and more blissfully, to go hunting for a new porn movie – the thrill often lies in getting there. The craving overpowers him like a repressed impatience that he can hardly contain any longer, something delicious on the other side of the immediate horizon of whatever he's doing, he next to Jack on the bed with plates of food on their knees: it's right there on the other side, he can even hear the change in his breathing. The difference is Jack. Jack has come as a bulwark and a barrier. He touches himself. He doesn't want Jack to see him touching himself.

When Jack goes to shower, the opportunity arises for a quickie, he stops at a video that he would have fast-forwarded if he'd had more time, but any port in a storm. He shoots his load and cleans up just as Jack returns with a towel around his waist. Mattheüs flings himself onto the bed, stretches out and indulges himself in a male image he can still recall: the snail trail of hair all the way from the centre of the chest down to the navel, a supreme snail trail, an ideal, he (or Jack) will never look like that or have one like that.

Jack bends over and dries between his toes, under his arms, wipes his bald head with deft strokes. His breathing still tight, Mattheüs sits looking at how attractive Jack is in the half-light: so, what about him and this man, then? What about his dear, beautiful Jackie, and he turns cold at the thought that he could, without wasting a moment, flap open his computer again to find his way anew as he wants to, as he must.

Jack looks at him, his towel around his hips again. 'Am I in this room for you, Matt? Do you at least know that I'm here?'

My dear son,

I'm nearing the end of the road, Mattie. The Lord is close to me. Do you know, even Samantha's chicken soup, no, really, I can't any longer. I can't taste it any more. They say you need to be able to smell food as well. At Luiperdskop last weekend I picked up a few of the farm's smells.

And now in the toilet too when I go to make water, I smell it hitting my nostrils. It must be a tremendous dose they give me each time in oncology. I'd say that's one of the last things I can still smell. Pa's own toxic urine.

Ag, my son, how can you when you're young and full of the lust for life and a bit devil-may-care ever predict what's going to happen to you in old age? It's good, too, that devil-may-care, that bit of naughtiness, the times you bend the rules a bit, Pa doesn't condemn that. But, of course, you should stick to your principles. That's what sustains you, day and night. Without that, ag, Pa doesn't want to preach at you.

I did still want to ask you whether you found a bit of serenity on the farm in the veld and in nature. Pa can see that at the moment you're on the go all the time, your day is full. Mattie, I wish you nothing but the best. I'm convinced that one day you're going to build up a really big business for yourself. Branches all over the city.

Do you know, way back, I remember it out of the blue now, her name was Elisabet. She worked for me for only a short while. A lovely person, but psychologically unstable. One afternoon I drove her out to the Kenilworth Race Course, I sold I don't know how many cars there to old Bertie Herselman. We were walking along the course while the jockeys were exercising the horses. I held her lightly around the hip as we walked. Suddenly the whole world around us shrank. It was just the horses, beautifully groomed, and the lovely green course and every now and then a horse making a dropping. That's about all. And the beautiful blue sky above us.

Do you know, that woman found such peace there. Just a bit of nature and the earthy smells and the horses and all the gulls there. It was as if scales fell from her eyes. She took out her handkerchief and dried her eyes. She told me: I feel like a new person. Later on, she lost her way again. There was something in her head that I never understood. All that I knew was that life was too much for her. She couldn't lead a normal life. And of course, I couldn't keep her on. Shame, I wonder what happened to Elisabet. She had the prettiest, longest white neck. That was the prettiest thing about her.

No, my son, Pa doesn't want to preach at you. On the other hand, I lie here and wonder, and before I know it I'm thinking about you. What

174

would happen to the world if everybody was like you and your friend? Where would our children come from? You must know, Mattie, these are things I can't easily put out of my mind. I'm only human after all, a man, please don't hold it against your old father.

When you get to where I am, then you do want something of yourself to remain behind on this old earth. Well, Duiker's Motors has long since ceased to exist and been given a new name. There are the earthly possessions I'm leaving behind, but that's all dust. It doesn't mean much.

In the end, all that remains are the people I leave behind, my blood relatives. Ag, my child, you must know that it's not easy for Pa to talk about these things like this. I've wrestled with it so much and prayed to the Lord to help me resign myself to it. Sissy has the three little girls I love from the bottom of my heart, but unfortunately they don't bear the Duiker name. Our bloodline stops with you, Mattie. There will be no more progeny. The bloodline runs dry. I suppose that's the will of the Lord, I don't want to kick against it. But let me tell you this today, Mattie, it's a bitter pill for Pa to swallow.

That's all I wanted to say. And I suppose it's more than enough. I know what you're doing for me, Mattie, I see it every day. Pa worries about you when you're old one day and you don't have children to care for you. What then? How will you get by?

Now I'm very tired. I'll stop here for the time being.

Your pa.

With his left thumb he posts on his Wall: Jack @ kitchen. *Mystery man also known as Wolfie will tonight fill all vacant spaces in Cape Dutch mansion with spaghetti bolognese. With bacon added. Parsley, celery and oregano. Yes! Too much of a good thing?*

He stirs the mince in the pan to flash-fry it for a while without burning it. The blinds in the kitchen have been lowered and he can do his thing unseen.

Charnie (seconds later): *So when can we come and party there?*
Jack: *You're crazy in your head. I'm not even supposed to be here.*

He fills a saucepan with water, adds a pinch of salt, and puts it on the hob to cook the spaghetti. The sauce must simmer to develop flavour. Jack sees to it that Matt never has to cook at home. In the mornings he makes the coffee, the toast, everything.

It remains strangely pleasant, but strange nevertheless, to be in the house. Without officially having signed the guest register. Uncle Bennie knows nothing or everything. He asks no questions, at any rate, not from Matt. Shame, when he does get to see him, in the afternoons or whenever he'd have visited anyway, the old man doesn't look good. A matter of time. But people can hang on by a thread for months.

Here's Charnie again. *Squirt of lemon juice at the end. Mmm.*

He puts the lid on the bolognese sauce and turns the flame down as low as possible. He helps himself to the white wine in the fridge, it's a Hermanuspietersfontein. He's talked in his classes about the use of Afrikaans in advertising. It works, even overseas. No need to go all English to sell. Eagle's Nest chardonnay and crap like that. No point in it.

He never contributes to the wine or beer he drinks here. He simply doesn't have the wherewithal. Not now. Once it's only the two of them in this house, then he'll try to do his bit. The prospect of living here alone with Matt is Jack's secret. He means, whenever Matt refers to *their* house, he prefers to keep his mouth shut. Better like that.

While discussing a Breyten Breytenbach poem with grade eleven the other day – the boys only have to write one or two lines to show their understanding of the poem – he sat down himself and wrote out a list.

He calls it problem number one thousand and one, at present insoluble. *No i: Matt's got a helluva fever blister. No ii* (Jack prefers Roman numbering, he always thinks it looks so good): *Matt's father is dying. No iii: Matt has started a new business.*

According to him, these three things are the sum total of Matt's stress. He's convinced that stress, no matter how much of it Matt's dealing with, doesn't account for limp behaviour. It's not that Matt isn't hot in the sack. But to sleep with Matt nowadays is like sleeping with a very good friend. Almost like your brother. He's gone lukewarm, the chemistry between them has fizzled out. It's as if he can sometimes hear the noise in Matt's head. Something's happened to him. Or rather, something is happening to him. He knows what the something is and that makes him unhappy and sad and desperate and what? What should he do about it? Is there a cure for people like that? What he does know and experiences intensely, is that he, Jack, is out of it. He's not part of it.

In class that day, Moenien, of all people, puts up his hand. He wants to know the meaning of *leedvermakerig*, line one, second stanza. It's from the collection *oorblyfsel/voice over*, a conversation between Breyten Breytenbach and the Palestinian poet Mahmoud Darwish. Hence Moenien's interest, the little fuckhead. Normally, he's as switched off as a stone in class.

He explains the word to Moenien with reference to the parallel English text. Then he sits down and leans back in his chair. From where he's sitting, he has a view of the boys' heads at their school desks. From where they're sitting, if they looked up they'd have a view of the back of Table Mountain, the part where Kirstenbosch is situated. It's one of the best classrooms.

He takes out his iPhone and posts on his Wall: @ Zilverbosch. *Mind adrift. Does anybody know anything about porn? How does it affect a relationship?*

Jack gets sixteen comments on the effects of porn, and six 'likes'. In the meantime he's gone to sit under the wild fig in the garden across from the main building, the area reserved for the grade twelves. He'd say he's a bit crabby today. Going to Duiker's Takeaway now and waiting for Matt to finish is not an option. Matt's room and Matt's bed even less of an option. He thinks of the house where he's so-called staying at the moment, and tries to delete the thought. He's not happy.

Charnie: *LOL you a porn junkie now?*

Jack: *Not me, stupid.*

Jaco (ex-lover, lives in Green Point): *Porn fucks with your sex. It's all in your head, ask me.*

Charnie (again): *Don't even know what it looks like. Is it guys swinging their schlongs?*

Koos Lategan (ex-lover, lives in Blouberg): *No-brainer. I mean, if you're in love, porn's second best.*

Jaco: *It's dream stuff. You can never have those guys. And can't do what they do. It's images in your head. Cyber-fucks. Unreal, except that that's not the way you see it.*

Steve (an ex-pupil): *You can learn a lot from porn. I did. Positions and stuff. Not healthy to watch too much. Your soul gets sort of messed up.*

Jack: *But if it's your partner?*

Charnie: *Oh my goodness, you poor thing, you need TLC. Come over tonight. You can sleep on the couch.*

Jamie (Even the redhead is chipping in. It's getting too public. Should he have opened it here on Facebook? Ja, why not.): *It's ambivalent like most stuff around us. Can be good and bad. There are counsellors.*

Steve (again): *Ag, they just feel you up under the table.*

Pete (a friend, lives in Mouille Point, rich, with two poodles and a helluva TV screen): *Bring it on. Mad about it.*

Steve (it's clear that he wants to participate fully in the conversation): *If you watch chronically, as in full-on addiction, you no longer get a hard-on with your partner. Only with porn. That's on the cards. Then you're in the danger zone. Point-of-no-return. You can watch porn, but you have to realise what it's doing to you.*

Jack: *Where do you get that from?*

Steve: *Read it. There's lots of literature.*

Jack: *Christian Family Circle kind of literature?*

Steve: *No, serious studies. I'll have a look.*

Charnie: *Just been out for the first time in my new boots. Very sexy. Got stares at the Waterfront. Are you coming around this evening? I'm making your favourite, ag pleez my dahling.*

Jack: *Kiss-Kiss. Can't. Must stick to the programme.*

178

Charnie: *I'm worried about you.*

Jack: *So sweet.*

Mikey comes sauntering along, the guy who pissed on Moenien at the Misverstand Dam. His piss. Jack's demise.

Mister Richie, just the man he's looking for. He wants to know if he can sit next to him on the bench. Polite. He takes out a memory stick. It's a present for him. There are a thousand songs on it to download on his phone. It's to say he's sorry he messed things up like that for Mister Richie. It was impulsive. He was being childish.

Jack laughs at this. Mikey sits staring straight ahead of him at the lawn to lend gravity to the matter. It's funny. He wasn't made for gravity. Prime specimen, Jack thinks secretly. Is this what Matt is hankering for with his porn watching? And does he think *he* doesn't know that's what he does or wants to do the moment they walk into that room?

Mikey holds out his hand as a final gesture of reconciliation.

'No big deal,' Jack tells him and shakes his hand. Mikey bends down quickly and gives him a hug.

Another comment from Steve comes through: *How deeply is he into porn, do you think?*

Jack: *Deep deeper deepest.*

Steve: *OK, so you've got a problem. Love him in the meantime. Love always works. I'll give it some thought.*

Jack: *Love you, Steve.*

He slips his phone back into his pocket, close to his kidneys where the pain is. (Could also be his heart.) It's a pain that registers gradually. Matt has given him the cold shoulder, sexually speaking. And the result is that he feels horribly inadequate. Like never before in his life. He walks to the tuck shop and buys a packet of Zoo biscuits. By the time he takes the bus to Obs, he's eaten them all.

In the fourth week of the existence of Duiker's Takeaways, his father by now extremely weak, little Emile worms his way right into his shop. The business is starting to take off and because of this he's behind with his preparation. Peeling garlic, onions, scouring saucepans, mopping the floor at the end of the day, his legs throbbing from the exertion and still throbbing when he eventually crawls into bed at night: all this makes him pick the nearest man at hand to help, the man who's nagging to be given a chance. (Is he perhaps making the mistake of his life?) Then, right underneath his arm, the short-arse briskly walks in on bandy legs, his pitch-black eyes looking everywhere and into everything.

No, says Mattheüs once he's inside, he thinks he'll have to get a testimonial from him first, surprising himself with the volte-face, usually he's not indecisive. He can't employ somebody just like that, that's not how things are done in South Africa (he bullshits). He simply has to listen to the inner voice warning him against Emile.

'Not starting today?' Emile folds his arms over his chest, still stony-faced. He's small, but he's strong.

Mattheüs nods and makes him march out again.

'No problem, I'll ask Father Raymond. He will come and talk for me. He will help me, always.'

By three o'clock that afternoon, he's sold out of his chicken curry; Emile is standing side by side with the Catholic priest across the counter. The man is wearing his dog collar and all, and has these feeble paedophilic peepers – an appalling thing to say.

In a velvety tenor voice, he starts laying out Emile's refugee history. Luckily, he keeps it short, and from that moves on to what he knows of him here in the Cape, his willingness to be of use in and around the church; it's just that there are already so many hands and that's why he's looking for work. He talks about his faith in human beings and how Emile has not disappointed him. Whether or not to employ him, is of course up to Mattheüs. But he does believe that Emile will yet make a worthy contribution to the Cape Town community. And if not here, then somewhere else. He thanks Mattheüs for his time.

The next day, he and Emile carry a wooden pallet inside, and now the short-arse is standing there at the work surface peeling onions, a whole plastic container full.

At seven o'clock in the morning when he reports for work, his wife and three children come to see him off. The whole family cut from the same cloth, all short-arses, and with the gaze of the victim. How long were they in a refugee camp before coming here? Very long time, too long. And the chained dog, he always comes along too, by Mattheüs's decree still a good distance from the shop. Long after they've started working inside – he must admit that Emile has proved to be a willing worker – the woman still hangs around with the children, one on the back and one at each hand. Most of the time, she just stands around or squats until he tells Emile his people must get going now, back to their single room in a backyard in Woodstock, the rent apparently three months in arrears; the church does help out a bit.

The cash register stands on the far right of the counter inside a steel chest, made by the same welder who did the steel door, and at the same sizeable fee, and the money drawer is under the counter in a concealed steel casing, like a safe, and, to tell the truth, he has never seen Emile's eyes rest on that – those pitch-black penetrators which, if they watch you long enough, become reproachful, and if a bit longer, there's also resentment; hatred, he hasn't seen yet.

Take the garlic, for instance. He only showed him once the quickest way to peel a clove of garlic. Place the clove on your board, tap it lightly with the flat of the knife, bruising the clove but not breaking it, and see, the papery skin will peel off by itself. He tries to love the short-arse as you're supposed to love your neighbour.

He has a new recipe here, actually one he came across in Galicia, northern Spain. It's a delicious peasant stew, perhaps more suited to midwinter, but still. It fits into his menu and it's cheap: a pig's trotter or two, chickpeas cooked to marrow-softness, a bay leaf (in Galicia you go out and pick yours from a hedge), potatoes, salt and pepper and a few tablespoons of paprika, not the pungent one.

181

Speaking of loving your neighbour, his mother is the only contender when it's a matter of unconditional love. Although, come to think of it, in her last years she turned inwards, to a bottomless, murky lake where nobody was permitted and where nobody wanted to follow.

He gives Emile a cake of soap and a towel to wash himself with in the back toilet that they share with the laundry. Under the arms, he indicates. A sour odour he refuses to tolerate on top of everything else, here in his takeaway. Personal hygiene – he doesn't baulk at talking to him on the subject. This is where his Duiker nature comes into its own. Man, if it looks as if any member of your staff doesn't want to cooperate or maybe doesn't have the temperament you're looking for in your business, you have to act quickly. Give him notice that very day, see to it that you part on a good footing.

Emile, with his knobbly shoulders and those sturdy, bandy legs that could be sexy, but alas are too short, and the frown followed by a deferential nodding when he's given a new task; a painful servility that prevents the man from growing on him.

Sissy phones him during the day at Duiker's and he loses his temper with her; she'd better come quickly if she still wants to see her father. No, she's getting into the car this very minute. The following afternoon she phones again, no, she's spoken to Professor de Lange, it's not the end by a long shot.

'Professor de Lange has no more business with Pa,' he says. He shuffles his feet impatiently because she's phoning him at work: he could have been halfway done with a new jar of pickles. Fatigue makes him even more tactless. She's cruel, he says to her, she's hard. He becomes so emotional because he's also unclear as to what exactly it is he wants to tell his sister, so that he loses his presence of mind in the shop and stares glassily at a customer who has apparently been waiting quite a while. Emile has, for the time being, been forbidden to deal with the public, and the customer shakes her head and walks off; it's an elderly woman with a headscarf, and when he ends the call he turns around to Emile, who is paging through his personal recipe book, his finger trailing the words of the recipes, some in Afrikaans, others in English.

'What are you doing?' Mattheüs says to him. (There is surely nothing wrong with kitchen staff looking at your recipes.)

Emile gets a fright as if he'd indeed had his hand in the biscuit jar, gets a fright at the harshness of Mattheüs's reaction, he doesn't know him yet, asks pardon, please, flaps his little hands in front of him, and then turns around abruptly and carries on with the mortar and pestle: whole cardamom, cumin, and roasted coriander that exude an irresistible aroma when crushed.

Sannie must please help him to get to his desk. He wants to make his last recording.

'But Bennie, man, really. In your condition.'

Something of the extra-sweet that she sprays on penetrates the air, making him light-headed and adding to his nausea.

It's no problem for her to help him there, she says. She could almost piggyback him by now. 'Bennie, you're breaking my heart.' Shouldn't she carry the machine to his bed and just give him a hand there? She won't listen to what he says if it's anything private.

'That will be the day. You. Not listen!' He's lost his spirit. A feebleness has taken possession of him. Sannie, ag, they've known each other for many years. Notwithstanding the overblown sentiment, she is after all a kind of mother to him. A person of principle, he can rely on Sannie always to be the same.

She need only lift the lid of the Philips and then move the machine into position, that's all. When she's done this, he signals that she can go, he needs his privacy. This is his final one. She tsk-tsks with her tongue against her teeth. When he hears the doors click shut behind her, he remains sitting, not knowing how he will ever get going. His thoughts are now coming more sluggishly, not like at the beginning of his confinement to bed, when they flooded his mind. It was the most beautiful and precious hoard of memories. And clear. Now he has to be on the lookout, or his thoughts run amuck like a herd of wild horses. He can't even remember his ID number.

If he wants to lift his hands from his knees and get started, he's going to have to do so now, otherwise he'll never do it. He lifts them. Like lead. He is drawing on his last reserves. His hands on either side of the Philips. His hands flop down. He picks them up again, searches for the Play button with his index finger, and drags the machine a bit closer:

My dear son,

This will be the last one. The need to talk to you keeps nagging at me. And it's also my fatherly duty. I can't get away from that. I no longer want to preach. You have chosen your way of life. That's how things are.

Imagine, the other day Dominee Roelf was sitting here and said to me, what we must remember, brother, is that they don't harm anyone. I was slightly shocked. I no longer have the strength to oppose him. Yes, my son, it's a different sort of world this, which I'm leaving, to the one I entered seventy-six years ago.

The doves outside my window have such a pretty way of talking to each other. And then every now and again the shrill old yaya-ya-ya of the hadedas. Ag, I love them too. I say it's a different world I'm leaving, but it's still a wonderful world. A gift from God, your whole life long.

Do you know, Mattie, sometimes I pray that I can spend just one more day here, right here in my chair at the window. Just one day without nausea. It's a long time since I've known how it is to feel ordinary and not nauseous to death. It's not the kind of nausea you get in a car on a winding road. Or perhaps from a bad oyster. It's a nausea that takes possession of you. It takes over your whole system, day and night. With every breath you take and every time you breathe out. There's no let-up. If only I could vomit to get some relief, but that is not granted me. My son, it will be a blessing to be rid of this nausea that's taken possession of me like a devil.

Now that I'm talking about oysters, I remember the Christmas holidays in East London, years ago. You weren't there yet, only Sissy, a floppy baby. In those days we could walk from the caravan park down to Orient Beach, everything safe, and clean as a whistle. Well, so I'd get up early in the morning and go for a jog along the beach and swim in that water, too, like champagne it was. I'd take along my towel and my pocket knife. Right there on the rocks, you could pick yourself some oysters. I'd rinse them in sea water and eat them just like that. They were the best oysters I've ever eaten, those. Of course, they say oysters make a man feel very lustful. Mattie, your father has never had a problem with that.

A wonderful life, Mattie. A wonderful life. That's what Pa still wants to get across to you for the last time. It was so short, so short, all of it, Mattie. I can't believe it. Everything over in the wink of an eye. A tiny little seed. What does that poet of ours say, like a grain of sand. Mattie, my dear child, if I look back over my life, I can't believe how quickly everything has passed. The old cot where my mother lay me down, painted a glossy light-blue, from there to where I'm lying here, worn to a frazzle, I can't believe it's all over.

Remember this, Mattie. Pa feels moved as he's sitting here. My wonderful life is over. And I can't believe how quickly. My tears have come too late, Mattie. It's all over, from beginning to end, in a wink. My life is over.

The Lord is coming to fetch me to his eternal home. I suppose I'll see your mother there too, but I'm not in the least concerned about that. You see, it is written, in heaven there's no man and wife, as on earth.

I'm ready, Mattie. You've been a good son to me. I believe I gave you guidance where I could. It was my privilege. You're now standing on your own two feet. May the Lord bless you abundantly, my son.

Your Pa.

'There's no need for me to see him again. I've said my goodbyes to Pa.'

'Well, then that's fine, Sissy. It's your decision. I respect it.'

'I've started baking for the funeral. If it's a fine day, we'll have to carry tables out onto the stoep. We won't have people messing and spilling on the floors and carpets then, for us to clean up afterwards. I'll be roasting a few legs of lamb too. There's nothing nicer than cold lamb with mustard. Everyone enjoys that.'

'I take it you'll be staying here.'

'That goes without saying, Matt. Or do you have a problem with that? You must speak up, man. It's your house, after all. Soon.'

'I need to know so that I can tell Samantha to make up the beds, Sissy. My time is divided between Pa and my takeaway. I don't have a minute to spare.'

'Oh.'

Mattheüs says nothing more. He stands there staring at the arrangement of strelitzias he's put in the hallway. Jack is showering.

'Does he ask after me?'

'Pa? He isn't really talking any more. I want to be with him when he goes. He asked me about that too. Mattie, sit with me till the Lord takes my soul away.'

'Oh.'

'I want to do it. I want to see what it's like when someone dies.'

'And if you're at work?'

'Samantha will phone me in time. The university is closed for the holidays and she's sitting with him while working on essays and stuff.'

'Ag, here on the farm we see how sheep die all the time. Nobody who lives on a farm is ignorant about death. Here you're too close to the earth.'

'I can't believe you're saying that. Those are animals, Sissy.

186

Sheep. It's Pa I'm talking about.'

'I've said goodbye to him. That's all I mean, really. And he knows it. He had all his wits about him. There's no point in my driving down to come and sit there. It'll just draw things out. Pa and I understand each other very, very well. We always have.'

Jack is a man who enjoys showering. If Sissy would get off the phone now, he could still get to his computer for his daily fix.

'Are you still there, Matt?'

'Yes.'

'You mustn't let us grow apart when Pa is no longer there, Matt. Remember, it's just the two of us. I love you, man, even though you're an otherwise kind of person.'

'Love you too, Sissy.'

'Well then, let me know if there's anything else I need to bring. How's Jack? I suppose he'll also be at the funeral.'

'Fuck, Sissy.'

'Okay, okay. I just wanted to know. Sleep tight, Matt. And phone me.'

'Bye, Sissy.'

It's the end of an era. Once Pa is no longer here, Sissy will have even less reason to come to Cape Town, she'll phone even less frequently, they'll become estranged and neither of them will have the will to put things right. It saddens him for a moment. He sees a future where he'll have to reorient himself, and the house with all its rooms and every space that for so long he's wanted to make his own, mainly the study, suddenly becomes a melancholy place. His hand in Pa's, then Pa's hand in his (he'll give himself another hour or so and then he'll go and sit there again), and soon enough the final severing of the old bond.

He enters his room (Jack is still showering) and for the first time the mustiness hits him. He'll have to clean up before the funeral, as one should, surely; the house must be vacuumed and dusted and polished inside and out so that his father's soul can depart this life from a squeaky-clean earthly home. Behind the drawn curtains on the windowsill is a vase of old proteas, almost as old as his mother's death, or even older; he's aware of their presence, sometimes something scrabbles around in their bone-dry flower heads. The big mother spider has her nest in the left back corner of the room, with hundreds of babies, and there, right in front of her nest, he's positioned the open mouth of a Consol jar that's supposed to entice them so that he can carry the whole family outside. And then there's the packet of soggy Romany Creams on the lower surface of the book table that he's going to chuck out. And there's all Jack's stuff that needs a bit of sorting out.

In all fairness, he's not going to blame Jack for the mildew, the grey-green growth, some of it already powdery. It's since he's moved in, no, this evening, that the room's felt so stuffy. There's the open wardrobe where Mattheüs emptied three drawers for him and that he hasn't used yet, the drawers are still pulled open as he left them. In front of the wardrobe, his running shoes sit gaping, with their worn inner rubber and a year's foot sweat. And there's the damp aftertaste, everywhere in the room, of the Ingram's Camphor Cream that he uses and that Mattheüs always rather liked on his mother's fingers rubbing it in hard all around his chapped heels, but now it bothers him.

He's exhausted. Torments himself mercilessly with the next day's work schedule, everything that has to be done before he can roll the shutter up at twelve. Late this afternoon, he discovered a piece of garlic peel the size of his pinkie nail in the leftover dahl. Emile gone already, so he couldn't question him about it. He sinks down onto the bed. Last one up is supposed to make the bed, he can't remember who it was this morning. He could happily sleep through a whole day and night's worth of dreams until he's slept his fill. Next to him on the pile of crumpled sheets the screen of Jack's iPhone lights up.

Mattheüs leans across and opens Facebook.

Charnie: *Meantime done lots of private research on porn, spoke to everyone who knows anything. Über addictive. You really need a professional to dig you out of the hole. Shit Jack. What are you going to do?*

Mattheüs turns off the screen and falls back on his bed, on

their bed, on the four pillows that smell of him and Jack, of their hair and their head sweat and all the things that happen to you at night when you're sleeping and tossing and turning, oblivious of everything except flashes in your subconscious, a primitive condition. He refuses to fill his headspace any further, certainly not with anything like regret, not about the condition of his room, his world in the house, and definitely not about his porn obsession; and he's done everything in his power for his father.

Jack comes walking in, towel around the waist, silvery sexy droplets on his shoulders. Mattheüs says to him (listlessly): 'Jack, it's a phase, the porn thing, it'll blow over. Just give me a chance.'

As Jack bends over to dry himself, light from the single reading light casts knobbly shadows all along his bent spine. He puts on some tracksuit pants and picks his T-shirt up from the floor and slips on his running shoes and paces up and down without sitting down as Mattheüs asks him to do; his slow-moving form – sometimes inside and sometimes outside the light cast by the reading lamp – disturbs him. The end of an era, he thinks, he is at last going to be on his own in this huge house, and then Jack begins to speak from a spot at the back of the room where Mattheüs can't see him, only his voice he hears, soggy like someone who's been crying a while and has phlegm in his throat, and in that sodden voice he cuts to the quick, Matt's and his own too, touches the most sensitive nerve.

He talks about the heightened level of sensation that Matt and he adore, or rather that he thought Matt adored, and that Matt has now sacrificed for the sake of porn. He talks about the sensation that you achieve only if you play the sex game for an hour or more without a break, okay, short breathers in between, no matter who takes and who gives, that breaking point you reach just before you reach it, the senses individually and collectively tuned to their most receptive key, and the breaking point that together they don't reach, deliberately withhold from each other so that neither the one nor the other can reach it, on and on until both of them have emptied themselves completely of all thought and all activity that could possibly occur in the rational sphere, both of them now surrounded

189

by a new smell that sweat carries and that both recognise precisely because they don't know it, because you don't smell it anywhere else, and then, at that moment: the overwhelming, all-inclusive sensation of pure animality.

Jack has in the meantime moved back into the circle of lamplight, and from where Mattheüs is lying on the crumpled bedclothes and listening and hurting, hurting nearly as much as in that condition of heightened sensation that Jack is trying to capture, except that that is a hurt which manifests itself through increasing degrees of pleasure, he dozes off and removes himself from Jack's words to reduce their checkmate effect, and then, looking up, he sees Jack's shaven head floating halfway between the bed and the ceiling, the glimmer of the low light on the stretched-to-breaking-point scalp, speckled with pinheads of shaven hairs, and he looks and looks until he succeeds in no longer taking to heart Jack's painful summing-up of their situation, but listening away, far away from the bobbing gleaming head that forms no part of him, of his existence, of the vision with which he now replaces Jack's damning words: a recent image from a porn movie of two Latinos on a sofa, bronzed on Rio's beaches and bulging with muscle yet without being out of proportion, and the approach to the whole thing, smiling and playful, that's what he remembers now and what makes him smile, he stretches out his hand and adjusts the lamp so that his face is veiled in darkness, and the memory of the image provides such pleasure, the total freedom with which those two interact. 'Jack, please, stop all that stuff,' and he turns on his stomach until he feels Jack's hand tapping his shoulder.

Then he looks back to see what Jack wants him to see. Jack is holding one of those foul running shoes of his right above his computer where it's in touching distance on the floor, *his* computer, his trusty partner. A blob of mud and dirty grass fall from the sole of the shoe onto the silver lid of the computer.

'Do it and you'll find yourself on the other side of the gate tonight.' (Imagine threatening Jackie, of all people, like that.)

Then Jack sits down on the chair under the string of sunglasses that will have to be dusted and Windolened, one and all. Mattheüs takes the end of the sheet and wipes the dirt off his computer lid and flaps it shut. He knows what Jack is saying. It's a phase. Nothing more. He can change again, after all, the brain is essentially plastic, everyone knows that. Arms folded across his chest, he lies thinking of some consolation for Jack; the man is shattered. He wishes he could tell him that he's come to the end of his porn cycle, that he's ready to walk away from it.

'Inadequate. Do you know how it feels, Matt? I might as well cut off my prick. You brought me in here and now you've swapped me for sex that doesn't exist. Think of it, Matt, it's all in your head.'

'I didn't bring you in here.'

The two of them sit there until it becomes unbearable. Mattheüs gets up, arranges his clothes, smoothes his hair, says he has to go to his father. He bends his head down between Jack's knees, lays it on his legs that smell of him and his tracksuit. Jack puts his hand on Mattheüs's head, says he doesn't know what more to say. At least he was honest.

Mattheüs tiptoes into the study and takes his father's hand. With his ear against his half-open lips he can only just discern some breathing. He's not in a coma: the hand in his performs tiny twitches of acknowledgement. Mattheüs asks if he has pain. This prompts a hardly distinguishable movement of the chin that has by now become completely beardless. He sits down without releasing the small, trembling bird in his hand.

For the time being he forgets about Jack's objection to the loss of the little death (a thing to cherish while you're still alive), but in the presence of death it's an objection that cannot be sustained; here, only death prevails, imminent, he can see it is upon them.

He doesn't cry. No need for it. He holds his father; with that frail hand in his, he'll hold him as he requested, that's what he'll do, and reminds himself of the most beautiful thing his father ever told him: you are a good son, Mattie. That's how he holds him, that's how he'll hold him to the end, the bequest of those words his only possible consolation.

Where is his father now, he wonders after a while. He tests for warmth over the nostrils. The unconscious is still operating, where is the old man wandering, with which person or thing is he still lingering?

A sob. 'Pa?' There will be no more words.

He unclasps his father's hand from his and quickly pours himself a double brandy that he knocks back, pours another double tot and takes the hand again, delicate now, the skin sacred to the touch because it covers the final human fragility with only the flicker of a pulse somewhere inside to preserve it.

The Sly Fox and Little Red Hen was one of his father's earliest stories. About the little red hen who sat on a rafter in the shed, trying for all she was worth to keep her balance while the fox, sly as sly can be on the floor below, marched and pranced and flattered and flirted so that Little Red Hen felt quite dizzy. That was Pa's best story; he on his lap. He cherishes that intimacy of his father's voice, warm as his own breath, exciting as it rose and fell, and the long whisper just before the hen succumbs and you don't want to know, even though you do know, what's coming.

That, and then later, his father as a man as he saw himself, and as Mattheüs saw him as a man, his father coming from work in his elegant tailored suit and always smelling of money and strange women and the leather of the seats of those dream-mobiles he spirited from the showroom floor (so clean you could eat off them) to the garages of his clients, his father returning from work, half past five or six o'clock or seven o'clock or even later, he always used to phone then, and he'd lean against the frame of the double door of his study while Mattheüs was in there reading or looking for something to do in his favourite room, and his father then, with one arm up against the varnished frame so that his tailored jacket pulled up and showed more of his shirt, a pure white or a pale-blue one, with the right tie knotted in just the right way, and if he then went to greet his father and walked past him, his father remaining in exactly that position, his appeal wasn't lost on his son, he could smell his father, his own private smell after a whole day's working and negotiating that took place without his taking off that jacket, at most a slightly loosened tie.

When he wakes up, he has the feeling that he's been sleeping into his own old age, right until he has arrived where his father is now, the hand in his has grown cold. Pa is dead.

He must have slept for a terribly long time, he can't tell, his mobile phone is in the bedroom, he can't name the hour when his father died. He was waiting for the death rattle; it was supposed to come, still.

Or otherwise he has slept for a very short time, maybe only minutes. His father was still with him a moment ago. *The Sly Fox and Little Red Hen*. Tumbled down. His father.

He takes the hand from his and carefully places it by his father's side on the bedspread. He tests again over the nostrils. It is so.

He'll go and tell Jack. Actually, he needn't really tell Jack anything, he'll just know. (Even though he's angry about their waning sex life, it won't interfere with his ability to read him correctly.) After that he'll go and phone. Sissy, Samantha and Auntie Mary, Aunt Sannie, Uncle Hannes, Dominee Roelf. He'll bring the tidings to each one in a different way, depending on how close they were to Pa. To Sissy he'll say: 'Sissy?' and then she'll know the time has come. She didn't fear Pa's end as he did. She didn't want to come to be with him at the hour of his death. Get finished and move on: she's made of different stuff to him.

He won't use the telephone in the study. His father's body is empty and cooling fast; in the next few hours it will become rigid, and if you place your hand on it then – he's decided already that he won't – the onset of death is more shocking and more incomprehensible than now when you might still, if you slid your hand inside the pyjama jacket and stroked the belly, discern a lukewarmth – that, too, he won't do. He pictures the lukewarmth as blinding-white in colour, tender as the skin of a newborn, more tender and softer than ever, just before rigor mortis sets in.

He goes out and closes the double doors infinitely slowly, and when he hears the soft click, he grabs his chest, his heart jolting, the pain fresh, tremendous, coming with a single, fierce stroke, and not again.

While his father's remains are lying in the mortuary, he decides to open Duiker's Takeaway after all for those two days. The show must go on, says Jack, frankly pleased that the old man has, as he says, got on with it. It's school holidays, and Jack is going to tackle the mustiness in his bedroom from the floor up, although, says Jack, he actually likes the dusty duskiness of his room in broad daylight, the smells and things that lie around just as they were left there.

Sissy talks nonstop about Pa lying so cold and lonely on his own, shame. He reminds her that he can't possibly still be there, it's just bones, dust, she can go and see for herself, she's silent and then eventually says: 'I still don't know whether I'll wear a hat or a mantilla to the funeral.'

Emile presents him with a slaughtered, badly plucked chicken as a mark of respect for his deceased father. He immediately puts the thing away, stuffed into one of those thin plastic bags, its skin is close to the touch. They never again mention his father; none of Emile's business.

Emile is energetic and efficient in all he does, to the point that it's difficult, Mattheüs even finds it disturbing, to explain how he so quickly managed to get on top of everything, even though he maintains that he used to work in a restaurant. He is even more deferential than in the previous week, and this hugely irritates Mattheüs. He doesn't want to work here with a sub-human: the short-arse he literally looks down on, even when he's standing on the pallet. That irritates him even more.

The only way he can counteract the lovelessness – and that's surely what it is – is to succumb to another disturbing tendency, which is to distrust the Congolese. Two of his people, poorly dressed short-arses, turn up with his wife and children over the next two days, supposedly to see him off, the dog also in attendance, as usual. The whole bunch of them some distance away on the pavement as he unlocks the steel gate and the door, and Emile enters underneath his arm and immediately takes the key of the cold room from its hiding place on the shelf under the bottle of sea salt, opens the cold-room door and starts carrying out the heavy pots – he's got these rock-hard little apples for biceps – or a pocket of potatoes or whatever is needed for the day; he knows without even asking or being told. Emile's lot sit there and chatter among themselves, one of the men rolls a cigarette for them all to share, until he asks Emile to tell them all to leave. He uses the dog as an excuse. (Its snout with the gums and fangs dripping saliva seems bigger every time.)

They get on very well over those two days, better than in the previous weeks. Emile doesn't put a foot wrong, even reminds him about preparation for the next day. His own mind isn't all that clear. He's battling with the last image of his father on the bed in the study, the face turned to the ceiling: bloodless, skeletal.

It's wearisome working right next to a person in a cramped space all day long, and then there's also the heat from the four flames of the hob. He hears his father: My son, there is such a thing as intuition, even in us men. Don't let them tell you otherwise. And with the staff working for you, man, you must have a fine perception. Doesn't matter how harsh it seems. It's your business, Mattie. It's your bread and butter, remember that. If it goes wrong, there's nobody to bail you out. It's yours, Mattie. Pa knows you're man enough for the thing, son.

Emile always prefers one of the meat dishes when they have something to eat in the afternoon, and a Coke that makes him burp every time he takes a sip. He makes a point of not using his hands to stuff his mouth. But as soon as Mattheüs has finished and goes to rinse his plate, the hands begin to roll the food into little balls, stuffing them in. Then he jumps up to go to the washbasin, chewing open-mouthed and still shiny with the delicious taste of the food. It's a child-like surrender and gratitude – it's not as if he's blind to the human being who probably for the first time in his life is being fed regularly. If only he could concentrate on that.

His fourth child, not by his wife here in Cape Town, is still in Kakuma, the refugee camp, Emile starts telling him, and turns around often from the washbasin to catch Mattheüs's eye and to convince him of the seriousness of the situation. It's a little boy, he says, and he's also coming out here now. His other father-in-law never wanted him to fetch the boy, even though the mother was dead; the way it works is that in the camp you're given a food coupon for every child you have. So if that child also left, the other father-in-law would lose a food coupon. But the boy has now been released, after all. Father Raymond helped him with this. 'Very good man. Very good heart.' The boy will arrive by plane on Saturday.

Mattheüs says he's glad for Emile's sake. It's his child, he belongs with him. He doesn't ask what the mother died of.

Afterwards, Emile washes his hands with a few drops of sterile soap from the wall-mounted bottle, as Mattheüs has shown him, and dries them with a paper towel. 'I want to make this business a big success, I want to build it and build it.' The pitch-black eyes glisten. 'I need a house, man. My family, we all need a house, I want to buy a house – then I will be a very, very happy man.'

'We'll see.'

Emile unties his apron and crams it into his rucksack, and walks out under Mattheüs's arm.

'You mustn't be angry. *S'il vous plaît*, Matthew.' And only then does he scrape up the courage to ask Mattheüs whether he'll fetch his child from the airport on Saturday.

He goes to the cold room, where he covers the soaking lentils with a cloth, locks the cold-room door, takes out the money, already counted, and puts it in the special reinforced leather bag that he has specially bought, which on cooler evenings he wears under his shirt or between his shirt and jacket, then he switches off the lights, locks the door and the steel gate, and walks briskly to the back of the building where his bakkie is parked.

He keeps coming back to the image of his father, which he cannot consign to oblivion. The ice-cold white log pushed into one of those oblong fridges. (That's not Pa, Sissy.) The night before the funeral, in the sultry, smoky air of Observatory, with taxis going up and down Main, that's the only way he can think of him: with a label around his big toe? His father made into a dead object. Rouge on his lips and cloth stuffed into his cheeks to fill out the hollow grimace. He resolves once again not to go and have a look at him.

When he's switched on the ignition (*B Duiker, number 102* or whatever, written on the label with an ugly old blue ballpoint pen) he remembers the Beretta. Uncle Hannes's. He can't really think of that weapon as his. It belongs to, but not with, Uncle Hannes. In that lonely rondavel on that man-forsaken farm, the poor man can no longer trust himself with it. It was never an altruistic gift.

He hides the leather bag with its cash under the seat, quickly unlocks again, jiggles the pistol in its pouch out from under the lentils, and this time pushes it into the front of his pants, 'You can wear it like that too, Matt, it's what you call a quick-draw position,' Uncle Hannes explained and they both had to laugh; it's so obviously gangster-style, and Matt such a pathetic candidate for a gangster.

Once again outside in the warm smoky air, this time with a Red Bull. And yes, he'll fetch Emile's child, it's hardly a request anyone could refuse.

@ De Waal Drive on the way to Uncle Bennie's funeral, Jack facebooks. *It's an auspicious day. Have you ever thought how heavy it is to take someone who was alive and is now suddenly gone and stone dead, and to shove him underground.*

There's no need for him to say anything. He sits there with the seat belt across his chest – the Mercedes belt holds you tightly – and tries to think in the way that Matt is surely thinking right now. It's a strange privilege to attend your father's funeral, so dressed up and all. Not going to happen to him. *His* father. If someone were to ask him now – he doesn't even know where the man is from whose loins he sprang. Last time it was East London. Maybe he snuffed it a long time ago.

Some way along De Waal Drive, they're signalled to reduce speed and to pull right over onto the shoulder. From behind looms another procession of police cars and motor bikes, the very big ones. With every available flashing light and siren and whatever switched on at full bore. In the middle of the procession of police vehicles there's a pitch-black official car, also a Mercedes, one of those stretch jobs. And this on the day of Uncle Bennie's funeral. Matt snorts. Matt, like no one else he knows, hates this kind of ostentatious crap. A policeman in blue signals to them to pull off even further.

'Fuck it,' Matt slides his window down.

And Jack, his presence of mind still intact, touches Matt's leg. 'Matt, just keep calm now. Please, Matt.'

'It's my father's funeral. You can see we're dressed for it,' Matt tells the policeman.

'I'm sorry, sir.'

'But you can't be late for your father's funeral.' Matt makes an appeal to the respect he knows the policeman, probably a Xhosa, has for the departed. Matt is icily calm, if that is possible. If only the policeman knew him. It's the king of Swaziland, says the policeman. And says again how very sorry he is. And Jack believes him. He can see the man means what he says.

'Oh, him,' says Matt, and Jack touches his leg again – the policeman goes over to the next car that must also move further over onto the shoulder – 'that little stoep-shitter!'

'Little palace stoep-shitter!'

'Tramples his people into the mud. Mud fuckhead!'

'Fucking pap-guzzler.'

'Virgin fucker. Slave-girl fucker. Fifty weddings or more. Twenty Mercedes S600s in his garage. If my father had to know this,' says Matt, 'that his son would be late for his funeral because some tin-pot king claims the whole of De Waal Drive for himself. If he had to know that!'

Jack aims his camera at the car with the king that is now almost alongside them. A policeman comes running to stop this, no photos, please, but has to rush to the next car and the next, where one after another, people are clicking away.

When the official car is right next to them, the back window glides open. Unfuckingreal, like in a movie. And King M III is sitting there, stuffed into his uniform with gold piping all over the show. It's totally over the top. A smug fat-arse on the soft leather seat made specially for his majesty. No longer the young king with his brown biceps and his triumphant pheasant-feather crown, but an old, overfed house cat bloated with arrogance and selfishness. As plain as daylight, they see him looking at the two of them with his fat eyes, maybe because they're also in a Mercedes. And would you fucking believe it, here's a gnawed chicken bone that comes flying out of the window, sailing gracefully through the air. Tink, they hear it strike the right-hand side of the bonnet of Matt's car.

'Fuck,' they shout together.

Mattheüs laughs so hard that the tears put out his newly lit cigarette. Jack too. Could you ever. They laugh and laugh, and when they recover, the procession has passed by. Mattheüs's laughter has changed into a falsetto. And he has to get out to piss next to the car, traffic or no traffic.

Inside the car, Jack smells the strange odour of the fart he's just released. Maybe Sissy's cabbage from last night, he doesn't recognise the green-barley smell of it. He looks over Matt's shoulder up towards the mountain at the crowns of the pine trees. Matt is still giggling. Probably also a reaction to the last few days. How faithfully Matt nursed his father. Bless him! And then the inevitable tension that follows death. Now the man who formed such an enormous part of his life is gone. For ever and ever. How is Uncle

Bennie's son going to react to this? Or how should a son react to the death of his father? The public is going to watch Matt. Is he up to it?

Jack thinks about all these things as they swing back onto De Waal Drive and drive on to the church. He tries to imagine all of it, but stops short in a kind of fatherless vacuum. There was never anyone in his life that he had such a fraught relationship with. He can't imagine Matt's state of mind.

Jack again posts on Facebook: @ funeral of Matt's father, Reformed Church, Gardens. *Matt sharp in black suit, black shirt with the small cutaway collar and an off-black silk tie.*

The previous evening at Matt's place, drinks were poured in the study. He and Samantha carried Uncle Bennie's sickbed and most of his stuff back to the main bedroom. Sissy placed a large flower arrangement on Uncle Bennie's desk. Feminine touch. Uncle Bennie's Philips was put away. On a stretch of open bookshelf to the right of the fireplace.

'Go and seal that machine. It's for nobody else's ears,' Matt says to him in between the funeral arrangements.

He takes a piece of red ribbon, the kind used by flower arrangers, and ties it around the Philips in the way you'd wrap a parcel. He rummages in Uncle Bennie's drawer and finds what he's looking for: sealing wax. Over a lighted match he drips raw-red wax onto the knot at the top of the Philips. He stands back: pleased that he could do it so nicely for Matt.

Uncle Bennie's clothes, all of them, were carted back. Samantha said she'd miss the old man. For her and her mother he really was one of the most genuine men they'd ever known. Troy, her mother's brother, isn't that bad either, he always comes to mow the tiny lawn in front of their house with the lawnmower that Uncle

Bennie himself had given them.

He's okay and also not quite okay with the family. Sissy especially is nice to him, over-nice, if you ask him. Apart from Uncle Hannes, he doesn't really know what the family makes of him and Matt. They're polite, but without being inclusive. For instance, he wouldn't be able to say to Marko, Sissy's husband, ag, fuck you Marko, without offending him. There isn't that kind of closeness.

Next thing, Sissy gets it into her head that he should also be one of the pallbearers, even though the list with the names of the six bearers had already been printed. She just talks without thinking through the suggestion. 'Let's face it, they'll be living together in Pa's house in any case. Jack is like family.' So he got up and left them all there with their wine and their stupid discussion: whatever.

For the funeral, Sissy wore the biggest broad-brimmed hat he'd ever seen. Black, with these black lace frills hanging down all around, fascinator-style. She doesn't actually need sunglasses, but she still wears them. The hat's brim sticks out so far that Marko can't sit shoulder-to-shoulder with her in the pew. To their left are Samantha, and Auntie Mary with a green pillbox hat. Auntie Mary has pulled her Zimmer frame in close and is resting one arm on it. Her lace-edged green satin handbag dangles from her other arm.

Matt's knee bounces up and down, beta blockers and all. When he touches Matt, his arm or shoulder or whatever, he's like one of those people who've cried for days on end and been gutted by it all. Matt said he wasn't going to cry in church or when the coffin is lowered. He wants to stay strong for his father. In spite of all the shit that Uncle Bennie caused Matt in his life. He was so straight, so straightforward. So set on his principles. On what he thought was right. This and this is how you must live your life. There is only one way. All those things that made Matt's life hell. And yet, Matt is the one who loved his father most. If you look at Sissy now, or listen to her when she talks, there's no question about it. Matt was mad about the man. The father and the son. The intimacy between them, almost brutal. Against all odds. Jack finds it a very, very beautiful thing to behold from the outside.

The whole time in church and throughout the sermon from the New Testament – the dominee had chosen the parable of the sower – Jack is moved. He's only been in a church once or twice in his life. His mother and father (when the bastard was still with them) never put a foot inside a church. 'I'm a child of Jesus,' his mother would say. She enjoyed doing her nails in the sun on the stoep on Sundays.

It's not much of a church inside. Dark wood and face brick. Stark, nothing to look at. And yet, the longer he sits there listening and switching off and listening again, the more he wants to cry. It doesn't matter that he's no longer following the dominee. The dominee has a melodious voice without any exaggerated rhythms. And doesn't pronounce Jesus with a drawn-out 'e' sound. (Uncle Bennie used to say it's a Reformed thing.)

Jack sits there in the midst of all the stuff he's experiencing and thinking. It's a comfort. That's what it feels like to him. He's right there in the pool of sunlight. Kitsch, okay, but he's so secure there. It's not as if he's going to join this church now, or any other church, for that matter. It's just that he suddenly feels provided for. Included. Snug in a basket of down. Something like that. He cries, he howls like a dog. It's enough to make him feel ashamed of himself. Sissy peeks at him from under her massive hat: what's the matter with him now? Matt even offers his handkerchief to him.

He's crying about his drug days, about that last sex incident that almost tore him in two. About Okechi the Nigerian who's squeezing him for payment with that shit voice of his that actually carries a threat, who sure as hell is going to sniff him out at Matt's house one of these days. He cries about the lovelessness of that house of theirs at 114 Villiers Road, Worcester, that he's been trying to get out of his mind for who knows how long. About the misery of those days, those nights when he had to go to bed. When? Seven o'clock or nine o'clock or twelve o'clock, makes no difference. Nobody ever told him: go and crawl into bed now, boykie. His mother with her eternal men's socks, summer and winter. And his sad, narrow bed in that back room with its high window where homing pigeons sat and crapped; to this day, he hates all pigeons. Sometimes it was only him and their cat in that empty house. Those days rise up inside him, everything he doesn't want to remember. He's crying about everything. And the recent thing at Zilverbosch. And Matt's obsession with porn that's messed him up. He noticed it the other evening when Matt approached him and the two of them tried to get going. He couldn't even get a fucking hard-on for the man. He cries about that. He cries so hard that he has to drop his head on his knees, and Matt puts a hand on his shoulder.

After the service, he stands to one side under a cypress that smells of resin. He couldn't wait to inhale smoke deep, deep into his lungs. Matt is fine. He's not going to cry. He's come through it all. In honour of his father.

Charnie on Facebook: *So how was it?*

Jack: *Fucked up. Bawled all the time.*

Charnie: *Ag, sweetie. And the coffin? Will you also be carrying?*

Jack: *No. Better that way.*

Mattheüs has shut the study door on the rest of the house with all its blown-in occupants: Uncle Hannes and Sissy and Marko and the children, fresh from a visit to the Castle, the children's cheeks inappropriately flushed, as if their oupa hadn't been buried the day before.

He inspects himself in the mantelpiece mirror: paler, older. Aunt Sannie has arrived with not one, but two of her milk tarts. (Death unites the living, Bennie was like her own brother, ag, even more than that.) If his father had still been here, he'd simply have chased her out. No, he probably wouldn't have.

Mattheüs walks past her and notices how she's managed to tie her apron symmetrically behind her bum, and involuntarily experiences a kind of fellow-feeling for the woman. Pa's attorney will be arriving soon to read the will, and Aunt Sannie is the one who arranges the tea for the occasion, all daintily, with cake forks and the small cocktail serviettes, all of which she manages to find without asking; this could easily have been her own home.

He paces around in the study so restlessly that he can't hear his own footsteps. His father's spirit lingers there as nowhere else in the house. For the time being, he won't move anything. All the books about cars, the ugly German guides to Stuttgart and the Munich Hofbrauhaus, for now he won't store them or throw them away as he'd intended. Even the *Battle of Blood River* painting – everything can remain right there to provide his father with a final earthly resting place. This is the only place he'll be able to sit down with his father for one last time. And if he eventually leaves, he'll be free. And be able to honour his father in his own way and not as his father wanted him to. Duiker's Takeaway – if he failed tomorrow, he wouldn't even have to report this to his father.

He moves the chair away from his father's desk without making a sound, sits down and picks up his father's paper knife, holds it under his nose, strokes the handle. The fact is that he still doesn't know what to make of his father's permanent absence. Words like *wastrel* and *loafer* – in all honesty he can't remember when last he'd heard his father use them, if indeed he ever did – have become redundant in the totality of memories of him, he doubts if even Aunt Sannie would still dare or wish to use them. He and Jack will just be able to walk in here and kiss each other however and whenever they like. He taps the paper knife on the desk: the liberation he'd so long hoped for hasn't dawned as he'd imagined it.

He hears the gates slide open outside. That would be the attorney; Sissy must have opened them. Tomorrow morning, early, they're all driving back to Laingsburg, and the house will belong to him and Jack. He gets up and stands in the centre of the room, on the carpet to the left of the circle of chairs where they'll all be gathering for the reading of the will; stock-still he stands there, aware of his own breathing as he exhales and inhales, in an attempt to guide himself in his thoughts about his father. It's the most unexpected phenomenon, slightly shocking to say the least, that he has no desire to shout out: the old dogmatist is dead, from now on you can make and break as you wish. A shaft of sunlight falls through the half-open curtains with hundreds of dust motes in free flight, and he succeeds in recalling his father's smell within that dusty sunlight, not as he later smelled on his sickbed, but before, with his expensive, sophisticated aftershave complementing the smell of his body.

The attorney, previously Uncle Frans to him, now simply Frans, is in every respect a grey man. Grey suit, grey temples, and a threadbare formality that you expect from lawyers of his age, but don't want anywhere near you. In actual fact, he doesn't know him at all. Just that one afternoon when he'd seen his father and the attorney together in a rather intimate situation. It was a fortnight or so after his father first had to go onto heavy doses of morphine; from then on it was only in the mornings, briefly, for a few hours at most, that he was able to give you the opportunity to reach him, their father, Pappie, as Sissy then started calling him. It was during that window period too that she phoned him, in fulfilment of her duty (that's how she saw it). It must also have been during those lucid periods that he'd made the recordings on the Philips for him. He'd noticed where Jack had put the Philips without actually looking in that direction. Jack was surprised that he hadn't started listening straight away, out of curiosity. In a year's time, maybe, he'll be able to listen to the tapes, when there's enough distance between him and Benjamin Duiker, just a man, nothing more than a progenitor, in the end. But maybe he'll leave the red ribbon sealed as is.

What had made the situation between his father and the attorney intimate – and Mattheüs recalls it now in an attempt to see the grey man as, in some sense, a friend of the father and the family – was that his father allowed the attorney to touch him. Mattheüs was walking past and stopped in the doorway – only one of the double doors was open – and he noticed that his father had lowered his pyjama pants slightly, without this in any way making him guilty of indecency, for in spite of his blindness, his father had always been as set on propriety as other people were on fresh air, and then guided the attorney's hand to feel the lymphoma lump just above his groin, a touching attempt on his father's part to share something of his path of suffering with him – his friend and confidant of years' standing. Here, take a seat, Frans, his father had then said. And this intimate recollection will, he hopes, enable him after all to treat the man with some cordiality.

Soon afterwards, everyone comes in: Uncle Hannes with his pipe and an intimate detachment, if such a thing is possible, probably because of his sharing of the contents of that last love letter to his Parisian lover, and maybe also because of the Beretta, who knows; and then Sissy, trim and well groomed, even and especially in a situation like the funeral of her father, which would have left other people rather pale and drawn; and then Marko, with the striped long-sleeved shirt and jeans with a sharply ironed pleat, his idea of city clothes; and following on their heels, Aunt Sannie carrying the largest tray in their house, with all the tea things, 'Thank you, but I may as well carry it myself,' to Marko, who offers to help her.

His phone rings and he goes and stands next to the window. It's Emile. He wants to know when the takeaway will reopen, his people have to eat, he says with undisguised impatience, which makes Mattheüs realise afresh that he'll be firing the bugger without any mercy the moment he walks into the shop again.

'Problems?' asks Sissy, with her ear for problems.

'The guy who works for me is so damn cheeky. Little shit.'

His choice of words makes the attorney look up from where he has in the meantime taken the will from the front compartment of his briefcase and placed it squarely on his grey knees, his left hand stuck inside the middle of the file, protective of the private stuff inside. With the wedding ring on his finger and the aged skin of his hand, also grey, it strikes Mattheüs that the man still retains something of that old-fashioned authority that is limited to the

206

male domain and which still intimidates him, even though he can see it for the hollow sham that it is.

Sissy pours. 'There's nothing, after all, like a nice cup of tea,' says Uncle Hannes as he reaches for his; he is served the second cup, after the attorney. And the latter surprises them all by asking if he might rather have a glass of Bennie's whisky, please, if it's not too much trouble, without ice, just with an equal amount of water, and Mattheüs – who gets up and looks down at the perfect circle of the man's bald spot, hairless for so long that it seems like old, tanned leather – experiences the slightest twinge of he doesn't quite know what, something like an itch in the butt.

'Anybody else for a drink?'

He places the crystal glass to the left of the attorney's cup, his poured tea untouched, and notices how the document under the left hand is still perched in exactly the same position on his grey knees, the attorney's arms protectively encircling *The Last Will and Testament of Benjamin Duiker*. While he's about it, he pours himself a stiff one too, and again takes his seat next to the attorney. Sissy has meanwhile sliced the milk tart and served it on the plates, each with a lace serviette, and he has to concede, if there's a woman who knows her milk tart, it's Aunt Sannie.

There is anticipation, there is a feeling of excitement, after all; he peeps at Sissy who's sitting right across from him, quietly tapping her nails against the side of her porcelain cup.

The attorney moves the glass of whisky a fraction to the left, the cup of tea and the plate with milk tart to the right, removes the document from the envelope, and then places the envelope on the space he's made for it on the coffee table. He takes a sip of whisky, presses his lips together, takes his handkerchief from his pocket and blots his lips with it, opens the document at page one, takes another sip.

@ 9 Poinsettia Road, he Facebooks Charnie. *Playing with children, Matt's sister's. When last did you play with children? Healing kind of thing to do. I = good space. Really. Believe it or not.*

He's gathered the children on the lawn. The lawn has been mowed, but not so short that the white shows through, and the edges have been trimmed. (He can hear Uncle Bennie on the subject.) Also, the inside of the house looks immaculate, specially for Uncle Bennie's funeral. Jack doesn't know how strongly Matt still feels the presence of his father with all his instructions. So the children have to be outside when the will is read: that's how it's done. Okay, he'll play with them. Cute, the three of them. Sort of country kids, innocent, with respect for adults, but also for bugs and birds and things they notice in the garden.

The smallest one hides behind her older sister's legs. She's instinctively wary of his shaven head, of a man with a different vibe to her father. He swings the two eldest around, first the one and then the other, by gripping their hands in his and then spinning them around so that the momentum of his body whirls them upwards and makes them fly horizontally over the lawn. Shrill little-girl screams. The little one is still holding back. Jumps up and down as she spontaneously shares in the flying delight of her sisters. No, not yet, she first wants to watch.

He digs a Coke can out of the rubbish bin and fills it with pebbles and teaches them to play I Spy. Chucks the tin way over on the other side of the lawn, so that the plovers scatter noisily. Their time to hide is as long as it takes him to fetch the tin. Shrieks trail behind them as they scramble for hiding places in their oupa's garden, which is not unfamiliar to them. He leaves the little one in her hiding place as she splutters with the tension. If he drags her out now, she'll definitely yell her head off. Funny timid little kid.

But their enthusiasm gives him more stamina. A loaded word, enthusiasm. He's explained it in class. From the Greek: possession by a god.

When, after the sixth turn, he collapses out of breath on the fanned steps, the little one shuffles closer and gingerly touches his shaven head: 'Does Uncle really not like hair?'

He can't tell when last he's felt so secure. First in church and now at this house and in this garden behind its walls. He and Matt. Here. He looks up when he hears something and points it out to the children. In the wind-swept blue sky above them, an aeroplane is writing the words *Happy Birthday Danny* in white smoke against the heavens.

Aunt Sannie comes out with a wedge of milk tart for each of them. When all four of them have taken theirs and sat down on the slate-paved stoep, Jack experiences the homeliness again.

Almost corny, he facebooks again.

Charnie: *Enjoy it my friend. It's yours.*

This is what it must have been like all those years for Matt and his sister, no matter how much grief there was in their family. Who didn't have their share? The house behind them, stylish and very beautiful, but above all a place, a kind of castle they could enter and feel safe in. Very. And this is where the two of them must also have sat, just as they're doing now, and then Matt's mother probably brought them cool drinks and cookies. And nobody could take it away from them. Maybe the cool drinks and cookies, but not their untouchableness here inside these walls with a mother and a father, and the rest of the world on the other side and who cares. Maybe here with Matt he'll be able to make a home for the first time in his life. Maybe he and Matt can be a family, just the two of them, but still a family, with a house and a garden. A security you can believe in. Every night you come back to it, milk and bread and food and things in the cupboards, beds with cool sheets or cosy flannel sheets in winter. Beds for ever! Always there, each one sturdy on its legs in its room with a door you can close behind you.

Matt is sitting in there now with his family, listening to the will that he claims he already knows. (The little one has now come to sit between his legs with her milk-tart hands: 'Uncle doesn't smell like my daddy.') He and Matt can sort things out in the safe haven of the house. Massive. He can't describe it in any other way. The privilege of becoming a permanent resident in such a house. He's going to grab hold of it with a passion, with everything he's got. Sitting here with the little one's blonde hair right under his nose, specially washed for her oupa's funeral with Sunsilk or whatever shampoo they use on the farm, he's not even bothered about his and Matt's pathetic sex life.

He hasn't even said it to Matt and maybe he never will. The guy's had a kind of furtiveness about him ever since he started with the never-ending porn thing. He knows it, he can see it now. Images and stuff, he doesn't know how hard-core the shit is he's been watching, but let's face it, it's completely changed him. He's not stupid. It's as if everything Matt does now and wants to do or is going to do leaves a kind of shadow trail. When he gets up in the morning and showers and prepares for work, Matt he means, he first has to open his computer and quickly check some site or other that's refreshed daily or even hourly. His pre-work breakfast. At first he was embarrassed with him in the room, but now Matt does it without batting an eye. That's how he's changed since he moved in. Matt also frowns more often. His takeaway is taking it out of him. He doesn't know how Uncle Bennie's death will still affect him. Maybe not at all.

And yet he loves him so much, that guy who is at this moment sitting there listening to his father's will in his father's study that he's prepared specially for the reading, the long curtains half-drawn to give the room a dimness. As he likes it. He loves the way he does things, everything in his special Matt way. Thoroughly, and with a sharpened pencil, not unlike Uncle Bennie. Even when Matt touches him, it's hard and all-embracing. So it's inevitable, he supposes, that he'll be thorough with his porn thing too. Burning to begin with, inextinguishable to the end. Let him get through it his way. And Matt will, for sure. There's no other way for him.

The children want him to play another kind of game. Wilder, faster. The little one the ringleader now. They make a circle around him and egg him on. Lovely, the children.

He makes them throw the Coke can now, and runs off to the back to the outside room where the mower and spanners and stuff are kept. In the darkness thick with oil fumes, his thoughts keep running. He's so glad he loves a man. Everything about Matt attracts him, and he's not only talking about his butt and the package in his Calvin Kleins. If he looks at Sissy or Charnie or some of the female staff at Zilverbosch – he simply doesn't know what it takes for a man to fall in love with women like that. He hasn't got it. And it's utterly okay with him.

'Where's Oom,' the little girls shout from way over on the other side of the house. He doesn't come out. Five, six minutes pass. And he starts his own game that he'll draw out until they can hardly take it any longer, he'll push them to the edge of little-girl hysteria. He goes round to the other side of the house, the south side where the people are sitting listening to the will, walks along the path of river stones leading to the lemon tree, hunches his back and slowly circles the tree. When they notice him, like that, they all scream, weak and barely able to breathe with the tension of it all. The game has switched: now he's going to catch them, they can sense it, they're afraid of him, and it's totally for real.

He can't remember when last he was so happy, he again thinks to himself. Even as far as the milk tart he can still taste in his mouth; it all completes the picture. A house with a pantry full of boxes of biscuits and Weet-Bix and jam, and cupboards full of linen and stuff, thick walls that will still be standing long after everyone is dead, full curtains to make everyone inside feel comfortable, nice and cool or nice and warm or nice and dim, and flowers and things that you smell when you open the big sash windows. And that's where he and his man are going to live. Believe it or not. Like people who respect their living space. And who inspire respect, he means, because if you arrive here at number nine Poinsettia Road, you know you've arrived. His breath comes fast and warm: he can't wait for it all to begin.

'I just want to mention beforehand,' says Pa's attorney, with his eyes on the open document encircled by his hands, 'I want to say the following in preparation. A will like that of your father, and brother, is carefully considered. Everyone must bear this in mind.' (The man's eyes still piously downcast.) 'And it's important to bear in mind that a will seldom turns out as expected by the heirs.' Now he looks up with a gaze intended to be benign. He looks first at Uncle Hannes, then at Sissy, and finally at Mattheüs. (How transparent the man is, without having the vaguest inkling of the fact.)

'Well, on that note I'll get going:

I the undersigned, Benjamin Duiker, ID number such and such, at present resident at (yes okay), *hereby rescind all previous wills, codicils* (get to the point), *and nominate Maria Anna de Witt, born Duiker, Mattheüs Duiker, Susan Helmien Strydom* (what's Aunt Sannie's name doing there?) *and the Reformed Church, Gardens, as the only heirs of my estate, movable as well as immovable goods, nothing excluded.*

The residence at number nine Poinsettia Road, Rondebosch, shall be put on the market as soon as is practicable, and after costs have been deducted the proceeds will be evenly divided between Maria Anna de Witt, born Duiker, Susan Helmien Strydom on behalf of the Silver Cloud Christian Fellowship, and the Reformed Church, Gardens.'

Sissy makes big eyes at him, then looks at Marko, and then he sees her pull her finger from the ear of her teacup and point at the door, in the direction of the passage, towards his bedroom where there's no Jack right now – he's in the garden with her children – at his bed, at Jack in his bed, at him and Jack on that messy, rumpled bed. Now she lightly waves her index finger from side to side, and Marko, with his stupid forehead and the stupid line that the sweatband of his felt hat leaves on it, nods his head in full comprehension, oh that, now he understands. You'd have to be a dumbfucking idiot not to know exactly what message Sissy is sending to Marko. And he, he's sinking, his whole body's sinking, and his hands in front of him on his knees, on his crotch, limply by the sides of the chair and back again on his crotch, his hands turn to blocks of bloodless marble.

For a moment, the shallow grey eyes of Pa's attorney rest on him before he carries on reading: *'The full contents of the house will with due discretion be divided between Maria Anna de Witt, born Duiker, and Mattheüs Duiker.*

'The Mercedes E-class is bequeathed to Mattheüs Duiker.'

(Sissy's eyes still on him.)

'Stop fucking staring at me!' Mattheüs jumps up and in one movement sweeps his whisky glass from the table so that it shatters on the antique tiles of the fireplace. Uncle Hannes splutters in pure discomfort.

'This has been cooked up. It can't be the truth. Pa wouldn't do it to me. I looked after him to the end. Not you. Not one of you!'

Sissy, also white as a sheet, jumps up, 'Mattie,' she nips around the back of her chair to fetch him, to hold him, but he pushes her aside and runs from the dining room, Aunt Sannie, clutching a dishcloth to her mouth, standing at the kitchen door, 'Yes, you hypocrite, Silver Cloud, my arse,' calls out to Jack while fleeing through the front door – Jack with the children way over there by the lemon tree – puts up two plovers that screech in terror, and sinks to his haunches, wishes he could cry about what's happening to him here, and all he can think of, all he's filled with, is how long it took him to love his father, how long, a lifetime he worked at it, the bitter nightmares and the sudden flare-ups when things went badly wrong between him and his father, he was eventually able to list each one of the occasions that were the original triggers for his hatred of his father, the sudden surge of nausea while sitting on the toilet or lying on Clifton beach; and how long hasn't it taken him to process it all and to see eventually that this is a man acting in good faith, his own father who wants nothing but the best (from the perspective of his set of values) for him. Towards the end, long before that, for years in actual fact, he'd felt compassion for his father, with all his whims and things, his mood swings, all his loves; it was no longer a matter of trying, he really did feel empathy for his father. When he'd started seeing more and more of Jack, there was a flaring up of objections that no longer affected him as they earlier had; he just wrote him off as the old man with drooping balls, a deliberately disparaging image to defuse his father's objections, that's how he'd thought of all his rubbishy old stuff that petered out towards the end and then stopped altogether. He'd believed that his father's change of heart had resulted from respect for him and respect for him and Jack (not a bad chappie, Pa called him), and he was always so very warm-hearted and polite to Jack. And in that last year or so he was constantly at his father's side – the devotion of a believer. He became familiar with his thighs, his arms, his buttocks, his cheeks, his dead eyes, every nook and cranny of his father's body, wipe and massage – it might just as well have been his own.

With his fingernail, he scratches a bit of moss off the slate path, gets up to go back and hear out the will, and persuades himself that this is not the latest, the last version, of the will of Benjamin Duiker, it's impossible; and realises as he walks into the entrance hall and smells their house, a blend of floor wax and wilting proteas and kelim dust and the Duikers, their characteristic smell, that it's nonsense what he's thinking right now. And: how would he manage it? This house is the only one that he knows intimately, he's never in all his thirty-two years had his own place, how on God's earth will he ever begin to hate such a house as a precondition to getting out of there, how will he ever banish from his consciousness this house with its history.

The people in the study are sitting in stony silence, with just the crystal shards of the glass, scattered on the rectangle of tiles, glittering as the light catches them, and both Sissy and Marko, who must in the meantime have helped themselves to a drink, take a sip as he enters.

'Well, yes,' says Uncle Hannes to no one in particular, 'old Bennie was a real old bastard, there's no getting away from that.'

'What else?' Mattheüs takes a long drag at his cigarette, 'What about the rest of his money, his shares?'

'Mattheüs, please, I think we must first try to get some perspective on the matter,' says the attorney. (How he despises the old-fashioned prick of a man.) 'Sit down first so that we can carry on reading your father's will like civilised people. Can someone pour the man another drink?' (He hates, *hates* his condescension, how could Pa ever have chosen such a piece of shit for his will.)

He requests that the will be read from the beginning, please, he'll sit quietly to the end, keep his trap shut, and now, as he hears it for a second time from that prim and proper mouth of the attorney with his sibilants and his tidy consonants – he's willing to bet that mouth has never serviced his wife – he knows that's it, that's how his father wanted it, 'codicil' and 'legal consequences' and 'Master of the Supreme Court'. He hears all the terms without considering or wanting to consider their context; he doesn't know what to do with himself. Maybe get up and go and look at himself in the mirror above the fireplace to see what his face is showing.

When there's a pause, he has no idea where in the will or why, Sissy comes and crouches next to him and takes his hand and drags the empty chair closer and sits down next to him, takes his half-smoked cigarette and has a pull, first time in years, and says very softly, as gently as she can: 'He knew about you and Jack here in the house, Matt.'

'How?' he asks. The attorney keeps gazing expressionlessly at the document, page four or five or whatever, and Marko looks straight ahead at his ironed jeans, both of them to sort of pretend that they can't hear what he and Sissy are saying. Only Uncle Hannes, the good old honest type, looks at the two of them, at what they're saying and what's happening.

'Pa told me on the telephone.'

'That he was going to change the will?'

'No, he never said that. You know yourself how he was, Matt. You know how he kept things to himself.'

'Don't come and tell me how Pa was. I knew him a thousand times better than you did.'

'Matt, it's a shock to me too. It's the last thing I want for you. Ag, for heaven's sake,' she looks at Marko, 'you can have my share, or a part of it, I don't really care. It's only money, after all.'

And Marko mumbles something about the drought, that she should think about them too, the conditions at Luiperdskop, and he thinks he's going to lose it right there, hearing such undiluted shit as if he's not even in the room. He looks up at the Blood River picture that always upset him as a child, the dark-green shadows, the jack-in-the-box Zulus and the terrified Boers with those hysterical plumes of smoke from their guns, the fact that *that* – that – should be named as the founding moment of a nation or a people, it's ridiculous, it's the first thing he'd wanted to take down and chuck out. But now, this house, everything, he wants nothing, just the things in his bedroom, nothing else, Sissy can have it all and stuff it into her already over-full house, he's decided already, none of this dreck to stir up all kinds of memories in him, he's done with everything in here.

The attorney's voice, crawling on, an oiled insect-thing penetrating deep inside every one of your orifices. 'Mattheüs, if I may say something about your father and me, about some of our conversations. I want you to know that your father himself wrestled with this, it was never a cut-and-dried affair. I guided him in all this to the best of my abilities. In the long run, your father, independently, and I want to stress this most strongly in the light of the emotional issue that it is, in the long run, your father decided on his own, after he'd made some careful calculations, that the financial support or monetary gift, depending on how one looks at it, that he provided you with for your four-year overseas trip, plus the funding of your present business plus the Mercedes, brings your inheritance in line with that of your sister; in fact, it is slightly larger.'

At this point, Mattheüs gets up and gestures to the man to be quiet, he is cold, that's how calm he is, and when he starts speaking, he is just as cool, and with that indomitable authority he's inherited from his father. (He couldn't stand it when his father carried on in that loaded tone of voice.) He walks to the liquor cabinet and refills his glass and speaks while walking, his back to the four people seated there. 'I don't need your explanation or anybody else's. I knew my father better than you ever could. I'm asking once again: What about all his shares? What happened to them?'

'There are investments that will mature in a few years' time. They are bequeathed to you and your sister, as stipulated further on in his will. I haven't come to that yet. Mattheüs, if I may add: You must, you have to also realise that your father lived well; he was not a man who stinted on things. That Mercedes E-class in the garage is less than a year old. He never drove the same model for long. Just think: he's been retired for more than twenty years. That's the first thing. And the second thing is that Motor & Allied Workers' Insurance didn't cover all his medical expenses. Your father was treated for three years with the very latest medicines, MabThera if I'm not mistaken, some of them not even approved by the Medical Council, but it was nevertheless his wish that they be used. But now you must all remember, these medicines were unfortunately not yet covered by his medical insurance. I'm talking about something in the region of R900 000 here. Then there are my own charges – your father unfortunately had his will repeatedly redrafted. There were administrative costs involved, I don't know how else to put it.'

Mattheüs doesn't sit down again. He buzzes around the study like a bee or something; he loathes the man so much that, unusually for him, he thinks it might be a sin. He walks past his father's modest collection of books, Pa always wanted to add to it, always said, man, if I have time, I want to buy a whole lot of books, you can help me with that, Mattie. His father was never a great reader. His father. What now? Whither, now, him and his father?

And whither him and Jack once the house has been sold? A flat. Where? In Sea Point?

He can't get past it: that the will is a refutation of everything he'd believed existed between him and his father. He'll be grappling with this for the rest of his life. He doesn't have it in him to get over the severed connections, printed here in black and white.

'Let me give you a refill, Matt,' and Uncle Hannes takes his glass and goes to pour him a drink. 'You know,' he says when he's right next to him, 'I gave my love away too cheaply to my Paul. That's what I'm thinking of right now. It's the same thing that happened between you and your father.'

'You've got no idea what you're talking about, Uncle Hannes.'

Sissy unhooks the copper dustpan and brush from the stand on the mantelpiece and starts sweeping up the shards without missing a single one. He looks at her hunched back that suddenly no longer reflects the youthfulness of her face and goes outside to Jack and the children.

'Just a quick call to hear how things are. Can't talk for long. I think of you so much, Boetie.'

'Since when have you been Boetie-ing me?'

'Ag, Matt, don't be like that. We have to pull together now. There's just the two of us left. Don't give up now, please, Matt. Have you and Jack found a flat yet?'

'Not yet. Don't know if we will.'

'But where are you going to live, Matt? The auction's in a week.'

'Nearly all the stuff is in storage now. The house is empty. All the walls have been stripped. Not a single portrait or painting left. It's horrible. I just about die when I have to get up at night and go to the kitchen. That echo of nothing, no carpets, no furniture.'

'It's better like that, then you can start taking leave of the place. Mattie. Think about it. It's reality, please, I don't want you to be hurt any more. The sooner the better.'

'The sooner the better what?'

'Ag, please, Matt. You must get out of there. Number nine Poinsettia Road's time has passed.'

'That's easy for you to say. This house is part of me in a way it was never part of you. Listen, Sissy, I broke open that old kist with ma's stuff inside. You remember, we could never find the key. There are some of her old dresses in there, everything still as she folded it in tissue paper with moth balls and all, just like that. There's that sea-green dress of hers, do you remember it?'

'With the beads down the front, Pa said it made her look like an ice maiden.'

'The beads are in a V, almost like the snail trail of hairs on a man's stomach.'

'I beg your pardon?'

'Are you coming to the auction?'

'Too tied up here with the children and everything. It's terribly dry here, you've got no idea. We have to feed all the sheep. I might still have come for your sake, but I don't actually feel up to it. I'd rather not know what happens to that house. It's over and out for me, Boetie.'

'Sissy?'

'What?'

'No, never mind.'

'Say it!'

'You know, it's not really the house I'm making such a fuss about. That's not what's making me feel so raw.'

'I know, Boetie. I know.'

'Can't sleep through any more. It's like a knife that's been pushed into me and someone twists and twists the blade till I want to go mad.'

'What about therapy, won't that be a solution? So you can get it all out of your system.'

'Do you think I've got money for that now? If anything goes wrong with my takeaway, I'm buggered.'

'Don't give up, Matt.'

'Okay, okay.'

'I must get going, fetch children and so on. Bye, Matt. Love you lots.'

'What must I do with ma's kist stuff? Those dresses are precious.'

'I don't know. Can't think now.'

Cunt.

It's three days or so before the auction. Mattheüs just knows that a house with a garden like this, a real gem, it'll sell like hot cakes, he's working like a man possessed to get Duiker's Takeaway going again: he doesn't want to miss the bus. When he says this to Emile, he nods and carries on chopping the pile of garlic on his board, understands absolutely nothing.

He pitches up every morning all shiny and scrubbed, extravagantly sprayed with Clicks deodorant, and always with a subservience you seldom come across in Cape Town, and smeared on top of all this, like rancid butter, is that wicked little smile of his. He no longer sees his wife and children and the dirty great dog, nor his comrades that he used to drag along with him in the morning as if they were a kind of gang or something, right up to the gate of Duiker's Takeaway. Mattheüs now realises that it's a form of security that he, a stranger in Cape Town, wanted to surround himself with. And there's his efficiency and dedication and the knowledge that Mattheüs won't just fire him, something he doesn't actually say, but Mattheüs knows it's what he's thinking in his struggle for survival, his own and that of his family; and by lunchtime, with the main rush of customers, he breaks out in a sweat, 'That deodorant you use is shit,' and to compensate for his wayward body, he tries to serve even more efficiently, to count change, to carry out instructions, it becomes impossible to think of Duiker's without the Congolese.

And Matthew must please not forget to drive him to the airport in his car tomorrow evening, please Matthew, that's when his son arrives from Kenya, it's a big day for him, he smiles sweetly to involve Mattheüs in whatever way he can, in the good and the bad of his life (right now, only good); and Mattheüs, who keeps shying away, looking away from this man, away, and self-tormentingly, almost like the adolescent satisfaction he repeatedly experiences after the umpteenth porn fix, struggles with what he's started calling the 'severed connection'. His father, who was simply not in a position to make the connection between his care for him, his openly expressed love, you could even call it blatant love, and then drawing a line from that indisputable point to making proper provision for him, Mattheüs Duiker, in his will.

The recurrent disappointment with the man overwhelms him, so that at times he's left standing there with one of the big saucepans as if his hands have been tied to its handles with a set of clever knots, and Emile notices immediately that there's something wrong, makes clicking sounds with his tongue, even touches Mattheüs's arm fleetingly, and would go so far as to hug him if he were given any encouragement by Mattheüs.

It eats at him: the total breakdown of the man he'd believed in, wanted to believe, the man he'd give another chance to, if only he could. So, that was Benjamin Duiker's defect, he couldn't possibly have been entirely without fault: his religious orthodoxy (thou shalt not crawl into bed with another man, not in his house) prevailed. His religion came between him and the affection (pure, anybody could see that) for his son. Fuck the house and the garden with the frangipani and the lemon tree and the entire contents of the house, the long family history, thick and thin, the love and hate that was grafted onto that house, fuck it all. But as the Lord is his witness, the fact that his father saw fit to sever that connection between him and his own son, that sticks in his gullet. The unforgivable, short-sighted – especially that – failing. And more: an arrogance as hard and cold as an old, old mountain; orthodoxy elevated over love. That's what it amounts to, and Mattheüs – 'Take this saucepan from me, please Emile,' can't, simply cannot, doesn't want to, and how, how should he – slides down onto his haunches against the wall warmed by the stove and hides his face with his food-hands until he feels the coolness of a glass of water pressing against the back of his hands.

It's up to Emile to put everything away, clear up, wipe and mop up, and then to count the cash without any mistakes, record the amount, put the money into five bank bags and then inside Mattheüs's leather bag before giving it to him, to switch off the neon lights and lock the steel door, rattling it to make sure it's properly closed as he's seen Mattheüs do, and finally to hand him the key.

'My son, tomorrow evening, please Matthew, arriving at seven o'clock at Cape Town Airport. Please, man. Can I ask you this one thing for me, please Matthew?'

Mattheüs stares at him, and Emile would have to be an imbecile not to notice this: the apathy, the unwillingness to get involved with him and his soon-to-arrive son.

At home, he realises that he's left the Beretta in the lentil drum again (Uncle Hannes wanted to know whether he still needed the thing, shouldn't he rather take it back to the farm) and, car keys in hand, he hurries down the echoing passage without a single carpet, portrait, or painting. Outside on the stoep, he decides against it. Nobody can get in there. Tomorrow when he gets in and before Emile arrives, he'll check quickly. On automatic pilot, he lights a cigarette and sniffs the herbiness of the evening air. It's nearly autumn.

Jack's friend Charnie goes to Johannesburg for a week's work and offers them her flat, a one-bedroom on a freeway in Pinelands. It's the last evening before the auction, and the last evening before Mattheüs finally has to surrender the spare keys to the estate agent, and he makes himself sick, he's so restless.

'So, go,' Jack says to him, at his wits' end and fed-up that Mattheüs isn't mature enough to accept his fate with the family home. He knows Mattheüs wants to go back to the empty house. To torment himself. 'Go, Matt. But then let that be your final farewell. What's the matter with you? It's just a house, after all. Bricks and a roof. I'm just as disappointed. More than you think.

Make no mistake. Do you know how I fantasised about you and me in that house? Then it turned out differently. Tough. It's between you and your father, man. And even if the house had become yours, I can't help wondering. I think it would still have haunted you and Uncle Bennie. Go, and try to get over the thing.'

Mattheüs doesn't answer Jack. Ever since the reading of the will, at the moment when the attorney said 'number nine Poinsettia Road', when the tip of his raptor's beak bent down and almost touched the exaggeratedly pursed lips on the 'poin' of Poinsettia, and the following flat announcement of the Silver Cloud Christian Fellowship as one of the three beneficiaries, Mattheüs has deliberately turned inward.

Reaching their house, now just the ghost of a house, he walks without even thinking about it into the study and inflates the mattress he's brought along, and places it on the exact spot where his father's desk once stood, not where it had been moved by him and Samantha to clear space for the sickbed, but in its original place to the right of the fireplace, the place his father had carefully chosen for light and proportion in relation to the furniture in the rest of the room.

He rolls his sleeping bag out on top of the mattress and takes a sip from the bottle of brandy he's brought along for the night – he won't be eating, he's got no appetite anyway – and with his knees pulled up he sits on the mattress without thinking of anything or even trying to recall anything from the past, any incident or conversation entwined with this room or this house. He takes another sip and enjoys the burning sensation down his throat and into his empty stomach. He's surprised at how calm he's become all of a sudden. And then remembers that that was often, though also not as a rule, the effect that his father's study had on him. After a while, sitting still in the darkening room – the electricity has long since been cancelled – he hears a chittering sound from the far left-hand corner where his father used to keep his steel filing cabinet. He peers in that direction and thinks he can make out the shape of a crumpled-up cloth or something similar – Samantha may have left it there with the final cleaning-up – and gets a fright when there's a slight movement. Or is he imagining things? He switches on the torch of his iPhone and accidentally activates the strobe function, then gets up and follows the sharp white flashing light that lends an unreal atmosphere to his father's study, and as he approaches, step by step, the crumpled thing in the corner, and the strobe light alternately lights everything up and wipes it out, faces come to him, shapes of himself as a child in his pyjamas. Briefly he sees himself entering his father's sanctum, maybe to come and say good night, and the image disappears just to let Sissy in for a flashing second, softly crying and rigid as if sleepwalking and noticeably calmer than he, and finally the figure of his mother who looks as if she's floating and not really touching the earth, which pleases him, she never liked the place, too overwhelmingly *Bennie*, too much of his sweat and breath; still, he's the one that Matthéus searches for in the flashing strobe, to loom also as an apparition, but nothing comes. His father is gone. Stone dead.

When he sees that it's a bedraggled sparrow hiding in the corner, he immediately switches the torch to ordinary beam and focuses the light away from the bird to avoid terrifying it any further. He stoops to pick up the sparrow so that he can let it out by the window, lightly holding the small pulsating body. The bird comes to sudden life and breaks free of the funnel of his hands, flutters up to the high ceiling where it circles once, twice, three times, and perches for a moment on the crystal chandelier where, in the beam of light, Matthéus sees the grip of its tiny claws around a glass arm of the chandelier. Then it flies off and begins to circle again. Matthéus strides to the windows, struggles with the catches and pushes both up all the way. It's dark out there, with none of the outside lights on. The sparrow isn't in the least interested in going outside. Matthéus goes to take a sip of brandy, switches off the torch and flops onto the mattress with his arm under his head.

For an hour or so, he lies like that until the triangle of his arm under his head starts throbbing. The whole time, he chain-smokes, eventually forgets the sparrow, its minimal bird stirrings mostly inaudible, and tries, as with his father during those final nights, not to fall asleep and to remain fully conscious. He doesn't succeed in thinking any thoughts other than those that have already churned through his mind over and over again; he doesn't succeed in reaching any liberating conclusions that might redeem himself from the one thing he keeps coming up against and which he clings to obsessively, the oppressive thought that his father sold him out for the sake of his religious beliefs.

A coolish breeze through the open windows makes him get up and close both of them, and for a moment the action clears his head. The sparrow swoops next to him once more as if wanting to acknowledge this other life in the room, then he no longer hears it. It's a consolation, after all, this tiny life that'll see the night through with him.

He lies down again with his arms folded under his head and concentrates on his breathing, shallow against the top of his nostrils. He chokes on a gulp of brandy and enjoys it, the burning alcohol has penetrated his nose and tickles his nose hairs. When the choking won't stop, he jumps up, again switches on the torch of his iPhone and starts systematically fine-combing the room. He makes out marks where the kelims used to lie, squares or rectangles against the walls where his father's things hung. (The *Battle of Blood River* picture went to Sissy in the end: 'Yes, you may as well give it to me, I'll make space for it somewhere. Terrible, even then, the violence, don't you think? Do you think it really happened like that?') He examines the wooden shelves where his father's books had stood, walks to and fro, starting at the left corner then the middle, to the right-hand corner. Shelf by shelf. Eventually he comes across something that remained behind, a small brown Betadine bottle on the fourth shelf. When he unscrews it, the hard plastic cap disintegrates in his hand. He sniffs at the mouth of the bottle. Stale antiseptic vapour hits him. It must have been his father's private bottle, because he remembers that his mother's bathroom cabinet also contained Betadine, along with all the other standard medications of those years. Would his father first have dripped the coffee-coloured liquid onto a handkerchief before rubbing it onto his wound, or would he have dabbed directly from the bottle? His father was extremely set on hygiene. It's more probable that he'd have dripped it onto a handkerchief rather than risking the mouth of the bottle touching the wound, transferring some of the infection to the container. Mattheüs rubs the last of the crumbly plastic from the ribbed neck and pockets the little bottle. Again he lies down on the mattress.

During the night – he must have dropped off – he smells boiled cauliflower with cheese sauce from the kitchen. He blows his nose and swallows and even flares his nostrils, but the smell remains unmistakably there. He considers getting up and going to find the source of the smell in the kitchen, but as soon as he sits up, the smell vanishes and he immediately lies flat again. The creamy, pale-yellow blanket of sauce over the soft-boiled billows of cauliflower, arranged in a Pyrex dish, and on top of the cauliflower, it goes without saying, the sprinkling of freshly ground nutmeg. More even than the other small life of the sparrow, the image consoles him, and he sees it as a gift sent to him by God's angels of mercy during the dark night of his soul.

At daybreak, when the sun from the east casts grey light around the house and into the high, uncurtained windows, Mattheüs reaches a terrible decision: he's not going to let go of the house just like that. It's the only stupid way, he knows it, to transform his father's treason into something else, though exactly what he doesn't know quite yet. His decision is terrible, he knows this only too well, because he's going to allow himself to commune obsessively with yet another thing, will tie himself to it to the very end, whatever that may mean.

He arrives at Charnie's flat at breakfast time; he detests the place. Her double sponge mattress with its brightly coloured floral cover is stained with body fluids, 'Matt, she's specially washed and dried her sheets,' and Jack said, 'I know she's only got this one set,' he hates the toaster furred with bread mould, he hates the forlorn pine tree the flat looks onto.

@ 9 Poinsettia Road, minutes before the auction. *Matt is so emotional. Trembling all over. Feel for the man.*

   Charnie: *The pits for him. Give him all your support. How are you settling into my flat?*

   Jack: *Matt's the problem.*

   Charnie: *What?*

   Jack: *He can't adapt.*

   Charnie: *Think I know what his problem is: Your Matt = snob.*

   Jack: *You don't understand what he's going through at the moment.*

   Charnie: *My flat's too trashy for him. Look at the house he grew up in. He probably thinks I'm white trash.*

   Jack: *Don't be hard on him, Charn.*

   Charnie: *Okay, forget it, love you both.*

   Jack: *Auctioneer's about to start, cheers.*

He and Jack stand some distance behind the thirty or so bidders and neighbours and nosy parkers, all more or less middle class or richer, close by the gate the two of them stand, and when the auctioneer gets going, Jack lights one of his expertly rolled joints, and amid the staccato barking of the auctioneer's voice and the exaggerated gestures as he and his assistant, a little squirt of a guy, acknowledge signals or nods from the bidders, he's dying in a way that no living being dies. Through the gate that is today wide open, and which as far as Mattheüs can remember has never been left open – and this upsets him anew – comes Aunt Sannie with her set of tiger's eye beads and tiger's eye earrings, in she walks and through the green haze around him and Jack without saying anything more than simply, 'Afternoon, Mattie,' a familiar sort of greeting with that intonation and all, so that he can no longer be pissed off with her, he isn't any longer; the will was, after all, the work of a man of invincible conviction, who would not allow himself to be swayed in any direction whatsoever, 'Ag, Aunt Sannie,' he says – and he dies a bit more on 'I have two and a half million' – when Aunt Sannie comes closer, closest she's ever been to weed, and presses him to her Estée Lauder bosom, making him shed a few feeble, pathetic tears.

'I shudder to think who might move in here, next to me,' says Aunt Sannie, and wanders off among the people to see who's here and who's serious, and looks sternly at those she believes to be strong contenders and shamelessly stands just a little way off to look them up and down, trying to fathom what kind of people she can expect next door.

He hasn't had a decent meal all day, has been off his food since the funeral, losing sleep, everything, and he can feel the weed messing with his empty stomach, slowly churning his guts like a winding road brings on carsickness, and then taking him further, and carrying on with him like you'd play with a child on a lawn until eventually the child got hurt and had long since lost all control over the game. His arms and legs come out in gooseflesh, which manifests higher up, in his head, as an intense sensation that overwhelms him and takes him away from the auctioneer to the pebble path on the right, the path with the lemon tree, where a child with a stick in his hand is now poking away at something, maybe a dead frog, then scurries away to the braai area that his father sketched and then had built – his mother was furious about the modern face-brick contraption so at odds with the style of their Cape Dutch house, one of the most unsightly things she'd ever seen in her life – used so often and with such pleasure by his father, so much sensual pleasure, and often just him on his own there with the ridiculously long braai tongs, so perfectly present in a den he'd created for himself, with the ever-present glass of dark-red shiraz, the blood of it still on his smacking lips, his shirt off, draped over

228

a garden chair, his chest hairs silvery-curly in the light breeze, his gaze sharply focused on the four T-bone steaks that he'd been given by his farming friend from Swellendam, tender beef fattened and slaughtered on their farm, which he watches closely through the fragrant smoke so that the flames don't suddenly catch them, so that they can be seared quickly and just enough to retain the succulence of the meat; and he and Sissy and their mother all get one of the enormous chunks of meat on their plate, just like that, the meat first, before the salad and the toasted tomato-and-onion sandwiches are added, with the red threads of blood seeping from the meat onto the white plate, meat that he, Mattheüs, found appetising and even tried to enjoy just for his father's sake – in those days he was far less emancipated in his relations with his father – while his mother and Sissy shuddered at the obscene blood, asked him please to put it back on the grid, whereupon he would collapse, plate in hand, onto the wire-mesh chair in the shade of the oak tree, his torso strong and sweaty, and laugh them to scorn, saliva gleaming on his lower lip, take a sip of wine and lustily, unashamedly animal-like, raise his T-bone and start tearing at the meat with his strong white teeth.

While he takes another drag at Jack's joint – the people in front of them have in the meantime started getting restless as the auction seems to be winding down and the auctioneer is hitting the high notes at the thought of the triumphant selling price he's going to achieve – with the stub of the joint between his thumb and index finger, he points out the barbecue to Jack and starts explaining a bit about his father's barbecue ritual, something at least, because in his befuddled state it's impossible to describe the magnitude of that ritual that belonged so utterly and completely to Benjamin Duiker, and to which the rest of the family was so averse, and in which he, Mattheüs, he tries to explain, may just barely have been included.

Then Jack says to him from somewhere on the other side of the place where he finds himself – Jack, a pin-sized presence seen through barely open lashes, as you experience people when you're getting high on weed – that he'd better start accepting that Uncle Bennie was a fuckup of a person, otherwise he's never going to get over the thing. Not that he wants to prescribe to Mattheüs what he should feel, that's the last thing he wants to do to Mattheüs. In any case, he's far too much of a Duiker for that. It's just that he's going to have to change his perception of his father; okay, he won't go so far as to call it idolatry. Uncle Bennie wanted a whole lot of little Bennies, finish and *klaar*. And he's going to have to get angry with his father, as in mad, as in completely beside himself with rage, otherwise he's going to remain stuck in his crippling disappointment. Limp. A victim. 'Matt, think about it. It's not the end of the world, man.'

The joint is finished. He puts it out on the driveway paving and with tearful eyes looks at Jack, whose pursed lips are shaping the word 'fuckup'. Even if his only remaining option were to die, he could never mention his father and say 'fuckup' in the same breath; at most he could include it in his arsenal of anger as a memento, as one of the descriptions encompassing the whole man. But as a primary adjective qualifying his father, never. And even the anger that Jack's talking about, which he'll have to rake up from nightmares and wounding incidents he's already dealt with, on his own, and how, *how*, do you reactivate an emotion or attitude that you know in your heart of hearts no longer sits well with your constitution.

And then he realises on the shoulder of Aunt Sannie (of all people) – she's come across to sympathise, Aunt Sannie with her fleshy shoulder and heavy-scented perfume, the woman he could never abide – that she is the one person who stands out as the embodiment of the old-worldliness of his father, a value system he was handfed with, and which he later, on becoming fully human, began to despise so passionately. And yet it's the constancy of that world that in an odd, almost repulsive way provided him with security, which he now misses so much, now that his father has ensured it's been taken from him, wanted to ensure that after his death it would no longer be left standing as his son's foundation; Mattheüs no longer qualifies for it, he would say, he could have, but he's made the choice himself, and now he's left on his own. He weeps for it, not openly with visible tears, but deep inside, an oozing internal wound. All that remains is the matter between him and his father. A one-sided story, because his father, after all, is dead. Isn't that the way it's always been?

The auctioneer's mallet bangs down on the lectern in front of his buttoned-down paunch, and Jack makes sure he's got a lit cigarette to pass to Mattheüs. Number nine Poinsettia Road has been sold. The auctioneer makes his way through the crowd to shake the hand of the successful buyer, an elegantly dressed Mr Anthony Bongani Mkhonza, beside him his wife, also all dressed up and now in tears, and with them their progeny, three children jumping up and down and tugging at their father's pinstripe trousers – 'swimming pool' comes fluttering from their babble.

Behind them, the two ADT guards come cycling through the gate, stop next to him and Jack, ask for two cigarettes, and want to know who bought the place. When Jack points at the Mkhonza family, they smile and shake their heads without really betraying how they feel about the new owners.

These are the two ADT guards that his father, and he, had known for years. Meat and cake were occasionally given to them, and a mutual trust developed that transcended the difference in class and wealth, or that at least is how Mattheüs thought of it.

'You've got bad luck here, man,' says Christopher with his ascetic face. 'You will not live here at your beautiful house any more, man.'

'It's all over, Sissy.'

'Ag, Mattie. Man, it was destined to be like this. You know, I went for a walk in the veld the other morning, it's just desert here now, and then I realised something about that house. We've done with it. I know Pa had his quirks, but that house is history now.'

'Pa trampled me one last time from his grave.'

'Let it go, Mattie. Let go of that stuff. He was damned good to both of us. He looked after us well his whole life. So how much did the house go for in the end?'

'Two point five.'

'Million?'

'What do you think?'

'Good heavens.'

'You're getting a third. Is it enough to fatten your sheep?'

'Ag, Boetie. It doesn't suit you to be like that. You're surely not going to hold it against me. For the rest of my life. It just gives me a pain here, in my side. Please, Mattie.'

'Jack says Pa was a fuckup.'

'Tell Jack I say he must keep his trap shut about our father.'

'I can't believe it's all over. All of it. I'll never again walk in that house just to feel what it feels like. In summer, barefoot on those cool clay tiles. I'll never get it out of my system. Never. Sissy, do you think that deep inside Pa despised me?'

'Matt, don't torment yourself, man. Pa is dead, he's had his life. I don't know what he thought. Do you think it matters any more? You know he had a big, big problem with you and Jack. It was never possible for him to square the two of you with his faith. That's the heart of the matter. He couldn't. It was much too much to ask of a man of his generation. But despise? You? Don't be silly, Mattie. You were his golden boy. Whenever you wanted to ask him for anything, he already had his hand open. Pa loved you, man. You have to believe it.'

'It was a conditional kind of love.'

'Aren't we all like that? Love, but just up to a point.'

'Hell, he was my father.'

'Matt, I must be off now. Fetch kids in town. They're all taking ballet now. Leona is already on pointe. A real little ballerina. You can see she has it in her. Now go and have a drink and celebrate, Matt. Enjoy your life.'

'Yeah, yeah, yeah.'

@ Charnie's. *Pinelands after midnight. For those of you who are still awake: a riddle. How do you sleep when you're stuck with another guy's problem in your head?*

Jack stares at the blue-lit screen of his iPhone for a while. Not a soul. All of them in dreamland.

'Talk to me,' Jack says to Matt, who has in the meantime got out of bed. The guy has clammed up. Pent-up anger. Jack doesn't know how to open it up and resolve it. It's not the first night that he's woken up on Charnie's sponge mattress and found Matt gone.

'Cheap and plastic. And a bit dirty too,' Matt says, standing in front of the only window, smoking and gazing out at the pine tree. He can't stay there any longer. She's got a heart, Charnie, that's true, but she doesn't know how to make a place cosy. Then he says, why don't they go and stay in the parking area at Rondebosch Common. They can make themselves comfortable on a mattress on the back seat of the Mercedes, eat at Carlucci's, Jack can shower at the Zilverbosch gym, he'll manage with the takeaway's toilet. He knows how to do a body-wash at a hand basin, all you need is a facecloth and soap. 'And every evening,' then he's quiet.

'What?' He knows what Matt wants to do. He wants to go back to number nine Poinsettia Road. That's why he wants to go and stay on the Common. To be close to their house. Jack is sitting down on the edge of the bed in his pyjama pants. He's got a late-night erection that's throbbing. He wishes Matt would concentrate on him and stop his shit. Go and stay on the Common. He's crazy. And yet it's the most he's heard Matt say in days. Okay, so they're going to stay on the Common like vagrants. Bergies in a grand car. Now he's seen everything.

He knows the Common well. Forty hectares of fynbos and veld. Milner Road is on the east side and Campground Road on the west. It's close to Zilverbosch Boys' High, and he likes walking there. In spring, the Common is a garden, with rare flowers that only grow on the Cape Flats. He doesn't know their names, only the white arum lilies he knows, a smaller species of wild arum. And then there are all the dogs that dog owners take there to run around freely. Pure joy. Up and down the paths among the grasses and flowers that have been trampled by people and by dogs' paws. He knows it sounds a bit silly, but he associates the Common with a zest for life. He's often seen two brothers who go there with their two chocolate Labradors. The men look alike, they could even be lovers. People say that after a while lovers start looking alike as a result of osmosis. He always watches them, those two. All tail-wagging hyperactivity, the Labradors run off in front of them. Sometimes the two men walk with their arms around each other's shoulders. The path trodden between the flowers and grass, the shiny-coated dogs, the brothers or lovers with that obvious bond between them, and to the east the beautiful dark-green backdrop of Table Mountain – to him it's one of the most beautiful scenes he's ever seen. When he comes across those two with their Labradors, he always feels a pang in his heart, wanting to have something like that in his own life, as complete as the two of them.

The next afternoon, towards dog-walking time, at about five or sixish, they pull up in the parking area. All the dog lovers come driving along in bakkies or 4×4s, then park, open the back for their dogs to leap out, walk and return after a while, dogs and owners all panting. Eventually, there's just the two of them. They've collected two takeaway lasagnas from Carlucci's, and each of them has four beers. The wind has turned nasty, and they sit in the car with half-opened windows. The whole car smells of lasagna. By now Jack is used to Matt saying nothing and clearly not about to say anything. He regards the Common as the last phase of the business of shedding the will. After that they'll take a flat together and maybe, just maybe, live happily ever after.

@ Common, he facebooks Charnie after supper. *Can you believe it? Common = our garden, Merc = our house. Two on a mattress on the back seat. Imagine someone peeping in on us in the middle of the night.*

Shock & awe.

Charnie: *Ag Jack, you're crazy, man. High-risk area that. People have been killed on the Common.*

Jack: *We = OK. You know about Matt's present from Uncle Hannes.*

Charnie: *What about those two gay guys who were chucked out near Klipfontein Road? Shot in the back of the head. Execution style. You've forgotten, haven't you?*

Jack: *Matt feels at home here. Healing, all that stuff. Try to understand.*

Charnie: *Where do you eat?*

Jack: *Carlucci's.*

Charnie: *And where do you wash? And all that?*

Jack: *@ Zilverbosch gym.*

Charnie: *Hope your nails = clean.*

Jack inspects his nails, which are not in fact very clean. It's difficult to keep everything tidy, his case this side in the boot, Matt's that side. Inside the Merc there's companionable chaos. Finding a sock's partner becomes more and more of a problem.

Jack: *Funniest thing is when somebody comes to walk his dog first thing in the morning and I have the Cadac on with our espresso pot on top. And the car with all its doors wide open. Mattress, bedding, everything. In a car like this. Nobody understands.*

Charnie: *You two scare me. Your life = a precious thing. Remember that.*

Jack: *I'm holding onto it.*

At bedtime, Jack props the Alsatian mask against the windscreen. He's begun to believe in the mask as a talisman. He refuses to connect Wolfie's moving into number nine Poinsettia Road with the will that turned out so badly. 'It was on the cards,' he tells Matt, who stares at him blankly. Nobody, Jack realises, can feed the man a line any more. He'll have to draw his own conclusions.

During the night, Matt goes outside with a roll of toilet paper to use the Common as the Common dogs do. Jack lies looking through the back window at the stars that he can make out in spite of the glow of city lights. It's cosy in the back of the Merc with the mattress and pillows and duvet and everything. And he enjoys it despite the deadly silence of his mate. He experiences a simultaneous tranquillity and low-level excitement, as if something tremendous is about to happen to them.

It's undoubtedly got something to do with Matt's ongoing silence. Sometimes it's even reassuring, because he knows what's happening in his head. But at other times he hasn't a clue as to what's bugging Matt. Probably because they're now living so intimately in the climate of the Common, he thinks of Matt's silence as dew, glistening and lovely in the early morning, and then again like frost, chilly and nothing more than that, and sometimes it's a sticky damp that makes him shiver, something you want to dry off, that you want to get rid of.

On the second evening, Matt's mouth opens and words issue from it. Grateful! The man has a clear idea of what he wants to do. And it's exactly as he thought. It's the reason for the squatting on the Common. Matt suggests that they walk past number nine Poinsettia Road. He wants to check what's happening there. Okay, he's got the picture. Matt's, that is. It's all been planned beforehand, Jack has no doubt about that.

When they arrive before the familiar gate with its fleur-de-lis spearheads, Matt orders him to stop. Then Matt takes him by the hand and he and his friend start marching up and down in front of the gate. (No, the man hasn't flipped. It's his way of healing.)

The house, garden and driveway have all been lit up in a way that the Duikers never did, except when there was a party. Every possible outside and inside light is on. Mr Mkhonza and his family are either very scared or they simply enjoy the luxury of all the lights. Next door, at Aunt Sannie's place, only the upstairs light of the TV room is on. Matt shows him the two eyes of her binoculars peeping out between her curtains.

Matt stands in front of the intercom. He looks at him over his shoulder. 'I want to see if I can still open the gate. Maybe they haven't had the code changed.'

'Don't, Matt.' And he puts his hand on Matt's, which is about to touch the numbers on the keypad. 'There's Mr Mkhonza,' Jack whispers in warning when he spots the man behind the right-hand window of the stoep. Matt ducks behind the gate. Only Jack's shaven head is still visible between the fleur-de-lis tips. When they see two ADT bicycle lights approaching from the far end of Poinsettia Road, they quickly take off in the opposite direction.

'Hey, Matthew,' they hear behind them. It's that Christopher-guard with his friend.

'Hello, Christopher,' Matt says in a friendly voice, so that Jack feels heartened: this is his final phase. After this, Matt will revert to his old self. And they'll fuck like rattlesnakes (maybe) to make up for all those dry spells. At least Matt is no longer watching porn. That is, he hasn't caught him at it yet. Only the occasional pissed-off glare as if it's Jack's fault that he's had to lay off the sleazy stuff. He's on a 3G connection and it's too expensive and too slow to download videos and play them. Matt is as terrified as Uncle Bennie was that poverty will grab hold of him. Duiker's Takeaway has gone rather quiet. The morose and silent person behind the counter makes the lunch trade wonder about the food.

But he has to add: Matt's morose moods don't last. And he knows him all too well. 'Let's go for a walk on the Common.' No, too late and too cold. Still, they put on their tracksuits and take one of the paths. It's not completely pitch dark, there are street lights on the four roads bordering the Common as well as an urban glow. They're not at all afraid that they'll be mugged. There are two of them. And neither of them is the fearful type. Jack takes Matt's hand as a father would a son's. He likes it, he knows the shape of Matt's hands. Broad and veined on top and rough on the inside from all the kitchen work. As they walk, Jack smells the early evening dew on the grass, and an odd whiff of exhaust gas blowing onto the Common. There's no need to say anything. All you have to avoid is possible dogshit on the paths. He suddenly ducks in behind Matt and tackles him slo-mo so that his knees buckle and he collapses onto the grass.

'Are you out of your fucking mind?' Matt lies there, propping himself with his hand on a tuft of grass.

'Matt. Matt.' He wants to tell him that all he wants is to bring him back. Make him ordinary again, like he always was. Happy. He pulls Matt up by the hand, but only halfway, so that they're both sitting on their haunches, heads level with the grass.

'What?' says Matt.

Jack looks north, west, south, east. 'Nothing. You can't see anything of the city from here. Only the grass and the mountain there, to the west. This is our hiding place in the middle of the city. Isn't that something. We're white tramps, bergies. With a Merc!'

'Let's go and sleep,' says Matt.

Matt doesn't relent. He doesn't want to, Jack realises. Matt's soul is worn out. But he still keeps hoping. Jack places a high premium on the happiness he associates with the Common. This is the right place for them. When they leave here, Matt's headspace will be okay again.

With the (forced) abstention from porn, Mattheüs experiences withdrawal symptoms that manifest mainly as grumpiness and impatience, twin symptoms he's deeply aware of without liking them – he doesn't want to be this way. Don't take that away from me as well, he prays, while rinsing a bunch of celery under the tap. But what god wants to listen to a porn addict? It's especially in the evenings after work when that particular circuit in his brain kicks in: he really misses it. He sometimes gets gooseflesh as a result of the absence of the dopamine fix after a porn session – his only relief from the muscle fatigue after nine hours of work – a physical lack of the pleasure he enjoyed with his old friends, porn stars, positions (studied), sounds (comical and/or erotic), the whole gang of old acquaintances that he wants to revisit to release the same triggers and to take him inside; he always thinks of it as a private domain, a single abode inside a cocoon nobody knows about or needs to know about, with him as the only occupant, success guaranteed on the first try or on the second or the third try at least. There are no restrictions in this domain; his friends never make demands, never get uptight if he doesn't do the right thing, and never disappoint with their carefully contrived offering.

It's a certainty he once had, in the past. Listen, if he thinks about it clearly, he blushes with shame. (His father would shudder in his grave if he knew that this was his pillar of support.) But the loss he experiences around five, six o'clock every afternoon is substantial; it's the deprivation of a physical pleasure that vibrated all the way to his fingertips. And so intimately connected with the person he's become inside it, that it's impossible to explain to Jack or to anybody else.

On the day Emile's little boy is due to arrive from Nairobi, business is slow. Mattheüs selects three chillis from the plastic bowl, finely chops them and stirs them into the curry that's not selling fast enough. Emile has been singing for days, today's song is happy. He refuses to be irritated by it. For the time being his feelings of compassion and self-pity and reproach, the whole spectrum, have been numbed. Standing next to him, washing the day's saucepans, is a man experiencing one of the most important days of his life; a man who, without asking, longs for the tiniest concession from him, even if it's just an iota of pleasure.

How does he feel about the arrival of his son, Mattheüs eventually asks out of politeness. Emile just shakes his head, laughs and carries on humming. Soon after five, his wife turns up in yards of brightly coloured damask. They can leave now, Mattheüs says almost immediately out of respect for the two people: their stray lamb is returning to the fold.

They lock up and walk round the building and Mattheüs unlocks the Mercedes with the remote. Emile's wife claps her hands about the car that's going to take them to the airport, she hasn't once looked him in the eye. Emile has in the meantime gone to the toilet to put on the going-out clothes that he'd brought along in a plastic bag. He emerges in a navy-blue suit, shiny on the seat and under the arms, the sleeves and pants too long.

'You look smart,' Mattheüs says, and this time Emile looks up at him defiantly. He is a man who is led by his emotions and knows where he stands with Mattheüs.

The stocky wife sits in the back, Emile in front, his short legs in their wide trousers crossed, fingers playing on his lap. 'Nice car,' he tries to keep things going well.

'My father's.' He pushes in the cigarette lighter.

'Your father was a good man,' he says, evidently without intending it as either a question or a statement.

Mattheüs lights his cigarette without bothering to reply. The two people have introduced smells into the car: a mixture of rose water and palm oil, their cooking oil of choice, and of the new cloth around the body of the woman, and the powdery, slightly toxic dye on the new cloth, and a light, excited sweat behind it, and all the time their breath, lukewarm and full, while talking to each other. Emile constantly fiddles with his seat and with the door handles; his excitement is tangible, on display, as if intensifying in relation to Mattheüs's dullness.

When they arrive, Matt says he'll wait right there in the parking garage. Level D-4, the colour is green, make a note of that now, and looks at the couple walking away: the colourful woman and Emile in his navy-blue suit and white shirt buttoned to the top and tieless.

He remains sitting there without listening to music on his iPhone or reading the book that he'd brought along for the purpose. Sometimes he registers people walking past to the lifts, wheeling their luggage, chatting as family members do after not seeing each other for a long time, the jovial, cruelly candid comments about so-and-so, and then he's wrapped up in himself once again, out of place and not knowing where to go. Deliberately so, but what's the use of saying this?

In the rear-view mirror, he sees Emile's group approaching from a totally different direction; they must have got lost. When they arrive at the car, with all the child's belongings in a single pink-and-blue plastic carrier bag, they are beside themselves with joy. Emile is glistening with pride: his son, look! The child is indeed lovely and is dressed in an old-fashioned suit with a blue shirt, white-and-navy-blue-and-gold sailor's cap with gold piping, and a short red tie that reminds Mattheüs of a rabbit's ear, and makes him smile at the precise moment Emile introduces his son to him.

And then he realises anew that the man sees right through him. He opens the boot and Emile stows the solitary bag and Mattheüs really wishes he could press a button to escape this reticence of his; he is powerless against it, or rather: he doesn't want to.

While the two in the back seat are chattering and giggling away, and Emile's wife every now and again strokes the child's head as if he were her own, Emile asks if he can tell him something. Mattheüs nods. Then he is informed: 'You are not my friend. You do not like me. There is nothing.' That's all the man manages to say, his only way of expressing his frustration with the aloofness that he can no longer tolerate.

In the rear-view mirror, he notices how the child has gone silent as they drive off the freeway onto the M5, his mouth literally hanging open at the sight of the roads, the tall freeway lights, the buildings and factories everywhere, the shoulders of other cars right up against them. And at times he bursts out laughing and shouts, pointing at things, so that Emile's wife repeatedly has to silence him.

'We will get a taxi here to take us to our home,' is all that Emile adds when he stops at the Shell garage closest to the Common. Emile doesn't look at him, doesn't say thank you either, as he's so fond of doing. The woman, though, does: '*Merci, merci,*' she has no inkling of the conclusion her husband has reached regarding Mattheüs.

Mattheüs waits there a while, his window open. Emile and his wife and the little boy with the pink-and-blue plastic bag huddle together to the right of the petrol pumps. For a moment Mattheüs relents and considers taking the family all the way home. The woman has taken some Fritos out of her handbag; she tears the packet open and offers it to the others. Emile has in the meantime put on that black leather glove he saw him wearing the very first day, the one with holes for the knuckles, and cut-off fingertips. When he sees Mattheüs watching them, he assumes a boxer's stance, left foot forward, heel of the right foot slightly lifted, left fist in front of the nose and right fist poised in readiness against his right cheek. The neon light catches his knuckles and the whites of his eyes. He pumps himself up and looks bigger than he is, and the show he puts on is more than a game; he is, in fact, threatening.

Mattheüs slides up his window, turns the air conditioner right down, and with his left hand he gropes for the Beretta under his seat. The Congolese knows how to unsettle him. In his unarticulated, intuitive way he's worked it out, from day one, in fact. At Duiker's, it's different; there, it's the deference that at times verges on servility that perturbs him. Emile knows this too, knows that he throws him off balance, just a shade, and in that vulnerable moment he holds the whip hand. He looks in his rear-view mirror one more time to where Emile's still standing like a bantam cock, his body turned towards the departing car.

When he stops at their spot on the Common, Mattheüs realises how heavily he's been breathing all the way there from the garage. At last he can make the decision he's always wanted to: he's definitely going to get rid of the man. First thing Monday morning. This much he can still decide, still feel: he's never liked him. Now Emile has put the noose around his own neck and he'll have to take the consequences. He'll just carry on on his own until he appoints a new assistant. And he's also aware of his own relief, at least that's some part of his emotional life that's come back. He hasn't become totally blunted, maybe he's in recovery. That's the first thing he'll tell Jack, who really has suffered enough with him.

He openly threatened him, Mattheüs tells Emile at work, and he doesn't put up with that kind of crap, not from anybody. And yet he can't bring himself to chase him away just yet, and gives him a week's notice. Emile tenses up, unpacking takeaway containers from a box and stacking them. He slowly straightens up, takes off his cap, rubs his bald head, pinches his nose as you would if you wanted to blow it, stands stiff and silent.

Then there's a pleading: he'll do his best, work extra hours, it was just a game, the boxing thing, he'll do his best, put him to the test, so many mouths to feed, the little boy as well now, on and on until the pleading starts hammering at his inner ear. Emile, who is standing with his back to Mattheüs and doesn't see him covering his ears, turns around slowly, and that's when Mattheüs realises the extent to which he's been restraining himself, how he's tried to keep up the subservience until he can't any longer and switches to the voice of a man who's empowered himself in this very shop: 'You can't kick me on the street. I work here,' he says. And repeats it.

A customer appears on the other side of the counter and asks for the lamb stew. Emile's the one who first gets a grip on himself and takes a medium-sized container from the pile and fills it first with rice and then with stew. Efficiently, faultlessly, and hygienically, as Mattheüs has taught him. Mattheüs leans against the cold-room door and experiences a sense of real danger in his own shop, which infuriates him, a fury such as he remembers on his father's face, the furrows that appeared on either side of his father's mouth the first and surest indication that trouble was brewing.

When Emile has given the change, and the two of them are on their own again, Mattheüs is the one to regain the upper hand: 'One week, and you're out of here. One word of shit from you in the next few days, and you're out straight away.'

He's welcome to leave, he says to Emile, he'll wash the last things himself and mop the floor. Emile says not a single word. Unties the black apron from behind his buttocks, neatly folds it and puts it in the rucksack he always brings with him. He's drawn in on himself, the shoulders bent forward on either side of the neck, the back hunched like a dog cowering after a hiding. A short little fellow, nothing more. A human being fighting to make a living and lacking the necessary words to help him. Is he understanding him incorrectly, then? Has he made an error, overlooked Emile's well-meaning heart?

When he gets to the door, he takes off his cap and turns towards Mattheüs without raising his eyes: 'There is no hate,' he says. 'I do not hate you.' Then he nods good night, puts on his cap and walks out, and Mattheüs follows him with his eyes, sees him quickly getting smaller and smaller, the rucksack eventually just a dark-blue hump on his back as he strides on his sturdy legs towards the stop where he'll catch his taxi, by now the rucksack with leftover food just a dark-blue dot, all that's left of him among the homebound workers.

Mattheüs clears up, fishes the Beretta out of the lentil drum and drives to the Common. He'd planned to wash his hair after work in the toilet washbasin, his shampoo in a box next to the broom and cleaning apparatus, but he's in too much of a hurry. When he arrives at their usual parking spot on the Common, he sees what Jack meant when he said that their life was getting a bit messy: somebody has moved onto that patch of ground. There are beer-bottle tops, an empty sardine tin that they hadn't noticed (they no longer eat at Carlucci's every night), the wooden pallet that they put on the ground behind the car as an extra room and that will certainly be carried off by someone. Jack had then said he didn't mind at all, that's the way it goes with possessions around here. Did he mind?

Mattheüs can't wait for the moment when he and Jack will set off for number nine Poinsettia Road. The past few evenings they've been playing 'Wolfie, Wolfie, what's the time?' on the pavement in front of the house. Jack has worked the game out so that each time he drastically changes the number of paces before shouting out the hour. Sometimes it's fourteen paces, sometimes just one big one. Mattheüs tries to anticipate the number and each time he's wrong, which releases an impatient desire in him, makes him blind to everything except when he sees Jack before him or hears Jack's voice, and when he comes, gruff and hoarse (Jack's very good at it), he can think of nothing else.

Mr Mkhonza, still wearing his suit and tie, comes marching out onto the stoep shouting at them: 'Voetsek, you white trash.' (Next time they must remember to wear gloves, all the exposed white skin must be covered up.) Soon afterwards, the ADT guards turn up on their bicycles. Christopher immediately knows who they are. Public nuisance, he hammers on. Cigarettes are distributed, he's not really serious, that's easy to see. But he did have to respond to Mr Mkhonza's call.

The following evening, they make sure that they arrive an hour later on the pavement in front of number nine Poinsettia Road. The Mkhonzas must have received their first electricity bill, because only one stoep light is on. Both he and Jack have dressed in black this time, gloves included, he with one of those ordinary black masks, and a black jersey draped like a scarf around his neck and face with only a strip of white skin visible on the bridge of the nose. The game commences.

When Mattheüs thinks the whole thing through, as he enjoys doing when they get back to the Common and snuggle up to each other, he can see what it still needs to be a perfectly choreographed game. Their steps, for instance, are perfectly coordinated – that's been sorted out. When Jack calls out the hour, he turns his head to the right. Mattheüs immediately swings his to the left. It's their arms that still need some work. When he reacts to Jack's shout, his arms feel loose and begin to windmill around his body. (He still gets a fright every time, just like a child, he can't help it.)

Most important of all, though, is how eagerly he looks forward to Wolfie throughout the day at Duiker's. He hardly takes note of Emile, the small, bitter ant scurrying around in his last few working days, and has an appetite only for the pleasure that will commence at twelve that night (they make it an hour later every evening). It's the same anticipation that he's successfully and quite by chance transferred from his porn addiction to this ritual game. And when Mr Mkhonza bursts out of his house pointing a desperate index finger at the gate – he's not really an aggressive man – his breath races and he becomes aware of a tingling in his muscles: the dopamine fix, but got in a different way.

On Sunday night they turn up as late as three o'clock, and a reckless Mattheüs is stoned and pissed, and on top of everything tensed-up because of the next day, Monday, Emile's last shift. After only two rounds of Wolfie – Jack never shouts twelve o'clock any more and he doesn't know when last he tried to catch him – Mattheüs goes up to the intercom at the gate, he hasn't been so present in his body and so absent in his head for a long time, and keys in the numbers that opened the gate for the Duikers. He's breathing so hard that inside the scarf-thing he's glowing. The gate glides open on its track.

'I don't believe it,' says Jack.

'Me neither.' Mattheüs is elated. 'Let's go and play *Wolf, Wolf* on the lawn.'

'Whoa! Now you're looking for shit. Mr Mkhonza trusts you. All you Duikers. That's why he hasn't changed the thing. I'm not going in. What we're doing is enough already. You're on your own now, Matt. You never know, he could even be armed.'

Mattheüs coaxes and cajoles, every which way, sweet-talks and soft-soaps: just this once, only two rounds, then they're done. He wants to go inside just one last time, to let Mister Mkhonza know that he can.

'Okay, quickly then. You're crazy in your head,' says Jack and they slip in by the gate that Mattheüs has opened just the width of a man before pressing the stop button.

Mattheüs takes off his shoes and socks, 'Fuck it, Matt,' he wants to step on the mowed lawn as they always did, like his mother who walked barefoot all summer on her two slender feet. (Hers not as perfectly formed as his father's.) Everything, all their games, their winters and summers, come to him like tastes in his mouth; all the memories still belong to him, even though he'll never live here again. Soon these will also fade, his mother's scent already much vaguer than his father's; and what do they actually mean after all, all the memories, what's the use of remembering that Pa's dog always chose the pebble path to the lemon tree to do his business?

'Matt, I beg of you.'

He's standing with his toes spread on the roughness of the lawn and doesn't respond to Jack's cajoling pleas.

'Matt, are you going to play or not? What's the time, Mister Wolf?' Jack manages to make his pleas sound more threatening than on any of the previous evenings.

'What's the time, Mister Wolf?' The grass cool and over-familiar as step by step he follows Jack. Mr Mkhonza is maintaining the place beautifully.

Then all the lights go on: those inside the house, the floodlights in the garden, and the six uplighters next to the driveway. Mattheüs swings round, grabs his shoes, drops one of his socks and takes off behind Jack to the gate that's starting to slide shut. He has to force his arm through the final gap, a police van comes hurtling along into Poinsettia Road. Mattheüs pulls off his mask and they try to stroll along like two friends out for a breath of air at three in the morning. The van's lights shine even harder on their bums.

The van stops, and a policeman's arm signals to them to do likewise. There are two of them in the van, both rather young. Pushovers, thinks Mattheüs.

'Have you just been at the house back there? The owner phoned with a complaint.'

'No, Constable. How would we get in?' says Mattheüs.

'The owner says you managed to get in somehow.' The policeman who's not the driver and hasn't yet said anything shines a powerful torch, first at Mattheüs and then at Jack.

'We didn't, Constable. That's not possible.'

'What have you got there with you?' The voice like a boy's that hasn't quite broken.

'Nothing, Constable. We've just come from a party. That's my car over there.' Mattheüs presses the remote and the car's lights flash.

When the policemen see the Mercedes E-class, it's enough to establish their innocence. 'You boys mustn't cause any shit here in this neighbourhood. Good night.'

Arriving at their parking spot on the Common, they prepare the mattress and bedding in the back. Matt takes up his spot under the pine tree where it's starting to smell of stale piss, and unbuttons his fly. Jack makes them take multivitamins every day and the smell of it wafts up from his stream. He can't say exactly what happened on the lawn in front of their house; no longer dopamine-induced, he just feels tremendously satisfied, refreshed, like after a prolonged sex session, say three, four hours long, and later you've got up to make tea with fynbos honey in the kitchen, all bare-arsed and glowing, and while you're stirring in the honey you realise that the session has become more than a physical thing, it's therapy, your mental gremlins and gruelling anxieties have been confronted without your even noticing it, they've cleared off. If he'd had Mr Mkhonza's phone number, he'd have phoned him now. Mission accomplished, may you and your family live in peace from now on in one of the most wonderful houses in the city.

He shakes off and looks up at the faint golden glow above the Common, sprints to the car, and with his cold limbs snuggles up to Jack.

'Where are you staying, Mattie? What's your address? I've still got a few bits of game biltong that I want to send you.'

'Sissy, we haven't found a place yet. It's hard. You know how picky I am. Just like Pa.' He laughs.

'So, where are you staying? Jack lost his flat in the hostel, didn't he? Honestly, the two of you!'

'Sissy, to tell the truth, we're living out of the car at the moment. We've parked here on the Common, you know where it is don't you, not far from Poinsettia Road. We're staying here for the time being.'

'Are you joking, or what?'

'I'm serious.'

There's a silence. She's changed towards him after all the will business. Okay, they've got the money now or they'll be getting it shortly, but he doesn't hold this against Sissy at all. She's less sarcastic, milder, as if she's looking at his life in the same way he does. Or is at least trying her best to do so.

'Matt, listen. I know you're going through a shitty time, but I don't want you to end up in the streets. Must I come to Cape Town? I don't want to ask if I can come and help, you're a grown-up man. But please tell me if there's anything I can do. Do you maybe want to talk to me or something? Ag, I don't know, Matt. I don't even know what I'm saying. I'm a bit shocked, please don't hold it against me. I thought you'd moved into a flat long ago.'

'That's the plan.'

Again silence.

'Matt?'

'Yes?'

'Pa always said: I'll never say die. Do you remember?'

'Yes, very well.'

'I'll send the packet of biltong to your takeaway. What's the address there? You were looking so thin the last time I saw you.'

'Sissy?' Now he's the one who's silent. The thing that would have pissed him off before, her concern that's never come across as sincere, now touches him. He'd seen some antique silver earrings in Observatory the other day, with a black onyx stone, he's going to buy them for her.

'What were you going to say, Matt? Go ahead.'

'We're okay. We're not going to stay like this for ever. It's just that I can't make a decision right now.'

'Good. Did I tell you it's started raining here? Such wonderful, gentle rain, started falling last night. Everything's soaked. It's a real mercy.'

'I'm glad for your sakes, Sissy. I must go now, it's Emile's last day at work. You know, the guy who works for me. The short little one. He's leaving today, I don't want him in my business any more.'

'You've got discretion, Matt. You'll know what to do when the time comes. You know the right thing to do. Love you, Matt.'

'Me too, Sissy.'

She's really trying, he thinks while reluctantly holding back the tearfulness and negotiating the morning traffic on Main, the cars and buses and taxis that gradually become less and less distinguishable from one another. He digs a hanky out of the cubby-hole: Sissy's trying to keep the remains of the family together now that the house and their father, common denominators between him and her, have fallen away. All that remains is a choice of words signifying sympathy, the expression of love, and a visit to each other two or three times a year. It's also, of course, a point of honour to be able to say to her friends in Laingsburg, when they're fishing for information: I do at least have a brother left, the two of us are closer than ever before, he's got his own business in Cape Town, it's just a bit too far otherwise we'd see each other just about every weekend.

Arriving at Duiker's, he finds Emile keeping to himself as always, though even more silent, and while they're preparing they only talk about absolutely essential things. Once, his hand touches Emile's on a work surface, and Emile jerks his away, and for the rest, the day doesn't pass too badly. By half past twelve the dahl is just about sold out, and he goes to the cold room to see what's available for a quick vegetarian curry, maybe one with large, firm pumpkin chunks and black mustard seeds, and is surprised to find the bowl of soaked lentils on the second shelf from the bottom, a low shelf, and he tries to remember whether he'd soaked the lentils the previous Saturday before closing time, while he walks out with the white pumpkin under his arm, looks at Emile's back in a black T-shirt, his hairline shaved to a perfect horizontal along the back of the neck, a hairstyle he's picked up here in Cape Town, and decides not to ask him about the soaked lentils, which he'll leave as they are for the following working day, for Tuesday, because it might just betray something of his hesitation or rather his concrete doubt (he is now turning the pumpkin around in the deep sink, with the tap half-open) regarding the dismissal of a conscientious worker.

He fries the black mustard seeds with wedges of brown onion in sunflower oil and adds a few drops of sesame oil: his father, he was such a fiery, proud man. He could never or would never have admitted that nothing remained of the family, that the family ties were in tatters (his relationship with Ma was a mess). Sissy is now following in his footsteps with words that he knows and actually yearns for, but has heard from her lips so seldom: love you, Mattie.

With half a pocket of oranges, a chunk of beef and one of the 2-litre cans of Italian tomatoes, and his pay up to and including his last day, plus an extra week, Emile leaves that afternoon.

The last thing they share is the customary triple handshake and 'Thank you, sir' from Emile, accompanied by a gaze from those dark, liquid eyes. What he should make of it, the 'Thank you, sir', he doesn't know. Emile has never addressed him like that, without his name. There is, to say the least, some malice in it, a trace of sarcasm, unexpected – he's always thought of him as not articulate enough to talk back like that.

Ag, fuck him, he's out of his life and thank heavens for that, and he pulls up at the Common, takes a beer from the cooler bag in the boot, looks for the nail clippers in the side pocket of the jumbled suitcase without finding them, goes and snaps off a sharp pine twig, and sits against the back wheel with his beer and the twig and starts cleaning his nails systematically. After each swipe from left to right under the edge of the nail, he examines the product – kitchen grime and soil and other unidentifiable detritus – and looks up when a sudden cold gust blows straight from the mountain towards him, and is surprised at how good it is just to sit there. He already has a new worker in mind, Eliad, a Jewish guy who came looking for work, had experience in a restaurant in Tel Aviv and then in Cape Town, and who reassures him about the future of Duiker's Takeaway, which, on top of everything else, did very well today. And he's still surprised at how mercifully little he has to mull over in the late afternoon while waiting for Jack, who arrives (the sun is setting earlier) either in the bakkie or jogging, his school stuff in his rucksack with the two straps expanding his chest, his sweatiness that cools down then and eventually dries on his skin, only to be rubbed off on him throughout the night, the man's smell of the day's dirt, his own, Jack's. He drains the last half of the bottle in one swig, takes out another and sits down again. In the meantime, about six bakkies and cars have arrived with dogs for their late-afternoon walk. He feels good about Jack, and hesitant about his slow, half-unwilling retreat from his porn cocoon: there's a life to be lived out there, with Jack.

Then he remembers that he's left the damn Beretta in the lentil drum again; with Emile being fired, the daily routine was disrupted. He lifts himself to stand up and get into the car to fetch the weapon when he sees Jack's figure approaching in the shadow of the row of pines along Campground Road, the road he'd have followed from Zilverbosch across Park Street. Rhythmically, he runs nearer, except that he swings his left arm less than the right (the practised eye) and passes Norfolk Avenue as far as the new traffic circle. At that point he's closest to Poinsettia Road: his father, oh hell, it's impossible to think of his father as a fuckup as Jack wants him to; he'd be knocking one of the most crucial, if not *the* most crucial, pillars from under his feet.

'Jack,' he calls out when Jack is close enough. How grassy Jack's skin is at times, almost a kind of cud, and if he keeps his nose against it long enough, say for instance against the part from his underarm to his hip where there'd be sweat trails after running, he eventually also smells something like meat, aged at room temperature.

Mattheüs leans on the roof, beer bottle in hand, and when Jack turns into the parking lot he notices how he grabs his white vest to wipe the sweat from his eyes and how the last light catches his white, flat belly: 'Hey, Jackie!' he calls. The Beretta will have to stay where it is. He's good-for-nothing-lazy, he feels good, pleased with the handsome man who comes walking towards him to greet him with a kiss, buggered if he's going to fetch that weapon now.

He parks behind Duiker's and takes the bag with his toothbrush and a fresh towel he found in among Jack's rubbish, and a bunch of rosemary for today, walks round to unlock the front (first thing, he always gets the dry beans and today's pot of potatoes boiling), when he sees it: 'Fucking hell.'

The shutter of his takeaway has already been pushed up, and he's looking down onto the back of Emile's round head busily at work in the kitchen. He runs closer and stops, completely overwhelmed – three builders in overalls walk past and notice his expression, instinctively realising that something is happening to him. The inside of his arms feels clammy as he tries to figure out exactly what's going on here, and: the Beretta is not in his pocket where it belongs.

One comes from behind and grabs him around the chest, a short arm with fingertips that only just reach his breastbone. Hot, his blood against his skin, he struggles, twists himself around in the iron grip and looks into the oil-black eyes of one of Emile's comrades, when two more come running through the crowd of early-morning workers, aiming swiftly and surely at their prey, preventing him from reaching his shop. A small hand grabs his pinkie and pulls it out of its socket. Emile has meanwhile turned around in the kitchen and is leaning on the counter; he's already dressed in his white chef's jacket, the dirty piece of shit, and is today wearing the black leather glove with his fingers and knuckles exposed, the glove he wore on the very first day, and next to him that monster of a dog jumps paws-first up to the counter, the dog's been taken into the kitchen in defiance of every health regulation, with Emile tugging at his chain to lift his dog's head even higher, the paws with their nails on the counter and inside its open mouth Mattheüs sees a thread of saliva forming from the upper canines to the lower jaw, and all the while a determined Emile holds him with his gaze and he looks manlier, bigger, than he's ever seen him, and under his right hand the Beretta lies flat on the counter.

'You fucking bastards, you can't do this. This is a country with laws,' Matt shouts, and with his fury at full bore he succeeds in dragging the three men with him right up to the counter of his takeaway, when Emile yanks the dog up on its chain, and eggs it on so that it snaps three-quarters of the way across the counter, inches from Mattheüs's spiky fringe. The three holding onto him again grab at him and wrestle him to the ground. People have stopped to watch; across the road at the Total garage on Albertyn Street, the attendants have dropped what they were doing.

'They've hijacked my takeaway,' he shouts at a man who's carrying a computer under his arm, 'call the police.' The man with the computer stares at him with blank eyes. Emile tugs at the dog again and spurs him on through his tiny teeth, it's only a matter of opening the steel door and that thing will tear him to pieces in full sight of everyone. Two policemen quickly arrive from the direction of the city centre and the three holding onto him let go. The policemen come right up to him, both with their right hand on their holsters, look at the three short Congolese who have formed a semicircle around him, at Emile who has calmed the dog and made it lie down on the tile floor of the kitchen, *his* kitchen. Emile beckons the policemen closer, smoothes out a form on the counter, and pushes it across to the dark-skinned guy with the pencil moustache and the neatly trimmed goatee.

Mattheüs manages to hold his aching pinkie with his other hand, his eyes blurred with his own sweat as he tries to make sense of what's happening here in front of him, the soaked lentils that he hadn't soaked, all the clues from yesterday and the day before, from the day the evil monster first greeted him, his plan probably already in place by then, and then wormed his way into his takeaway, always against his will, always against his better judgement.

When he again tries to break free to see the form for himself, the form that has become the main focus of the operation (it's clear that that's exactly what it is), the three Congolese pin him down right there, two around his legs, one around his waist, until the policeman with the moustache, almost a work of art, comes across and addresses him in Afrikaans.

'You'll have to read it for yourself, sir. Cape Town Municipality. His name,' he points at Emile, who's standing there showing his teeth, the Beretta suddenly gone, 'appears here as the registered licensee of the food enterprise Duiker's. There you are,' he taps the form, 'he is the legal operator of the shop.'

He grabs the form and speed-reads. It's the official licence to trade as a food business, made out to Emile Guillaume Youlou, and at the bottom, like a slimy smear, the signature of Lucinda Symes of Media City Building, second floor, the one and the same woman who way back had so wholeheartedly assisted him: a business like this is exactly what Cape Town needs.

'Where is his contract with Mr Alexopoulos, the owner of the building? I have proof. I can call all my customers here. This is my shop and it will always be mine. Are you too damned stupid to see what's happening here?'

'You'll have to watch your language, sir. We are the law,' says the policeman with the moustache, and takes the form back to Emile.

Mattheüs calls the policeman aside, the three Congolese at his heels. He's fuming, he's been driven to an extreme, and for a few seconds there's a gap, where the physical demands of his work, the funeral and everything before and after it, don't weaken him but give him strength. When he makes his case to the policemen, he is calm and collected, he speaks clearly and concisely, in every respect it's the way a grown man speaks. My fingerprints are on all the pots and pans, they're everywhere here, this is my shop. From the very first day to this moment. That short guy has just been working here.

He's got an unlicensed weapon with him, go and see for yourself. And watches the one with the moustache, how comprehension dawns on him, these words are real, hard-hitting, the shop there, right in front of them, indeed belongs to nobody other than him, Matthéüs Duiker, it would be beyond all reason to conceive of it in any other way; but then, at that moment, the policeman's eyes shift once, twice, three times, this side and that side, reptilian, and he sees how he deliberately switches his understanding and follows another, insane logic, and without saying a single word, his decision is made: he'll turn his back on this whitey even if he is the legal owner.

Then he realises that he's up against superior numbers, like the enemy at the Battle of Blood River, only more cunning; the two policemen and Emile and that dog of his and his three comrades are all in cahoots, bribed cunts all in place at the planned time this morning – he hasn't got a chance.

'How much did he pay you?' And the moment he says this, he knows that his last chance to win them over has just been buggered. They're furious, or so they claim, one more word and they'll chuck him into the van.

Smoked paprika he smells, Emile is busy cooking *his* lamb stew. He'll have to retreat for the moment and work out a strategy that's smarter than theirs. Slowly, a numbness takes possession of his calves, then his thighs and eventually his torso. He sinks down between the two who are still clinging to his legs and squats on the pavement, sucks his pinkie, takes a cigarette out of his pocket and lights it upside down and remains sitting like that, hollowed out from the inside (that's what it feels like), overpowered, no matter how hard he's fought it up to now.

My attorney, he wants to say and can't, he doesn't even have one, and then gets up so suddenly that the three men surrounding him are caught unawares. 'I'll kill you,' he shouts at Emile, the dog's docked ears showing above the counter, and rushes around the corner to his car.

In the car, his shirt sopping wet and his heart still galloping, he phones Jack immediately, then remembers that he's invigilating an exam, which will keep him busy till four-thirty that afternoon. He jumps out again, grabs two bricks from a pile to the right of the entrance to the laundry and rushes back, but the three Congolese are waiting for him around the corner. They make an immediate grab for his arms, one tries to tackle him again. Behind them, he sees the steel door at Duiker's swing open on its sturdy hinges and the dog bearing down on him. He manages to free his right hand and throws a brick at the charging animal, turns round and dashes back to the car. He's in, safe, speeds across Main, the light on the corner changes from yellow to red, and almost immediately he takes the ramp past Groote Schuur that puts him on De Waal Drive, then past the bare patch where District Six once was, and he refuses to see the correspondence between those people who were so hideously thrown out of their homes and his own expropriation, he'll never give up, he'll fight to the last drop of blood, as people always say.

He's now remembered Uncle Wannie du Plessis, Colonel Wannie, one of his father's best friends. Whenever anything went wrong, old Wannie du Plessis was there to lend a hand; he was a high-up. Even though he's retired, he's the man he'll ask for help, Uncle Wannie will still have some contacts operating outside the present police system, from that shadowy realm, its powers only revealed to the criminal when the crackdown happens, that little scumbag with his underhand operation will be nailed.

He drives along with the city on his left, his legs only just capable of braking and accelerating, his state of mind in constant flux, revving up to fury and then subsiding again, and by the time he finds parking opposite the Sea Point swimming pool and has paid the security guard R5 to keep an eye on his car, he's cleared a space for a mix of hopeless failure followed by grief, a raging, tearing grief, like a fury, but (he suspects) lacking the punching power of rage that he needs. He has a terrible attack of heartburn and gets out of the car, tears in his eyes.

After a while, he thought he was going to puke, he leans in and takes a swig from his water bottle, locks the car, checks that it's locked and starts walking along the broad promenade to Mouille Point, presses the remote of his car once again and then carries on next to the narrow strip of beach with its black rocks and black kelp washed up by the tide, wishing he felt free to shout it out here in public, vomit it out, anything, about the unreal situation he's been forced into and which he now has to solve, but he can't rid himself of a recurring sadness that now, under the gaze of Benjamin Duiker, makes him a child again: and now, my son, what now? The power of that challenging voice knocks him over: so he has not succeeded after all, not with his business, not with anything, he simply isn't able to.

After a while, he swings to the right and shelters under one of those clumps of windswept coastal trees, lies flat on the lawn on his stomach, his head on his arms; he really doesn't care any more.

He wakes up when his bare, sweaty arms start itching on the grass, and phones Jack again, but he's on voicemail. He walks up one of the side streets to Main Road, Sea Point, to buy a plaster for his pinkie and phones Sissy, but he can't reach her and is pleased at this – with her do-or-die attitude that she's acquired out there on the farm, she'd put the blame on him: so where was Uncle Hannes's Beretta?

He again tries to phone Jack, and ten paces further on tries again, keeping to the shade of a block of flats on the left-hand pavement. In the end he phones Samantha; she's between classes on the UCT campus, and clearly, even on the phone, she's overjoyed to hear from him, really, he can feel it, and he'd always thought that she didn't have much time for him.

Law and order, she says when he tells her about the hijacking of his takeaway. No way, she says. That can't happen in this country. She believes in this country. Okay, she's heard of flats in Hillbrow being hijacked by Nigerians, but this! Has he been to the police? Must she come and help him? Oh dear, she has to go, her class starts in a minute. Won't he please phone her mother, she's been nagging for ever, she's got something she wants to tell him. She'll business-card the number to him.

When he receives the number, he stands under an overhanging loquat tree in the sun on Main Road and phones Auntie Mary. As children they called her Mary; as times changed, 'auntie' was added out of respect. His parents should never have permitted the disgrace of calling the woman, older than his father, by her first name like that. Oh well, that was the way it was. It's not his fault that he was born in those times and his father and mother were of their time, if he now has to make excuses on their behalf.

'Auntie Mary? It's Mattheüs.'

'Ag, my dear child.' He sees her at the kitchen table covered with a plastic cloth with a rose pattern; he remembers it from the time he and his mother drove to Jakkalsvlei Avenue, something urgent, he remembers his mother's mouth that said not a word the whole way, on a mission to get Auntie Mary as a witness to something bad that had happened between her and his father, his mother insisting on getting proof that he'd been wrong. Tea was served at the table with the rose tablecloth, and they could hardly hear each other over the congregation next door in the church, singing or rather jubilating evangelical hymns; it was a Sunday morning that they'd gone there – that's his strongest recollection of that house in Athlone.

She just wants to say, says Auntie Mary, she's discovered an old photo in a shoebox. It's of him as a boy and of Mister Bennie and she's even in the photo, all three of them on the steps of their nice house. He's sitting on Mister Bennie's lap, too cute, waving his little hand. Must be his mother who'd taken the snap.

'You know, Mattees, I just want to tell you what the snap made me remember again. That day of the funeral there wasn't time. Look, Mister Bennie didn't beat about the bush. Very honest. Sometimes hard. But ag, you know, he was the first white man that I learnt you could really detest and then you can also love him in your heart. The crease of his pants wasn't pressed straight, oh my goodness, Mister Bennie calls me straight to his study. Thought he was going to bite my head off. The power of that man. Okay, I'm leaving, I'm giving notice. Goodness, Mattheüs, then he's good to me again. I get a lawnmower for Christmas for our lawn here in front. I'm sitting in that very same study this side of the desk and Mister Bennie talks his loudest to tell me something of how things are now going wrong in his house. I can see he wants to share it with me, because I know that house from top to bottom. He can't. I'm sorry for Mister Bennie. Mister Bennie speaks to me from his heart. That's how he was with me. The first white man that I can say: I care about him. He's a human being, I like him, warts and all. That's all, Mattees. I'm wasting your money with all this talking. Now Mister Bennie's also been put away. A path we'll all have to walk one day.'

Long after he's ended the call, Auntie Mary's story stays with him, punctuated by sounds of spit-swallowing and breathing, the story that she'd kept to tell him in a special way. And the perfect timing that she can't have guessed: he's fired up now. When he walks past an internet café, he goes inside and googles the recipe for a Molotov cocktail.

He walks back to the sea, and goes and sits in the bar at La Perla restaurant opposite the Sea Point swimming pool. The place has a luxuriously high ceiling, full-length mirrors and soft black leather couches, and a TV soundlessly broadcasting Manchester United versus Barcelona FC; in the dining room next door, mussels are being carried out on top of mountains of linguine to tables laid with linen and which are now, at dusk, slowly filling. He crumples up the piece of paper with the Molotov cocktail recipe, orders a neat double brandy and a beer, and phones Jack again, twice, and one more time again, and then he sees that his battery's flat.

He laughs to himself: the Merc cruising slowly up Main past Duiker's, Jack driving, and right opposite his business he slides down his window and accurately lobs the cocktail into the oblong skylight above the steel door, which takes the burning IED right inside the takeaway. He orders another double. The waiter is an older Indian man in La Perla's spotless black-and-white waiter out-fit, a man he recognises after years of visiting the established Italian restaurant.

With the brandy on his tongue, he scans Bellville in his mind's eye, searching for the colonel's house, Uncle Wannie, who's going to help him with the shit his business has temporarily – everything is temporary – landed in. Over the Tygerberg Hospital he floats, there, no, it was closer to the city, more to the north-east, across Voortrekker Road and further north to Boston, that old, leafy part of Bellville. What he clearly remembers about Uncle Wannie's house was the budgie cage in his back yard, the grass-green and yellow and blue budgies twittering in their small prison covered with chicken wire that Uncle Wannie always painted exactly the same green as the green-feathered budgies. He'll have to search for the exact street by driving up and down, but find it he will. Colonel Wannie will help him, he'll fetch a pitilessly cunning plan from his strongroom (just like the old days): Emile, his dog, the whole pile of rubbish will crawl, they'll beg.

Mattheüs sinks back into the sofa. As far as he's concerned: even if it's just a mustard seed of hope, he must keep believing he has it in him. And he has. Downstairs in the lobby near the toilets, still seventies-style with gilded mirrors and embossed wallpaper, there's a pay phone where he'll phone Jack in a minute. He'll tell Jack the whole thing and tell him he's got nothing to worry about, everything will be okay. And he wants to tell Jack he loves him, for once he also wants to say this to the poor, dear, sex-starved, handsome little fuck.

@ 9 Poinsettia Road, Jack facebooks. *Matt, where are you? Looked everywhere, thought you were here. For old times' sake came as Wolfie! Love you, as in heaps.*

@ 9 Poinsettia Road. *Charnie, where are you hanging out? Long time no talk. In deep shit again at school. Moenien's ma, you remember, that's the fucker who got pissed on at Misverstand Dam. Anyway, the*

261

thing's still eating at her. Went to complain to Mister Richardson:
Afrikaans teacher's nails = dirty. Where's the example now? That kind
of shit. And Moenien apparently swears he can smell me in class. Can
you fuckin' believe the cheek? Stay well, darling.

Jack peers through the fleur-de-lis tips of the gate at the house. Only the study light is on. Learnt fast, the Mkhonzas; an electricity bill can get out of hand. Nothing's moving, not inside or on the lawn or in any of the trees. Far to the right of the lawn, a blue heron stands with a raised claw, waiting for its frog dinner. An in-between time.

Jack turns his back on the house. Must take a photo of Wolfie. His wolf ears make a comical two-pointed silhouette in front of the fleur-de-lis tips of the gate. Looks like a Chinese paper cutting. Behind him the house is out of focus, the Cape-Dutch gables recognisable only to an insider's eye. He immediately sends the photo to Matt.

What Jack facing backward does not or cannot see, is that the sash window to the right of the front door is being pushed open, so that the frame of the top window is level with that of the lower one. If it hadn't been for the fact that the Duikers kept their sash windows well-oiled, actually Mattheüs's father did, Jack might have heard the window sliding down. On the two parallel frames the barrel of a rifle now appears. The tip of the barrel moves slightly to the right, corrects to the left, and finds its target right between the wolf ears. Then a bit lower. The barrel drops a fraction lower so that the aim is not too high between the ears; it's a mask after all. Now. The plan is in place. The trash around the house must be got rid of, once and for all.

Jack's mobile phone flies from his grip. The black plastic cover comes apart and scatters on the side of the pavement.

Matt has a double espresso to temper his drunkenness, pays and walks down to the promenade. The waves are booming and crashing, their foam lips clearly visible in the evening light. It'll be like this with him and Jack, he decides. He'll work hard and transform his brain, and as far as Jack goes, he'll position himself somewhere between desire and love. If it's just desire, he won't be able to be with Jack alone, that's too much to ask of a man and far too much self-control to ask of him. And if it's love only, what becomes of his God-given desire? He'll drift along at some point between the two poles.

He sniffs at the seaweedy salty air that blows sharp and cold against him from the Atlantic Ocean. That's the first thing he'll do with Jack: he'll hold that lovely bald head of his in both his hands and explain it all to him, and then he'll let go of him, and from the expression that lingers in his eyes he'll know whether Jack will be able to live with the self-styled position that he still has to teach himself.

Much more than that he can't offer – not to Jack, not to anyone.